THE FIRE BABY

Praise for Jim Kelly

'A significant new talent' *Sunday Times*

'The sense of place is terrific: the fens really brood.
Dryden, the central character, is satisfyingly complicated
. . . a good atmospheric read' *Observer*

'A sparkling star newly risen in the crime fiction
firmament' Colin Dexter

'Kelly is clearly a name to watch . . . a compelling read'
Crime Time

'Beautifully written . . . The climax is chilling. Sometimes a
book takes up residence inside my head and just won't
leave. *The Water Clock* did just that' Val McDermid

'An atmospheric, intriguing mystery, with a tense
denouement' Susanna Yager, *Sunday Telegraph*

'Excellent no-frills thriller with a real bite. 4 stars' *FHM*

'A story that continuously quickens the pulse . . . makes
every nerve tingle. The suspense here is tight and
controlled and each character is made to count in a story
that engulfs you while it unravels' *Punch*

'Kelly's evocation of the bleak and watery landscapes,
provide a powerful backdrop to a wonderful cast of
characters' *The Good Book Guide*

The Fire Baby

JIM KELLY

PENGUIN BOOKS

PENGUIN BOOKS

Published by the Penguin Group
Penguin Books Ltd, 80 Strand, London WC2R ORL, England
Penguin Group (USA) Inc., 375 Hudson Street, New York, New York 10014, USA
Penguin Group (Canada), 10 Alcorn Avenue, Toronto, Ontario, Canada M4V 3B2
(a division of Pearson Penguin Canada Inc.)
Penguin Ireland, 25 St Stephen's Green, Dublin 2, Ireland
(a division of Penguin Books Ltd)
Penguin Group (Australia), 250 Camberwell Road, Camberwell, Victoria 3124, Australia
(a division of Pearson Australia Group Pty Ltd)
Penguin Books India Pvt Ltd, 11 Community Centre, Panchsheel Park, New Delhi – 110 017, India
Penguin Group (NZ), cnr Airborne and Rosedale Roads, Albany, Auckland 1310, New Zealand
(a division of Pearson New Zealand Ltd)
Penguin Books (South Africa) (Pty) Ltd, 24 Sturdee Avenue, Rosebank 2196, South Africa

Penguin Books Ltd, Registered Offices: 80 Strand, London WC2R ORL, England

www.penguin.com

First published by Michael Joseph 2004
Published in Penguin Books 2005

1

Copyright © Jim Kelly, 2004
All rights reserved

The moral right of the author has been asserted

Typeset by Rowland Phototypesetting Ltd, Bury St Edmunds, Suffolk
Printed in England by Clays Ltd, St Ives plc

For John

Acknowledgements

I would like to thank Beverley Cousins, my editor, for providing inspiration and advice in perfect measures, Faith Evans, for her determination to elevate the quality of writing in *The Fire Baby*, and Trevor Horwood, for creative and meticulous copy-editing. This book again centres on the case of a car-accident victim locked in a coma. I am grateful for the welcome extended to me by the Royal Hospital for Neuro-disability, Putney, and am happy to point out that donations can be made through its website: www.rhn.org.uk. I would like to thank Donald and Renee Gillies, and Jenny Burgoyne for helping with the text. Darren Fox, of Ely Fire Station, provided technical advice on the properties of fire. The US Air Force let me tour Mildenhall base, a privilege for which I am grateful. The oddities of the East Anglian weather system were expertly explained to me by Weather-quest, the forecasting company at the University of East Anglia. Midge Gillies, my wife, stepped in brilliantly to break the occasional logjam of ideas.

The Landscape of the Fens is, of course, real but topographical and historical details have been occasionally altered for the sake of the plot. All characters are entirely fictitious and any resemblance to real persons is entirely coincidental.

Tuesday, 1 June 1976 –
The Great Drought

East of Ely, above the bone-dry peatfields, a great red dust storm drifts across the moon, throwing an amber shadow on the old cathedral. Overhead a single, winking plane crosses the star-spangled sky. Flight MH336, just airborne from the US military base at Mildenhall, flies into the tumbling cauldron of dust.

The diamond-hard sand begins to shred the turning turbines and the dislodged blades scythe each other like spinning knives. The fuselage dips as the engine suffocates, and begins a descent of such violence that the passengers float, despite their seatbelts, in a weightless fall towards their deaths.

At precisely 11.08 pm, according to the pilot's watch recovered at the scene, the fuselage buries itself in the soft earth. The distant cathedral tower shudders with the impact and the crows, roosting on the Octagon Tower, rise in a single cloud. Heads turn ten miles away at Littleport with the earthy thud of the crash, followed by the crackling combustion of the airfuel.

A fireball marks the point of impact at Black Bank Farm. Here there is too much sound to hear. At the heart of the fire a cold white eye burns where 50,000 gallons of kerosene turns to gas in a single second. Then the flames come, licking the stars.

At the foot of the vast white pillar of rising smoke the air crackles with the heat. And in the ashes of what had been Black Bank Farm she stands alone. Her, and the baby.

They are the only ones alive. Her, and the baby.

The family died at the table: her mother caught in the act of drowning in a flame, her father's blackened arm still stretched towards his throat. His last words will stay with her to her deathbed: 'The cellar, Maggie.

1

A celebration.' She'd gone to get the bottle, leaving Matty in his cot by the empty fireplace. Celebration: a family christening to come, now that Matty had a father.

In the dry damp of the stone cellar she heard it coming. Machines, like people, can pretend to scream. But the pretence was gone in the final wail of the failing engines, the ripping metal, and the blow of the impact.

Sometimes she wished she had died then, as she should have.

Instead she saw the light and heard the sound that was the fire, the dripping fire, falling through the floorboards. The liquid fuel from the tanks, the quicksilver light that saved her life. So she found the stairs and climbed up to count the dead, hung, like game, from the burning rafters. Then the real horror, in the tiny swaddled bundle with the blackened limbs.

Outside, with her secret in her arms, she felt him kicking, and nudging, with the jerky half-conscious movements only a child can make.

Even here, in what had been the kitchen garden, she felt the heat prickling her skin. She smelt her hair singe, as the black hanging threads turned to ash-white corkscrews. A lock ignited, and burnt into her cheek. She had a lifetime to feel the pain, but even now it terrified her with the slow, insidious intimation that the worst was yet to come.

A fire in her blood. And the baby's.

A silent fire. The only sound a flapping inside her ear, like a pigeon's wings.

She took a limping step towards the coolness of the night. These ashes weren't cold like the ones in the grate at Black Bank. These were white with heat, an ivory crust beneath which breathed the cherry embers. She smelt flesh burn and knew, with the clarity of shock, that it was hers.

And then she saw him. A hundred yards from the house, shielding his face from the heat with an out-turned palm.

He'd been waiting to join the celebration. Her father had been confident Maggie would change her mind that night: 'Come at eleven. She'll come round for Matty's sake. It's the baby. She'll come round.'

And with the intuition of a lover Maggie knew where he'd been, knew where he'd been waiting in the night. The old pillbox. Their pillbox; the concrete hexagonal space that she had once dreamed of in the damp and guilty night, the place where they'd made Matty come to life.

She heard a siren then. The first. From the base. They'd be at Black Bank soon, but not soon enough to save him. Not soon enough to save him from the life she planned for him in those few seconds. It was the best decision of her life. And the quickest. Taken in the time it takes to light a match.

And then they were together. So she smiled as she trembled. The yellow-blue light of the kerosene was in his eyes and briefly she remembered why she'd loved him once. But she saw that he looked only down, at the baby. His finger turned back the fold in the blanket. He saw the face for the first time, the tiny red wandering tongue. And the fool smiled too.

'Our boy,' he said, wishing it was so. 'He's safe. Our boy.'

She let him believe it for another second.

'Dead,' she said, and pulled the blanket back to let him see the stencilled blue capital letters on the soft linen: USAF: AIR CONVOY.

He looked at the ruined farmhouse then: 'Dead? You can't be sure.'

He looked at the blanket again. 'I'll get him,' he said. 'Stay here.' She watched him run into the flames, until they closed behind him, like the hushed velvet curtains of a crematorium.

Saturday, 14 June 2003 –
27 years later

The single glass of water stood like an exhibit on the pillbox shelf. When the sun reached the western horizon it shone directly into the hexagonal room through the gunslit and caught the liquid, sending a shifting rainbow of incredible beauty across the drab concrete walls.

It haunted him now. He could see it with his eyes closed. Its cool limpid form was held for ever in his memory: but then he knew that for ever, for him, was not a long time. As the heat rose towards midday he could see the level of water drop, and he sucked in air to catch the memory of the moisture.

It was his life now, trying to reach the glass. But he knew, even as he stretched and felt the handcuffs cut into his wrist, that he would never touch it. He'd marked the full extent of his passion on the floor. On the first day he'd stretched out and left a line in the sand, three feet short of the far wall. By the third day he'd stretched until he heard his joints crack, a sickening pop of cartilage disengaged.

The next day he won six inches in a single panic-stricken lunge, the pain of which had made him swoon. When he came to, the blood had dried and the cut at his wrist showed the glint of bone, like a gash of knuckle glimpsed on the butcher's counter. That night the fox came for the first time, circling, sniffing death.

His jailer noted his efforts to reach the glass with obvious satisfaction, smoothed clean the sand and re-filled the glass with bright water from the sparkling plastic bottle. Then he took the carved knife from its place, sticking out of the door jamb, and held it to his victim's throat. A minute, maybe two, then he returned it, unblooded.

There was something familiar about the jailer. Something in the way he leant against the concrete wall by the glass and smoked. Something in the downcast eyes.

He yearned to hear his voice, but the jailer hadn't spoken.

The routine was silently the same. He'd hear first his footsteps on the tinder-dry twigs beneath the pines. The iron door pushed open, the glass re-filled. Then he'd stand and smoke. A packet sometimes. How long does that take? An hour? Two?

Sometimes he came twice a day, the sound of his car suddenly loud as it parked beyond the trees he could see through the gunslit. But he'd always go without answering the questions. And then once at night. He was afraid then, for the first time, that the jailer would kill him before the thirst did. His tormentor was drunk, and the storm lantern put tiny red flashes in his eyes, but still he said nothing.

He'd speak before the end came. He felt sure of that. But he wanted to know now. Know now for which of his crimes he was being punished.

Nine Days Earlier
Thursday, 5 June

I

Philip Dryden looked down on the taxi cab parked on the neat shingle forecourt of The Tower Hospital. In the front seat was a large sleeping figure encircled by an Ipswich Town sweatshirt. The driver's delicate hands were clasped neatly over an ample tummy. The slumbering cabbie's tiny mouth formed a perfect O.

'How can he stand it?' Dryden asked, turning to the figure laid out under a single white linen sheet on the hospital bed. 'It's eighty-four degrees. He's parked in the full sunlight. Fast asleep. All that meat. Cooking.'

The figure on the bed didn't move. Its immobility was a constant in his life, like the heat of that summer, and equally oppressive. He turned back to the large Victorian half-circle window and put his forehead to the glass.

Heat. Inescapable heat, like a giant duvet over the Fens. He felt a rivulet of sweat set out from his jet-black hair and begin a zig-zag journey across his face. His features were architectural. Precisely, Early Norman. The head of a knight, perhaps, from a cathedral nave, or illuminated on a medieval parchment. Illuminated but impassive; a dramatic irony which nicely summed him up.

He tipped his head back and turned his face to the ceiling. He had a powerful imagination and he focused it now, as he had done a thousand times that suffocating summer, on conjuring up a snow storm. The ice-cold flakes fell on his upturned eyelids. He listened to them falling in the silence, punctuated only by the tick of the bedside clock.

When he opened them it was 11.57 precisely. Three minutes.

He closed his eyes again and tried to wish the heat away. The Tower was on Ely's only hill. A precious hundred feet above the limitless expanse of the Black Fens which stretched in a parched panorama to the distant wavy line of the horizon. A tractor, wobbling in a mirage, trundled across a field slightly smaller than Belgium.

He looked down at Laura. His wife had been in The Tower nearly four years since the accident at Harrimere Drain. Dryden had met the other driver on a lonely fen road head on, swerved over the verge, and the two-door Corsa had plunged into twenty feet of water in the roadside dyke. Harrimere Drain. Whenever Dryden saw the sign he could feel the seatbelt cutting across his chest and the dull, distant, double click of his collar bones breaking.

He'd been dragged to safety, but Laura, unseen on the back seat, had been left behind. He tried never to imagine what she must have thought when she regained consciousness. Alone, in the dark, in pain, and gasping for breath in a remorselessly diminishing pocket of damp air.

Three hours later the emergency services got her out. She was in the coma then. Locked In Syndrome: LIS. Locked away from the horror of those 180 minutes of total isolation, locked away from the knowledge that she'd been abandoned, locked away from him.

The clock flipped over a number: 11.58. Dryden pulled at the frayed linen collar of his white shirt and fingered the gold chain around his neck. He pulled on it until the single brass Chubb-lock key came out into his hand. The car crash had been two days before his thirty-third birthday and he hadn't got back to their flat in London until a month later. That's when he found his present where she knew he'd stumble on it, in the top drawer of their desk. A single white envelope, a card showing a black and white landscape shot of the Fens near Ely, and a newly cut key. The inscription on the card read 'Love, Laura'; nothing else.

He'd tried the locks in the flat first, then her parents' café and flat, but nothing. He tried the local locksmiths in the North London suburb where they lived but none could recall a visit from the Italian girl with the copper hair. He'd tried the two cottages out on Adventurer's Fen they'd inspected during their long debates about moving out, starting a family. But the doors were rotten and the keyholes rusted. Ivy obscured the sign engraved in the bricks: Flightpath Cottages.

How many other locks had he tried since Laura's accident? A thousand? Two? But nothing. Only Laura knew which door the key opened, and she hadn't spoken since the night of the crash. It was a mystery which tormented him subtly because it seemed the perfect symbol of his life since the accident. That he should have the key, but not the door. An answer without a question.

'Unbearable,' he said out loud, and the heat seemed to intensify.

Eleven fifty-nine, and one minute to the news. He flipped open his mobile and rang Humph's business number: Humphrey H. Holt, licensed mini-cabs for all occasions. Not quite all occasions. In fact, hardly any occasions at all. Humph's cab, a battered Ford Capri, looked like it had been retrieved from a dump on the outskirts of Detroit.

Dryden's face, normally stonily impassive, creased with pleasure as he watched the cabbie start awake and fumble for the mobile.

'It's me,' he said, unnecessarily. They knew each other's voices better than they knew their own. 'Put the radio on. Local. Last item. I need to hear.'

They zoomed dizzily over the wavebands until Humph picked up the signal.

'The headlines at noon on Radio Littleport . . .'

Dryden, for a decade one of Fleet Street's sharpest reporters, listened with complete indifference to the usual tales of political intrigue, international violence, and lurid showbusiness before the station moved on to local items.

'. . . with an entire lorryload of turnips. Meanwhile on the coast at Cromer the heatwave again brought havoc to the holiday beaches. A huge cloud of ladybirds descended on sunbathers by the pier. A spokesman for the local council's environmental health department said the insects were breeding in huge numbers and were desperate for food. Apparently they can live quite happily on human sweat. And with that thought the time is now four minutes past twelve.'

There was a short jingle, a digital version of Fingal's Cave. Dryden swore at it.

'This is Radio Littleport. The Voice of The Fens. And now an important announcement from East Cambridgeshire County Police Force.'

Dryden had his reporter's notebook ready on the window ledge. His fluid shorthand left an elegant scribble across the page. Elegant but unreadable: he was only fooling himself.

'This is an urgent message for Estelle Beck, the only daughter of Maggie Beck of Black Bank Farm, near Ely. Please contact immediately The Tower Hospital, Ely, where your mother is gravely ill. I'll repeat that –'

Dryden clicked off the mobile without thanking Humph. He brushed away a fly which had settled on Laura's arm. Then he walked across the large, carpeted room and folded his six-foot-two-inch frame into a hospital chair beside the room's only other bed. In it lay the curled, wheezing body of Maggie Beck.

'Why now?' he asked nobody.

There had been four radio appeals, each as urgent as the last. He hoped her daughter came soon. He had seen very few people dying but the symptoms were shockingly clear. She held both hands at her throat where they clutched a paper tissue. Her hair was matted to her skull. She seemed to draw her breath up from a pit beneath her, each one a labour which threatened to kill her. Her skin was dry and without tension – except for the single mark of a livid burn which cut across one side of her face in the shape of a corkscrew.

'They'll come,' he said, hoping she'd hear.

In the oddly detached way in which he expressed almost all his emotions Dryden had come to love Maggie Beck. When his father died in the floods of '77 Maggie, still a teenager and newly married, had moved in to look after his mother. Dryden had been eleven. Maggie had taken the spare room and helped his mother through the few weeks before the coroner's court inquest, and then the excruciating absence of a burial. His father had been presumed drowned, swept off the bank at Welch's Dam, and the body never found. For his mother this had been the final burden which Maggie helped her bear. The heartache of grief without a corpse to cry over. After that they combined their sorrows in often companionable silence. Maggie had her own tragedy to carry – the air crash at Black Bank which had killed her parents and her infant son. They shouldered their grief together, farmers' wives who didn't want to subside under the weight of their misfortunes, at least not without a fight. They'd travelled together – day trips and weekends which took them far from the memory of their lives. He'd met her many times at Burnt Fen in his mother's kitchen, a big woman with farmyard bones as familiar and comforting as the Aga, with that corkscrew burn like a tattoo on her face.

Maggie knew she had cancer. The radiotherapy would last six weeks, the convalescence longer still. Dryden had gone out to Black Bank to see her and knew instantly that she expected to die. The specialists had suggested that it might be good therapy for Laura if she shared her room. Maggie said yes without a pause and raided her savings to afford The Tower's substantial fees. She would spend her last months in comfort, for she had a task to complete before the cancer took her life. She wanted to tell her story. Dryden gave her a tape recorder so that each day she could spill out her tale to a silent audience. The story she wanted to tell, the one she wanted Laura to witness. And Laura, if she could hear, had a story to listen to.

Dryden had visited in those first weeks and found in her a desperate insecurity. She'd hold his hand and tell him that her life had been a failure, that she'd failed Estelle, that she'd failed Black Bank. But she still hid the heart of this failure, a secret Dryden sensed was burning her from within. And then she'd turned to him one night just a week ago, as he sat with her enjoying the breeze that came through the open windows. They'd heard the cathedral clock chime midnight and she'd taken his hand and held it with the intensity of a bullclip: 'Promise me they'll come,' she'd said.

She'd been in The Tower a month and each day Estelle had visited – until now. Each day she had come to sit with her mother. But the best days for Maggie were when she brought the American. Dryden had met him twice, by Laura's bedside. 'Friend of the family,' said Maggie. A pilot, tall and slightly wasted, with the drawn features of a victim. Every day they came – until this last weekend. The doctors assured them that the end was months away, if not years. Maggie had agreed to a break, to let her daughter go. Let them both go.

The moment they left, Maggie's health had rapidly collapsed. The cancer cells had begun to multiply in her blood and she had felt the change within her, the subtle beginning of the process of death. She had to get Estelle back, she had something to tell her. About the secrets that had consumed her life.

'Promise me you'll find them in time,' she said. Dryden noted the plural.

He didn't like telling lies. 'I can't,' he said. 'The police are trying; what more can I do?'

Her eyes pleaded with him, with a look which seemed, prematurely, to cross the divide between the living and the dead. 'Then promise,' she said. 'And promise you'll forgive me too.'

'Forgive you for what?'

Her hand fluttered, searching out the bedside table where the tape recorder stood. 'I've said it here. But I must tell them too. Promise me.'

He'd always remember the white arthritic knuckles and the parchment skin clutching his fingers. He stood, angry at the suggestion he needed a public oath to make him keep his word, and angrier still that she'd penetrated his emotional defences.

'I promise.'

She cried. The first time he'd seen her buckle after all the months of pain.

'I promise,' he said again, and by some peculiar transference of emotion he felt vividly that he'd made the promise to his mother, to her memory, to the gravestone on Burnt Fen. Even now the thought produced a fresh surge of sweat on his forehead. He was doing all he could. The police appeals, ads in the papers along the coast where Estelle and the American had gone touring. Why didn't she ring? Why didn't she answer her mobile phone?

He walked back to his wife and touched her shoulder through the white linen sheet. 'Laura?'

Her eyes were open. Seemingly sightless, but open. He imagined she slept – why not? So she needed waking like anyone else. And he liked using her name, now that he knew for certain that on some level, however deep and however distant, she could hear him.

The caretaker walked by in the corridor outside, dragging laundry bags and whistling the 'Ode To Joy', each note perfectly pitched.

Maggie Beck turned in her bed and struggled, as she always did, not to cry out.

Humph beeped from the cab. They had a job. Dryden had to go, back out into the world where people talked. But Dryden knew there was no real hurry. *The Crow*, the paper for which he was chief reporter, had a final deadline of 3.00pm. The handful of stories he had yet to file would take him an hour to knock out, probably less.

'Loads of time,' he said, sitting on the bed and taking Laura's hand.

They'd made the breakthrough three months ago. Dryden, unable to sleep, had spent the night on the deck of his boat at Barham's Dock. The sunrise had driven him to walk and a fox had dogged his tracks into town, scavenging across fields of sunburnt crops. The Tower had slept, the night nurse looking up from her studies to wave him through. He'd tried the routine a thousand times: taking her hand and beginning the endless repetition of the letters. Waiting for the tiny movement which would signal intelligent life, like a radio blip across the galaxy.

That first time, she'd done it perfectly. L-A-U-R-A. No mistakes. He'd sat on her bed and wept for her. Wept for joy that she was somewhere. But wept most for himself, doomed perhaps to spend his life beside a hospital bed, waiting for messages from another world.

Humph beeped again. Dryden placed the smallest finger of Laura's right hand in his palm so that it barely touched his skin. The neurologist had shown him how. They had a machine too, the COMPASS, but Dryden liked doing it this way – the way they'd first done it. The communication was intensely personal, as though he were a lightning rod, channelling her energy to earth.

'OK. Let's concentrate.' The specialist, the one with the dead-fish eyes, had told him to give her a warning.

Humph beeped again and Dryden suppressed a surge of petty anger.

'Loads of time.'

He counted to sixty and then coughed self-consciously: 'OK. We're starting. A, B, C, D, E, F . . .' and on, a full two seconds for each. He felt the familiar tingle of excitement as he got nearer: 'J, K, L' – and there it was, the tiny double movement.

It didn't always happen. One out of five, six perhaps. They'd always got the next bit wrong until Dryden had hit upon the idea of beginning at M and running through the alphabet rather than starting at A. He moved on, with the two-second gaps, but she missed it. Two tiny movements – but on the B.

He felt irritation, then guilt. The neurologist had explained how difficult it must be. 'It's about as easy as playing chess in your head. She's learnt to combine certain muscle movements, small tremors in the tissue, to produce this timed response. We have no way of knowing how much time she needs for each letter. How long she has to concentrate.'

He did the rest to spite Humph. L-B-U-S-A. Three letters right, two just a place away in the alphabet.

He felt fierce pride and love burn, briefly, at her achievement. The specialist, an expert from one of the big London teaching hospitals who had treated his wife like a specimen preserved in a Victorian museum jar, had told him to be patient – a word which always prompted in Dryden an internal scream. Laura's messages were halting, disjointed, sometimes surreal. He must wait to see if she would ever emerge from the confused penumbra of coma.

'Patience,' he said out loud. A virtue, if it was one, of which he had no trace.

2

Humph parked up in a lay-by three miles east of Ely. It was a lay-by like all lay-bys, distinguished by nothing. The A14 east–west trunk road linking the coastal port of Felixstowe with the industrial cities of the Midlands was punctuated by them. At this hour – lunchtime – it was a canyon of HGVs ticking over and spewing carbon monoxide into hot air already laced with cheap grease from the Ritz T-Bar.

'Coffee. Four sugars,' said the cabbie, unfolding a five-day-old copy of the *Financial Times* with casual familiarity. He played the stock market in the way that many people play the horses. He lost a lot; but when he ran out of things to read the *FT* made a snug, pink blanket.

Humph was Dryden's chauffeur. There was no other way to describe it. They had shared a life of aimless motion for nearly four years since Laura's accident. Humph had a few regular customers who paid well – early morning school runs, and late night pick-ups for club bouncers in Newmarket and Cambridge. The rest of the time he was on call for Dryden. *The Crow*, Dryden's newspaper, was happy to pick up the modest bills as it made up for the fact that they appeared to have forgotten to pay their chief reporter a salary. Humph's home life was as non-existent as Dryden's, in his case owing to an acrimonious divorce. He had a picture of his two girls stuck on the dashboard. Dryden and Humph shared an insular view of the world, if that is possible, for the most part without sharing a word.

In the lay-by the combination of the noon sun and the

exhaust pipes of fifteen heavy wagons was headily reminiscent of Athens under a smog. Amongst the lorries were two Milk Marketing Board tankers, common now on the Fen roads, converted to carry water for irrigating salad crops in the drought. The air along the roadside was a shimmering blue advert for global warming. Dryden tried a cough and produced a strangulated lead-fuelled squeak.

The Ritz T-Bar was a regular meeting place for Dryden and the crew of stragglers he counted as his 'contacts'. He noted that Inspector Andy Newman's car was already parked up on a grass mound at the end of the lay-by. The detective drove a clapped-out Citroën with a sticker in the window for the Welney Wildfowl Trust. Andy Newman – 'Last Case Newman', as he was known to his fellow officers on the force – was more interested in catching sight of a sparrowhawk than a crook. Mentally he had been on the allotment for a decade. Or in his case, in one of the hides from which he could spy on his beloved birds. He had twenty-three days to run to statutory retirement age. He wasn't counting, but that didn't include two days' holiday and a doctor's appointment.

Dryden queued for a cup of tea. The Ritz was standard issue in the mobile tea-bar world. Sugar bowl with one teaspoon and several lumps of coagulated glucose. One copy of the *Sun* – tied to the counter with a piece of string. A hotplate with a row of sausages sizzling in six-point harmony. And one oddity: a bird cage hung from the wooden awning in which sat a moth-eaten parrot. It was not a pretty boy.

A blackboard on the rear wall of the kitchenette read: THURSDAY'S SPECIAL – DOUBLE SAUSAGE SANDWICH 99P.

The proprietor was tall, with blond hair tinged nicotine-yellow. His conversational powers, which Dryden had tested before, were strictly limited to Premier League football, female lorry drivers and the weather in a two-mile radius of the lay-by. He kept his hands in his pockets and smoked a roll-up with the lung-pulling power of a set of doll's house bellows. As he pushed the styrofoam cup of tea across the counter Dryden noticed the livid raised mark of a skin graft on his hand.

'Johnnie,' said Dryden, putting his change on the Formica top.

'Steamin' again,' said Johnnie, shuffling coins between the lines of five-, ten-, twenty-, and fifty-pence pieces on the counter-top he had arranged in the long hours of boredom which came with being proprietor of the Ritz.

Dryden left it at that. He got into Newman's car and sat pretending to sip the tea for five minutes. Newman, binoculars pressed to his face, was scanning the vast field opposite. Eventually he placed them on his lap with a sigh. 'Herring gull,' he said. Even his voice was tired. Knackered. Ready for retirement with the rest of him.

'Not long now,' said Dryden, referring to Newman's favourite topic – retirement.

'Nope. Not long.'

Dryden produced a single piece of white paper. It was a five-paragraph story put out by the Press Association that morning. *The Crow* paid for the wire service PA provided – a regular series of news stories churned out online to the terminal on the news editor's desk. Dryden had a search mechanism on his screen which alerted him when any story came up with a headline containing the key words 'TWITCHER(S)', 'BIRD(S)', 'RARE' or 'EGG(S)'.

He'd rung Newman that morning as soon as the story had appeared on the wire. It might make a paragraph in the nationals the next day, or even the local evening papers, but Dryden's favour bought Newman the best part of a twenty-four-hour lead on his fellow enthusiasts.

'Rare Siberian gull spotted', ran the headline. The bird had been blown, exhausted, on to the bird reserve at Holme on the north Norfolk coast. Once the news hit the papers thousands of twitchers would descend on the spot, with enough photographic hardware to cover a Paris catwalk. This way Andy Newman got there first.

'Thanks,' he said, stuffing the paper in the glove compartment. He always seemed mildly embarrassed by what, Dryden had to admit, was a not very subtle process of police bribery. They had long since dispensed with any pretence that their relationship was anything other than cynical: Newman got the tips and Dryden got a story. It was as simple as that.

Newman retrieved a large brown envelope which had been stashed in the Citroën's glove compartment. Dryden gingerly extracted some photographic prints from it. 'They're X-rated,' said Newman, as he raised his binoculars to watch a flock of flamingoes rising from the distant waters of the Wicken Fen nature reserve.

And so they were. Twenty prints, black and white. Two bodies. One female. Her face was to the camera in a few, the eyes glazed. Dryden guessed she'd been drugged. The man's face was crueller. A professional. A pornstar's body. Hairless and smooth. But ugly. They were always ugly in these pictures, whatever they looked like.

She'd have been beautiful anywhere else. Blonde, bright eyes, leggy. Dryden guessed twenty – perhaps younger. The stud was older, late twenties; the cynical smile added another couple of decades. But it was the room that left Dryden uneasy. Walls, but no right angles. Bare concrete. Graffiti: layers of it, decades of it. Coats and clothes on the floor, and under that, what? Straw, perhaps.

The camera angle never changed. It was outside looking

in, through a narrow horizontal slit. Night time. A peeping Tom by arrangement, looking in and recording everything.

Dryden put them back in the envelope and fished in his trouser pockets for the pear drops he'd bought that morning. He hardly ever ate a decent meal, preferring instead to graze on the crop he could harvest from his pockets. He wound the window down but it made no impression on the stifling heat. A fly head-butted the windscreen without enthusiasm.

'It's a pillbox,' said Newman, lowering the binoculars and putting them carefully in a box lined with immaculate green baize.

Dryden nodded as if he knew what the detective was talking about.

'Is that a clue?' asked Dryden, fighting off an urge to yawn. Sometimes Dryden was aware that of the two he got the poorer bargain in their little game of bribery. Newman had to find a story at very short notice to get his tips, and sometimes the Fenland underworld failed to come up with anything even moderately exciting.

'Not really,' said Newman, already trying to work out if he could lose himself for a few hours driving north to Holme over lunch to get a snap of the Siberian gull. 'There were thirty thousand built in the late thirties, forties. There's probably ten thousand left. Most look like the one in the pictures. There's a club – apparently – which spots them.'

Dryden imagined Newman joining up. 'People should get out more.'

'They did,' said Newman, nodding at the brown envelope. 'The pictures turned up in a house in Nottingham. A raid – illegal immigrants.'

One of the HGVs shuddered past, drowning out for a second the whine of the cars on the A14. Dryden felt one of the small bones in his ear vibrate in tune with the diesel engine.

'Operation Ironside,' said Newman. 'April 1940. They thought the Germans were going to invade on the east coast. Plan was to blow up the sluices at Denver and flood the Fens. The Isle of Ely was the HQ for the region post-invasion. So they built pillboxes. About a hundred and fifty of them across the region, mostly around the edge of the island and on the old cliff-line.'

Newman handed Dryden the binoculars and pointed north across a field of dry peat soil to a windbreak of poplars.

It took Dryden a minute to find it. One of its six sides caught the sun. The narrow machine-gun slit a jet-black shadow like an ugly mouth.

'That one?'

'Nope. Roof's collapsed.'

Dryden looked again through the binoculars. One side had crumbled and the roof did indeed sit at an angle on top. While pillboxes came in many guises, this he knew was the standard design. Hexagonal, single-storey, with gunslits on up to four of the sides. A door would be located to the 'rear' depending on the engineer's guess as to the direction of attack. Once inside with the door locked a small group of soldiers could hold out for days, even weeks. Dryden had been inside a few in the Fens covering a variety of stories from devil worship to juvenile drug taking. Most were squalid, with ash-covered floors, and all the detritus of low-life from used syringes to discarded condoms. One had been daubed with the signs of the zodiac.

Dryden didn't believe in ghosts or devils but some places, he felt, radiated evil. He could sense it now, even across the open fields of a summer's day, a palpable sense of menace focused on the pillbox.

'And there's this,' added Newman.

One of the prints Dryden had ignored was a blow-up of

part of the wall. He'd thought it was just a duff picture but now he could see faintly stencilled letters neatly set out by a wall bracket.

'It probably held a phone,' said Newman. 'The number identifies the pillbox. At least it would if we had the records. Which we haven't.'

'But?' There had to be more.

'The first three numbers give the area: 103. Isle of Ely. Local TA boys still use them for orienteering.'

Dryden didn't move. He considered the 150 or more pillboxes circling the city, each, perhaps, protecting its own sordid secrets. 'So what's the story? More to the point, what's the crime?'

Newman got out and leant on the Citroën's baking roof. Dryden followed suit and they faced each other over the hot metal. 'We're looking for anyone who's seen anything unusual around a pillbox. Cars at night. Lights. Clothing left in them. Kids might have seen something. The crime? My guess is the girl's drugged. She's somebody's daughter, somebody's girlfriend.'

Dryden let the sun bake his upturned face for a few seconds. He thought about the girl in the pictures, considering the six grubby walls pressing in, and the stench of decay: 'Could she be missing?'

'It's possible. You can say we've got the national police force computer on the job and the missing persons files have been scoured.'

What a place to be trapped, thought Dryden: his claustrophobia made his pulse race at the thought. Six walls, pressing in. He remembered Harrimere Drain and the vanishing air pocket in which he and Laura had been trapped. The car, forced off the road by an oncoming driver, had plunged into the icy water of the deep ditch. He had been pulled clear by the other driver, letting himself rise through the dark water towards the air above. As consciousness faded he had told himself then, and always, that he had given Laura up to get help, but he knew others doubted his motives. Had he simply fled the nightmare of the underwater cell? The panic-stricken retreat of the coward?

He thought of the girl in the picture and the look of bewildered fear in her eyes. He didn't have much pity left, even for Laura. But he had some anger.

3

The Crow's offices stood on Market Street between a seed wholesalers and the old town gaol. It had a single door to the street which boasted a catflap and a flip-over plastic sign which could read 'Open' or 'Closed'. Inside, the floorboards were bare and behind a single counter sat Jean, *The Crow*'s half-deaf receptionist and switchboard operator. As a front lobby it hardly compared to that of the *News*, Dryden's one-time Fleet Street employer, which had been manned by two jobsworths in quasi-military uniforms and contained a fountain and enough seating for a planeload of waiting holidaymakers. *The Crow* had three wooden chairs, a flimsy coffee table and a pile of magazines so dog-eared they had adverts priced in pounds, shillings and pence.

The Crow. Established 1846. Circulation 17,000 and steady. The *News*, circulation 3.6 million and rising. Dryden breezed through the door, checked his watch at 1.30pm and flipped over the sign to 'Closed'. Ely was still a member of that sleepy band of towns where some of the shops close for lunch just in case someone wants to buy something. Besides, Thursday was early closing and most of the shopkeepers had headed home for a siesta. Jean was knitting and singing to herself a tuneless ballad. Outside, Market Street cooked in the midday heat and nobody moved. The girls in the shoe store opposite had opened all the doors to assist the air conditioning, not realizing they were asking the system to cool the whole of East Anglia before it started on the inside of the shop.

He took the wooden, uncarpeted stairs three at a time and pushed open the hardboard door at the top marked, with misplaced confidence, NEWSROOM. The room on the other side wouldn't have qualified as a cupboard on Fleet Street. Dryden had left the *News* after Laura's crash. *The Crow* paid the bills for his floating home and gave him plenty of time to be at Laura's bedside. The insurance company paid for The Tower, an arrangement on which they were, at present, unable to renege. Laura's accident had resulted in a media blitz and the story had taken up the front pages of the tabloids, on and off, for a month. At the time she had been one of the principal characters in the TV soap opera *Clyde Circus*. Her condition, once diagnosed, had kept the story going. Locked In Syndrome – or LIS – was news. Victims appeared to be in a deep coma but could, at times, be entirely conscious despite their lack of movement.

Dryden had met the onslaught of Fleet Street with resignation – after all, he'd been on their side for the best part of a decade. At every opportunity during interviews he'd dropped the name of the Mid-Anglian Mutual Insurance Company into the story, praising the way they had paid up instantly for Laura to be cared for at The Tower and for treatment by some of the world's leading coma experts. They had little choice but to go on footing the bills. But he knew it wouldn't last. One day, probably fairly soon, a polite letter would inform him that less expensive care would be appropriate. It was a corrosive anxiety, made real by the image of Laura lying in some forgotten ante-room in an under-funded, and over-stretched, local hospital.

But for now he needed only an income to pay his bills, to be near enough to visit Laura, and to have something else to fill his days other than the image of his wife laid out beneath a single linen sheet. The position of chief reporter on *The*

Crow, offered after a month of casual shifts, had been an admirable solution to all three problems.

The newsroom's bay window was open to the street. Outside it was lunchtime and nothing moved. Siesta, Fen-style. Across the street the local ironmonger's had dropped its white linen blinds. Above the shops the cathedral's Octagon Tower loomed, while crows soared in the thermals over its hot, lead-clad wooden pinnacles.

For a city centre it was a touch on the quiet side. Dryden could hear his watch tick.

The news desk was along one wall. Charlie Bracken, the news editor, was by now in the Fenman opposite administering stress relief at £2.30 a pint. Brendan had a drinker's nose, which was not as noticeable as it might have been, because it was embedded in the middle of a drinker's face.

Dryden tried the coffee machine. It took a variety of foreign coins which *The Crow*'s staff collected on holiday. The editor, Septimus Henry Kew, always referred to this as a principal staff benefit. It was probably the only one. Thursday was press day, as well as early closing, so by 3.00pm the newsroom would be as full as it ever got. Three subs, the news editor, the editor and Splash, the office cat. *The Crow* had two reporters, Dryden and his junior side-kick Garry Pymoor. In the midday silence Dryden could hear Garry coming up Market Street. He'd had a bout of meningitis at the age of four and the result had been the complete loss of his sense of balance. The cure was simple, the doctors told him, and his shoes were fitted with metal 'blakeys' so that he could bang them on the pavement when he walked. The result was a kind of stereo sonar which allowed his ears to function properly as stabilizers. Garry thudded through the front door, plodded up the stairs and flopped into his desk.

The junior reporter made sure the editor was not behind

his smoked glass partition and lit up a cigarette. The news-room was officially non-smoking. He flipped open his note-book. 'What's a Fen Blow?' he asked, sniggering. Dryden considered the obscene answer Garry was hoping for but thought better of it. The post-adolescent junior reporter had hormones that humped each other.

'It's a dust storm, Garry. In dry weather the fields in the Black Fen can lose their topsoil. Dry peat is effectively weightless. If a strong wind hits during a period when there's no crop cover a field can literally take off, and once airborne the dust cloud can travel for miles.'

Garry nodded. 'There's one coming. I did police calls from the magistrates' court. They said they'd got one out on the Fens to the west, near Manea, coming east.'

'Great. Phone Mitch. I've got a job that way – I'll keep an eye out.' Mitch was *The Crow*'s photographer. He was a miniature Scotsman with a passion for fake tam-o'-shanters. Fen Blows made good pix but poor stories. Unless they hit town the only damage they did was to farmers' incomes, which even for a paper like *The Crow* was a minority interest given that automation, and chronically low wages, had taken thousands of farm workers out of the fields.

'And there was more on the Beck appeal,' added Garry.

Dryden had told no one at *The Crow* that Laura was sharing a room with Maggie Beck. He tried to keep his emotional life separate from work. In fact he tried to keep it separate from the rest of his life. But he found it hard to disguise his interest in the increasingly frantic appeals being made by the police for Estelle to return home. His promise to Maggie haunted him. Was he doing enough to track her down? Would she get back in time?

'They've had nothing from the radio appeals. Police say she could be dead in twenty-four hours. Apparently they think the daughter is away on holiday – north Norfolk coast. So they've contacted the tourist boards, RNLI, B&Bs – the lot.'

'Fine,' said Dryden. 'Knock out two pars for the front page. And three on the dust storm.'

'According to someone at Black Bank – one of the farm hands – she's travelling with some Yank.'

'Name?'

Garry laboriously leafed through his notebook. 'Koskinski. Lyndon. Apparently he's based at Mildenhall on temporary leave or something . . .'

Dryden saw again the tall, willowy pilot standing by Maggie's bed. 'Knock it out,' he said, and booted up his own PC. He wrote quickly and fluently in perfect, objective reportese. He had a court case about a man who stole cabbages at night and an appeal for a lost snake.

Then his phone rang: 'Hell – oo . . .' Inspector Newman's voice always sounded as if it was ten feet away from the phone.

Dryden could hear evidence of birdsong in the background and guessed Newman had it on his PC's screensaver.

'A bit more. The stud. His face. It's on the records. Although his face wasn't to camera most of the time. East Midlands Police have picked him up. Coupla hours ago, at his flat. Few hundred videos in the spare room – Vice Squad are checking them out now.'

Dryden scratched a note as Newman spoke. 'Name? Charge?'

'Can't release. No charges yet.'

'Local?'

'Rushden.'

'The girl?'

'Says he can't remember. Said it was all consensual. She led him on. Blah, blah.'

'So he knew the cameras were running?'

'Looks like it. Not surprised to see his bum in the frame, anyway.'

'Occupation?'

'Besides shagging? Long-distance lorry driver, apparently. Surprised he had the time. And, Dryden . . . Nothing sensational, OK? Just an appeal for information.'

'Would I?' It was one of Dryden's favourite questions. The answer was 'yes'.

There was a pause on the end of the line which was filled with birdsong.

'Hold on,' said Dryden, pulling up the PA wire online. Newman's extra information warranted an update.

Dryden found a second take on the rare bird story which had run at 1.16 pm: 'Rare gull finds love on the beach'.

'There's an extra paragraph on your gull: "Ornithologists at Holme Nature Reserve on the north Norfolk coast made a further plea for twitchers not to descend on the remote spot after news leaked out that a rare Siberian gull had been spotted by enthusiasts late yesterday. They said that two of the birds, which normally spend the summer in northern Scandinavia, had now been sighted and appeared to be a breeding pair."'

'Thanks,' said Newman. 'I might run out and do some crowd control.'

4

The Sacred Heart of Jesus was about as spiritual as a drive-in McDonald's and twice as ugly. This was brutally apparent because that is exactly what it was built next to. The two shrines crouched like colonial monuments up against the main wire perimeter fence which surrounded USAF Mildenhall.

Dryden hardly ever went to church, haunted as he was by a disastrously ineffective Catholic education, but he was prepared to make an exception to keep his promise to Maggie Beck. The police appeals might not work. He needed to do something else, and he needed to do it quickly. He let Humph take five minutes picking a parking spot in the otherwise empty lot the church and drive-in shared. There was enough room to re-enact Custer's last stand but Humph cruised for a few minutes considering his options.

'Who's paying for the petrol?' snapped Dryden. Humph ostentatiously took his time parking precisely between two white lines marked RESERVED.

On the far side of the base fence a smoke-grey military DC-10 sat motionless on the tarmac. The only signs of life were its winking tail-lights and a steady plume of hot exhaust which turned the horizon into a smudgy line.

The church lacked frills. It was a red-brick 1950s statement of solid devotion to dull values. Inside, it was even worse. It was so bad, Dryden concluded, it could have been Roman Catholic. But it didn't even have the candles and the pictures. The only vaguely spiritual presence was the almost tangible smell of furniture polish.

Major August Sondheim was sitting in the front pew smoking, an act of calculated sacrilege that was typical of him. He was tapping the ash on to a copy of the *Wall Street Journal* laid out at his feet.

August and Dryden had two meeting places: the church, or Mickey's Bar by the other public gate to the base. The church meant August was sober and intended to stay that way until nightfall, which was a sacrifice of supreme proportions because August was a major league drunk. His CV, however, was decked with glittering prizes: degree from Stanford, West Point, Purple Heart in Korea, Pentagon in the Gulf War. Who knows when the drinking started? August was head of PR: USAF Mildenhall, with oversight of Lakenheath and Feltwell, the two other US bases which ran north on the flat, sandy, expanse of Breckland. Three air bases with the capability to destroy European civilization. An arsenal of brutal power which could be flung into a war in Europe in the time it took to press a few buttons. It was a sobering thought: unless you were August.

August didn't look round. Sober, August could see the futility of life and the faults which made people want to live it. It didn't make him jovial company but Dryden enjoyed the edgy intelligence which underpinned his cynicism. August drew on the cigarette and sent the nicotine coursing round a few miles of narrowing veins.

'Well?' There was a note of impatience, directed not at Dryden, but at the world in general. Dryden rarely wasted August's time, which was one of the reasons the American liked him. He also admired the un-English lack of stuffiness and envied Dryden's ability to have four drinks and go home.

Dryden had met August a year before when Fleet Street's news desks had got hold of a story that the US military were stockpiling nuclear weapons on the base in case they needed to be shipped quickly to war zones in Iraq, Afghanistan or North Korea. A couple of the quality broadsheet news-papers rang Dryden and asked him to check it out. As a reporter Dryden had always put more store in trusting his contacts than diligent research. In the long run his copy had turned out to be more accurate that way, and he delivered it quicker. In this case he had also been hampered by an inability to spot a nuclear warhead even if it had been riveted to the roof of Humph's cab. But he could tell when someone told him a lie. He was pretty sure August was honest: before or after closing time. August might not tell him something that was true, but he liked to think he'd never tell him something false.

Dryden had killed the story. August said they'd had a shipment on the base for twenty-four hours and now they were clean. Dryden had charged the papers three days' money for research and surveillance and £258 for a telephoto lens, the receipt for which Humph had forged after drinking two miniature bottles of Grand Marnier. Dryden had rung the papers and told them the base was clean. Only time, or a very nasty accident, would prove him wrong.

'Well?' said August again, lighting up a fresh Marlboro Light. He was tanned, with silver-grey hair swept back as though his days as a pilot had shaped his body for speed. The pupils in his blue eyes swam like coins in a fountain. An expensive French eau de cologne failed to mask the whiff of the ashtray and last night's alcohol.

Dryden said: 'I need some help. A woman's dying. She wants to see her daughter. They lived at Black Bank Farm.' Dryden held a compass in his head and never lost the ability to find north. 'Over there,' he said, pointing through the wooden panelling beneath the first station of the cross. 'She's on a break. A holiday. But her mother's fading fast, faster than anyone thought. She's going to die, August, very soon. The daughter is called Estelle Beck and she's travelling with a family friend – a relative of some kind, I think. Lyndon Koskinski. He's a US pilot here at Mildenhall.'

Dryden took a card from his shirt pocket. *Major Lyndon Koskinski. c/o PO Box 569, Mildenhall USAF.*

August nodded, trying not to think about families. His wife had left him ten years earlier, but in more conventional circumstances than Dryden's. With dreadful predictability he'd come home to their clapboard house in Georgetown to find she'd flown to Hawaii with the family accountant. She'd remembered to take two things with her, their twelve-year-old daughter and her cheque book. The girl was called April and she must be a woman now, but whenever August thought her image might pop into his mind he conjured up a glass of Bourbon instead.

August stood and stretched. 'So there's a story in this, is there? Deathbed plea from dying mom – that kinda thing.'

'I guess. But she asked me to do this. There may be a story, sure. It's not the only reason I do things. I am capable of independent action. I'm bound,' said Dryden. It was an odd phrase, but he meant it.

They walked to the door, their shoes slapping on the cheap wooden parquet flooring. There was a table to one side with a small pile of orders of service in the middle, some books for sale, and a small box with a slit in the top for coins. August shook it and was surprised to hear money inside.

'Jesus,' he said. 'People are honest round here. Gives you the creeps.'

Dryden had spotted a locked door beside a utilitarian concrete font. August looked the other way as Dryden retrieved the brass key around his neck and tried it in the lock.

'No go,' said Dryden, genuinely surprised as he always was not to have unlocked Laura's secret.

'You're mad,' said August, with envy.

5

Dryden had been turning the microfiche for several minutes, struggling to focus on the tumbling blur of newsprint and headlines, before he finally caught sight of the picture for which he had been searching. Black and white, grainy even then, it smacked of an age when newspaper drama was still monochrome and flares were in fashion. It was from the *Cambridge Evening News* of 2 June 1976. A front-page picture showed a pall of smoke shrouding a distant line of poplars, while in the foreground the tail-fin of a plane stuck up from a field of wreckage. The fuselage lay twisted, melted like the cellophane from a pack of cigarettes incinerated in an ashtray. A house, clearly demolished by the impact of the falling aircraft, was blackened stone, with a few tortured beams exposed to the sky, and the single pine in the kitchen garden a narrow spear of blackened wood. A figure stood in the foreground with a clipboard, a respectful distance from what was, after all, a grave.

The caption was in the best traditions of stark news reporting: 'The scene yesterday of the Black Bank air disaster in which 12 died.'

Dryden looked up from the microfiche as the cathedral bell tolled 4 o'clock. He had decided to refresh his memory about the crash at Black Bank Farm. Maggie Beck's life had been unremarkable but for this tragedy, which had swept away her parents and her only son in a catastrophic accident. Dryden sensed that the torment of her dying was linked to this one traumatic event.

An ice-cream van played a version of 'Greensleeves' on a distant estate. Dryden's medieval features remained immobile as he closed his eyes. His ten-year-old self had not been far away that night in 1976. He remembered the blast rocking the old farmhouse at Burnt Fen. Did he remember the orange glow in the sky and his father holding him at the open attic window? Or was it a family memory inherited? They hadn't gone to gawp the next day with the others, but he'd saved the pictures and the newspapers until they'd been replaced by other obsessions.

He opened his eyes and went back to 1 June 1976.

PLANE CRASH KILLS 12.

The headline was set above the black and white picture of the scene of the crash. Below it a strap aimed at pathos: 'Mother saves baby from flames but sees her own son die'.

Dryden turned the knob on the side of the microfiche reader and the page slid down. Most of the nationals were agreed on the main facts by the second day. The death toll put it on the front page of the broadsheets. The coverage was objective and largely avoided criticism of the US Air Force. It was thirteen years before the Berlin Wall would come down and still the height of the Cold War. The US was a trusted ally in a conflict which was, despite the absence of actual warfare, very real. None the less, the facts spoke for themselves. The Met Office at Norwich had issued warnings that night that dust storms would criss-cross the Fens. Light aircraft at Cambridge were grounded, but the tower at USAF Mildenhall let MH336 begin its journey on schedule. In the aftermath of the crash the Civil Aviation Authority ruled, as an urgent priority, that all aircraft using the aerodrome should have filters fixed to air-intake valves.

The tabloids put the issue of blame to one side and concentrated instead on the personal tragedies of those who died. Dryden chose the *Daily Mirror* for an in-depth account, and had read it twice before he identified exactly what it was that was tugging at his memory. On board that night, according to the *Mirror*'s man on the spot, was the pilot, Captain Jack Rigby, his co-pilot and three servicemen travelling home on compassionate leave with their wives and children. One couple, Captain Jim Koskinski and his wife Marlene, were travelling with their two-week-old baby son, Lyndon. Marlene's father had died two days earlier in a car crash in San Antonio. The USAF had a transport flight booked – carrying field equipment stored in Manila back to Texas – and they owed young Jim a favour after fifty straight bombing missions in the last months of the war in Vietnam. The transporter had limited passenger capacity, but they offered to fly the family home.

'Koskinski,' said Dryden, out loud. The librarian, a stunning redhead with a figure far better than any of those described in the romantic fiction section, looked up and scowled. Dryden scowled back.

'Lyndon Koskinski,' he said, louder still. The Becks' family friend, the man now travelling with Estelle. The man he had to find.

Dryden discovered a half-eaten sausage roll in his jacket pocket and munched it, remembering he'd had nothing substantial since the ritual egg sandwich with Humph that morning.

Overhead he heard the familiar rumble of a transatlantic air tanker flying into Mildenhall, the air base from which the fateful flight had taken off that summer's evening more than a quarter of a century earlier. The aerodrome had opened as an RAF base in 1934 but by the fifties the Americans had moved in in force. By the time of the Black Bank crash the base, with its outliers at Lakenheath and Feltwell, was already the US 'gateway to Europe'. Today, with 100,000 passengers a year and billions of gallons of fuel ferried in to support US operations in the former Yugoslavia, the Mediterranean and the Near East, it was an exotic American township of nearly 7,500 people.

The sight of a shadow dashing across the Fens as one of the giant B-52s flew in to Mildenhall was now as familiar as the turning sails of a windmill had once been. And up there, beyond the clouds and on the edge of the stratosphere, something else circled. Two airborne command centres were kept aloft in a shift pattern providing a permanent flying nerve-centre from which a putative war in Europe would be waged. From this impossibly distant metal cylinder the US would direct the death rites of a continent. By that time, Dryden comforted himself, he'd be a small pile of radioactive ashes beneath an atomized cloud of best bitter.

He dragged himself back to the night of the Black Bank air crash, trying to imagine the scene as the transatlantic flight took off that June night. He'd been up in one of the new transporters that summer, a Lockheed Starburst, on a facility trip from Lakenheath, just north of Mildenhall. Passenger space was small and cramped, the noise terrifying, the porthole view obscured by racks for kit and stores. But that night in 1976 most of the passengers on flight MH336 would have been just happy to be flying home. Marlene, though, would have been struggling with two competing emotions, grief for her father and the coming ordeal of the funeral, and her excitement and pride in showing her mother the new boy. For Jim, Vietnam behind him for at least a period of extended leave, the flight must have offered a rare opportunity to collapse into sleep, haunted perhaps, thought Dryden, by the rhythmic thud of turning helicopter rotor blades.

Dryden saw the scene as the dust storm hit the aircraft. All the servicemen would have heard the sudden change in the engine noise, the metal of the turbine blades screaming as they were shredded in the diamond-hard dust. He tried to shut out the image of the aircraft stalling, the fuselage tilting violently, nose down, into a dive, a sickening spiral fall into the black peat below. A savagely short journey, but not short enough for Marlene and Jim, joined, Dryden imagined, in a single embrace across the tiny body of their infant son Lyndon.

He re-focused on the microfiche with tired eyes. The only survivor from amongst the air passengers had been Lyndon Koskinski, aged thirteen days. Maggie Beck had found him in the rubble of the farmhouse, still secure in a travelling cradle strapped into his seat. She'd walked out of the flames with him wrapped in a USAF blanket, having seen her own child trapped, and clearly dead, in the ashes of the farmhouse. She'd saved Lyndon's life, thought Dryden, and now he was here to see hers end.

The next day – 3 June 1976 – the *Cambridge Evening News* had a picture of Maggie Beck coming out of the mortuary at Cherry Hinton. The caption caught the horror of the moment: 'Maggie Beck leaves the city mortuary after identifying the bodies of her parents, William and Celia Beck, and her 15-day-old son Matthew John'.

The good news came two days later. James Koskinski, Snr, and his wife Gale were shown holding their grandson at a photocall at USAF Mildenhall. They had flown the Atlantic to take custody of the child, saved from the ashes of Black Bank. 'We have met Miss Beck and extended our thanks for her courage in saving Lyndon's life,' said Koskinski, according to the *Daily Telegraph*. Both tried and failed to deliver a smile for the cameras. They didn't look thrilled to be parents again, and certainly not a few days before the funeral of their only child Jim. They flew home with their grandson, and two coffins.

Inquests on all those killed were held on the same day. *The Crow*'s reports were the most detailed, but given the cataclysmic forces involved in the disaster the verdicts – of accidental death – were a foregone conclusion. The heat of the crash had made most post-mortem examinations on the passengers impossible and irrelevant. Dental records were required for formal identification of most victims.

President Gerald Ford sent a message of condolence which was read at the military service of remembrance at Mildenhall's bleak, brutal, 1950s chapel on the base perimeter. All US personnel killed in the crash were flown home for burial or cremation. An official USAF inquiry cleared the pilot of any negligence but severely admonished the air traffic controllers at Mildenhall and the senior officer in command of the base. He finished his tour of duty in the UK, and then returned to a desk job in the Pentagon.

Maggie's parents were buried at the church on Black Bank Fen. It had been their last wish, according to an interview with William Beck's sister, Constance, shortly before the funeral. *The Crow* carried a brief report of the ceremony itself with a single-column heading: 'Crash victims buried within sight of home'. An honour guard from USAF Mildenhall escorted the coffins to the graveside. Matthew John, known as 'Matty', was cremated at his mother's request.

The Revd John Peters, team vicar for the parish of Feltwell Anchor, which embraced Black Bank, delivered a eulogy at the Becks' funeral, fully recorded in *The Crow*. 'They were transported from here to eternity in an instant,' he told the congregation. Dryden wondered how often Maggie Beck had relived the few seconds which had destroyed her life.

6

Dryden lowered the window of the Capri and let the breeze buffet his ear. It was evening time but the heat of the day still made the cab stink. Hot plastic, socks, and sump oil merged in an odour that Humph liked to call 'Home'. The promise Dryden had made to Maggie Beck weighed heavily on him, but he felt he had done everything he could, short of touring the north Norfolk coast himself on the off-chance he could spot her missing daughter. In the meantime he had a job to do, which meant he had to find a decent story for the next edition of the *Ely Express*, *The Crow*'s downmarket tabloid sister paper.

Dryden had spent many hours that summer scanning the national papers for stories to follow up in the Fens. The so-called 'silly season' had struck early that year. Nobody could be bothered to make news in the heat, or even make it up. Last week *The Crow* had splashed on the drought for the sixth time in a row. From 'It's a scorcher!' to 'Mains water to be cut' the soaring temperatures had dominated everything.

The Crow's meagre editorial budget did not stretch to a full set of national papers each day so Dryden spent an hour in the library every afternoon. He'd begun to spot the pattern in the first days of May. The odd paragraph here and there but, essentially, always the same story. Police raids on lorry parks on the motorways. Illegal immigrants in small, bedraggled groups. Mainly sub-Saharan West African in origin, all Francophone. They probably crossed the Med from the North African coast to the ports of the South of France. Then north to the Channel and via container ship to Felixstowe where they could be shipped across country by lorry. Some had got out en route for the West Midlands. At night, in roadside lay-bys, welcomed by silence and fear.

And the same promise. Jobs. Pickers in the fields. An idyllic picture, laughably misplaced. Dryden scanned the horizon. Miles of empty dry peat. Thousands of acres and not a single living thing on two or four legs except the wheeling birds and a single conspicuous black cat picking its way across the ridges of a vast field. No pickers. Even at harvest time you couldn't see them in the fields. They shuffled along in the shade of the picking machines. An ambling production line. Then they disappeared inside the sheds for the rest of the summer. Sorting, cleaning, and packing, but always hidden.

He knew that several police forces were tracking the illegal trade. 'Operation Sardine', as it was called, had been coordinated by East Cambridgeshire and the East and West Midlands forces with help from Norfolk and Suffolk. He'd been given a briefing in Coventry at the regional crime squad's HQ by the detective leading the operation. Dryden had been on several raids but little of substance had been found so far. So he'd started to made his own enquiries, which was why he was going to try his luck at Wilkinson's celery plant.

'Appointment's at six o'clock,' said Dryden, checking his watch.

Humph grunted and pressed the tape button on the dash-board. All the cabbie's copious spare time was devoted to taped language courses. Each Christmas he would take a holiday in the country of choice, neatly avoiding the necessity to endure the festive season alone. Greek this year, Polish last year. Only France was taboo. He and his ex-wife had gone there for their honeymoon. That was before she'd run off with the postman. Humph had seen him once, loitering outside the divorce courts in London. He'd been balding, with sloping shoulders and a paunch and Humph's daughters had held his hands with, he judged, obvious distaste. So not France.

On the tape Andreas, his imaginary friend from Thessaloniki, asked him the time. Humph repeated the question and gave an answer in what he understood to be elegant Greek.

Then he asked Dryden a question, a rare enough occurrence in itself. 'Why Wilkinson's?'

It was a processing and packaging plant for celery, one of several small-time businesses which had sprung up on the Black Fen. They employed a silent workforce several thousand strong. The big operators, like Shropshire's outside Ely, had multi-million pound premises and a workforce recruited from agricultural colleges across Europe. To compete, places like Wilkinson's had to cut corners. That meant cheap labour and safety regulations stretched to breaking point.

'Illegal immigrants,' said Dryden, reaching into his pocket and extracting two-thirds of a miniature pork pie gently dusted with fluff. Humph was steering using his elbows as he tore the cellophane off a diet sandwich. He loved diet sandwiches: hundreds of them. 'Who says?'

Dryden was guessing. He'd recognized long ago that his interest in the people smugglers went beyond a story. Claustrophobia was one of the many things that terrified him. The thought of being entombed in a container lorry was a cliché of hell, but no less real for that.

He flipped down the sun-shade as the car turned due west on the old road by the Forty Foot Drain – a drove known

46

with affection by the locals as the Fen Motorway. A large reflective sign shouted: 5 DEAD, 18 INJURED in the last TWO years. Dryden considered briefly the chilling horror behind those bald statistics: at least three of those killed had drowned in their cars.

The sun was setting on the razor-sharp edge of the horizon and cutting its throat as it slid out of sight. Dryden felt his spirits rise; a sure sign something was about to go horribly wrong.

To the south a farmstead stood about a mile back from the road. The only way to get to it by car was over a small private cast-iron bridge across the Forty Foot Drain. A wind pump on the roof span in the evening breeze. It was the kind of place he and Laura had talked about the last time they'd talked at all. Since then it had been four years of monologue. He'd talked for both of them as she lay in her coma. Sometimes he would imagine her part of the conversation, and when the messages started he would say the words out loud, trying to recall the exact inflection of her voice, the subtle combination of a Neapolitan childhood and a north London adolescence.

The last time they'd talked, really talked, they'd been on their favourite walk, along the bank-top by Little Ouse, past the old Victorian grain silos at Sedge Fen, then over the iron bridge to the north side and the wide desolation of Adventurer's Fen. It had been the day before the crash in Harrimere Drain. It was their spot, the place they'd daydream about most. But there were only two houses – two pathetic brick semis built for farm workers in the 1920s. Both were criss-crossed with cracks in the brickwork, the peat beneath their flimsy foundations shrinking as the new electrical fen-land pumps sucked the moisture out of the peat below. Tiles slipped from the roof as the houses tipped forwards into the fen, the window frames twisting and splintering with the movement.

Mist that day. A swirling soup of it which opened up for half a mile and then descended like a cotton-wool blindfold. They'd stood in the solid whiteness of the day and held each other close.

'A house,' said Dryden. 'We should decide. Move out of London and start a family.' He kissed her hair but she hadn't answered, and in the long silence a crow had called from the rooftop of one of the crumbling cottages.

He wanted to walk on, towards Adventurer's Wood, but she pulled him back. Something was wrong. He knew it then, and he knew it now. But what? A house and a family were what they wanted, but only after: after she'd done one last series of *Clyde Circus*, after he'd done one more year at the *News*. After – the word he hated most now, after Harrimere Drain.

What did he doubt in those final hours they were together? Her love? Commitment? Whatever it was, it had disfigured that last memory, possibly for ever.

It wasn't as if money was a barrier to fulfilling their dream. One of the many aunts from Campania who had emigrated with Laura's parents to help run the family restaurant in north London had left her a nest-egg: £80,000. It was all they needed out on the fen. It sat in Laura's trust account, getting fatter, and it sat there still, administered by the solicitors and her parents. None of Laura's family had mentioned the bequest since shortly after the accident, an act of faith which signalled their belief that one day he and Laura would buy the house, start the family, and begin again.

Humph flipped open the glove compartment and fished out two bottles of vodka. He collected miniatures on runs to Stansted Airport. Some of his regulars gave them as tips. He handed one to Dryden, sensing that his friend was descending into a rare bout of depression. Since Laura's accident they had maintained an almost constant mood characterized by either irrational exuberance or mutual indifference.

'Cheers,' said Humph, repeating a few random phrases in Greek.

They'd reached Manea. At least that's what the sign said, otherwise you wouldn't know. It was the archetypal Fen town. Most of the houses lined the sinuous main street with back garden views that stretched twenty miles to the horizon. Manea had a claim to fame, a railway station. Unfortunately it was three miles outside town.

Wilkinson's stood on the edge of Manea. A triple set of mammoth MFI-style blocks with a windswept car park full of the kind of cars which spend half their life up on bricks, and the other half breaking the speed limit. Most of the workforce, which had to support a twenty-four-hour production line, were picked up by the company coach on bleak street corners in the middle of the night.

Humph swung the cab in off the road and met an articulated lorry coming out. The stove pipe belched black exhaust as the driver swung the wheel with his forearms so that he could roll a cigarette and light up before he hit the road. He wore the sort of vest which only lorry drivers can, the colour of dirty snow with ash highlights.

They parked under a sign which said: Wilkinson's Celery Ltd. UK Headquarters. Below that another sign hung from one hinge: Research Department.

The staircase was steel and ran in a zig-zag tower up the outside of the main block. At the top was a door with no handle but an entryphone, so he pressed the button and after ten seconds of crackle he heard the lock turn automatically. He pushed the door open and walked down a long neon-lit corridor to another single door, which was half glazed with milky-white glass reinforced with chicken wire. There was a strong smell of disinfectant and his shoes stuck to the featureless cream lino.

He knocked once and walked in before anyone could stop him. A man in a shabby suit stood up from the only desk. He was a bit like a stick of celery himself. About six feet six, with white hair and narrow shoulders. 'Mr Dryden? Ashley Wilkinson. Don't think I can help you any more than I did on the phone. But sit down.'

Behind his desk was a plate-glass window, a good ten feet long and five feet high, looking down on to the shop floor. The light, entirely artificial, had the flat depressing effect usually reserved for deserted seaside aquaria. Dryden expected to see a bored shark cruising over the three identical production lines. On the conveyor belts salad crops, a livid lichen green, shuffled forward between lines of workers in bleach-white overalls.

Meat-eaters' hell, thought Dryden.

It was the celery shed. Tractors brought the crop in off the fields and dumped it down chutes at the far end from Ashley Wilkinson's office where it tumbled on to conveyor belts. By the time it got to the other end it was cleaned, trimmed, and neatly packaged. Radio 1 blared from a crackly tannoy system and the workers, each with a white plastic hairnet, moved with that odd combination of listlessness and physical economy born of the production line.

Dryden decided to be nice, a little-used tactic in his repertoire, and one invariably unsuccessful. But the blood-red sunset had lit up his mood. 'I understand West Midlands Police have been making enquiries. Illegal immigrants. I'm told two men have been arrested and removed to the Home Office detention centre outside Cambridge . . .' Dryden flicked open his notebook until he reached a page which contained an illegible shorthand note of three tips for the weekend's race meeting at Newmarket. 'Two West Africans I understand. Sierra Leone.'

Wilkinson didn't look wildly interested in the geography of the Dark Continent.

'Sub judice,' said Wilkinson. This, Dryden recalled, was 'fuck off' in Latin.

'This is all for my background, Mr Wilkinson. No names.' Dryden shut his notebook, slipped a large rubber band round it, and lobbed it on to Wilkinson's desk.

'Your numbers are wrong. They had papers. There's no suggestion we knew they'd come through Felixstowe. We'll check the references next time,' said Wilkinson.

Dryden noted the disguised admission. 'Where were they living?'

'Police never found out. Out there somewhere – plenty of places.'

'Good workers?'

'Fine. Darn sight better than the locals.' Wilkinson looked down through the plate glass at his workforce. 'Lazy bastards, most of 'em.' British management at its motivational best, thought Dryden, as he produced another miniature pork pie from his pocket and popped it, whole, into his mouth.

Outside, the musical wallpaper was interrupted as a voice cut in: 'Mr Wilkinson to the loading bay. Mr Wilkinson to the loading bay.'

'I'll show you out.' Dryden noted relief in the voice, and made a silent bet with himself that the call had been pre-arranged to cut short his visit.

'Ever been done before for employing illegal immigrants?'

But Wilkinson was already hitting numbers on a mobile phone. Interview over.

A door led out of the office to an observation balcony, from which a stairway dropped down to the shopfloor. They made their way between the production lines, watched by every worker in the shed. In a whites-only fastness like the Fens, the workforce looked like an outpost of the Notting Hill Carnival. Three women working together on the first line were black. Almost the entire second line was ethnic Chinese. 'Cheap labour,' thought Dryden. But he said: 'Mind if I have a chat with one of the workers?'

Wilkinson hesitated. Dryden decided to push his luck: 'I could always just hang around by the gate and catch them on the way home.'

'This is Jimmy Kabazo,' said Wilkinson, leading him over to a half-partitioned office at the side of one of the production lines. 'He's the day-shift foreman. Talk to him, if you like. He'll show you out too. '

Jimmy was black. Night black. Dryden guessed he was Nigerian.

'Follow me, sir,' he said, the voice pitched high and sing-song. Jimmy was short and wiry with tight-curled hair and the kind of smile that could hide any emotion. He wore the regulation Wilkinson's white overalls with a laminated badge: 'Foreman'.

Dryden told him what he'd heard about the police raid. The smile never flickered: 'Yeah. Bad news for the rest of us.'

'Police?'

Jimmy nodded, still beaming. 'They bin round. Yeah. Times. Everyone upset now. We're legal. We got the papers. They left a poster – you want to see it?'

'Why not?' said Dryden, and followed Jimmy down the production line and into a small staffroom. There was the girlie calendar, of course, with Miss June's thighs spread to reveal an anatomical level of detail. Some dried-out tea-bags stained the worktop while a spoon stuck up out of a tin of powdered milk. On the table the *Mirror* was open at the racing pages.

Kabazo closed the door to reveal the police poster.

£500 REWARD

Police at Ely and Peterborough are investigating the illegal entry into the United Kingdom of immigrants lacking correct documentation. Several lines of enquiry are ongoing and arrests are imminent. A reward of £500 is offered for any information leading to further arrests and conviction of any person involved in the organization or execution of such activity. Contact may be made via the dedicated freephone hotline number below or by e-mail. All information will be treated in the strictest confidence. Immunity from prosecution will be considered in exceptional circumstances.

Issued on behalf of the chief constables of the
East Cambridgeshire, East Midlands and
West Midlands Police Forces

An 0800 number and an e-mail address followed.

'Tempted?' said Dryden.

Kabazo tried a smile. 'It's not a joke.'

'Sorry. You're right. Any interest in the reward among the workers?'

Kabazo picked up a wooden chair effortlessly with one hand and swivelled it round so that he could straddle it. 'Not that I hear; it's a dull place. Nothin' happens at all.'

'How d'ya hear about it – about Wilkinson's?'

'Good news travels fast.' He must have been joking, but it was difficult to tell.

'Family local?' asked Dryden, enjoying himself.

'Some,' said Jimmy, biting his lip.

They talked about life in the shed. The six o'clock start, the mindless work, the wages. 'The worst thing is the windows,' said Kabazo, meaning the lack of them. 'The summer goes, the winter comes, we don't know. They ship in the stuff from abroad. We just work. Always the same.'

They shook hands. 'See you again,' said Dryden, somehow knowing he would.

Outside, Humph was asleep in the cab. Dryden leant on the roof and ate a packet of mushrooms he'd sneaked into the glove compartment and followed that with some small but perfectly formed Scotch eggs. He chased them down with a Grand Marnier. Now he felt even better. The evening sky was a stunning bowl of rose-tinted blue. He fished around for another miniature in the glove compartment and settled on a second Grand Marnier.

About a mile away an HGV cut the landscape as it powered its way on the arrow-straight back roads towards the Midlands. Dryden imagined the dark, fetid interior of the container and wondered what, or who, was on board.

7

Dryden drank some more on the way back to Ely while Humph, enthused by the general air of gaiety, made a spirited attempt to knock a passing postman off his bike on the edge of town on the off-chance it might be his ex-wife's lover. The cabbie wound down the window as the postman's bike mounted the pavement and embedded itself in a hawthorn fence: 'Bastard!'

There was deep, satisfied silence between them. 'It wasn't him, was it?' said Dryden.

'Nope,' said Humph happily.

They parked up at The Tower. Dryden's life was largely marked by random motion, but at the end of each day he came back to Laura. He grinned stupidly at the nurse at reception, making a half-hearted attempt to hide the effects of the alcohol, and tried not to skip to the lifts.

He walked to Laura's bed, touched her arm briefly as he always did, and checked Maggie, who was asleep, curled in the same tortured ball as before. Then he stood over the COMPASS machine, running a finger along its cream metallic paintwork. The specialists had brought it in two months ago. It consisted of a PC and computer keyboard. On the screen was an alphabet grid.

ABCD
EFGH
IJKLMN
OPQRST
UVWXYZ

The concept was simple, and familiar to anyone with a modern remote control. A small electronic trigger was placed in Laura's hand which she could use to navigate the grid and highlight individual letters. Clicking on a highlighted letter printed it on a tickertape which chugged out of the COMPASS.

The first problem was random erratic movements and mishits on the trigger. These distorted the printout record. The second problem was much bigger. Laura was not 'conscious' in any accepted understanding of the word, although she could clearly see the COMPASS screen, if only intermittently. She drifted in and out of Dryden's world to bring an occasional message; few made sense. For Dryden this had made her recovery painfully frustrating. On one level she was 'back', back from the coma which had so completely enveloped her after the crash in Harrimere Drain. But her visits were swift, unannounced, and often cryptic. A long line of tickertape lay folded in a neat concertina at Dryden's feet, ready to be deciphered.

He'd met Laura while working for the *News* on Fleet Street. Her father owned a north London Italian café, Napoli, where the regular clientele squeezed themselves down a long corridor from the café counter to a small room with six tables decked out in checked tablecloths. The food was simple but sublime: fresh figs, golden balls of mozzarella, piquant ragu, and pungent Parma ham, all washed down with the Vesuvio her father prized. One evening Dryden had found himself in the suburbs on a job, doorstepping a politician who'd had to resign over allegations of fraud. He'd sneaked into the Napoli while the police were inside the house taking a statement. Hurrying, he'd spilt his pasta course into his lap. Laura had helped mop up the mess in an oddly erotic dance of embarrassment. Love, as Dryden liked to recall it, at first fumble. Despite Laura's long apprenticeship in food she had kept her figure, and avoided the fate of her plump aunts, by smelling food rather than eating it herself. While her mother helped run the business she had brought up three younger brothers, and cooked most of their meals, without adding an unnecessary pound.

So each evening Dryden tried to fill her room with the aromas of the past. It was a ritual he found deeply satisfying. Beside Laura's bed stood a bottle of the same Vesuvio, the cork drawn and replaced. On a plate he put fresh fruit, cutting the figs to let them breathe. He poured out a glass of the wine and set it down beside her. And he lit one cigarette, a Gauloise, which he knew would remind her of their honeymoon. Then he would chat for half an hour. About his day, about Humph's planned Greek holiday, about what he'd seen in the world outside The Tower. Then he'd tear off the tickertape, and take it out to Humph's cab.

Tonight inspiration failed him: 'Maggie's dying.' He let the silence hang, as he often did, trying not to rush and fill the gap where Laura's voice should be. 'You must know too. But the doctors . . . they say days. We're trying to get Estelle back. Back in time, I guess. Forgive me, it's been a distraction . . .'

He stood and walked to the wall beside Laura's bed. The nurses had put up a cork-board and Dryden had pinned up most of the messages she'd been able to send using the COMPASS machine. He'd cut out the letters that made sense from the background jumble. He was acutely moved by the fact that he understood each as only a lover can.

SGDFDYFYJF FLIGHTPATI SGD PK ABI YCND

He ran his finger along it, enjoying again the thrill of deciphering this opening message. The first time she had used the COMPASS to say anything other than her name. It said so many things about how well she was, at least in her mind. But for the missed H at the end the single word was perfect: Flightpath. Flightpath Cottages; the now derelict houses they'd discovered together on Adventurer's Fen. A vision of where the future could be, if Laura recovered. A home, a family, and everything they'd wanted before the accident in Harrimere Drain.

SHSHFT ROSA SDGDU

Rosa was her mother. He'd photocopied the tickertape and sent it to Turin, where her parents had retired. He could only imagine the tears that had flowed. And he'd taken a copy to the family restaurant in north London, which was now run by Laura's three brothers. They'd embraced him, cried, and promised to visit soon. When they came the brothers crowded in to Laura's room with their families, while the children ran riot. When their time was over Dryden stood with them outside on the lawns, waiting while the kids climbed into the cars. There were tears then, too, and bitterness that this should have happened to Laura. Of all people. That was the phrase that Dryden always heard echoing around the family: of all people.

Dryden's favourite was the simplest. It's straightforwardness an echo of the life they had lost.

SGDHFYU MY HAIR SHDSIDK

He had then, and he did it now, because he was lost for words. He raised her head and ran the brush back through the auburn hair, feeling the warmth of her body through the nape of the neck. He kissed her once and left.

Humph was waiting in the Capri in the midst of an Athenian street wedding. Three tiny empty bottles of Ouzo were lined up on the dashboard. Humph wasn't a drunk driver, which meant they were going to be parked for a long time.

Dryden got in the cab but left the door open. Humph gave him a miniature bottle of Greek brandy and went back to the wedding. Dryden read the tickertape and spotted the four attempts at LAURA. The tickertape had a digital timecheck along one side. All four had come just after seven o'clock that night.

Then he saw it. At 8.08: a burst of nonsense with those two words. His hair stood on end despite the fact that he told himself it must be a bizarre, random chance.

PDGUT WLGHJKOR T HISKFOT HJKKDHSGSI
THGYUS GHJYOU JNKOWFGH THEY
WHISPERKKJTNFMR
AEWGHCMI GKIAKA JEJUOIFK

But even as he tried to dismiss it he had to ask himself: did she mean the nurses? Visitors? And what, he wondered, did they whisper about?

He led her through the trees to the cast-iron door and even as the blood pumped in her ears she noticed that when he turned the key in the lock it clicked over with a barely audible, oily ease. She remembered later, on the park bench, thinking that he'd been there before. That he'd done it all before, with others. She knew that now, when it was too late.

That was the first time that night she'd felt like crying for help, and the last time she could have. She watched his body move ahead of her with a sinuous sexuality which had struck her dumb despite the fear. She'd never craved sex like that, never found its promise so intoxicating. And only now, looking back, did she understand that it was the drug which had made her blood run hot.

But before the drugs she'd seen him, she had to admit that, and called him over with her eyes. He'd breezed through the door of The Pine Tree that Monday night with an easy, athletic, grace. Mondays: the quietest night of the week, with a few locals and the quiz team. She was bored, and she must have radiated that, like a lighthouse seeking a ship.

She got closer, collecting the glasses, close enough to see the tail of a tattooed dragon that curled around his collar bone before plunging back beneath the white cotton top. And the face. A face she'd seen a thousand times and never, the face of a comic book hero, her very own Action Man. Blond cropped hair, and pale fingers with spotless nails. She wondered then what he might do. And there was another question: how could he be interested in her? How could someone so beautiful, so clean, so perfect, be interested in her?

She should have known when he made the call, on his mobile, walking away from the bar, cupping his hand to smother the words. He

60

winked then, something which normally made her laugh at men. But she just beamed, stupidly, knowing already that something wasn't right, but not caring, now she sensed that his body could be hers.

She washed the glasses, served the locals, and pretended to laugh at their jokes, but watched him at the end of the bar. She hated the Pine Tree, she told him that. Hated it, but needed it to pay the university bills, for the clubs, and the clothes, and the holiday to Spain with the girls in her house.

'University?' he'd said, smiling.

'Yeah. East London. It's great,' she said, shouting to herself to shut up.

'The heat,' he'd said, his smile confined to his red lips. 'You want a drink?'

She'd taken for a vodka and tonic and left the drink on the bar beside him as she worked, returning, sipping, feeling lots of things which should have made her run. She'd been confused then, getting the change wrong a couple of times with the locals. And she dropped a glass: 'Sack the juggler,' they'd all laughed. She felt her legs buckle but thought it was the vodka and the heat of the night.

He licked his lips and she sipped another drink and heard her laughter, overloud, in between the CD tracks. She sang too and the locals laughed again, eyeing the stranger at the bar. She never really drank much, even in the clubs, which is why she didn't taste it, didn't catch the metallic edge which laced the vodka.

She asked Mike, the landlord, to lock up and do the ashtrays. He was a friend of her dad's from way back when they were together in the army in the Far East. But he'd been upstairs all night with his feet up in front of the telly. So he hadn't seen, hadn't sensed, as he surely would have, her disorientation.

'Date,' she whispered, and brushed a kiss across his cheek. He'd smelt it then, and kicked himself later for not stopping her. Not the vodka but something else, the drug sweating out through her skin.

The moon hung over the Pine Tree like a giant sunlamp. The car

61

suited him, she thought, opening the silver-grey door and catching the sickly scent of the air freshener. Alfa Romeo? Perhaps, she told the police later, but she couldn't be sure.

She got in the car, aware of her long legs, the tight jeans around her bum, and the tight T-shirt which tucked under her breasts. She couldn't stop thinking about her body, and his, together. It almost happened then. In the car park in the long knife-blade shadows of the pines.

He took her hand and put it on his crotch: 'I know a place,' he'd said and she imagined a flat, with sophisticated lighting and a bed a mile wide. And mirrors, she thought, giggling and letting him kiss her neck.

They drove into the night along the main road, the headlights passing them leaving long dizzy, neon lines in the night air. By the time they turned down The Breach she didn't care where they were. The stars seemed to be darting across the sky and she felt her heart racing hard, pushing against her ribs. They parked and she stumbled through the ditch grass by the moonlight, laughing as he tugged her forward, laughing as the thorns scratched her legs. And then she'd seen it for a second between the trees and she felt the grip of his fingers tearing into her wrist.

The pillbox.

Friday, 6 June

8

He'd first seen the Mollies dancing by moonlight on the water's edge one evening soon after Laura's accident. He'd wandered aimlessly for hours during those first weeks, trying to throw off the depression which clung to Laura's room at The Tower like the sweet smell of lilies. The first specialists to examine his wife said the chances of her breaking out of the coma were infinitesimally small. Dryden walked in search of an answer to a question he could not dare articulate: what was to become of his life? Would it be spent in a dismal vigil beside the bed of a woman who would never speak his name again?

It was past midnight when he'd come upon them first, in the water meadows beyond the town quay. The Mollies danced, laughing, and collapsed by their narrow boat to drink and smoke. He'd written stories about them for *The Crow*, but had never thought of them as embodying a way of life, a style of escape, a glimpse of freedom. A largely female band of singers and dancers, their black and white costumes reflected the darker side of rural life in the Fens. They spent the winter nights preparing the muscular routines they would perform in spring and summer. To the rhythmic thud of a drum they danced, knees brought high and suspended for a beat, before descending with crack of boot on gravel or stone.

He'd sat with them that night around their fire. He'd even talked about the accident and Laura. They'd talked about the New Age, about living on the boat, about the river and its life. And he'd seen Etty's eyes in the firelight, a forthright promise that he could have another life.

They danced now in front of the Cutter Inn, a sunbaked audience of shoppers and mums with pushchairs arranged in a dutiful, even fearful, semi-circle, with the river as a backdrop to the high-stepping Mollies.

Dryden raised his beer glass to the sun. The liquid was honey coloured and already warm. He raised it again to Humph, parked by the riverside twenty yards away. The cabbie waved a small orange juice back. Humph had a headache, a big blue headache with an Ipswich Town sweat-shirt. The cabbie avoided the word hangover, as if this made it impossible for him to have one, but there was no doubt his fragile state was associated with five small bottles of Ouzo consumed during an imaginary celebration in Nicos's taverna.

'Mollies,' said Dryden to himself. 'The military wing of the Morris Men,' and drained his pint.

Dryden listened to the rhythmic thud of the drum and thought about Maggie and his promise. There had been no news from the police – he'd checked that morning when doing the regular round of calls – and he'd left another message for Major August Sondheim at Mildenhall air base. If there was nothing by nightfall he'd have to do something dramatic, even if only to salve his conscience. A tour of the north Norfolk coast in Humph's cab loomed.

In the meantime Dryden had time to kill and a story to stand up. He had enough to run something on Wilkinson's celery plant and the people smugglers but it needed some padding, some colourful background to bring the story alive. The Mollies were among his best contacts. By turns anarchic, naive, streetwise and mundane, they provided a vivid view of Fen life. Once he'd got the job at *The Crow* he'd tapped into the knowledge they collected pursuing their unconventional lifestyle. Often asleep during the day, roaming at night, working out in the fields when they needed the money, they knew more about the real life beyond the town than a Panda car full of detectives.

The lead Molly, with a black hood and the hangman's noose round her neck, stood, blindly watching, as the others danced. Decked out in coloured rags with black and white painted faces they paced out metrical steps to the thud of the drum. But the one with the noose was a study in black. Still death.

Mitch was taking pictures for the *Express*. 'Bunch o' dykes, if you ask me,' he whispered in his bleak Glaswegian accent, missing his own Fen pun. Mitch was short, trim and wore his fake tam-o'-shanter with no sense of irony.

'Shall I get ye a pint, boy?' It was Mitch's turn, and a rare offer.

As Dryden waited for his drink he squinted at the Fens on the far side of the river, a seemingly limitless expanse of sun-drenched water meadow stretching to a wobbling horizon. Humph had picked him up at 9.00am, armed with two egg sandwiches, and they'd polished off two Golden Weddings before hitting the library to read the papers. That just about completed his official duties on a Friday. This pace of life suited him in the week but he knew he would wake on Saturday morning burdened down with the time to spend, and no one to spend it with, except Humph. And for two days at least nothing to legitimately distract him from Laura's bedside.

Something about the motionless girl with the black hood and the noose caught his eye. Even he jumped when she moved. Some kids in the crowd squealed as her dance began, threading its way between the rest of the Mollies who stood still, only their chests rising and falling as they fought to recover breath. It was an eerie but simple trick. The black hood, made of flimsy gauze, let the dancer see her way in the bright noon sun as she danced up to the crowd, right to their faces, her knees brought to waist height, before backing off. A youth with a red face and tattooed shoulders tried to laugh it off, but the jeer died in the silence of the little crowd as the black-hooded figure swirled past.

She stopped when she got to Dryden. The drum beat climaxed and stopped dead as she raised the noose with a jolt and let her head loll on the broken neck. Snap!

It was a finale guaranteed to kill any applause. The crowd moved away with indecent haste. The Mollies were associated in local legend with what the locals called the Water Gypsies – drop-outs who lived in a line of damp, dilapidated narrow boats on the edge of town and grew vaguely exotic, and strictly illegal, substances in gaily painted decktop pots. According to whispers they indulged in pagan rituals, including naked moonlight dancing and group sex. The Water Gypsies struggled hard to live up to this reputation, but still spent more time playing Scrabble than dancing under the stars.

Dryden sipped his beer. 'Hi,' he said. The girl whipped the hood off and a bun of blonde hair dropped to her shoulders. She had several beautiful features, dominated by the hair, and the kind of brown eyes you can swim in. She was naturally tanned by her work – crop picking. Her figure was, like Laura's, full and the lack of a bra always seemed to give her nipples ample opportunity to puncture her T-shirt. Etty, always just Etty, for all the Mollies who lived on the narrow boat had forgotten their surnames.

'Dryden,' she said, taking a gulp from his pint and wagging her tongue in the amber liquid. 'You got my text message, then. Nothing like a throbbing pocket, is there?' She smiled, revealing too many teeth, and extravagant laughter lines.

Mitch, who had returned with the drinks, gave Dryden a suspicious look and excused himself.

Etty flopped into a seat while Dryden went and got her a pint of cider from the bar. She downed a third of it, when it arrived, in a single gulp. 'The people smugglers. We saw them.'

She eyed Dryden with thinly disguised lust. What she liked most was the emotional distance, the six-foot two-inch frame, and the Early Norman features. She imagined him scanning the sky for a comet in a long-lost section of the Bayeux Tapestry. That was the key to the New Age after all – a passion for the past.

'What's it worth?' she said, her eyes wide from the effects of a plump spliff. She put her hand on Dryden's knee and let it rest there.

Dryden pretended not to notice. He'd been a journalist long enough never to show interest when a good story surfaced. It simply upped the price, even if it was being measured in pints of cider. He turned his medieval features to the sun and closed his eyes. He heard water lapping against the bank and the gentle tinkle of wine-glass toasts from one of the floating gin palaces on the far bank.

'A Friday night. Last Friday night. We were out in the van,' said Etty, filling the silence.

Etty and the rest of the crew from the *Middle Earth*, one of the narrow boats, ran a VW caravanette. It had curtains, which, considering what went on inside it, was a blessing for everyone.

'There were two artics parked up by the lay-by on the A14 where the tea bar is. They let three out. They were black. Poor bastards. Imagine – around 'ere.'

They surveyed the crowd, which displayed about as much ethnic diversity as a stable of thoroughbred racehorses.

'Time?'

She jiggled her empty pint. Dryden completed another bar run, aware as always with Etty that the more they drank the lower his defences fell. But for Humph's brooding presence they were defences which may well have been breached some time ago.

Refilled, she took a glug. 'One o'clock. The tea bar was closed but that creepy bloke was there who's usually behind the counter. It looked like a drop. There were other people to meet the lorry, a group of them – all black, 'cept one. The driver was a white guy – really odd, he looked like NF to me. Shaved head, really mean looking. We buggered off in the van.'

'Were they putting them back in the lorries?'

Etty nodded, slurping down the cider and letting her eyes swim over the Fen horizon. 'Last thing we saw they were all back on except a group of them – half a dozen maybe. They went off overland. East from the lay-by, across Black Bank Fen. Like a chain-gang.'

9

The phone was black, Bakelite, and bang in the middle of the news desk. When it rang everyone jumped. Luckily it rang very rarely. It had been installed nearly fifty years earlier by Sextus Henry Kew, the present editor's father and then sole proprietor of *The Crow*. It had no dial, and its twin sat on a shelf on the public side of the counter below. When Dryden first arrived a small metal label had sat beneath the phone marked 'Complaints'. He had snipped the wire one evening after a brief drinking bout with Humph, and then stolen the label, which had reappeared in Dryden's boat, neatly screwed to the panel above the toilet roll in the loo.

The editor, ever vigilant on behalf of his heritage, had spotted the fault within a week. Thereafter Septimus Henry Kew would pick up the receiver, every Friday, and check the dialling tone as he opened up the office. Dryden had suggested mice were gnawing through the cable. Henry sent Garry out for a trap, and called an electrician. 'The readers,' said Henry, recalling an aphorism of his father's, 'must be heard.'

When the black phone rang, it was every man for himself. It rang.

Garry, confidence buoyed up by his normal Friday lunchtime diet of four pints of India Pale Ale, picked up his own phone immediately and dialled an imaginary outside number, leaning back in his seat and closing his eyes as if steeling himself for a particularly difficult interview. Charlie Bracken, the news editor, flinched. Charlie had got the job on the basis of Henry's bizarre concept of inverse qualification. Being the news editor demanded an ability to make hard decisions under pressure: it took Charlie twenty minutes each morning to decide which side of the bed to get out of. But when the black phone rang he knew exactly what to do. He had his coat on in seconds and was heading for the stairs. 'Ciggies,' he said, patting a pocket.

Now that this week's edition of *The Crow* had gone, 'ciggies' was code for the Fenman bar, which stood opposite *The Crow*'s offices and offered customer-friendly opening hours. They wouldn't be seeing Charlie again that day.

The phone rang again. Dryden failed to move, befuddled by the effects of a liquid lunch of his own at the Cutter and Etty's frank offer of an afternoon of sex on water. He had also been trying to work out why he was so unsettled by the news that the people smugglers used Black Bank Fen. Just when he was trying to put Maggie Beck out of his mind, the scene of the 1976 air crash seemed to be haunting him.

The phone rang again. If it rang four times Henry would be out of his office. Dryden, who liked nothing but a quiet life, walked over and picked up the receiver, leaving a slight imprint of sweat on the cool black Bakelite. Despite having spent more than a decade as a reporter, Dryden retained a deep-seated fear of meeting any member of that mythical but terrifying group: the readers. He had long since realized that advancement in his profession relied on the simple truth that journalists wrote newspapers for other journalists to read. The readers? Who cared what they thought? Who cared, that was, until they turned up on your doorstep demanding to talk to a reporter.

'Hi. Newsroom. Philip Dryden speaking.' He always hit a confident tone. That way he had plenty of room for what was, inevitably, an occasion for abject apology.

'Hello now. I didnae think this thing would actually work,' said a voice dipped daily in nicotine. 'The name's Sutton. Bob. It's no' really a complaint about yon paper. It's the polis I'm after complaining about.'

'I'll be right down,' said Dryden, who loved little more than landing a well-judged boot upon the idle rump of the local constabulary. He clattered down the newsroom steps with enthusiasm. Bob Sutton turned out to be the human incarnation of the Tate & Lyle sugar man: a cube of muscle with arms and legs hung from the corners of a barrel chest. Each fist resembled a solid two-pound bag of sugar. He wore a cheap security man's jacket in black. He was in his forties, with sandy thinning hair and a dollop of an accent which Dryden guessed originated somewhere on the Clyde; somewhere with a big crane. He would have looked menacing if he hadn't clearly spent most of the last twenty-four hours crying. He rubbed butcher's fingers into reddened eye sockets.

'It's my dau'ta. Alice. She's gone missing. I've had the polis round. Bloody useless, man. They seem tae think she's run off. It's crazy.' He spread his hands out on the counter as if they were proof of his determination to find his daughter. 'She'd not go with a fella like that. You know? She's a good girl,' he added, taking a cigarette from behind his ear and gripping it between his teeth.

Dryden reflected that it was every father's lament, that his own daughter could not fail but be a grown-up extrapolation of an innocent five-year-old. But he took a note. Alice, aged twenty-one, had last been seen leaving her job as a bar maid at the Pine Tree pub, three miles west of Ely, five days ago shortly after closing time. The landlord had told her father, and later the police, that she had spent most of the evening chatting with a young man in a white T-shirt, jeans, and a pair of wrap-around reflective sunglasses which were held in his short blond hair. The landlord had described the man as late twenties, with an athletic build and a confident manner. The landlord's wife, who had seen him briefly on popping down during the evening to put out sandwiches and hot sausage rolls for the quiz teams, said he looked like a male model. She'd seen him walk over to the bar from a one-armed bandit by the door and told the police that his movements were 'silky'.

Later, said the landlord, Alice had asked to go early, explaining that she had a date. He'd watched her get into a car beside the Pine Tree. It was silver, he said, a sports car, with an expensive badge on the bonnet. He was sorry, he told Bob Sutton, but he was bad at spotting cars. She'd been seen sitting in the front with the bloke: kissing, he said, trying to find euphemisms for what he'd seen.

'He chatted her up,' said Bob Sutton. 'No way she'd just be going after someone. It was him that made the first move – no question.' He produced a box of matches and moved to light the cigarette. Dryden pointed timidly at the 'No Smoking' sign that Jean had knitted herself.

Sutton glowered.

'Done it before?' asked Dryden, judging the moment badly.

'Never,' said Sutton, thumping a fist on the counter, which jumped on the rebound. 'Can you do anything?'

Dryden shrugged. Missing teenagers were two a penny, the small change in the currency of the disappeared. He could do something for the *Express*, but that didn't publish for four days. And a freelance paragraph on a missing adolescent would sell nowhere on Fleet Street. Alice was probably having the time of her life with her dream man; either that or he'd dumped her and she was making her way home, pausing only to delay the inevitable humiliation.

Sutton searched his jacket pockets and flipped a passport-sized snapshot over the counter.

Dryden felt the hairs rise on his neck. He knew immediately, but took a long second look. The last time he'd seen those eyes they'd been glazed and staring out of one of Inspector Newman's X-rated snaps. It was the girl in the pillbox, but this version was quite different: college scarf, excited smile, and the sheepish grin that said 'Daddy's Girl'.

He calculated rapidly and decided Inspector Newman needed to hear first. 'I can try to find her, Mr Sutton. Perhaps use the pic? Would that be OK?'

'Sure, laddie. You do that. Anything comes up, ring me.'

The card said: Bob Sutton Security, The Smeeth, Wisbech. Dryden considered, not for the first time, the ability of the Fens to add a sense of mystery to English place names.

Sutton paused in the doorway letting the sunlight flood in behind him. 'Meanwhile, I'm lookin' too.'

Dryden wondered what Bob Sutton would do if he knew that the place to start looking for innocent Alice was under the counter at the local backstreet video shop.

10

Humph swung the Capri through the gates of The Tower and grinned as the tyres scattered the loose chippings. Dryden gave him a long-suffering look. 'Every time? Do you have to do that every time?' He kicked his feet out in irritation to try to find more room in the suffocating heat radiating from the cab's labouring engine. He seemed annoyed that the standard model was not built for someone of his height. Dryden's petulant mood was not entirely due to Humph's idiosyncrasies. He was dreading bad news. Maggie's life was perilously close to its end.

They parked where they always parked, about a hundred yards short of the neon-lit entrance lobby to the hospital, in a lay-by under a monkey puzzle tree. Dryden eyed the fore-court of the hospital. Most nights he delayed his visit by sitting on a wrought-iron bench on the edge of the lawn. Tonight, when he would have treasured ten minutes of solitude, there was someone there already.

Humph slipped his language tape into the deck. The imaginary Greek village was celebrating: a new taverna was opening and Nicos was looking forward to the food, a tasty platter of small delicacies. 'Methedes,' said Humph, spraying the dashboard with a light shower of saliva.

Dryden pushed open the cab door and noticed that a talcum of rust fell on his worn leather shoes.

He was almost past the bench when the man on it spoke. 'Mr Dryden? Philip Dryden?' The man stood, stepping into the pool of neon light shed by The Tower's foyer. It was

Lyndon Koskinski. Dryden felt a surge of relief that he'd managed, at least in part, to fulfil Maggie's wishes.

Koskinski brushed down the creases on his uniform, that of a major in the US Air Force. The physique was anything but GI – there was nothing general issue about the tall wiry frame and almost complete lack of puppy-fat. He radiated a shy intelligence and a civilized reserve which made Dryden wary.

'Hi,' said Dryden, walking back.

The pilot's face was handsome in the light, spare of flesh and still with a desert tan. He was bare-headed with his forage cap folded and held under one epaulette. The hair was brown-blond and longer than military regulations normally allowed: the eyes were hooded and held a permanent squint, like someone looking constantly into the glare of the sun. Dryden felt himself in the presence of a personality which habitually radiated an almost tangible sense of calm and self-possession. But Koskinski's air of complete physical control was undermined by his hands, which fluttered awkwardly at his pockets. Dryden concluded this man liked his own company, and possibly even prized it. He felt like an emotional trespasser but pressed on, sensitive only to his own curiosity.

'Hi, Lyndon,' said Dryden, his tone light, insincere, and almost perfectly pitched to avoid any real emotional contact. They shook hands. Koskinski's eyes, dimly seen beneath the heavy upper eyelids, seemed to brighten a few watts. 'Major Sondheim got the message to me. About Maggie. We're both back. Estelle's up in the room.'

Dryden saw again the newspaper picture of the baby saved from the crash at Black Bank being held up by his grandparents for the *Evening News*'s photographer. He'd be twenty-seven now. The only survivor, with Maggie Beck, of the 1976 air crash.

Koskinski looked up at the half-moon Victorian window: 'I phoned the base to see if I could get my treatment in the UK extended. The medics said Major Sondheim had left a message. So we came back . . .'

Nobody seemed in a hurry to go up to Maggie's bedside. Dryden sat. 'I was reading, yesterday, about the crash. The crash in '76. She saved your life, that night. Bringing you out of the fire.'

Lyndon, not answering, took out a lighter. It was a Zippo, the kind pipe smokers use, and roll-your-own fanatics; standard issue for GIs. They were icons, if original, and this one was worn to a golden sheen by years of use. Koskinski flicked the top up expertly, sparked it, and examined the blue flame. Dryden noted the smell of the fuel, and a pronounced shake in the pilot's right hand.

'This was Dad's,' said Koskinski, gazing into the flame.

'They found it?' said Dryden. 'At Black Bank?'

Koskinski shook his head: 'They didn't find anything at Black Bank. Not even a body. The coffin just carried his medals and a dress uniform. Grandpa told me that, later. I never forgave him. No, their luggage went separately from the air convoy. Clothes, some furniture, stuff from 'Nam and Cambodia. This was in a trouser pocket. Not much else.'

'What happened to you?' Dryden was pleased with the ambiguity of this question.

'Nerves got shot,' he said, examining the shaking hands.

Dryden nodded and let him fill the silence. 'I spent some time in Al Rasheid. Baghdad Hilton. The war. Four weeks in a cell. Shit happened, every day, like the sun coming up. You don't want to hear.'

'Solitary?' asked Dryden, imagining it would be better if it was.

Lyndon shook his head and took so long to answer that

Dryden thought he'd have to ask again. 'Nah. I was with Freeman, Freeman White. We came down together – engine failure. Freeman was bad. But we stayed together.'

'Where's Freeman?'

'Mildenhall. Medical treatment like me, then home, I guess. Ejector seat made a mess of his head.'

Dryden winced. 'You kept in touch with Maggie Beck. It's been nearly thirty years.'

Koskinski seemed to think this was a question. He held his hands out, palms up, as if mystified. '*She* kept in touch. She lost her kid, didn't she? It must've hurt plenty, so I guess I help in some way. I don't like to think of it like that, but that's the truth. I guess I'm a consolation. Second prize. I don't have to do anything. I just seem to help.'

'Why now?' said Dryden, relaxing visibly, trying to put his interviewee at ease. 'Why visit now? Did you know Maggie was ill?'

'No.' He shook his head both ways as if trying to dislodge persistent desert flies. 'They knew at home but, I guess, they felt – my folks – I had enough to deal with. I was just going home. To Austin, to Texas.'

'Folks?'

'My grandparents. They brought me up after the crash. We've talked about Maggie and they think I should stay too, hang around while she needs me. We all owe her. I was flying back to the States but they've got the medical teams here. I had some treatment to wait for – that's when I ran out to Black Bank. I didn't plan to. It just kinda happened. I'd never been. Weird.' He shook his head again.

'Why weird?'

'Coming back through Mildenhall like that. Just like Dad did in '76. I'm glad. I'm glad I'm here.' He smiled again, and Dryden sensed a real joy, even excitement.

Lyndon flicked the Zippo lighter again, pocketed it, then looked at a watch on his wrist which would have embarrassed James Bond. 'We'd better go. She's out cold but the doc said I should be there when she comes out of it. If she comes out of it.'

'We?' said Dryden, standing reluctantly. 'Why we?'

'She asked. She asked both of us — Estelle and me — to make sure you were here too. She's got something to say — to all of us.'

11

Dryden and Lyndon walked towards The Tower. It stood against the dusk like a cheap set from a horror film, its Gothic tower a pin-sharp silhouette against a sky which had finally relinquished the sun. But the heat remained. The moon blazed down like a scene-of-crime lamp on the hospital's Victorian façade.

Inside, the irritating background music which normally enveloped the foyer had been turned down to an almost imperceptible level: a far more emphatic signal than any doctor's opinion that one of the patients was about to die.

The curtain had been drawn around Maggie's bed. Lyndon slipped inside while Dryden sat beside Laura's bed, holding her hand with a pulsing grip, watching the shadow-show. Spasmodically a brief flame flared, like a struck match, seen through the gauzy material of the mobile screen. A doctor came and went with the over-careful steps of a mourner.

Dryden looked into Laura's eyes. Did she know what was happening?

'They've come,' he said, gripping the fingers still harder. 'August found them. Trust August. She'll be fine now.' He tried a smile and hoped Laura couldn't see its fragile confidence.

One of the shadows stood and parted the curtain. Lyndon Koskinski stood over Laura's bed. 'I've wondered, you know, about her,' he said. 'When we've been visiting, we've often sat here, talking, and thought about her. I'm sorry.'

Dryden, confused by kindness, shrugged. For the first

time he'd caught the tension in Koskinski's accent: the preppy college correctness only just obscuring the twang of the Deep South.

Dryden looked at Laura too, catching again a regular sensation that he was seeing her for the first time. 'She's getting better. That's what they say, anyway.'

'She wants you now,' said Lyndon simply, turning back towards the screen. Dryden stood, aware that he was about to be asked to play some role other than sceptical observer. He felt unease seep through his guts like a bad curry.

Estelle Beck sat at her mother's bedside. Her slim, athletic body squeezed into a pair of stone-washed jeans and a white T-shirt. Her hair was a trendy blonde bob cut asymmetrically, which captured what little light surrounded her mother's bed. The bedside lamp showed a face younger than her twenty-five years. The unmarked, olive skin held a bloom in both cheeks; the eyes a sensational lichen green. She could have been looking out of a sixth-form end-of-term picture. Dryden had met her at visiting time, and once out at Black Bank before Maggie had been admitted for the cancer treatment. She'd told Dryden her daughter was a teacher, in a primary school out on the Fens. He couldn't remember where: Ten Mile Bank, or Barrowby Drove.

She smiled now, seeing him. 'Hi. Thanks, for everything. I just feel so guilty we were away . . .' she said, her hand seeking out her mother's on the counterpane.

The heat was suddenly overpowering. Dryden felt a trickle of sweat begin on its long journey from his hairline down one temple. It wasn't just the heat. Since childhood he had feared being asked to play any role other than bystander. Why did Maggie Beck want him now?

Estelle must have known it was going to happen just before it did, because she leant forward and stretched out a hand towards Maggie's face. Her mother's eyes opened slowly and she raised her head from the uncreased pillows with surprising force.

'She's not going to die,' thought Dryden, mistaking the morphine-induced serenity for self-possession.

'Estelle?' Maggie said, taking her daughter's hand. She smiled then, and Dryden saw the truth – the irrational exuberance the drugs were pumping through her bloodstream.

'I'm here,' said Estelle. 'And Lyndon. And Dryden, as you asked.' Dryden felt even less comfortable, like an interloper. He saw the fear in her eyes as she clutched at her own wrists, as if seeking a pulse. Lyndon crouched down beside Estelle and the three held hands together. Maggie's other hand covered her mouth, afraid perhaps to tell a secret she had vowed to keep. Suddenly exhausted she slumped back and let her hand fall, the eyes closing and rolling back. Lyndon stood, retreating to the shadows. In the long silence that followed he retrieved the lighter from his pocket and sat, rhythmically flicking the flame on and off. On and off.

In the silence Dryden considered Maggie's life. A life of predictable Fen insignificance, flat and featureless except for that single night of unspeakable horror. What had it done to her? What scars had lingered within, as the corkscrew burn on her cheek had faded with the years?

They all jumped at Maggie's voice, suddenly loud in the hushed space around the deathbed. Her eyes remained closed and still but the tendons in her neck flexed visibly with the effort of speech. 'I lied,' she said, and Dryden was astonished to see tears running in a beaded stream from one eye. She struggled with herself, twisting in the bed as if resisting questions in an interrogation.

They waited. The windows were open in the heat and the sound of a bus changing gears came across the fields from the main Cambridge road. Dryden watched skylarks in the patch of china-blue sky which marked where the sun had set. The Tower was silent except for the cool snapping sounds of linen being folded by a nurse in the corridor outside. The caretaker whistled, perhaps outside, crossing the lawns.

Maggie's eyes opened again, but this time she saw nobody, at least nobody there.

'Dryden. My witness. I lied.'

She raised a hand. 'Lyndon?' He came forward from the shadows and folded long tanned fingers around hers, enveloping her wedding ring, which had caught the light like a candle in the darkness in the shadows of a church.

'We all lie,' he said, and Dryden noticed a glance of complicity with Estelle.

'I'm sorry, Lyndon,' Maggie said. 'It was your life. I stole your life and ended it. Matty didn't die, Lyndon. He's never died. I lied. I lied to the coroner. To the police. To . . .' She fought for breath for the first time and Lyndon made to get help. 'No. Stay, please stay. This is all I have left to do. I lied to give you a different life. You're Matty . . . You're my son . . .'

There was silence as Lyndon half-knelt again at the bed-side. Estelle sank back into the shadows, regrouping as the fixed points of her life were scattered by a single confession. She had a brother now, not a yard away, while she'd been putting flowers on the grave of a stranger for twenty years. And Lyndon? He'd gained a mother, on her deathbed, and lost a father he'd loved as a hero, but had never touched.

Dryden thought about Maggie's confession. She said she'd given Matty away to give him a new life. Could that really be all that had driven her; driven a new mother to give away her only child? What was so terrible about the life he would have had? From what did Maggie want to save her son?

Maggie struggled to say more. She turned to Estelle and offered a hand. Dryden watched her daughter's arm rise up, as if from under water, to clasp the fingers. And Dryden saw fear for the second time in Maggie's eyes. But this time the fear was specific and had an edge. The whites of her eyes were oddly vibrant in a dying face as she scanned their circled faces, pleading, searching. She had more to say, more she had to say, but she couldn't say it. Like a scream for help in a nightmare, the sound wouldn't come. Estelle kissed her mother's head and held her tight. But still there were no words.

Lyndon went for the doctor and a nurse gave Maggie more morphine, despite her feeble struggles.

'She'll sleep now,' said the nurse, so they went outside to take in lungfuls of cool air. Then Lyndon and Estelle went back and sat by the bedside again. But when Maggie spoke it was only with the echo of a whisper, so they didn't hear. There were just two words, spoken as she died that morning at 3.30am.

'The tapes,' she said.

Saturday, 7 June

12

The cathedral clock tolled four, a cold light tore the black edge of the horizon, and rooks rose in a cloud over the town. But it was the nightmare which woke Dryden. Always the same, and always in red. The gurgling blood, slipping past, with Laura clutching for his hand. He stretched out but never reached her, screaming silently for her to reach out to him. But she never did. Her eyes just asked a question: 'Why did you leave me to die?'

He jolted awake, his heart racing, and the fear so vivid that his hand still stretched out for Laura's.

Dawn greyed the hospital's Gothic tower as two orderlies carried Maggie Beck's body out of the foyer on a sealed stretcher. The silence and the lack of urgency told Dryden all he needed to know. He got out of the cab and stood, shivering, as the ambulance crept past.

Lyndon Koskinski walked behind it to the gates and then stood, watching until the curve in the road must have taken it finally out of sight. They were twenty feet apart but in the stillness of dawn they could almost whisper.

'I'm sorry,' said Dryden.

Koskinski's shoulders sloped, and his hands fluttered to his face, pushing back hair, and rubbing eyes.

'She should have told us. Before. She should have told us,' he said, walking closer.

'It was her secret.'

'It was my secret,' said Koskinski, his voice suddenly

angry. 'She should have told me. At least. What can I do now?' he asked, wanting an answer.

'Look after Estelle,' said Dryden.

He laughed then, the sound of a cynical lover rather than a grieving son, and Dryden's skin crept.

'Estelle,' said Koskinski, pulling out a letter from his pocket. He stood holding it, uncertain what to do. 'Maggie left this for you. I must go back,' he added, looking up at Laura's room with dread.

Dryden took the letter. 'Can I do anything?' he said.

Koskinski laughed again. 'No one can do anything. Believe me. No one.'

Dryden sat on the iron bench and opened the letter. It was in Maggie's elegant copperplate.

My Dear Philip,

When you read this I shall be dead, a thought which I'm forced to admit is not entirely repugnant to me. I have felt that my life is at its natural end for some time. I have made a dreadful mess of things, Philip, as you must now know. My illness has shortened what could have been a joyless old age. I have made my peace with God. As your mother knew, that is the most important thing.

There were many things I wanted to say in person before I died to the people whose lives I have disfigured. That is the word I have decided on, Philip – and it is the right one. I am conscious that I have done many wrongs, to many people. I have tried to deal with each. I have discharged my two secrets. They have weighed me down, Philip, and I shall be glad to be free of them.

There is one further matter left. What I have to say to you is best written. It is, after all, your medium. I want you to do something for me. Yes. Something more, I'm afraid, than the many things you have done already.

This letter concerns Lyndon's father. For the sake of absolute clarity, and I am aware this is a legal document, I am talking about his natural father. I know that this man, whom I once loved, has never been far away. I have not seen him since 1976. Indeed, I have made sure of that. But I have watched his life, at first with some satisfaction, later with misgivings and a growing sense of my own guilt.

At first his identity was well known, at least within the family, although I doubt if they ever uttered his name after Matty was born. I certainly never did. We expunged him from history. I will not name him here, but for more complex reasons than shame and anger. I feel now that he deserves his anonymity if he wishes to keep it. He is a victim too. The only person who can rightly name him is himself. I tried to keep his name from Estelle, with success I think, and he deserves his obscurity still, if he wishes to keep it.

Whatever his faults, and believe me they were grievous, I have robbed this man of his son. I want to give him a chance to recover some of the life he could have known had I not done what I did. I admit, freely, that I do this more for Lyndon than for his father. But never mind. Both will benefit and it is time for charity and forgiveness. If you meet him, Philip, tell him I am sorry. Ask him to forgive me if he can.

Philip, we have often talked about the value of truth and I know that newspapers can carry the truth to many. I want you to tell my story. Tell everyone I lied. Tell everyone that Matty did not die in the air crash at Black Bank. I believe that his father will come forward. He loved Matty and I know that, if it was as strong as mine, this love will have endured and even deepened over the years. But I know I may have killed that love with my lie. So I want you to say, Philip, in the newspaper, that if he comes forward he will be eligible for a portion of my estate. In many ways I cheated him out of it in 1976. I have set aside the sum of £5,000 for him alone. It is not much but in his present circumstances I think it is enough. The solicitors dealing with my will – Gillies & Wright – are in a position to confirm his identity. They will hand over the money only in the presence of my son, and only in person.

I know these requests are onerous and may seem baffling to you but please carry them out without change or delay. I would wish the story you write to appear after my funeral, the details of which I have set out separately for Estelle and Lyndon.

And one final request. The memorial stone marking the site of the 1976 crash carries Matty's name. I have no wish for it to be removed, but please see to it that Lyndon Koskinski's is added. My solicitors will find the sum of £100 in my will to cover the costs of the stonemason. I shall lie in the same graveyard as that child, whom I wronged so completely. I shall have to deal with the consequences of that if, as I hope, there is life after my death.

Your loving friend, who will always be in your debt

Margaret Alexandra Beck

Witnessed by John R. R. Gillies, solicitor

1 May 2003

Nothing moved on the Jubilee Estate except the burglars returning home after a good Friday night's work. Kettles whistled and pots brewed as bags of third-rate jewellery and fourth-rate silver were excitedly examined by bedside lamps. Outside No. 29 Wissey Way Humph had parked by his own front gate and, flipping open the glove compartment of the cab, he exhibited no desire to travel the last three yards to his own front door.

Dryden was equally overcome by the need to go nowhere. Humph passed him a bottle of Bell's whisky and then switched off the interior light. This was a minor ritual in their relationship, allowing them to view the world outside without being seen themselves.

A white cat with a collar that sparkled like the glitter-ball in a cheap dancehall selected the middle of Humph's blistered lawn to expel a sizeable pond of piss, the black creeping lake expanding stealthily several feet in all directions. On the other side of the road a couple shouted at each other beneath a bare lightbulb in an upstairs bedroom.

'. . . fucking Cymbeline . . .' shouted the man. But surely not, thought Dryden.

Humph tried to weigh up whether Dryden's silence was due to Maggie Beck's death, but as he was silent most nights it was a difficult call. 'Nice old girl then,' he said eventually, judging the moment badly.

'Yeah,' said Dryden, swigging the tiny bottle and accepting another. He shrugged as if it didn't matter. He told Humph about Maggie's confession. 'But there was more, I think, something else . . .'

'Perhaps it's on the tapes,' said Humph, who knew as much about Dryden's present life as the reporter did himself.

'The tapes,' said Dryden. 'I guess they're Estelle's. Yes. You're right. It must be on the tapes.' Dryden had given Maggie a tape recorder to let her tell at last the story of her life, and to encourage her to talk out loud for Laura's benefit. He'd never imagined the result would be a vital testament, a key, even, to the real mystery of Black Bank: Why had Maggie Beck given her son to strangers?

He stretched out his legs and took out the letter, handing it to Humph. Then he took out that night's section of tickertape torn off the COMPASS machine. As he read each foot of the tape he passed it over to Humph, tearing it off along the dotted lines. The cabbie was a crossword puzzler of strictly limited ability, but Dryden valued the double check. If he ever missed anything he could always blame Humph. He read the first take and passed it over, wordlessly, to the cabbie.

DHFVIUROIF SUFJJF SUFT DKJOO J J INDIGA
FGJGF
SHFDUTH ABABYGHTUKDN FHGFHFO SHOSJ

Dryden searched in his jacket pocket for the chocolate bar he had bought earlier that day.

Humph squirmed in his seat. 'A baby?'

'Maggie said she swapped the kids on the night of the Black Bank air crash. The one that survived – the Yank pilot – is her son.'

'Jesus!' said Humph, actually turning in his seat. 'How does Laura know?'

Dryden considered this: 'I guess she heard Maggie using the tape recorder. If that's the baby Laura means.'

The last torch had faded three hours ago and Emmanuel had wanted to cry then. Others did. He heard them when the lorry stopped and killed its engines. But the fear had shut them up.

No one talked now. The blackness was total. But that wasn't why they were afraid. They were afraid because of the heat, and the way it seemed to be stealing away the oxygen they craved. Emmanuel's chest hurt as he breathed, and he had to suck the air just to stop the screaming pain in his lungs. He pressed his forehead against the coolness of the metal walls and he tried to do what his father always said: 'Emmy. Act your age.'

Sixteen. He was proud of that. A man at last in the village. Just in time to leave.

He felt the self-pity well up so he thought about home: his touchstone. Almost thirty-one days now, counted out and marked up in his diary. He'd written down what he'd missed most; the way the dogs barked at night and the cool, overwhelming presence of the great river. He'd spent his childhood feeling it slip by, never ending, perpetual. Their lives depended on the river because his grandfather's boat meant they could all eat. He ferried the foreigners to the mine and back, and Emmy could hear, even now, the high intoxicating whine of the outboard motor. But it hadn't been enough. First his father had left and sent money. Now he too must send money home.

He reached out a hand and touched an arm. It jerked away. None of them were friends now. He felt the indignation swell into tears. They were supposed to look after him. There was Kunte, Josh and Abraham from the village. His guardians, his grandfather had said, in front of everyone. The village would never forget what had happened to Emmy, but then he thought they might never know. Could that really happen? Could he die and no one would know?

The fear had started at sea. The panic swept over them with the first big swell, which piled them in a thrashing heap against the food boxes. When the lantern failed Emmy felt better: he couldn't see the faces of the others. He had been a lucky child to live so long and never see betrayal in another's eyes. But he saw it then.

He'd seen England for the first time that day sometime just before dawn in a lay-by on a busy road. At least it was busy to Emmy. In the village they'd come out to watch the oil tankers go by, and the cars driven by the well-fed Americans. Here the cars were perpetual like the river, not cool and comforting, but alien — harsh.

In the lay-by the driver's torch beam blinded them. They hadn't been let out. Something was wrong.

'There's no choice,' the driver said.

They let them have the air for a moment and then crashed the tailgate back down. A fight started as the bolts shot into place. Emmy touched his fingers to his forehead later where someone's nails had clawed and he felt the stickiness and smelt the hint of iron on his fingertips.

They'd driven on and then Emmy had heard the sound of gates opening. Then silence. How many hours now? The driver got out and a car started up. Then nothing.

The night had gone, Emmanuel knew that. Now the sun was rising. Just beyond the thin aluminium curtain which kept him from the air.

He wasn't the first to panic. Even in the dark he knew it was Abraham; he'd known him all his life. He heard his fists hit the walls. Then everyone moved. Blindly in the dark. And Emmanuel felt the pain across his chest, and as he panicked too he knew, with the true insight of the living nightmare, that this was just the beginning of the end.

Nine Days Later
Monday, 16 June

14

Aboard *PK 129* Philip Dryden had not slept. That was the lie he always lived with: the truth was that he had slept, but could not face the nightmares which proved he had. Who said you cannot dream in colour? The blood was red and Laura always bobbed to its surface. She floated past his outstretched hand, each time a little nearer, but each time he could not reach, and each time he shouted out her name until he woke himself free from the torment of repeated failure. This time his anxiety had been doubled by the presence of Maggie Beck in his dream, still curled in her death-bed like an aged foetus, but floating on the sticky surface of the blood.

As always, with the dawn, the darkness lifted like the lid on his chest of guilty secrets.

He went up on deck with a mug of coffee to watch the sunrise from his deckchair. When he'd bought *PK 129* shortly after Laura's accident it was chiefly for the unspeakable romance of the small teak plaque in the wheelhouse which read 'Dunkirk: 1940'. The deckchair was less romantic. Tired of repeated efforts to put the thing up he had nailed the wooden stays in position and fixed the legs to the deck with steel brackets.

The sun wobbled free of the horizon and Dryden felt some joy seeping back into his heart. He liked his floating home: it combined permanence with mobility and a pleasing sense of the temporary. And if he ever got bored with the view he could just pay for a new mooring. She was a steel-built inshore naval patrol boat for which Dryden had extracted £16,000 from the joint savings account he'd held with Laura. He would have paid twice that for the plaque, but money management was not one of his strong suits. He had few determinations, but one was to make sure his life wasn't pinched by a lack of pennies.

He made a fresh batch of coffee in the galley. Two cups, tin. Through the porthole he spotted Humph's Ford Capri parked up at Barham's Farm. He laughed out loud at Humph's biggest joke: the only cabbie in Britain with a two-door taxi: a triumph of indifference over reality.

An automatic irrigator sent a plume of water back and forth across the intervening fields. The first rainbow of the day formed and appeared to end in Humph's cab. Dryden doubted it ended in a pot of gold, recalling instead the murky glass specimen bottle the cabbie had collected to make sure the occasional call of nature did not result in him having to leave the car.

Dryden looked up and checked his watch: 8.10am. He'd arranged to get to Black Bank early. The call had been difficult: they were busy, said Estelle Beck, arranging for the next day's funeral. He sensed animosity in her voice, even fear. Getting up early suited him. It was press day for the *Express* and he wanted to run Maggie Beck's deathbed confession and the plea for Matty's father to come forward. He was happy to follow Maggie's stipulation that his story should run after the funeral – but he still needed an interview, and a family picture, to make sure it got the space it deserved.

'Have you listened to the tapes?' he'd asked Estelle.

'At nine then,' she said by way of reply. 'At Black Bank.'

Dryden knocked on the cab's bonnet and held up a cup of coffee. Peace offering. Normally Humph's working hours began at 9.00am.

Humph was chatting to Nicos again about the village olive festival. Reluctantly he sipped the coffee: 'No egg?'

'No egg,' said Dryden. 'Full English at the Bridge after the interview.' The Bridge was a greasy spoon in town which specialized in fried everything on fried bread. For Humph they did a drive-in service complete with an improvised in-cab food tray.

Humph wiggled in his seat by way of indicating mounting excitement at the prospect of such a feast. They pulled out into the busy A10, already nose-to-tail with sleepy drivers heading for the academic sweatshops of Cambridge seventeen miles to the south. 'College sweater shops,' said Dryden, and laughed at his own joke.

Humph remained in a silent, brooding world. Dryden imagined the cabbie's sunrises were fried-tomato red.

Dryden flipped down the vanity mirror on the passenger side and looked himself in the face. His jet-black hair had been sandwiched in a strange cone towards the left, the result of sleeping heavily and avoiding early morning brushes and mirrors. He was fingering the sallow skin beneath his eyes when he saw a motorbike in the rear-view mirror. The bike was black, with cow-horn handlebars, and the early morning light touched the chromework in a series of minor sunbursts. The rider was in oxblood-red leathers with a matching helmet and a black tinted visor. A silver line of chrome crossed the helmet along the ridge of the cranium. A flag flew from the aerial which Dryden failed to recognize: a white star on a blue background took up one third, the others were red and white.

'Easy Rider's a bit close,' said Dryden.

Humph made a point of never consulting his rear-view mirror. It was angled to provide a squint view of his own face. He felt too much information was confusing and a curse of modern life.

The motorbike trailed them at varying distances along the A10. Dryden guessed from the size of the air ducts to the front of the engine cowling that it was a 2,000cc at least. 'Why the hell doesn't he just breeze past?' he asked.

'I said . . .' Dryden glanced back at the vanity mirror but shut up when he saw the bike had gone. 'Where . . . ?'

But then Humph swung the cab off the main road and on to a drove. Originally cattle tracks, the network of drove roads provided the Fens with a latticework of shortcuts and dead-ends the map to which did not exist. Dryden skewed round in his seat but couldn't see the biker. Then he made a nearly fatal mistake. He told himself that only paranoid people think they're being followed.

'Only paranoid people think they're being followed,' he told Humph.

Humph considered this. 'Who'd bother?' he said – an eloquent insult.

The road to Black Bank was the loneliest Dryden knew in a landscape disfigured by solitude. It ran for seven straight miles through the fen. The drought had killed the mid-summer crops and the soil had been left to the sun. Even a light breeze raised clouds of red dust. As Humph's cab bumped along the drove it left in its wake a series of miniature crimson whirlwinds. Dryden wound the passenger window down as far as it would go and put his elbow on the already hot metal of the bodywork.

The sun was low into Humph's face as he drove east, a disc of murky orange already weaving and rippling with the heat from the land. He flipped down the sun-shade and hummed tunelessly. Devoid of curiosity he never asked questions. He was happy going nowhere, as long as he knew the route.

A mile into the fen Dryden saw the tail-fins of the trans-atlantic fuel tankers parked on the apron of the main runway at Mildenhall US air base. It must have been six miles away but the tall, battleship-grey tail fins stood up like a glimpse of whales breaching the surface of a calm ocean. Then came the fields of landing lights. The inward flightpath was marked by formations of steel posts with green, white and red lamps. For the pilots of the Starblazer fuel tankers that had flown non-stop across the Atlantic this would be their first sight of Europe from under 30,000 feet, save for the illuminated Octagon Tower of Ely Cathedral.

Airport flotsam littered the landscape. Nissen huts from the war held hay and sugar beet and just short of Black Bank they saw their first Stars-&-Stripes, flying from a Dallas-style bungalow complete with a triple-doored garage which could have held the fleet cars of a platoon of travelling salesmen. And the Mildenhall Stadium. A dog track boasting US fast-food outlets, a bar with draught Schlitz, and popcorn stalls. Six days a week it was deserted, but its car park was big enough to take an incoming B-52 bomber.

With the sun now up, and the dust kicked airborne, they could have been anywhere west of the Mississippi. Dryden expected to see a wagon train threading its way across country surrounded by twenty thousand head of longhorn.

Black Bank Farm stood on a wide plain of Fen peat which stretched to the edge of sight. The farm's façade had survived the air crash which had killed Maggie Beck's family, but the stone had been burnt a deep carbon black. Foursquare, with a central doorway and Georgian windows, it faced south across a small kitchen garden. To the east end of the old house were the remains of a single pine tree, a pencil-black fossil, distorted into a twisted tapered finger. A new kitchen block stood to the west, an unadorned example of seventies utility, and beyond that a large steel-framed barn. A line of poplars grew in a natural shield at the rear of the house, protecting it against the north winds. The sash windows had perished on the night of the air crash, to be replaced with single-pane double-glazing which managed to unsettle the building's otherwise classic proportions. Dryden felt it looked like what it was: a house with an ugly past.

Humph pulled up short of a cattle grid by a sign: 'Black Bank Farm Ltd: Salad Crops'.

'Bit grim,' he said, and laughed. He really enjoyed other people's misfortunes.

'I'll walk from here,' said Dryden, throwing open the passenger-side door. Humph didn't argue.

Dryden squinted east into the rising sun: 9.04am. The sweat popped on his forehead and he felt a rivulet of salty water begin a long journey down his back. Just inside the gate was a large granite memorial stone which listed the victims of the 1976 crash: the three UK civilians first, then the nine US citizens.

WILLIAM VINCENT BECK
CELIA MAUD BECK
MATTHEW 'MATTY' BECK

CAPT. JACK RIGBY
MAJOR WILLIAM H. HOROWITZ
MAJOR JIM KOSKINSKI
MARLENE MARY-JANE KOSKINSKI
CAPT. MILO FEUKSWANGER
LT RENE FEUKSWANGER
AIRMAN JOHN DWIGHT MURPHY
KYLIE PATRICIA MURPHY
JOHN MURPHY, JNR.

IN MEMORIAM, it said simply, followed by the date. Dryden fished in his pocket and found a round beach stone he'd picked up the last time he and Humph had run out to the coast. He put it on the top of the memorial and walked on.

Ahead of him he heard the engines first, and looking up from the dust saw the B-52 rise, heaving itself out of the distant haze like a swimmer breasting the pool. Its four turbines screamed and the pregnant black belly seemed to rear straight out of the fields: a nightmare crop. Dryden looked directly up as it went overhead, and saw the undercarriage enfold itself into the fuselage with a satisfying mechanical thud. It was so close he could see winking safety lights inside the undercarriage bay as they switched from red to green before the doors closed.

And then it was gone. A stream of grey fumes uncurling in the warm morning air.

He stood in the sudden silence before the front door of Black Bank Farm, which was green, varnished, and massive. Dryden looked at it from the gate of the kitchen garden and thought *Dogs*.

In the full litany of Dryden's fears dogs were not in the same class as water, enclosed spaces, heights, authority, or emotional attachment. But they moved faster than all of these, and the bone-white teeth and chopped-meat gums had always held a potent power to terrify. Dogs stood, growling, in a long queue of terrifying dangers which pursued him with tenacity. But nothing he was afraid of was as frightening as looking like a coward, even to himself. This fear ruled all others and produced occasional acts of misunderstood courage which had earned him an unwarranted reputation for valour. So he pushed the gate open and walked up the path. Which is when he actually got to hear the dogs. Their claws skittered on quarry tiles on the far side of the door. Dryden knew what they were thinking. They were thinking they could smell fear, and they were right.

He knocked, praying it wouldn't open.

But it did. Estelle Beck leant against the door jamb in US combat fatigues which Dryden guessed had cost her half a week's salary. Her T-shirt carried a single Stars & Stripes across her bust.

She held a large Alsatian, the size of a small horse, by the collar while eating a tomato.

'He won't hurt you,' she said, with a smile that never touched the lichen-green eyes. She looked like she hadn't slept for a week and her carefully cut bob of blonde hair was completely lifeless, like straw. Her knuckles were white as she gripped the dog's collar. Dryden noticed that the leather was decorated with tiny studs in red and blue with white stars at their centre.

'Then I won't hurt him,' said Dryden, failing to move any of his limbs. 'What's he called?'

'Texas,' she said, a laugh dying in her throat.

Pitch, thought Dryden. *The difficult bit.* He took a half step backwards: 'Maggie asked me to be a witness for a reason. She wants me to find Lyndon's father. I sent you a copy of the letter?'

She nodded. He looked beyond her to the dark interior of the house and saw a foot poised on the staircase. A trainer, Nike, new and still shop-white below a pair of jogging pants.

'It's what she would have wanted,' he said. Experience told him that if he had to say anything more she wouldn't let him in.

Estelle dropped the dog's collar and it padded nonchalantly past, pausing only briefly to smell Dryden's testicles. In the darkness beyond her Dryden saw a lighter flare, then snap out.

'Come in. It's a mess.'

He met Lyndon in the hall. He was putting a large bottle

of mineral water into a rucksack. He didn't have to explain why he was there. He was home, but he didn't look like he was staying. Dryden looked from brother to sister and searched for the tell-tale signs of their mother.

Lyndon was in a less self-conscious outfit than his pilot's uniform but it was equally American: grey sweatshirt with US Air Force crest, running trousers in white, and the new Nikes. He twisted a basketball in his slender hands. 'Excuse me,' he said to Dryden, and fled into the shadows of the house.

Estelle turned right into the front room. It was stuffy and about as homely as the Victoria and Albert Museum. An upright piano supported a clutch of family photos, a mockery of the truth they now knew. The newest showed Maggie in bed at The Tower with Lyndon on one side and Estelle on the other. It had 'last picture' written all over it.

Dryden picked it up. Best to ask first, get it over with. 'Could I borrow this? We'll need a picture. I can give you some copies too – bigger size.'

Estelle shrugged. Dryden thudded down into a moth-eaten armchair beneath a stuffed fox's head. He took out a notebook and tapped it with a ballpoint. 'I'll keep it short.' It was a phrase he loved, and like most of the phrases he loved, it meant nothing.

Estelle sat at the dining-room table sorting through some papers. A will? Dryden hadn't even thought of that. A will: the sudden possibilities multiplied as he considered Maggie's hastily re-drawn family tree.

'So. Where to start?' said Dryden. Clearly she didn't know. There was a long silence while somewhere music played. Folk. An American voice just audible: Bob Dylan perhaps.

'You were born after the crash?'

'In 1978. Two years,' she said. Dryden sensed she wanted to go on but was diverted by a greater truth.

'And your father . . . ?' He knew much of the story himself, largely retold by his mother. But Fen gossip had clouded the detail.

'Donald. Donald McGuire. Mum went back to the Beck family name after Dad died. They married in '76. A few months after the crash. She never said why. He was older, much older. I think she loved him in a way, he certainly loved me. It's odd, isn't it? I don't really believe I remember him at all, but I can remember that he loved me.'

She shuffled some of the papers on the table. 'Why do you think she married?' asked Dryden.

'Yes. She talks about that on the tapes – we've been listening together. It's such a help, hearing her voice. Thank you – it was your idea, wasn't it? It must have done Mum so much good in those final months, to talk about her life. She felt very guilty about what she did but she had a very noble life in a way. Steadfast. That's the word that Lyndon uses. We're still listening. It's painful – very painful for him.

'We left the tape recorder in Laura's room. We've cleared out the rest of her stuff – but we thought you should have it back.'

She returned to Dryden's question. 'I don't think she ever regretted marrying Dad. But I got the feeling she did it to get away from here, from the memory. I think she fell in love with the idea of a new life. Away from Black Bank. He had a farm on Thetford Chase, Forest Farm, it's sold up now and a private house. Mum moved there and that's where I was born. He died in '82. Heart. He's buried out there,' she said, nodding towards the fen. 'The church on Fourth Drove.'

Dryden knew it. A wooden chapel built by the Victorians

for the crop-pickers. Dilapidated now, it stood at an angle to the land, tipping its cheap tin belfry to the east. 'St Matthew's,' he said, and made a squiggle in his notebook. 'But you came back.'

'When Dad died we sold the farm. There'd been a manager here and it had made money, it's always made money. Black Gold, Mum called it, the peat . . . you can grow anything ten times a year. Mum wanted to come back.' She looked out over the kitchen garden. 'God knows why.'

'You didn't want to return?'

'The place was haunted. It's just the identity of the ghost that's changed.'

Dryden tried to imagine it, a childhood overshadowed by the death of a baby she thought was her brother.

From somewhere to the rear of the farmhouse came the rhythmic thudding of a basketball hitting a wall. Dryden heaved a sigh and decided it was time to ask the only question that really mattered: 'Any idea why she gave her son away?'

Estelle rose. 'Drink?' He followed her into the kitchen. By the door a noticeboard held snapshots covered by a clear plastic sheet. Most were of Lyndon, from the naked baby in the paddling pool with the sunburnt arms to the proud airman by his warplane on a windswept New Mexico airstrip. In several of the shots a grey-haired couple in expensive leisure clothes hovered in the background.

Estelle offered Dryden black coffee from a filter machine while she got herself a Pepsi from the fridge. She pulled the tab, slipped it back into the can, and studied the pictures.

'Mum always made a point of keeping in touch. She'd not met Lyndon since the crash until this summer. There was a real spark – I guess now we know why,' she said.

Dryden sipped the coffee and felt the promise of the caffeine lift his mood: 'Jealous?'

She laughed then, forgetting whatever it was that was the backdrop to her life. 'Of Lyndon! No way. It was dead exciting. An American cousin. And the family – the grandparents – sent presents. Toys and stuff. Clothes for me. It was great. He couldn't be a threat – he was an ocean away. And it gave me an identity at school – the American kid. Least I wasn't the Fen kid like the rest. That counts. No, I never resented Lyndon.'

'And then he just turned up?'

'He knew Mum was ill. We'd written. I'd even telephoned – we always did at Christmas. But he was out in Iraq and then he got shot down and we didn't hear until the Koskinskis – the grandparents – sent Mum a letter. About Al Rasheid – the prison. It's in Baghdad. They've always held their political prisoners there, tortured them there. Some US personnel were taken there too – for interrogation. But Lyndon had nothing to tell them. So they let him rot. That was how lucky he was.'

She turned her back on the kitchen table, put her palms down flat on the top, and jumped up to perch on the edge. 'I'd never seen her cry like that. When she got the letter. She wept for days. I guess he'd died twice for her. It must have turned her inside out – and nobody to tell.'

'But then he came back,' said Dryden.

She crossed her legs in a perfect lotus position on the table top. 'Yes,' she said, and began to cry. 'She was in The Tower by then. With Laura . . .' She dabbed at the tears. 'It's odd. I feel I know Laura. But I never thought of her having a . . . family. Having you . . . I mean.'

Dryden wondered why this sounded so depressing. 'He's well? Lyndon? He seems withdrawn – I guess that's hardly surprising. When he came back, had he suffered psychologically? There are scars, surely?'

She picked at the T-shirt at her neck, as if to lessen the heat. 'Four weeks in confinement in a windowless cell is not something one can feel fine about, is it? I think he emerged remarkably unscathed. But who knows? Who knows what's going on in someone else's head? And whatever, it was hardly an ideal preparation for news like this . . .'

'He must be disorientated.'

She nodded. 'We both are. Lost, I think. And wary, very wary, which is understandable. I think it will be a long time before either of us trusts anyone again.'

'Except each other?'

She smiled with her mouth. 'Yes. Of course.'

Dryden closed his notebook. They listened again to the dull percussion of the basketball in the farmyard. The kitchen wall was covered in children's art. Blue cows, green cats with giant whiskers, loads of tractors. Dryden walked over and got a closer look.

'They're my kids,' she said proudly. That was it, thought Dryden – a teacher. Maggie had told him.

Then they heard it, the unmistakable sound of a highly polished limousine creeping sedately over gravel. Estelle grabbed at her throat. 'It's the undertakers. They just want to run through the details.' She looked towards the rear of the house with something which again looked closer to fear than anxiety.

Dryden made for the back door. 'I can tell Lyndon,' he said.

Relief flooded over her. 'Thanks. We should both see them. She's his mother too.'

15

The dead crows, strung like beads on a line over the kitchen garden, were the only signs of life in the farmyard. It was one of the landscape's ironies that the only sign of life was death. Black Bank, like most Fen farms, had no livestock. The soil was too precious for fodder. The peatfields stretched east to the limit of the eye, but nothing moved, nothing breathed.

A dead landscape, and silent but for the rhythmic pounding of a basketball. Lyndon, sporting black wrap-around pilot's glasses, didn't acknowledge Dryden's arrival. The reflective black lenses mirrored the panorama of Black Bank Fen, an image as lifeless as the landscape itself. Then Lyndon stooped, tilted his chin and sent the ball in a loop high against the sky, from where it dropped into the hoop without touching the sides.

Lyndon loped across the farmyard, his brilliant white Nike trainers kicking up knee-high clouds of red dust, collected the ball and thrust it with surprising force at Dryden's midriff. He pushed the glasses up into his hair and looked around. 'It's like home.'

Dryden nodded stupidly.

'There,' said Lyndon, pointing to the far eastern horizon where a turning red-black miniature twister teetered like a child's top. Common that summer in the Saharan heat they did little harm, touching down on the earth for a few short seconds to suck up the weightless dust. Dryden always felt uneasy at the sight, which recalled a nightmare vision of a length of disembodied gut twisting in pain. This one was corkscrewing harmlessly over a field and visibly fading as it lost touch with the hot earth.

'At home they could take the roof of your farm. Here they can't get the tops off the carrots,' said Lyndon, leaning against the barn wall with the easy grace of the natural athlete, his chest muscles filling out the all-American sweatshirt. His height, which must have been at least two inches greater than Dryden's six feet two, didn't make him look skinny. He flashed a smile that was a testament to the efficiency of Texan dentistry and an affluent US childhood.

'This must have been a difficult time,' said Dryden, proud of himself for finding the right opening question.

'Difficult? Hell, no. I've just found out that the life I had was someone else's, and that my life never got lived. I'm buried out there at that clapped-out church. I've visited my own graveside. Confused? Cheated? Pissed angry? You said it.'

He grabbed the ball, ran back to the edge of the yard and shot directly at the hoop, twanging the metal and sending the ball on a zig-zag bagatelle course around the farmyard until it rolled into one of the sheds.

'What sort of life was it – Lyndon's?' asked Dryden.

The US ace pilot walked towards him with the hint of a military swagger and slipped the glasses down again, cloaking his eyes. 'Great. Texas. The big country, makes this look like Central Park. San Antonio. You know it?'

Dryden shook his head. He and Laura had made New York and New England for a week in the Fall before the accident but hadn't fancied the South: they lynched people and drank out of beer cans so cold they stuck to your lips.

'The big country,' said Lyndon again. 'I'm always near folks here. Kinda gets ya. It looks like a wilderness but it ain't.' He lifted the sweatshirt from his chest to let some air circulate.

Dryden shrugged. 'There are places. Go north. The fen gets deeper. You can lose yourself there. Adventurer's Fen. That was our place. Is . . . our place.'

'Yeah?' said Lyndon.

Dryden got back to his past. 'So the life you had. In the States – there was money?' he asked.

'Yeah. Loads. Grandpa Koskinski was US Navy. Big shot. Pentagon. We had three cars, a pool, tennis court with AstroTurf. A maid, a gardener, and an air-conditioning system big enough to cool an English county. That qualify as wealthy?'

'Sure.'

'But not classy, eh? That's the thing with you British. It's class, not money.'

'Happy childhood?' tried Dryden.

Lyndon took some steps back and squatted down on his haunches in the dust. He took out the Zippo lighter from his pants pocket, flicked it open and lit it once, before holding the cool chrome case to his forehead. Dryden caught a faint whiff of lighter fuel on the hot breeze.

'You can't miss what you don't know – that's what they say here, yeah? Well, I missed 'em. I thought they died here,' he said, running his fingers through the red dust. 'Mum and Dad. Jim and Marlene. I know their faces better than I know my own. But they're always the same age. Twenty-seven years ago, right here. But guess what – they're total strangers. I might as well have your picture in my wallet.'

'Maggie had kept in touch?' asked Dryden, sensing a tailspin into depression.

'Yeah. Christmas, birthdays, pictures of Estelle, that kind of thing. I think my grandparents were grateful and they felt some compassion for her. I guess they'd seen what the crash had done to her life. They went to Matty's funeral. They felt . . . implicated in some way.'

'But this visit. This was the first time you'd met your mother.'

He nodded. Watching the twister grow faint, fading in the east. Dryden should have thought longer about the next question: 'And your sister . . .'

'Half sister,' he said, too quickly. 'Different dads. Not that I knew either of them.'

'You know about Maggie's letter? About your father?'

He nodded. 'Sure. Means nothing. Nothing means nothing. Brother, sister, father, mother. You tell me. Who can I trust?'

He flicked the Zippo one last time and, standing, pocketed it. 'I've had enough of the past. I'll leave the rest of the questions for Estelle. And that's a good question, isn't it? Why the questions . . . ?'

'Maggie wanted me to write her story. You saw the letter. I just want to get things right. But no more questions . . . Except one,' he nodded at the Zippo lighter. 'Ex-smoker?'

'Ex most of the time,' he said. 'Not always.' Lyndon walked off towards the barn to fetch the basketball and Dryden followed. Inside, out of the blinding light, something crouched in the shadows.

It was a Land Rover. Dryden knew nothing about cars except that they killed people. But this looked expensive, a 1970s gem, lovingly restored. The metal top had been taken down and the leather seats showed a lifetime's wear. The paintwork was cream-white, the blue letters UN emblazoned on the bonnet and side doors.

Lyndon took off the dark glasses. 'It's a 1973 model. In great shape. I got her off a guy on the base who couldn't afford to take her home. They'd used it for the peace keepers in Bosnia – so I left the colour. Kinda history, I guess.'

'It's beautiful,' Dryden said, noting that the bonnet was still hot and the red dust of the fens lay in a film over the paintwork.

'Yes, it is,' said Lyndon. 'Class. Makes a Jeep look cheap.'

Dryden changed tack. 'I passed the memorial to the Black Bank victims. I guess they'll have to make some changes.'

Lyndon smiled then, and flipped the Zippo open to watch the flame. 'And I used to think, you know, that I could have died here in the crash with my folks. I used to think that would have been better. And now look – I did.'

'But they weren't your parents.'

'It wasn't my life. That's the real point, isn't it? If she hadn't given me away I'd have had another life. A life that didn't have three garages, a college education, West Point, and a cell in Al Rasheid. None of it.'

'But what would it have had? Your other life?'

'Her.' He looked back towards the farmhouse. 'But she chose differently. Which is something I have to live with.'

They walked back outside. 'The hearse has arrived,' he said. 'Estelle said to say.'

Lyndon slipped his glasses into his sweatshirt pocket and held out his hand. 'Do you have family, Dryden? Brothers, sisters?'

'Only child,' said Dryden.

'Me too. I guess I always will be – despite what Maggie said. You can't change a life with a few words, Dryden. It shouldn't change things. I'm the same person. She's the same person – Estelle. What does it change?'

Dryden didn't answer, but he thought, *Everything*.

16

Humph dropped Dryden in Market Street and he took the steps up to the newsroom three at a time. He felt a sense of elation now that he was able to discharge his debt to Maggie Beck. The story had hung over him for ten days since her death at The Tower. And there was some real excitement at the prospect of writing what he knew would be a wonderful tale. It was childish really. He'd been a reporter for more than a decade but he still got a buzz from the job. It was like drinking lager through a straw.

Up the wooden steps and through the door marked NEWSROOM he found the *Express* in full flow – the deadline was an hour away at noon. Copies would be on the street at going-home time and delivered with the evening newspapers to homes in Ely and the surrounding villages. The *Express*'s circulation was 13,000 and as weak as a dying man's pulse. Twenty years earlier they'd sold 25,000 – more than two copies for every household in the town.

Charlie Bracken, the news editor, looked pathetically pleased to see his chief reporter back in time. He let rip a tremendous beer-sodden burp by way of greeting.

'You got it?'

Dryden nodded and chucked the family picture he'd got from Black Bank into the darkroom where Mitch was printing up a landscape shot of another Fen Blow for the front page.

'Picture too,' he told Charlie.

'Great. It's the splash, kid. Human interest stuff,

eh?' Charlie picked up his jacket and headed for the door. 'Ciggies,' he told nobody.

Dryden sat at his PC and knocked out the story in ten minutes.

By Philip Dryden
Chief Reporter

A deathbed confession by an Ely woman has rewritten the history of one of the Fen's most famous disasters.

The crash of a US Air Force transporter on to a farmhouse at Black Bank, near Ely, in 1976 left twelve people dead and only two survivors.

Until now they were thought to be the farmer's daughter, Maggie Beck, and a newborn child being flown home with its parents to Texas.

Ms Beck, then 16, walked out of the wreckage of the farm, where both her parents were killed, carrying the baby. She said her own two-week-old son Matty had died with the rest of her family.

But on Friday night at The Tower Hospital, Ely, Mrs Beck told close relatives, shortly before her death, that she had swapped the children.

After the crash her son was flown to the US and brought up by the parents of the US pilot who died in the crash – Major Jim Koskinski.

The boy – Lyndon Koskinski – became a pilot in the US Air Force and, having kept in touch since the 1976 crash, was visiting the Beck family home when his mother fell seriously ill with cancer.

He was at her bedside when she died.

Major Koskinski is on leave from the USAF after active service in Iraq, where he was forced to bail out of his aircraft while patrolling the no-fly zone in January and spent two months in a Baghdad gaol before coalition forces liberated the city.

He spoke exclusively to the *Express* about his feelings.

'I'm a US pilot. That's my life. This doesn't change anything, shouldn't change anything. I do feel cheated and angry. And lost. I can't imagine why she did it. We never had a chance to speak.

'Yes, I'm confused. Who wouldn't be? I've just visited my own grave,' he said. It now appears the grave marked Matty Beck at St Matthew's Church, Black Bank, is that of Lyndon Koskinski.

Dryden, who'd decided to leave his notebook in his pocket during his discussion with Lyndon, made the quotes up. He didn't so much rely on his own memory as the poor memories of others.

Military police at USAF Mildenhall will be investigating the original crash records to see how Mrs Beck was able to fool doctors and officials at the time.

Ely police will be informed of the confession and will have to re-open the inquest into the reported death of Matty Beck in 1976. But detectives indicated that they are unlikely to take the case any further, given the length of time involved and the death of Mrs Beck.

Before her death Mrs Beck left instructions that the father of Matty Beck should be allowed to contact his son now that the truth had been told about the events at Black Bank in 1976.

She has made provision for him to inherit a sum of £5,000 if he contacts solicitors Gillies & Wright of Ely. They are in a position to verify his claim.

Dryden re-read it once, made some small changes, and filed it to the news-desk computer basket with a note attached to make sure the subs left the last two paragraphs. He would track the story down electronically later to make sure they had respected his instructions.

He was pleased: it was a good story, and now that he had written it he saw how clearly one question still hung over Black Bank Farm: why did Maggie Beck give her son away?

Charlie Bracken had not returned and was clearly administering emergency stress relief in the Fenman bar opposite *The Crow*'s offices. The rest of the team was hard at work. Garry was exploring his nose with a Biro and behind his glass partition Septimus Henry Kew, editor in chief, was reading the proofs for the edition. Either he was distinctly unimpressed with his news editor's efforts, or he was sniffing cocaine.

Dryden checked his watch: nearly noon. He picked up the phone and ran through the usual litany of last-deadline calls to the emergency services. The fire brigade had two fires, less than average in that incendiary summer. The first had started in a lock-up garage on the edge of town, swept through a nearby allotment and gutted two council houses. The smell of burnt vegetables apparently hung, even now, in the air over the Jubilee Estate.

'Anyone hurt?'

'Nah,' said the control-room operator. 'It was mid-morning. Mum at work, kids at school, Dad's a travelling salesman. Nice to come home to, though – a real fire,' he said, laughing at the old joke.

'Cause?' asked Dryden.

'Kids. Mucking about round the garages. They found some matches, traces of lighter fuel . . . but I doubt anyone can be nailed for it. The other one's a bit different.'

Dryden heard the inexpert two-finger tapping of a PC keyboard. 'Here we are. Register Office – at Chatteris. Someone broke in, smashed the place up, set fire to the filing cabinets – destroyed all the records. Every last one.'

'Bloody hell. Someone's honeymoon went wrong.' Dryden took the details for a par in the Stop Press. With almost telepathic timing the phone rang again as he put it down. It was Jean. 'Dryden!'

Dryden felt his ear-drum pink like an overloaded loudspeaker.

'There's a girl here to see you.' Jean had taken up a voluntary unpaid job as Dryden's chaperone. 'Shall I tell her to go away?'

Dryden took the stairs four at a time on the way down, missed the last one and went flying. The girl helped him get up.

'Hi,' said Dryden. She was tall, leggy, with blue eyes and dyed blonde hair held up in an untidy coconut top. She didn't look eighteen but the last time Dryden had seen her she'd been posing in Inspector Andy Newman's illicit porn shots. Alice Sutton was holding a cutting from last week's edition of the *Express*. It was Dryden's story on her: Father's Plea Over Missing Girl, with her picture, across two columns. He'd run it dead straight without any link to Newman's pillbox porn story which he'd got into *The Crow*. But he'd left Newman a message telling him the ID of his snapshot star.

'It's about this,' she said.

Dryden nodded. He took her over to an alcove where they conducted interviews. Jean watched with eagle eyes from the switchboard.

'You turned up?'

She nodded. 'I've been to the police. OK. It's all over. I told them everything. I want to leave it at that.'

Dryden shrugged. 'Sure. And your dad?'

Which is when the tears started to flow. Dryden put his arm round the girl and he felt Jean's eyes boring into the back of his head. Jean was one of those extraordinary people who live entirely moral lives. A hospital visitor, she had spent many hours beside Laura's bed in the months after the accident, when Dryden had been too traumatized to endure lengthy visits. She'd read Laura books, knitted her a bedspread and believed, far more vehemently than Dryden, that her coma would one day end in a miracle return to full consciousness. She was determined that when that time came Dryden would be in the perfect position to resume his married life. She was a woman with a romantic mission and nobody, least of all Dryden, would be allowed to get in her way.

She appeared now beside them. 'Tea?' she asked, and Dryden nodded.

'We can't find him,' said Alice, as soon as Jean was out of earshot.

'We?'

'Mum. I got back last night. She said he'd gone a couple of days ago – on Saturday. Said he knew what was going on. Who'd done those things to me, and taken the pictures. Jesus,' she said, burying her face in her hands. 'The pictures.'

'How did he get to see them? The police normally keep that kind of thing pretty much under wraps.'

'He had friends, didn't he? He has friends everywhere, that's how he does his job. He got an attachment by e-mail. That made it worse. He said they'd be all over the net, just like real porn.'

'How'd he take it?' asked Dryden, wishing he hadn't.

'Mum said he sparked out. Broke some furniture. He wouldn't let Mum see them, carried them with him so she wouldn't get close. Then he drank some whisky on his own. All night, Mum said.'

'Do the police know he's gone?'

She nodded, snuffling. Jean appeared with a cup of tea. Just the one.

'Any idea where he'd been looking? Did he say anything to your Mum?'

She shook her head. 'Nothing. He just said it was something to do with the lorries.' She slurped tea noisily from the cup. 'He works in transport security – HGVs – so he's always talking to the drivers. I guess it's his job. And he likes talking,' she smiled, but it faded quickly. 'He told Mum someone had said something. About . . .'

Dryden let the silence lengthen.

'About . . . the pictures.'

The pictures. How could he forget? He held Alice's hand.

'And nothing else?'

'Mum's upset. She's in pieces, really. I shouldn't have gone away.'

'What happened that night? The night in the pillbox . . .'

Alice's hand trembled slightly as she brought the cup to her lips. 'You tell me. God. I . . . I sort of remember the sex, I guess.' Tears welled up and plopped into her tea. 'This bloke started chatting to me at the pub where I work – The Pine Tree. It's dull, you know? But I need the money and the landlord is a friend of Dad's, so it's OK with them too. The police said he put something in my drink – but they couldn't prove that. The dishwasher took all the traces off the glass. Anyway, it's a drug, OK? It . . . makes you feel sexy.'

'It's used for date rape. It's illegal. Do you think he'd done this before?'

Her eyes widened. She hadn't thought of that. 'Yeah. Sure . . . he didn't put a foot wrong. He just let me do what I wanted to do. He was good looking, I guess. Slim, with a tan.' The embarrassment flooded back. 'Jesus. How could I? Look – you ain't gonna put this in the paper, are you?'

'No,' said Dryden. 'But I should write about your dad, yes? See if anyone has seen him.'

She could have left it there but she needed to tell the whole story. 'He took me to the pillbox. I must have slept . . . afterwards. I woke up on a park bench, on the river bank by the Cutter. There was a fiver in my purse which hadn't been there the night before. I guess it was to get home. Thoughtful, eh? But I couldn't. Mike, the landlord at the Pine Tree, had seen me leaving with that bloke, all over him. I'd been out all night. And . . . and they'd left me a picture. In the purse with the fiver. One of the snaps. I just sat there looking at that picture and thinking what they'd think, at home, if they ever saw it. I guess it was a threat. To keep me quiet. So I ran. Friends in London. I'm at East London University – Docklands. The halls of residence are closed – and Dad would have checked there anyway. I should have phoned but I was scared, scared Mum and Dad had found out . . .'

Dryden nodded. 'And you can't recall anything else your mum said about your father? About the lorries . . . ?'

Then she remembered. Dryden saw it in her eyes.

'And?'

'Mum said something about a lay-by. Where the drivers stop. He spends a lot of time in them, watching, you know? It's his job to make sure the drivers aren't flogging the stuff or carrying cargo for other companies. Greasy spoons, that's what he calls them. He hates them normally, always told me off for eating rubbish. Mum packs his sandwiches. But he said . . .' and she bowed her head again. 'He told Mum that was where you could buy the pictures . . .'

'The police will find him,' said Dryden.

'That's what we're afraid of,' she said, pushing her chair away.

17

Humph pulled into the Ritz lay-by and stopped the Capri in a cloud of red dust. The cab reeked of overheated plastic. Humph, disturbed in the middle of his afternoon nap to make the run, moodily flicked through his language tapes. 'I need my sleep,' he said. Dryden could see the logic in this in that it was one of the few times Humph could be sure he wasn't putting on weight.

'Well take a nap now. Be my guest. I'm paying.' Dryden, irritated, gazed pointedly out of the passenger-side window at a mechanical irrigator standing in a field of burnt kale.

Sometimes he wanted to tell Humph how he felt. How the cabbie's immobile insolence pissed him off, like almost nothing else pissed him off. He turned to face him but Humph had the earphones on for his tapes – not those little plug ones that tuck inside the ear, but the big ones, like rubber dustbin lids.

Dryden thumped both palms as hard as he could on the dashboard but Humph didn't move. So he braced himself for the shriek of rust and pushed the door open with his foot.

He'd wanted to visit the Ritz ever since Etterley told him about the 'people smugglers' using the lay-by as a drop-off point. Now Alice Sutton had given him another good reason to get a cup of tea and a carbon monoxide sandwich. If Bob Sutton had been checking lorries passing through the Fens he'd have got to the Ritz eventually. Perhaps it was here he'd been offered some dirty pictures which featured his daughter.

But the Ritz was closed. The shutters were down and a

note stuck on it in childish capital letters three inches high said: SHUT 'TIL FURTHER NOTICE.

Dryden noted both the apostrophe and the motorbike which had pulled up on the opposite side of the road. It was black, and the rider wore oxblood-red leathers. He thought about walking over to confront his uninvited shadow but an HGV rolled into the lay-by and obscured the view. The driver got out and walked over to read the note. It took him quite a long time.

'Bastard,' he said, kicking one of the wheels of the kiosk with a boot the size of a horse trough.

It rocked for a few minutes, red dust slurping off the roof.

'Closed, then?' said Dryden.

The driver wiped a hand across the stubble on his chin. 'Fucking thirsty too.'

'Odd.'

The driver read the note again. Up close. 'Never closes, Johnnie, not while it's light. Never.'

Dryden tried to modify his personality to suit that of his prospective interviewee: a professional trick made considerably more difficult by the need to look shifty, man-of-the-world, physically tough and permanently stupid. The fact that the lorry driver achieved all of this without trying, and no doubt on a daily basis, made Dryden's task only more challenging.

'Johnnie runs quite a business,' he said, offering the lorry driver a jelly bean.

Nothing. Lights out. The driver looked at the sweets as if Dryden were peddling ecstasy tablets to nuns.

'Worth a fortune.' Dryden stepped closer. 'And what about the immigrants, eh? People smuggling must pay,' he added, edging closer and catching a whiff of industrial-strength BO. 'Bloke told me those poor bastards pay six

127

hundred quid a time. He runs the lorries through,' he said, tilting his head towards the empty T-Bar. 'Gets 'em jobs. Amazing, eh? Wonder what his cut is?'

The driver looked both ways, and used his T-shirt to wipe sweat from his chin. 'Should drown the fuckers.'

Dryden hesitated before executing his next tactic, sensing at some subliminal level that he might have already stepped outside the strict etiquette laid down by the Road Hauliers Association. 'Then there's the dirty pix, of course. Hmm? You had any of them, have you? Apparently they get stowed away with the immigrants. Sort of reverse trade. I'd be interested. You know, to get a cut too.'

Dryden leered hugely and tried a wink, which in the circumstances was a bonus. It meant he got to see the fist which hit him with just the one eye. He heard rather than felt the thud of the bunched knuckles pushing his eye back into its socket. The pain came a second later. A red-hot electric pulse which collapsed his spine and knees with frightening efficiency.

Then the guy picked him up by the shirt and pushed him hard up against the metallic side of the Ritz. Dryden's vision blurred. His assailant was so close he could smell the scraps of food between his teeth.

'Who told you that?' he said, surprisingly quietly. Over his shoulder Dryden could see Humph in the Capri, eyes closed, headphones still on. The motorbike had moved on. Cars swept past like they always do, innocent of any crime.

'Just heard it,' he said, and the guy laughed in a friendly way which made Dryden's heart freeze. Then he took Dryden's arm, twisted it round his back and began to apply his weight. The elbow joint began to give with a series of plastic pops. Dryden screamed but the passing cars drowned him out.

The bloke was whispering in his ear now. 'Let's keep that to ourselves, yeah?'

'OK,' said Dryden, pathetically eager to comply. The vice-like grip was released, so he sank to his knees and threw up. He kept his eyes down, viewing the puke, until he heard the lorry rumble back out on to the A14. He knelt there for some time while he waited for his breathing to return to normal, and for his little fingers to stop vibrating like windscreen wipers.

Out of the hot dust of the road Inspector Andy 'Last Case' Newman's battered Citroën appeared. He got out, walked over and rattled the roller-shuttered front of the Ritz before turning to Dryden. He gently opened the fast-closing left eye, looking for broken blood vessels: 'That's gonna be a corker. Care to tell me who did it?'

'A driver. I suggested he was after buying porn. He took exception.'

'We can put him down as a "No", I think, don't you?' said Newman.

Dryden wanted to laugh but still felt too sick. 'Bob Sutton. Little Alice's father, picked up something about the pornography racket in a lay-by, according to his wife. But I guess you know that already.'

Newman nodded, thumping the roll-up shutter one last time. He peered in through a gap between the door and its metal frame. A green parrot lay silent in an ugly little bundle.

'Parrot's a stiff,' he said. 'Shame, he could have told us where the proprietor's gone.'

There was a whiff of putrid beefburger on the air so they moved up-wind. Newman took out his notebook and flipped over the pages. 'Ex-wife of the T-Bar owner came in yesterday. Sub-station at Shippea Hill. She hadn't seen him for a month – six weeks.'

'Why'd she wait so long?'

Newman shrugged and watched with rapt attention a swift dipping over a field of burnt celery. Then he remembered that he knew the answer: 'They were separated. Ten years. But he paid her some cash, every month. He missed the date, she smelt a rat and went looking for him.'

'Smelt a rat,' said Dryden, and they moved even further up-wind. 'It's like the Bermuda triangle around here. Alice Sutton goes missing, then Bob Sutton goes missing, now this guy.'

Newman stretched his arms above his head, revealing two large splodges of sweat. 'Doesn't bother me. People lose themselves. It isn't a crime. Alice Sutton is back. I'd like to find her dad but my guess is he's still on her trail, and it led to London. When it goes cold he'll be back.'

'And this guy?' said Dryden, circling the Ritz, massaging his shoulder.

'Is more interesting,' said Newman. 'We've had him down for the illegal immigrants for some time. It's a drop-off point. Frankly we just let him carry on so we could get an idea of when the lorries were coming through. Try and spot the ones with the human cargo. Now it looks like he's mixed up in the porn too. Perhaps he's stepped out of line. They wouldn't like that. These people are capable of anything . . . More.'

Dryden fingered his swelling eye and walked back to the mobile T-Bar. He pulled at the gold chain around his neck, and tried Laura's key in the lock of the chipboard door. Nothing. Newman watched with the exaggerated patience of a nurse on a psychiatric ward. 'Johnnie Roe's the name,' he said. 'Villain. You should see his file at the nick. Takes up a whole drawer. Petty in every sense of the word plus two really black marks, a GBH five years ago in a town pub. And procuring, that was ten years ago. Nottingham.'

'Procuring?'

Newman sighed. 'He was a pimp. He sold girls. Got it?'

They strolled back to the cars. Humph was just unscrewing the top of a glove-compartment gin bottle. He shared few pastimes with Dryden but baiting coppers was one. He waved the bottle at Newman and grinned hugely.

'I'll leave you two gentlemen to it, then,' said Newman, getting slowly into his car.

Humph waved him off with a feminine flutter of the fingers.

Dryden slumped into the passenger seat and checked his injury in the vanity mirror.

'Shit,' said Humph, noticing the blackening eye for the first time. 'Sorry. I was . . .' and he weakly shook the earphones.

'Not your fault,' said Dryden. 'Drink?'

Humph fished out two Bacardis. The mood had changed and suddenly Dryden felt the uncomfortable certainty that their carefully concealed friendship had been exposed.

Dryden looked for the maps in the passenger-side door compartment. He went for the OS four inch to the mile. The question was simple: Where was Bob Sutton? Like Inspector Newman he must have been searching for the pillbox in which his daughter had been raped. He came to the Ritz because he'd heard this was where you could pick up the pictures. Newman had said that the pictures had turned up in Nottingham during a raid on illegal immigrants. So there was more than a circumstantial link with the people smugglers. And Etty had told him the Water Gypsies had seen the illegal immigrants being decanted at the Ritz, and then setting off across Black Bank Fen.

Dryden found the Ritz lay-by on the map. To the east, about a quarter of a mile, the tiny symbol for a pillbox stood in a stand of green shaded trees. But Newman had pointed out that it had a different roof from the one in the pictures. Etty had said the immigrants were led east which meant they were heading across Black Bank Fen. A single drove cut the fen in half and was marked on the map: The Breach. Half-way along, about three miles from the Ritz, a small plantation of pines was marked: Mons Wood. The OS map showed the wood as a stylized green rectangle shaded with little, childlike Christmas trees. And at its heart there was a small hexagonal symbol. A pillbox. Dryden tapped his finger on it. 'There,' he said. He tried not to notice that it was less than a mile from Black Bank Farm. He didn't believe in coincidences, so he couldn't believe in this one.

18

Dryden needed two things: a bag of ice and a copy of *The Crow*. Humph realigned the rear-view mirror so that he could see the black eye burgeon. 'Corker,' he said, swinging the cab out on to the main road and heading for *The Crow*'s offices.

'Thanks for the bodyguard service,' said Dryden unkindly.

'If I'd known you were going to wink at a seventeen-stone HGV driver I'd have been keeping my eye out,' said Humph, letting the smile take root.

'I think his reaction points to more unsavoury motives than effrontery, don't you? I'd guess he had a cab full of hard porn, or even a container full of it. That's why he was looking for our mutual friend Johnnie Roe.'

In *The Crow*'s front office there was a pile of *Expresses* for sale, the ink still wet. Dryden took one and jumped back into the cab. His story on Maggie Beck had made the splash – complete with the picture from Black Bank of Estelle and Lyndon with their mother. There was a chemist next door who advised him that he needed a cold compress for his eye.

'Brilliant,' he said, rudely walking off.

Dryden knew exactly where he could get one. 'Five Miles From Anywhere, quick as you can,' he told Humph, getting back in the Capri. Humph tooled the cab down Market Street expelling a cloud of exhaust which would have looked extravagant trailing behind the Zeebrugge ferry.

Five Miles From Anywhere was a pub at the confluence

of the Ouse and the Cam. It stood on a lonely promontory accessible only via a dispiriting three-mile drove road. Most of the clientele were families from the pleasure boats which used the moorings beside the pub or the marina which had been dug out of the bank in the sixties. Most days there was dust in the bouncy castle and a small pyramid of empty Calor gas bottles in the car park. It was a place haunted by the ghost of holidays past. Dryden loved the ambiance of gentle disappointment and the spectacular view: directly north along the wide conjoined rivers Ely Cathedral patrolled the horizon like a bishop's battleship.

They parked up on the tarmac forecourt with a satisfying screech of bald tyres. Humph killed the engine. 'G&T please, and a packet of cashew nuts.' He began to fumble with the language tapes.

Dryden fingered the black eye in the vanity mirror and for once his infinite patience fled. 'No,' he said.

Humph froze. Dryden pressed on. 'No. I'm not getting your fucking drink and nuts. You're coming with me. We're gonna sit outside and have a drink and . . . and a chat.'

'Chat?' said Humph, horrified.

Dryden wasn't going to argue. He got out, but leant back through the open passenger window. 'I'll see you at one of the picnic tables. No hurry.'

The bar was empty so Dryden rang a bell. He waited for a bleary-eyed barman to organize his trousers before ordering drinks, nuts, and a bar-towel packed with ice. He considered Humph's lumbering progress from the Capri towards the picnic tables, as viewed through the bar window. Already he was regretting baiting his friend. Did he really want to talk? No: what he wanted was to sit on his own with a pint of beer and contemplate both the river with its immutable beauty and his bad luck in being thumped in the face by a thug in a lay-by. Now he'd have to talk to Humph instead. He cursed himself, and friendship, and upped the order to two pints for himself.

'Medicinal,' he told the barman, touching the eye. Humph, astonishingly, had reached the picnic table by the time he walked out with the drinks.

'I hope you're bloody satisfied,' said Humph, wiping a curtain of sweat from his forehead with a handkerchief the size of a pillowcase.

Dryden sat back and held the ice to his eye, sipping from a pint at the same time. The silence between them deepened like a grudge until Dryden set the ice aside. He considered the normal rules of friendship, a pertinent subject as Humph appeared ignorant of the basics. 'So,' he said, heavily, 'how are you? Who's cleaning the house these days?'

Dryden had initiated several conversations that summer about the problems of finding someone to clean clothes and homes – a not too gentle hint which Humph had finally taken. The cabbie fumbled with the nuts. 'The woman who does,' he said.

'Does she indeed?' said Dryden, smirking.

'No, she doesn't,' said Humph emphatically.

'And the kids?'

Humph had two daughters: Grace, six, and Naomi, three. They lived in a nearby village with their mother and the postman of doubtful parentage. Humph got to see them every other weekend for outings arranged, down to the smallest detail, by his ex-wife.

'Next Saturday. Pantomime apparently, in Cambridge.'

'A pantomime in June?'

Humph shrugged. 'It's avant garde.'

'Oh no it isn't,' said Dryden.

'Yes it . . .' Humph stopped himself just in time, grunted

and reached for the G&T. All the liquid disappeared as if inhaled. So Humph got to his feet and said words never previously uttered in Dryden's presence. 'Same again?'

He tottered off like a hot-air balloon trailing its basket along the ground. He returned with what looked suspiciously like a double G&T, a pint, and an astonishing array of bar snacks from pork scratchings to cheesy whatsits.

'Snack,' he said, pulling open a packet of crisps with the kind of ease a polar bear exhibits when gutting a mackerel.

Humph took a big breath. 'So, Laura, how is she then?'

Retaliation, Dryden realized, brilliantly executed. Suddenly his insistence on communication seemed ill-judged. 'What can I say?' Dryden's emotions on the issue were complex. He wanted Laura to be returned to him as she had been a few minutes before the crash at Harrimere Drain. He didn't want to be tied to an invalid unable to speak for the rest of her life, or, more to the point, for the rest of his life. He wanted to take her back in time to the woman she had been. He didn't want to be a 'carer' – a word he hated. If she was going to exist in some world beyond his reach then he'd rather it was completely beyond his reach. At the moment they existed neither in nor out of the real world, but in separate universes which shared only a diaphanous boundary across which they might fleetingly touch. So her present condition was not the point. The point was, where it was all leading, and how long it would take. And since the answers to these questions were almost certainly not what he wanted to hear, he had avoided asking them even of himself.

But then he'd insisted on having a conversation in the first place. 'I . . .' he said, and then he spotted the motorcyclist. The one who appeared to be trailing the cab, and had been parked opposite the Ritz. The motorcyclist with the monochrome oxblood leathers. He was just getting out of

Humph's cab. Even from a distance of 200 yards Dryden could see that he was taking a hammer out of his pocket. Then he pulled it back and crashed it through the passenger side window. Dryden saw the fractured glass suddenly catch the light and the sound reached them a second later, like the call of some exotic bird off the marshes.

Dryden's jaw dropped and he pointed stupidly. 'Oi,' he said, so softly even Humph didn't hear him.

But Humph turned to see what the reporter was pointing at and an emotion close to murderous anger crossed his childlike features. Fate had taken many things away from Humph: his wife, his two daughters. They had all gone without a fight. His cab was a little peripatetic island of security, and now someone was defiling that sanctuary. So Humph was mad, and when he shouted 'Oi!' everyone on the Great West Fen heard – including the motorcyclist.

Dryden would recall afterwards the lack of panic in the rider's movements. He folded something and put it in a zip-up pocket. Then he put on the helmet with the black visor and the single chrome line along the cranium and ambled to his motorbike. The engine was already purring, drizzling a stream of hot hair out of the double exhaust pipes: and then he was gone, visible only as the invisible centre of a dwindling red dust storm.

Humph got to the cab first. The seats had been slashed with a knife and his beloved fluffy dice snipped off. The contents of the glove-compartment bar had been swept to the floor, with a few breakages, and the picture of Humph's daughters torn into pieces. A single knife scratch crossed the bonnet in an ugly zig-zag.

Dryden, who had stopped to finish his pint, came in second. He looked inside the Capri and decided to try for a laugh. 'It's the mark of Zorro,' he said.

Did Humph have tears in his eyes? He looked at Dryden now. 'You made me get out,' he said, by way of accusation.

The newspaper cutting was taped to the windscreen with a single piece of masking tape. It was Dryden's story about Maggie Beck.

19

Dryden sat on the roof of *PK 129* long after sunset. There was no moon, but the starlight burnt through the holes punched in the night. It was the kind of sky that comets love to cross. He leant back to stare heavenwards, gently fingering the swollen skin around his black eye. But the river stank. Reduced by the heat, like a good soup, it was sixty per cent ducks' piss with a hint of incontinent rat. The pleasure boats had fled to the moorings up-river at Ely leaving the silent waterways to slip stickily towards the sea.

Dryden lolled back in the deckchair, cradling a cup of cold black coffee, and flicked on the heavy-duty torch he'd retrieved from the tackle room. The beam cut the night like a searchlight, catching moths in a holding pattern overhead. The wind had dropped and the temperature was still in the mid-80s. A trickle of sweat slipped into his ear and gurgled like a drain. He checked his pockets: mobile phone, OS maps, notebook, binoculars, and a quarter pound of wine gums.

He picked at the damp white linen of his shirt and raised it from the skin of his chest. A tiny zephyr of breeze brought a flood of relief.

Monday night. 10.30, the pubs were still open. What did he think he was doing? One of his many vices was inertia, punctuated with sudden bouts of often ill-advised activity. He knew that such a bout was imminent. Would it help to work out why?

So far nobody had acted on the information published in the *Express*. He'd asked the solicitors at Gillies & Wright to leave a message on his landline if Lyndon's father made contact. But it was still too early. The *Express* was delivered to most homes that evening and would be read, piecemeal, over the coming days. According to Maggie Beck's last letter Lyndon's father was likely to read the story. Dryden's eyes swept the horizon. It was one of the many dramatic ironies of the Fens that it appeared to be an open landscape, when in fact it could hide so much.

Maggie's last letter had suggested another mystery: she had planned to divulge two secrets on her deathbed. Had she died before she could say more? What remained unsaid? He knew the heart of the mystery was on Black Bank Fen and he planned to return. There was no doubt he was drawn to what he feared. He had a suspicion that water would kill him, but he lived on a boat. Even before the accident in Harrimere Drain he'd been claustrophobic. Now it was the central anxiety in his life. So two images were pulling him back to Black Bank Fen: Alice Sutton, drugged and abused in her pillbox nightmare, and the unseen hell of the smuggled people, crammed inside their black, swaying boxes. And a third. Lyndon Koskinski in his tiny, dark, breathless cell cradling the salvation that was the Zippo lighter.

So, tonight, he would visit the pillbox on Black Bank Fen.

He heard the familiar clatter of the cab's exhaust pipe hitting the sleeping policeman on the lane which ran down to Barham's Dock. Humph's assaulted limousine coasted into view. He liked driving by moonlight without lights. It appealed to his sense of romance and adventure and it radically increased the admittedly slim chance that he would accidentally kill the bastard who'd run off with his wife.

Dryden pulled open the passenger door, winced again at the screech of tortured rust, and passed Humph a mug of bitumen-black coffee.

Dryden was about to close the door when he saw by the interior light track marks in the dust. Barham's Dock was a lonely spot. Occasionally hikers walked past on the seventeen-mile path to Cambridge – otherwise traffic was restricted to migrating birds and the cows which grazed on the river bank. But this was a set of motorbike tracks in the thick moon-white dust which coated the surface of the drove.

'Odd,' he said out loud, and giggled inappropriately at the fear which made his skin prickle.

Humph ignored him and was silent, a subtle and contrary indication that he was prepared to talk. He turned the ignition key and the cab coughed like a camel.

'Why?' he said. 'Where?' Humph was good at questions.

'Why? I'm haunted by a small hexagonal room,' said Dryden. 'Where? Black Bank Fen, follow The Breach from near the Ritz lay-by. Anything else?'

Humph saluted and flicked on the local radio, pulling the cab round in a screeching circle of grit and dust. Dryden wound down the passenger-side window. Humph never appeared to sweat in the cab, he'd noticed, but there was no missing the smell.

They hit the drove road across Black Bank Fen twenty minutes later. The Breach was unsigned, unsurfaced and deserted. They hadn't passed another car on their entire journey. It was 10.50pm and neither had spoken, lost in worlds which were unlikely to collide.

Dryden used the torch to read the map and guided them east. Black Bank Fen lay around them like a hundred-mile stretch of the Doldrums. The occasional light of a farm cottage twinkled in the tumbling hot air like a passing round-the-world yacht. Overhead a fuel transporter heaved itself towards Mildenhall, a tiny city of lights twinkling in its loading bay as it flew overhead.

After ten minutes Dryden spotted a tall stand of pine trees which stood out, charcoal-paper black, against the sky. 'Mons Wood,' he said. Humph ignored him, parked up, and began to rummage among the language tapes.

Dryden guessed the pines had been planted as a windbreak after the Great War. As Humph killed the engine an owl flew from a top branch of one of the trees and failed to hoot.

As the dead engine ticked to silence Humph repeated his question. 'Why here?'

Dryden sighed. 'Newman has a set of pornographic pictures taken in a wartime pillbox. At night. The girl's drugged. The pictures turned up in the Midlands in a police raid on a house used by illegal immigrants. They're dropping groups off in the fens and finding them jobs as pickers. I talked to Etty. She's seen lines of them crossing the countryside. Immigrants, using The Breach, crossing Black Bank Fen. I checked the map. This is the only pillbox on the fen.'

It sounded daft even to Dryden. He shrugged. 'It's a night out.'

Humph was asleep. Tiny snores popped like a coffee percolator. That was the great thing about Humph, he was always there for you. Right there, in his seat.

Dryden got out of the car and stood in the deafening silence that only a very large open space can produce. He recalled once as a child going early to the cinema to sit and munch sweets and the weight of anxiety which had fallen on him when the lights had momentarily failed. It was as if he could sense the space with bat-like sonar. He stood now, shivering in 80 degrees of heat, his anxieties crowding round like witnesses at an accident.

The woodland around the box was thin and dry and his footsteps crackled with broken twigs and dead grass. He sensed the presence of the pillbox rather than seeing it, a hard-edged blackness within the shifting shadows beneath the pines. He picked his way forward along an animal track and met a fox coming the other way. The torchlight caught the eyes and the nose, and the shiny liquid which caked its snout and teeth. At night, by a thin beam of light, there was no way Dryden could see the colours, but he knew with the sixth-sense of the born coward that the liquid was a lipstick red.

Dryden had that strange sense which signals disaster, a sense that told him this wasn't him, padding through a deserted stretch of Fen woodland, but someone else, some-one he could safely watch from his front row cinema seat, comfortingly surrounded by an audience of several hundred representatives of the real world. The fox's retreat had unnerved him further, and he knew that if he didn't move quickly he'd fall down.

He could see the pillbox now, one wall catching the moonlight, decorated with the Grimm fairy-tale shadows of the pine trees. He walked quickly to the wall and touched it, confronting a fear which helped allay his anxiety. He moved carefully anti-clockwise, tracing the hexagonal outline of the box, until he came to the door. The silence was oppressive now, so he rattled it loudly, the sound helping to quell the panic which was rising in his throat. The door was iron, rusted, but with a newish-looking deadlock and stood slightly ajar. He pushed it fully open and sent a beam of light into the dark space within.

There were shadows, and out of them came a figure, head down and running. Dryden, paralysed, later recalled hoping the figure would simply run through him – an insubstantial nightmare's demon. As a result his head met his assailant's with the kind of crack that is muffled only by two intervening layers of skin. A dagger of pure pain stabbed him in his black eye. What did he recall? An eyeball, white. A flash of ivory teeth beautifully arranged in tombstone order. Nothing more. Except the smell. It was what Dryden imagined carbolic would be, but with a bitter edge: up close and impersonal.

Then he did pass out. A curtain of cosy blackness fell before his eyes and he was no longer there to feel the fear. In the cab Humph dozed dreamlessly. But Dryden, plunged into the fetid well which was his unconsciousness, returned to his ever-present nightmare. Laura floated in the viscous blood, just beyond his outstretched hand. It was a river now, he could see that, and on one bank stood a pillbox. The blood oozed from the open wound of the gun portal.

Dryden was shouting Laura's name when he came to with a start that seemed to stop his heart. The torch lay beside his head, illuminating the straw. Its beam slightly yellow, the battery fading. Had he been out for hours? If so, where was Humph?

He would have run from the pillbox if he could have stood up. But his overriding emotion was thirst, prompted by the taste of blood in his throat. Which is when he saw, by the torchlight, the glass. It was on the opposite wall, immediately below the rectangle of black, star-studded sky, that was the gunslit, on a shelf. It was exactly in the middle of the shelf, like a chalice left on an altar.

Dryden knew two things immediately; that the glass was polished and without fingerprints, and that it was completely empty. He needed water. It was really spooking him, that single, untouched glass. He held the torch beam on it. Sweat popped from a thousand pores in tiny globes. He was panicking now, and trying to suppress the reason why.

He knew the body was there. In the moonlight its pale form had begun to emerge, like secret writing, from the straw-lined confusion of the pillbox floor. He rolled the torch in the straw and let the light give the corpse all three dimensions. It cast a shadow now, low and lifeless across the straw, and it was the shadow of a man. And for this victim there was to be no fourth dimension: time had fled for ever.

The body wore jeans, no socks, but the torso was naked. One arm was outstretched behind the torso where it was manacled to the pillbox wall. The rest of the body was in a ball, except for the other arm which stretched out forwards along the floor, towards the shelf and the single, empty glass. The index finger was outstretched again, as in one of Michelangelo's touching angels. The chain to the wall was taut and still appeared to be supporting part of the weight of the corpse.

Why reach out for an empty glass? Easy. It hadn't been empty once.

Dryden stood and circled the body until his back was to the shelf. He could see the top of the head now, tucked down into the straw, and the thinning blond hair was tainted with the yellow of cigarette smoke. The fox must have eaten from a wound on the leg where the manacle had cut in. Dryden puked, gagging until he could breathe.

His head swam and he knew with certainty that he was about to pass out. The darkness came but he went into it carrying a single image: the victim's skin. It looked unnaturally dry and parched and across the outstretched arm and the arched back it was streaked with livid patches of discoloured flesh: flesh pitted and blue like a Christmas turkey's. He recalled, instantly, his last visit to the Ritz and the cup of coffee placed on the counter by the owner, the vacuous empty conversation, and the hand that held the cup, crossed with raised purple skin grafts.

20

The beam of light from the pillbox gunslit shone out across Black Bank Fen like the lantern beam of a landlocked lighthouse. Dryden had watched from the Capri as first the scene of crime team, and then the pathologist, had picked their way through the edge of Mons Wood towards the box. The interior now, he knew, would be bathed in the super-light of halogen lamps. The body was still in situ, awaiting the medics who sat patiently in the ambulance drawn up on The Breach, its emergency beacon pulsing silently. Humph offered him a malt whiskey and he took it thankfully. His throat was dry with fear, and his guts were still churning.

There was a sharp tap on the near-side window which made them both jump. Inspector Andy Newman's head appeared: 'OK. When you're ready.' The detective took him under the arm, partly to keep him on the narrow path marked out by the forensic team's white flags, and partly to hold him up. 'Just talk me through it, Philip, step by step, OK?'

It was the first time Newman had ever used his first name and he was pathetically grateful for the kindness, and at the same time aware of how visibly he must be radiating anxiety.

'I met the fox here,' said Dryden, and Newman gave him an old-fashioned look.

'Mr Tod, was it? Peter Rabbit not at home?' Their laughter drew resentful looks from the forensic team combing the woodland. Newman placed a hand on his shoulder to stem the almost hysterical escalation of good humour. 'A fox, Philip?'

'No. Yes. Seriously – a fox. I couldn't be sure, but I thought it had blood on its snout.'

A man appeared at Newman's shoulder in a head-to-foot plastic shell-suit. The policeman did the introductions with exaggerated care: 'Dr Beaumont – Home Office pathologist – this is Philip Dryden, chief reporter on *The Crow*, Ely. He found the body, Doc. An hour ago.'

Beaumont had the eyes of the true professional: intelligent, alert, even excited, but certainly inured to death by the sight of a thousand corpses before his thirtieth birthday. 'Mr Dryden is right, inspector. There are clear signs of animal activity around, on, and to some extent in the body.'

Newman refused to ask the obvious question.

'Most of those injuries being inflicted after death,' finished Dr Beaumont, a smile suggesting itself through his eyes. 'Shall we?' he added, turning back towards the pillbox as though he was ushering forward dinner guests.

A scene of crime tent had been erected over the entrance to the pillbox, and here Newman and Dryden donned blue plastic suits. Then Dr Beaumont led them into the pillbox. The most striking feature of the victim's body was the tautness of the limbs. The chain which linked the manacled hand to the wall was still taking the full weight of the corpse. It was as if death had struck at the exact moment the victim had stretched out to the edge of physical endurance.

'Cut the chain,' said Beaumont, and a scene of crime officer stepped forward with bolt cutters. Beaumont put an arm under the corpse's chest and took the weight. 'OK – now.'

The chain sheered and bounded back to the wall while

the torso of the corpse slumped forward the last two inches to the straw floor.

Beaumont got close to the victim's face, still unseen and tucked beneath the shoulders, and examined it with a pencil torch and a forensic scalpel. He filled several plastic bags with minute traces of hair, blood and skin.

Newman walked across the floor between two white chalk lines until he got to the shelf under the gunslit. 'And this was like this? Empty?' he said, tapping the glass with a ballpoint.

'Yup,' said Dryden, wishing he could drink some water now.

'Let's turn him over,' said Beaumont, and the room suddenly filled with the forensic team. They flipped the corpse over and he lay, awkwardly, like a crab with his limbs raised.

It was the owner of the Ritz. His mouth was stretched open in a frozen scream, the eyes tinged pink with broken blood-vessels. The skin was caked in what looked like salt, with a rim of rime around the thin, blotched lips. The nose had been destroyed by a violent blow which had folded the cartilage back into the skull.

'I think we can assume that death was unnatural,' said Beaumont, scribbling notes.

Dryden knelt and examined the face. 'What are those?'

They directed one of the halogen lamps on to the face. On each cheek and across the chin were a series of livid puncture marks, with blue bruising around each.

Beaumont didn't answer but used a gloved finger to slightly massage the skin.

Newman lifted the chain which had secured the victim to the wall, using the ballpoint looped through one of the heavy iron links. The manacle contained a single lock and was smeared with blood and skin tissue where the man had lunged forward towards the glass and injured his wrist. The other end was looped through an iron ring in the wall and secured with a simple padlock.

'That's interesting,' said Newman, turning the pencil torch on the manacle. A line of script had been stencilled into the metal.

Dryden shrugged. 'An African language? Indian? Arabic? It's not European, that's clear.'

The ambulance team arrived with a bright neon-yellow body bag.

Dryden waited outside, watching the stars turn above, while the corpse was removed.

'Any sign of the killer?' he asked Newman, as they walked back to the Capri.

Newman shook his head. 'There are some tyre marks further down the drove. Looks like a four-wheel drive. You can't remember anything about him at all? The bloke who bowled you over.'

Dryden shrugged.

Beaumont came out, peeling off the white surgical gloves he had worn to examine the body.

'The punctures in his face; any idea?' said Dryden.

The pathologist consulted his notes. He held out his right hand: 'Three puncture marks on the left cheek.' He held out his left hand: 'Four on the right.' He stepped forward and held Dryden's face in a grip with his fingertips, gently applying pressure. 'My guess is someone held him like this, and then went on applying the force. Some of the nails dug in. The thumbs raised bigger welts, to the centre, the fingers less so, trailing off towards the neck.'

Dryden looked into Beaumont's eyes. He could see the irises widening as they accommodated the drop in light level outside the pillbox.

'Then he hit him?' said Dryden.

Beaumont nodded, releasing his grip. 'Yes. Hard. Some of the cartilage has been forced back into the brain.'

'Did it kill him?'

'No. No, I don't think so. I think he died of thirst.'

21

Dryden, released from police questioning at 12.30am, got Humph to drive him straight to *The Crow*. He filed stop-press single pars to all the broadsheets and most of the tabloids for the Tuesday morning's late editions. He'd agreed with Inspector Newman to withhold most of the details – but there was enough there to flog the story: wartime pillbox, semi-naked corpse, partly eaten by wild animals. What more did they want? Newman had signed-off a form of words to cover how the body was found: the time was withheld, and the discovery attributed to a local farmer – name also withheld.

Having finished filing he woke Humph to drive him to The Tower. There was no way either of them would sleep so they shared what was left of Humph's Greek picnic and rammed that home with a couple of Metaxa 3-star brandies. He brought Humph up to speed on the investigation by reading out the copy he had filed. The cabbie listened, whistled once, and settled down to sleep.

Dryden decided it was visiting time. Laura's breath whistled like a cat's. Dryden, and the nursing staff, had long since agreed that her sleeping time should be respected, and despite her open eyes the room was darkened, and the COMPASS machine turned off, between 10.00pm and 7.00am.

Dryden sat quietly for a minute, studying her face in the blazing moonlight. He stood and went to the window. Below, the caretaker was sweeping the forecourt. Clearly an insomniac, he whistled happily. Beethoven again, perhaps 'The Emperor', thought Dryden. In the cab Humph read his language primer by the courtesy light.

He turned back to the room. It had changed since his visit the evening before. Estelle and Lyndon must have been in to ferry out Maggie's stuff, large amounts of which had accumulated in her final weeks. A bookcase had been filled with gifts from family, neighbours and friends and a wardrobe had held clothes for when she was judged well enough to walk in the grounds of The Tower. The cardboard box in which Dryden had stored Maggie's tapes had been emptied shortly after her death, the box left under the bed. Her life, in her own words, was back at Black Bank. The cupboard stood open and empty. The only thing left of Maggie's in the room was the tape recorder on the window ledge.

Dryden sat down by Laura's bed and examined her hands, which lay lifeless on the single sheet. The image he was trying to suppress seemed to be etched on his retinas – the outstretched hand of the corpse in the pillbox and those undulating, angry, skin grafts. Who had killed Johnnie Roe? Had Bob Sutton's inquiries disrupted the trade in pornography? Had the crooks behind the business come looking for Johnnie? Or had Sutton got there first?

Quietly he stood and walked to the COMPASS machine. For once his curiosity seemed dimmed. He stuffed the tickertape in his pocket unread, and went back to the cab.

SHFYTJF SHDURIT DHEOFJO DJDO
GHGEIKOW WATCHWHITE KRUBBYO
ASAIUDSJ HD UCANSEETIERIVERGHHUJI

Over the months he'd learned the telltale signs. The tiny sounds which said the light was coming.

First there was the outer gate. A rusted hinge grated. Not like the others he could hear at dawn and dusk. The hundreds of iron doors opening and closing in the prison of Al Rasheid.

This one had a note. He'd played cornet at high school. Was it a G? Perhaps. Middle register. Pleasing.

He had only a few seconds then to prepare. He had to close his eyes, he must, because the pain would be sweeping, a burning poker of agony thrust into his eye sockets and down into his brain. That first time the nerve ends had sizzled, like tiny caterpillars shrivelled on a hotplate.

But he had to open his eyes to savour the light, to relieve the human inkwell of darkness which was his life. An absence of light so total he sometimes forgot what sight was. So to ready his eyes he pressed his fingers into the sockets, producing the dancing colours which helped prepare for the light, even though they danced now with a half-hearted flickering voltage.

After the rusted hinge came the dog biscuit. He knew the dog, Atta, lived at the end of his corridor. Many people kicked him; some, surreptitiously, patted and fussed him. But only the jailer gave him the biscuit. He imagined the dog tossing the biscuit and crunching it further each time it was caught. A joyless meal which made the jailer laugh each time.

Then came the keyhole. There must have been a disc of metal covering the keyhole on the outside. The jailer flipped it up to insert the key and for a second a magical key-shaped beam crossed the cell and fell on the wall.

154

So he'd moved Freeman there, to catch the light. Freeman, who'd survived like he had, drifting down inert to the desert. Lyndon blamed himself for the injury. He'd panicked, hitting the button for the ejector seats before his co-pilot was ready. So he'd caught the canopy with his head, breaking the skin and the skull, and blackening his eyes. He held Freeman's head in his hands sometimes, tenderly, feeling for the fractures beneath the skin, and the sickening click of the cranial plates which had been dislodged by the cockpit canopy.

But when the keyhole light fell on Freeman's face his eyes never opened. For eighteen days they'd been in this solitary silence. And Freeman hadn't moved; even though Lyndon gave him most of his food and cleaned the head wound with the water he craved so much to drink. But Freeman White lay still, stiller with each passing day. One day soon, Lyndon knew, the keyhole light would find his eyes forever open.

The jailer knew his business and the key turned in the lock and the door flew open with military swiftness. The light engulfed them. Direct sunlight. Lyndon's eyes hurt so much he always cried out, while he scrabbled to his knees beside Freeman's body.

And then the jailer showed his pity, smoking a single cigarette in the doorway as Lyndon tried to see out on the world. Once he saw the leaves of a cedar tree over the far wall flickering from lime green to silver grey in a breeze. And once the flag. Three green stars on a horizontal white band, a red band above, black below.

And he always made the same plea for Freeman: 'Take him away, not me. Take him away. He needs a doctor. Look!' And Lyndon would draw back the bandage on the forehead to reveal the purple wound, with its iridescent greenish tinge. He'd take some of the water then, and bathe away the pus and the flies.

But the jailer smoked; not cruelly, but with his back turned. There was never ever any warning of the end of the light. Just the sudden diminution of the sunburst and the rocking percussion of the iron door crashing against the jamb. And then the darkness again, and the terror of the small space he knew so well.

Tuesday, 17 June

22

Dryden held the cup of black coffee to his lips and watched the tiny tremor in his right hand translated into concentric wavelets on the surface of the liquid. He gulped the caffeine with an addict's concentration, then picked up Humph's flask and, tilting it, confirmed it was empty.

A surge of panic, less potent than the caffeine, made his muscles tighten. The events of the night before were still a cartoon strip of indelible, technicolour images – from the blue-spotted skin grafts on the victim's back to the bright yellow fluorescence of the body bag in which they'd taken him away. And finally the cell in which he waited, briefly, for Newman. The cell that smelt like a cat's tray without the comfort of the litter.

Had he slept? Humph had taken him back to *PK 129* but they'd drank little bottles until dawn without speaking. Dryden rubbed his fingers in his eyes and heard the gritty squeak of dust and eyeball grating.

He looked at the ceiling and remembered where he was: church. Precisely, St Matthew's – The Pickers' Church on Black Bank Fen. Newman had fended off a clutch of media inquiries overnight by scheduling a press conference for 10.00am close to the site of the murder. Educated as a Catholic in a grim north London grammar school, Dryden had always found that organized religion left him with an overwhelming urge to laugh out loud. He tried it now, the echo bouncing back off the thin clapboard walls of the church.

The light inside the church was extraordinary; instead of the play of medieval shadows this was a display of sunbursts, making the charged air more substantial than the rickety church itself. The ten lancet windows on either side of the main body of the wooden ark-like nave were of plain glass, a sea green mixed with milky white. It was like sitting in a fish tank. Ten sunbeams with the concentrated energy of lasers thrust through the nave as the sun climbed into another featureless blue sky.

Despite the summer drought Dryden could still sense the damp of more than a hundred Fen winters. The smell was as cloying as a memory, and as vivid as the names in golden script above the altar. These were the vicars of the strange whitewashed wooden church on Fourth Drove, Black Bank.

St John Reginald Dawnay. M.A. Cantab. 1868–90.
Reginald Virtue May. Ph.D. Oxon. 1890–1901.
Conrad Wilton Burroughs. M.A. 1901–

That open ended dash said it all. For more than thirty years they'd fought to save the pickers from Methodism – and lost. They even called it 'The Pickers' Church', but they still wouldn't come. More than 2,000 of them had lived on the fen according to the census taken at the turn of the century, living along the dykes and banks in skewiff homes which creaked in the wind. Then the Great War swept the men away. Even the evangelical Methodists retreated, closing the Bethel, and falling back into the Fen towns. With peace the machines came and the Revd Conrad Burroughs melted into the past, without the time, or energy perhaps, to pause and mark the date.

The church, and its tiny bell tower, had sagged with the years into the rich peat soil. For more than eighty years the building had limped on as a machine store, estate office, and finally a community centre. A single pool table stood on the altar, a razor-blade slash exposing the chipboard beneath the sun-bleached green baize.

Dryden laughed out loud again, enjoying the atmosphere of ingrained disappointment.

Inspector Andy 'Last Case' Newman, arranging papers on a trestle table, looked up. 'That's them.'

They heard cars bumping along the drove road. Her Majesty's Press was on parade. There was plenty of interest. Dryden had filed early morning pars for the late editions of the Fleet Street papers, and a full story for the first editions of the local evening papers in Cambridge, Norwich and Peterborough. He'd left an answerphone message for Charlie Bracken telling him he was at the press conference and would be in the office by ten. Then he'd called Mitch and told him to get some scene of crime pix at the pillbox, if he could get near.

Newman had pinned the cuttings from the nationals to a large board by the church door marked 'Incident Room: PRESS'.

'Pillbox Killing Baffles Police', was Dryden's favourite, from the *Mirror*. Although 'Gruesome Pillbox Killing in Fens', from the *Daily Mail*, had more lip-smacking sensationalism.

There was a small room to the left of the church doors where the local branch of Darby and Joan met. Newman's sergeant, Peter Crabbe, was making tea. Half a dozen uniformed coppers were trooping in having spent the early hours combing the fields for evidence. A woman PC was sticking photos and maps to the main incident room board. Nobody appeared to be in a hurry.

'You'll miss all this excitement,' said Dryden, smiling.

Newman was sitting on a plastic chair, tilted back, examining a swifts' nest in the roof.

Dryden stood. Even now, as the sun began to rise above the treeline, the cotton of his shirt stuck to his back where it had touched the pew. 'So why here? Why not use the nick in Ely? It's a long way for the press to come.'

Newman parked an ample backside on what had been the wooden altar rail. It creaked like a door in the wind. 'Exactly. Some peace and quiet – once I've got rid of you lot.'

Dryden considered this explanation more than sufficient. 'I'm a key witness. I can haunt the place. I might even have done it.'

'I wouldn't push your luck. I've managed to get through an entire career without a miscarriage of justice. But I could just fit one in . . .'

The press arrived. They shuffled in like the extras from *One Flew Over the Cuckoo's Nest*. The man from the *East Anglian Daily News*, Joey Forward, was the best dressed, and he had his flies open. PA's man, Mike Yarr, appeared to have his pyjamas on under a jumper. The rest headed for the free coffee. They all knew each other, so nobody said hello, a subtle indication that there were no strangers in their sad little world.

Dryden had one more chance for a private question. 'What about the porno shots? Is it the same pillbox?'

Newman showed his irritation by pulling at the tight collar which had helped turn his face red. 'Too early, Dryden. Looks the same – but then most of 'em do.'

Dryden knew he was bluffing. The military code-number Newman had spotted on the pictures could be easily matched if it was the same pillbox. He kicked himself for panicking the night before and not checking the walls before he'd rushed back to the cab to phone the police.

'Are you looking for Bob Sutton?' He knew Sutton's search for his daughter's rapist must make him a leading suspect.

162

Newman's patience snapped. 'For Christ's sake, just wait, Dryden. Patience. It's a virtue. Look it up.'

The press pack, fired up by mugs of Nescafé, took their places. In the mid-morning heat there was indeed a whiff of something unwashed, something, Dryden noticed with satisfaction, that liked a drink. He felt a twinge of admiration for his trade.

Newman flicked open a manila folder. Someone farted loudly and the press giggled. Newman adjusted his reading glasses and wished, with an almost religious intensity, that he was in the metaphorical bird-hide of his retirement, removed to a world where communication was not only inessential, but a liability.

'The body of a white male was found last night in a Second World War pillbox about half a mile from this church. He was manacled to the wall.'

'We can read the papers. Tell us something we don't know.' It was Mike Yarr. The PA needed fresh information to wire to its customers, mainly evening newspapers with first editions which went to press before noon. But for now Yarr was gyrating a pencil in his ear. 'Like an ID.'

'Enquiries are continuing into the identity of the victim. We expect a positive ID this afternoon. I can tell you he appears to be between forty and fifty years of age. Now, if I may continue . . .' There was some irritable shifting in chairs and some dark looks at Dryden. Most of the press pack suspected he knew more than he'd given away in his copy for the dailies – they feared being scooped again, and this time on a story they'd been sent to cover.

Newman pressed on. 'I am prepared to release details of this man's death but one aspect must remain under embargo until you are otherwise directed to print it. Agreed?'

This was standard procedure in murder cases. The police

often withheld details in order to weed out cranks who rang up to confess to the killing. Dryden had not been told to keep anything out of his reports except his own name – and the fact that an empty glass had been found at the scene. So whatever Newman had to say it had to be something which the pathologist had found, or the scene of crime team. The rest of the press pack nodded wearily. 'Bound to be the best bit,' said Yarr, yawning and revealing a sliver of yellow-green cabbage caught between yellow incisors.

'Fine,' said Newman. 'The cause of death is to be ascertained, but at the moment we are working on the theory that he was poisoned.'

That did it. Silence.

'With?' asked Dryden, surprised. The pathologist at the scene had guessed he died of thirst.

Newman flicked through some notes. 'Samples are at the lab but the stomach contained benomyl, carbendazim, and thiophanate-methyl. Fungicidal weedkiller to you lot. But this wasn't the garden variety. Industrial strength. Usually sold for crop spraying.'

Mike Yarr, a typical wireman, took a perfect note in 200-wpm Pitman shorthand. He weighed eight stone soaking wet and drank Guinness in buckets. His eyes were marbled like a pickled egg. 'And he drank it, did he?' he asked.

'Yup,' said Newman, still reading. 'Which was hardly surprising, given his condition.'

'Which was?' asked Dryden, remembering the empty pint glass on the shelf below the pillbox window.

'Severely dehydrated,' said Newman. 'The pathologist who got to him first on site reckoned he hadn't had any fluid for at least six days. It was eighty-two degrees in the box at two o'clock this morning. In the day – a hundred and twenty, possibly more. In the pathologist's words, the victim's body tissue was about as moist as a Jacob's cracker.'

'But it didn't kill him?' asked Joey Forward. Joey was scratching his beer belly, his fingernails screeching on the white nylon shirt.

'No. But it would have. I won't go into the specific details, but let's say it would have been a race between gagging on his own swollen tongue or drowning in his own stomach juices. His last meal had been taken even longer ago than his last drink. Two sausages with beans: pork.'

Several full english breakfasts rearranged themselves in the room. There was another fart, but this time nobody laughed.

'When was his last drink – the poison cocktail – taken?' It was Mike Yarr again.

'About twenty-four hours before his body was found. Pathologist at the scene believed he would have died within an hour of drinking the poison. But in his case it would have been quite a long hour.'

'And the body – found by a farmer it says 'ere,' said Yarr, now ostentatiously reading a copy of the *Mail*. 'No name given here.'

'Those details we are withholding – for the time being – while investigations continue.'

The press corps examined Dryden, and he examined a wine gum he'd found in his pocket.

'Further points of interest – and you can use all this, gentlemen. The victim was naked above the waist but fragments of clothes were found amongst ashes in the pillbox.'

'What kinda clothes?' said Forward.

'White linen. With traces of animal fat. Tomato ketchup.'

'Suggesting?' said Yarr.

'Anything you like. Now. There was also a lot of loose

change on the floor, more than a tenner's worth in coppers and silver.'

Newman pinned a black and white photograph to the incident room board. It showed a narrow-bladed seven-inch knife sticking horizontally out of a wooden door jamb. The hilt was gilded and decorated with raised, geometrical patterns.

'And this. No traces of blood and no knife wounds on the victim. The designs are Arabic.'

'Fingerprints?' said a voice from the back.

Newman thought for a second. 'Yes. Partial prints. We're putting them through the computer now. I'll keep you up to date on any developments.' 'Plus,' he added, putting up another print. A plastic Tesco bag with its contents, presumably, laid out in military rows on the green baize of the pool table for the picture. Torch, pre-packed sandwich, apple, two motoring magazines, a small cassette player with earphones and two bottles of mineral water. And a cheap metallic picture frame. The quality wasn't good enough to see the subject of the photo which sat inside, slightly off-centre, with one corner folded down.

Dryden leant forward in his chair. 'The snap?'

Newman put a third print up on the board – it was the photograph blown up. A dog, a mongrel, with a piece of rope round its neck. There was a cheap plastic water bowl at its feet. In the background was a sluggish river, mulligatawny brown, and some tropical vegetation floating by. It was an astonishingly mundane image. A childhood pet perhaps?

Someone yawned. 'Well, it ain't the Thames, is it?' said a voice at the back.

'No,' said Newman. 'Our guess is tropical Africa, south of the Sahara. Which narrows it down to an area about twice the size of Europe.'

'So what do we think happened?' asked Yarr.

Newman shrugged. 'He was tied to the wall. Left. Tortured? His wrist was broken in the manacle. Skin very badly cut. And the pathologist says his vocal cords were in shreds.'

'Shouting?' said Dryden, knowing he was wrong.

'Possibly, but the pathologist said the damage was violent. Screaming, more like,' said Newman.

Dryden closed his eyes and tried to imagine what that would have sounded like. A human voice, shredded, echoing across Black Bank Fen. And then he tried to imagine who would have heard it.

23

As the press left Black Bank Fen in a caravan of cars Dryden checked his answerphone. There was one message: 'Hi. It's Gillies & Wright, solicitors. You asked to know. Someone has contacted the office with a claim to Maggie Beck's five thousand pounds. Name . . . Richard G. Mere. A farm labourer from Manea. We can't check it against the name Mrs Beck gave us until tomorrow when the will is read. Then we'll know if it's a genuine claim. But it looks good – I've dropped a copy of his letter in at *The Crow*. He certainly knew Mrs Beck and the farm.'

Dryden slapped the dashboard. '*The Crow*, chop, chop.' He'd phone Estelle from the office and tell her a claim had been made. Lyndon should be told as well – after all, it was his father. And the will? Had Maggie left Black Bank to her son, or her daughter?

They led the cavalcade along The Breach and watched the rest of the press turn south towards Cambridge and London. The Capri turned north towards Ely, where the cathedral's distant image was already buckling in the heat of the day. A cloud was so unusual that summer that when a large shadow dashed across the landscape Dryden watched its flight like a hawk. Peering up through the Capri's windscreen his eyes filled with cobalt. 'Blue sky,' he said, a seagull crossing it with motionless wings. Humph pulled the cab up by the side of the road. Dryden got out and scanned the horizon. The sun was behind them but it wasn't a cloud which had blotted it out. It was a column of smoke, rising from the fen just west of the city, and widening as it rose into a chef's hat a mile high.

'Jesus,' he said. It looked like an oil painting from hell.

Dryden rang Mitch, who was still at the scene of Johnnie Roe's murder. 'I guess it's a field fire. On the peat. But it's a biggy – get as close as you can, Mitch – I want to see the burn marks on that bloody hat of yours. The pix are for *The Crow* on Friday – so no rush.'

Humph slung the cab off the main road and headed south along a drove made of concrete slabs; the tyres thudding over the cracks as they traced a zig-zag route around parched fields.

'It's the old airfield,' said Dryden, already tasting the smoke in his mouth.

. Witchford Aerodrome had been a Lancaster bomber base in the war. Dryden had done a colour piece the year before after a farmer had ploughed up the remains of a German Heinkel which had come down in a raid. It had buried itself in the soft, wet peat of the winter of 1941. Dryden had been there when they'd got the pilot out of his sticky grave. He could see now the splayed bones of one of the hands in the mud, caressed by worms.

But Witchford's days of glory were long gone. Now the old hangars and conning tower were derelict and deserted except on Saturdays and Tuesdays, when the grass runways were used for car boot sales. The weekend sale was for general goods – white elephant and tatty; the Tuesday market for antiques or items which might be mistaken for antiques in a poor light. Entry was for 'trade' only – dealers, restorers, and general London or Brighton sharks. Hundreds jostling for the chance to buy 1920s china, Edwardian furniture, and First World War medals. As the cab got closer they could see the parked ranks of cars through a mirage of tumbling hot air at the base of the column of smoke. The drove road ran through a derelict section of the old perimeter fence and then across a mile of parched grass towards the runways. Heading towards them was a crowd of a couple of hundred bargain hunters pursued by the drifting, noxious cloud of straw smoke. And they were coming at quite a speed, most of them holding handkerchiefs or clothing to their mouths.

Humph pulled up and killed the engine. The silence was filled by a distinct sound Dryden knew well: panic, with crackling grass as a background motif.

Coughing, screaming, laughing and crying the crowd parted to sweep past Humph's Capri and kept going.

Through the drifting red-brown smoke Dryden could see two fire tenders working their way towards the seat of the fire in a field beyond the car boot sale. Through the purple-red flames Dryden could make out the shape of a bright yellow combine harvester. They were death traps in hot weather, with sparks flying and enough grease and oil caked to the machinery to make sure the chaff and straw caught fire with a satisfying BOOM! The top soil had caught alight as well, a common danger that summer. The peat fields of the Black Fen were essentially a huge open fireplace waiting for a light. As Dryden watched the fire advancing traffic-light orange flames flared at the edges of the dense Brown-Windsor smoke.

The fleeing crowd re-grouped beyond the flimsy remains of the wartime perimeter fence, as if the criss-cross wiring was a magic shield against the drifting pall of smuts and dust.

Dryden grabbed a rag from the cab boot, poured the contents of a bottle of mineral water over it, covered his face and set off for the parked cars. Ten years on Fleet Street had taught him the value of on-the-spot reportage. If there was a story here he needed to go and get it. Even as he did it he knew it was an act of bravado designed, like so many, to conceal a profound level of physical cowardice. Humph had no such demons to struggle with. He sat happily watching the fire spread, munching a diet chicken sandwich.

Dryden walked 200 yards towards the blaze, his eyes streaming as the smoke swirled around him, before a fireman emerged from the gloom in full breathing gear, and grabbed Dryden by the arm muttering: 'Idiot. Follow me.' Dryden tried to say 'Press' but the breath of air he would have used turned out to be 60 per cent carbon monoxide. The fireman led him to a door in one of the vast 1930s aircraft hangars and pushed him in with enough force to leave him flat on his face. 'Stay in there,' he said, fading back into the smoke.

The open door faced west so the drifting smoke was slipping harmlessly round the building. Dryden lay still, catching his breath. He heard a muffled thud which could have been a car exploding, the echo bounded around him like a giant ping-pong ball. The hangar had skylights but the thick smoke from the field fire was cutting out the sun. Somewhere very close he heard the crackle of tinder-dry grass burning.

He stood and surveyed the building, which must have been nearly eighty yards long and a hundred feet high. The hangar's floor wasn't entirely empty. In one corner an old RAF fire tender stood, a leftover prop from a Will Hay film. Along one wall aeroplane tyres had been stored in tall rubber stacks. The decaying carcasses of trapped birds littered the floor, and an oil slick ran from a punctured tank like blood from a head wound.

Up against the vast closed hangar doors a white van was parked. Dryden walked over and put his hand on the bonnet.

'Still warm,' he said. The side of the van was painted a light green with a white-lettered sign: 'Wilkinson's For Celery'. On the passenger seat there was a clipboard and a mobile phone. He peeked inside the windows in the tailgate doors and estimated there were about fifty boxes of fresh celery neatly packed in cellophane. He looked round the hangar again, but it was still empty.

Where was the driver? In the far wall, which was almost obscured by piled tyres, there was a single door marked 'Flight Group'. Dryden pushed it open and looked down a long corridor listening. He could hear music, African, with a solid rock beat.

He inched open the second door to find a Nissen hut: a curved corrugated iron roof over a concrete floor. The windows were all skylights again and high enough to give no view. Moss and lichen had covered them anyway, giving the whole room a sickly green tint. Rows of iron bedsteads crowded against the side walls. The springs were rusted and shot. At the far end Jimmy Kabazo, the foreman from Wilkinson's celery plant, stood watching him.

Dryden walked in and decided to try easy informality. 'Hiya.'

Jimmy turned and tried a door in the end wall, indicating that this ploy had failed. It was locked and when he turned back the smile had returned. He bent down and turned off a portable CD player. Dryden noticed that not all the beds were bare. Two or three on each side had sleeping bags on them, and fresh twenty-first century rubbish under them, from sandwich wrappers to tin cans and empty crisp packets. A modern Calor gas heater stood in the middle, with four plastic milk-bottle crates drawn up as seating.

Dryden picked one of the bare beds and sat where the pillow should have been, bringing his legs up off the floor.

'Looking for someone?' he asked, nodding to the sleeping bag on the next bed.

Kabazo grinned. 'Nope. Just waiting.' But he wasn't listening.

'Friend of mine saw them,' said Dryden, knowing he didn't need to spell it out. Evidence of the people smugglers was all around them. He guessed Kabazo was an illegal immigrant too, or at least mixed up in the trade.

'We safe?' Kabazo asked. Dryden couldn't be sure if he was referring to the fire, or to the likelihood that he would go to the police over what he'd found.

Dryden decided innocence was best. 'Just a peat fire – the combines start them. We're fine – it's mostly smoke.'

'Saw dem where?' said Kabazo.

'Black Bank Fen. Going across country – east. From the lay-by on the A14. That's where they took them out of the lorries.'

'Ritz,' said Kabazo, nodding, trying to calculate what Dryden knew and who he would tell.

Dryden folded his arms in a sign, he hoped, of patient informality. 'This is between us, OK? I'm not after anyone – just a story. No names. No need for names.'

Kabazo nodded but didn't move. 'I'm waiting,' he said again. 'My boy. Today maybe. Tomorrow. Police mustn't know.'

Dryden shrugged. 'Sure. Why should they?'

'Who you tellin' den?'

'Nobody. It's not my job. I'm interested in the story. I mean it; I don't need names.'

Kabazo nodded. 'He'll come. The skinhead said. Winston. He said last week, this week . . . maybe later. I don't trust him.'

'Winston?'

Kabazo stood at the foot of Dryden's bunk. 'The driver.

Our people pay him, he does the dirty work. With the Ritz man – Johnnie.'

Suddenly sunlight blazed down through the green sky-lights, indicating the runway fire was out.

'They've found a body. On Black Bank Fen,' said Dryden, cruelly, but didn't let the silence last more than a second. 'A man. In his forties. I think it's Johnnie – but they won't say.'

Kabazo's eyes widened. 'How long?'

'A few days – perhaps. What would they have done if Johnnie hadn't been there? Where's the next drop?'

Kabazo shook his head. 'Nottingham. If the driver knew. Perhaps Winston doesn't come, then they don't know.'

'I can ring you with a positive ID on the body at Black Bank. OK?'

Kabazo shook his head. 'Yes? Ring the factory. Leave a message.'

They walked back to the main hangar in silence and stood in the sunlight at the door. Outside the crowd was being marshalled towards the cars. Two vehicles had been dragged away from the rest into the middle of a field where they smouldered still. The bones of the combine harvester were black and crumpled, fire still licking around the driver's padded seat. A scene of incident officer in a bright orange jacket was examining the threshing mechanism, pulling scorched straw from the blades.

'Can you contact them? Get Winston?' asked Dryden.

'They don't like it. They got the money. And I left them a bag for Emmy. Food and his things. His music. I sit tight some days. Wait some more. Sensible boy, my boy. He's the first I send for with the money. Emmy's a good boy. '

Kabazo took a wallet from his jeans pocket and flipped it open to show a snap: a boy, maybe fourteen, stood grinning under an African sun. In the background a great river, too wide to offer a view of the far bank, swept past. But it was what the boy was holding that made Dryden's blood freeze: a mongrel dog with a rope collar. They looked happy together: impossibly happy.

24

Dryden stood alone in the graveyard of St Matthew's, and looking at his shoes in the dust, observed that he had no shadow. The sun beat down vertically on Black Bank Fen for Maggie Beck's funeral. Despite the discovery of the corpse in the pillbox the fen was deserted. Andy Newman's team had finished their trawl for clues and were now out interviewing Johnnie Roe's friends, relatives and lovers. The pillbox body lay in a mortuary at Cherry Hinton, its chest torn open by the pathologist's knife, its dull eyes sightlessly open to the white-tiled ceiling.

The funeral cortège had left Black Bank Farm a few minutes earlier. He could see it now zig-zagging towards St Matthew's. A brief ceremony had been held on the farm first – he'd checked the details with Samuel H. Gotobed; Undertakers. Private burial. No flowers. Donations to Cancer Research. Humph had parked the Capri under a stand of lime trees by the churchyard gates and stood beside the cab, a mark of respect only Dryden could truly appreciate.

By the time the hearse crunched to a halt a thin layer of red peat dust had taken the shine off the immaculate paint-work. The heat was pulsatingly intense. A trickle of cool sweat set out across Dryden's forehead from the thick black hair above. He thought it was a good day to bury Maggie Beck. No splash. No clawing slurp of dark peaty water over polished pine. It was the first burial at St Matthew's since Maggie's husband Don more than twenty years earlier. The newly dug grave lay open next to those of Maggie's mother and father, which, according to the stone, also contained the small corpse of Matty Beck, aged two weeks. 'Even stone can lie,' said Dryden, touching the warm marble.

Estelle rode in the first limousine, alone, her black, tailored shirt the only concession to funeral etiquette. Her shoulders were hunched in a silhouette of sadness. The second car carried a woman who had to be helped into a wheelchair. She wore a small pillbox black hat and veil, which had been fashionable in at least three different decades. The rest of the funeral party walked behind the cars led by a priest in white and black. A dozen farm workers followed in ill-fitting suits, their heads bowed by the heat rather than grief. But no Lyndon. Dryden considered his emotional state. The last time they'd talked, the anger had been visible. Anger at Maggie for giving her son away. Bewilderment as to the reason for that betrayal. Determination to find some sort of justice amidst the mess that his life had become. And Estelle? What part did his half-sister have to play in the rest of his life? He'd felt a distance between them, a fracture opened up by Maggie's deathbed confession.

Estelle saw Dryden as she walked to the graveside and seemed to shrink further into herself at the sight. At their first meeting Dryden had detected anxiety and anger; now she radiated something else, something far more dangerous: defiance?

Dryden retreated to the shade of a lime tree as they gathered around the letter-box trench of the grave. The priest's vestments, which hung lifeless in the heat, drank in the light. Dryden squinted at the white surplice, and looked away to rest his eyes on the horizon, where he found a lone figure standing in a group of pine trees. He felt his skin prickle as he shaded his eyes to try and see more. The trees had been planted to provide a windbreak for a storage barn which stood on what had once been a small island of clay in the peaty marsh of the fen. A white Land Rover was parked on its far side, the open tailgate just visible beyond the barn's end. The figure, Dryden could now see, was dressed in USAF grey. He watched the head fall in a brief bow, then someone touched Dryden's arm.

Estelle Beck's eyes were bloodshot but bright. 'Thank you for coming,' she gripped his arm. 'The police came, this morning,' she said, watching the funeral party shuffling out of the graveyard. 'About the man they found, in the pillbox. It's terrible. It feels so close,' she added, clutching at her throat. 'It's frightening – I'm frightened. Out here.' She looked to the distance where the heat of the day was beginning to distort the strict symmetry of the fens.

'They'll find who did it,' said Dryden, realizing quickly just how unlikely that was. 'Newman – the inspector. He's an old hand, and they've got a whole team on the job. Try to put it out of your mind – at least for today.'

'Out of my mind?' said Estelle, too loudly. 'God! The torture . . . how could anyone do that? Such an inhuman thing . . .' She covered her mouth. 'Like Tantalus.'

Dryden considered the classical allusion and how perfect it was. The king chained to a pillar in a pool of water and left to die of thirst. The perfect torture.

The woman in the wheelchair was pushed towards them by the priest. Estelle stooped to kiss her. 'Come back to the farm, Connie, at least.'

The woman shook her head: 'God bless, dear. I won't, forgive me. But come and see me soon.' The priest pushed her on towards the waiting cars.

Dryden took his chance. 'The solicitors have had a call. A letter, actually, delivered by hand. A man claiming to be Matty's father – Maggie's lover.'

'Yes. I know. They rang here. We won't be able to verify his identity until the will is read. I'm going into town this afternoon. I can let you know . . . You are interested?'

Dryden nodded looking round. 'No Lyndon? I thought he'd be here.'

Her features softened but Dryden still struggled to see a shadow of Maggie's humanity in the bitter green eyes. 'Well, he's not. I told him he'd regret it – but he said one more regret wouldn't change his life. He may be right.' She paused, looking briefly north towards the old barn.

'Give him time. His life is in pieces,' he said.

She shivered despite the heat. 'Yes. Pieces.' She looked about.

'At least he has you. And a home.'

'Lyndon isn't comfortable at Black Bank, I'm afraid. He went soon after Mum's death. I don't know where. Perhaps back to the base. He won't tell me. Says he needs the space and the time. The farm is suddenly very empty. And very frightening. It's amazing how much you can hate a place, isn't it? Really hate.'

Dryden wondered why Lyndon Koskinski did not want to spend time with his newly found half-sister, but he said instead: 'Ring me after the will is read? Please. I'd like to know.'

Estelle looked to the funeral cortège. 'I must go. Some of the hands are coming back for a drink. It's the least I could do. They've run this place for Mum.'

'Will you sell?' asked Dryden.

She shrugged. 'It may not be mine to sell. Lyndon's the oldest child. And male.'

'You should sleep,' said Dryden. 'You can't do anything for Maggie now.'

She smiled. 'I've been listening.'

'Listening?'

'The tapes. The tapes Mum made. Her life.'

Dryden thought of the long hours Maggie had talked and Laura, perhaps, had listened.

'And does she say why she gave Matty away?'

She shook her head and looked north. Dryden saw that the white Land Rover had gone.

'Not a word,' she said. Dryden sensed the lie, and wondered if she'd listened to the tapes alone.

25

Mickey's Bar stood by one of the giant concrete blocks the Americans had used to block Mildenhall air base's residential roads from terrorist attack. Beyond the wire stretched the fen, but this side Mildenhall was like any other small Mid-Western town of 7,500 lost souls. Most of them needed a drink and a reminder of home. The place was riddled with homesickness. The barman had given Dryden a small draught Schlitz and was now staring into the middle distance. There were two other customers sitting at the long bar on high stools praying over their drinks. One wore a lumberjack's checked shirt and was reading *USA Today*, the other smoked Lucky Strikes with obvious enjoyment. Mickey's had a third customer – he stood, legs set wide apart, playing a one-armed bandit while swaying slightly to the piped music.

Dryden pulled his glass closer and sat watching the bubbles rise. One puzzle had brought him to Mickey's Bar. How could Maggie Beck swap two babies and get away with it? He'd trusted her, and so had his mother. But even dying women lie. He found it difficult to believe she could have got away with the subterfuge. He'd promised to help her put right the damage her lie had done – but he couldn't go on without being sure he wasn't helping to construct a greater lie. And the good reporter in him told him he had to check the story out one last time, now that it seemed Lyndon's new father had come forward. At least then he would feel confident that only one question would remain: why had she swapped the babies?

The walls of Mickey's were hung with pictures of fighters, bombers, transport planes and their crews. The haircuts and the technology changed over the years, but not the over-confident smiles. Dryden checked the three clocks behind the bar. 13.30 GMT. 08.30 NY. 05.30 LA.

He drank his cold beer and looked at himself in the bar mirror. He was unaware he was handsome, an oversight which had saved his character from vanity at least. What he didn't look like was a US serviceman. The jet-black stubble and the unruly hair were reasons enough to mark him down as local civilian staff. The gleaming blue-black eye added to his eccentric appearance and explained why the barman having served him and moved off, was continuing to watch him surreptitiously as he washed a small tower of glass ashtrays.

The bottles behind Mickey's Bar shook as a B-52 lumbered overhead bound for the US.

Major August Sondheim walked in briskly and took the next high stool. He looked like he owned the place, which considering his position as head of public relations for the base, and the amount he spent in Mickey's, was close to the truth. The barman needed no prompting: double Bourbon on ice minus the fancy umbrella.

'Philip. Good day,' said August, draining his drink and pushing the glass back across for the barman to refill. Dryden put a ten-pound note on the bar top and looked forward to the small change.

Today August was a drunk, just like every day. He ran a hand through his militarily trimmed white hair. 'Laura?'

That was the problem with Dryden's friends. They all asked the same question.

'Same. Better. I get messages. Sometimes they make sense.'

August slapped a twenty-dollar bill on the counter but the bartender was way ahead of him.

Dryden started his second beer fighting off a dual attack – hiccoughs and burps. He'd phoned August the day before to ask for details on the Black Bank air crash, 1976. For Maggie to successfully switch the babies she would have had to hoodwink the US military authorities into accepting that her own son, Matty, was in fact Lyndon Koskinski. How had that been possible?

August never wrote anything down but luckily he had a good memory before lunch. 'I read the file on the crash. Not much. Why would the woman lie, after all? This kid, her kid, was about the same age as the Koskinski boy – a few days' difference. Their colouring and weight were similar.'

'How did Maggie know that?' asked Dryden.

August shrugged. 'The dead child was found amongst the wreckage of the farm house. The body was clearly visible. The boy had died instantly from massive internal wounds caused by the impact. He had been travelling in a baby seat with a belt and had been thrown clear. My guess is Maggie found him, quickly realized the similarity in age and saw her chance to swap the babies. It looks like Maggie removed the blanket the Koskinski kid was wrapped in and used it to swaddle Matty Beck.'

Dryden paid for another round, feeling the room begin to gyrate on oiled wheels.

August was smoothing down his uniform in Mickey's bar mirror.

'The child who survived was examined by the base medic on duty that night, a different one had delivered the child at the US clinic. By the time of the crash the original doctor was Stateside, his tour over. The Koskinski child had been

183

cared for twenty-four hours a day by his mother, they lived in married quarters on the base. Jim, the father, had returned for the birth from Vietnam.'

August downed a fourth drink, but Dryden wasn't counting. 'There was a problem they should've checked out,' said August. 'But hey, the grandparents had been told, they wanted the kid, the rush was understandable.'

'What kind of problem?' said Dryden, aware he was slurring his words.

'Blood. They gave the kid a transfusion because of a slight head injury. He'd lost some blood. Luckily they double-checked the type. It didn't match the records. They put it down to an error. Sounds incredible now, but remember, Dryden, this woman had given her own son away. Nobody could have imagined she was lying. The base medics took him that night and as far as I can see she never saw him again until this summer. Never looked back. All the Koskinskis had seen was a few shots taken after the birth – and we all know what newborn kids look like, right? Walnuts. What was anyone supposed to think? Perhaps they didn't want to think. And don't forget, Maggie Beck went on to identify the kid in the mortuary as her son. Who's gonna step forward and ask: "You sure about that, lady?"'

'What about the autopsy?'

'Not our jurisdiction. Local coroner. It'll be in the records. But apart from weight and vital statistics they had nothing else to go on. She identified him, for Christ's sake.'

August sipped the bourbon, realizing that he'd reached that point where the rest of the day was going to be spent in a fog of alcohol. 'Any idea why she did it?'

Dryden burped into his glass. 'Nope. She left some tapes – recordings she'd made setting out her life story. Perhaps the reason is in there.' He burped again. 'What do you know about Koskinski? What happened to him in the desert?'

August gave him a sidelong look and pushed the empty glass across again. 'Let's sit down.'

They took a booth.

'He came down in Iraq. Engine failure. Captured and taken in for interrogation. He was held in Al Rasheid – the Baghdad Hilton. I don't need to paint pictures, I'm sure, but every expense was spared. So when they did fly him out it was felt, understandably, that we owed him some R&R, and not least some time to recuperate. He's under medical treatment as well – base hospital unit are dealing with that. Enough?'

Dryden nodded but remembered his golden rule: there's always one more question.

'And he's back on the base?'

'He has a room. We don't keep tabs. As I said, we owe him. He has accumulated leave and the medics wouldn't let him back anyway. The base commander has requested an interview, as have the local police. Clearly there's the issue of the paternity – which affects nationality. I can't imagine it's an insuperable problem. But who knows? Bureaucracy can kill. He needs the passport checked – that kind of thing. There's the issue of the crime that Maggie committed. But there seems little to gain from anyone taking that any further.'

'Grandparents been in touch?'

August flipped the coaster on the table top and siphoned up an inch of whiskey. 'They're anxious to talk to him. I've taken a call. It's clear they don't know about Maggie's confession. They've been informed of her death.'

Dryden tried again. 'Medical treatment, you said. Anything

specific?' August stood, indicating that it was time to change bars.

'Claustrophobia,' he said, and gave Dryden a genuinely happy smile. Six bourbons, thought Dryden, that's all it takes.

26

Dryden walked to the Capri with the light steps of someone propelled by alcohol. Humph was holding his mobile, which had a text message from Inspector Andy Newman. It read simply: 'Sardine'. Dryden told Humph to head north to the coast to West Lynn, Gifford's Haulage Yard. The raid had been on the cards for weeks and Newman had promised Dryden the story once the police decided to go in. Code name Operation Sardine. But Dryden's expectations were low, he'd been on similar outings which had produced a string of dull down-page stories. The idea was to catch the people smugglers with their cargo on board, but so far all they'd found had been empty containers and parked-up cabs. But now, at least, Dryden's interest in this illicit trade had quickened. The pillbox on Black Bank Fen was at the centre of the operation, and Jimmy Kabazo was waiting for a consignment to be dropped with his son on board. And then there was the porn. Bob Sutton had discovered that the import/export of the pictures was running parallel with the people smuggling. And Bob Sutton was still out there.

They drove north in companionable silence. Humph was still sulking after the attack on his beloved cab. He'd put masking tape on the seats and the fluffy dice had been re-attached to the rear-view mirror. The cabbie had acquired a tape of Greek balalaika music from Ely Market and he played it now, aware that it would drive Dryden to despair.

Gifford's lorry park was the size of six football pitches; acres of bleak concrete, enlivened by nearly two hundred

HGV containers. A modern-day maze. A Saharan heat haze was already rising from the baking metal boxes and the smell of blistering paint was like a heady drug on the air. Dryden mistook a heavy sense of foreboding for the beginnings of a hangover.

The northern perimeter fence of Gifford's ran beside the beach. The sea was the only thing moving in the landscape, sucking at a bank of baked mud. The coast appeared a feature-less foreshore on the estuary of the Ouse, except for the plastic cartilage skull of a conger eel which stuck up like a pagan symbol from the beach and was collecting early morning flies.

Dryden, pressing his face against the diamond-weave electric fence, picked up an electric charge which made his watch run backwards for a week. Humph, sitting in the cab, was beginning a Greek conversation with Eleni. The great Romantic, thought Dryden, trapped in a 1974 Ford Capri with soiled swinging dice and surrounded by the corrosive aroma of old socks.

'Claustrophobia,' said Dryden out loud to nobody, kicking the wire fencing. That's local journalism for you, he thought, unbearable excitement in exotic locations. He felt tired and drained. The black eye throbbed and made him feel bilious. The pillbox murder had shocked him far more than he had admitted, even to himself. People smugglers and porn pushers made his flesh crawl. He had no interest in meeting them and a positive fear of them trying to meet him. The newspaper cutting left on the Capri's windscreen was a clear enough warning to leave the story of Black Bank Fen to history. He felt threatened, confused, but most of all defeated by his inability to see clearly how events were linked. But he had little doubt that they were.

Then the dogs arrived. At least that prompted a sharp emotion: fear. Three vans pulled up and half a dozen uniformed coppers spilt out. Inspector Andy Newman arrived in an unmarked police car. Unfortunately he *was* marked, having had 'copper' inscribed on his forehead at birth.

One of the uniformed PCs rolled up the backs of the three vans: Dryden counted fourteen dogs, and every one an Alsatian with a regulation string of saliva hanging from custard yellow canines. 'Dogs,' he said, to Newman. 'I don't like dogs.'

'Who cares?' said Newman, looking at a map upside down.

Two of the dogs, immediately aware that Dryden was an international-class coward, nosed his crotch with indecent interest. Briefly, as if from another world, Dryden could hear Humph laughing.

The keyholder was in the second van. He was tall, with the kind of fissured face reserved for those addicted to illegal substances in commercial quantities. The gates swung open on the sunlit maze of the container park and the dogs ran, abandoning Dryden's privates.

Viewed from above, the scene must have been bizarre; a laboratory maze with the role of the mice taken by fourteen skittering dogs. They were using their noses, but if they'd used their eyes they would have seen the gravid cloud of flies hanging, despite the onshore breeze, over a lime-green container marked ZKA-RAPIDE.

It took the dogs twenty minutes to find it. While they were waiting Dryden told Newman about the Nissen hut at the old airfield at Witchford. 'Looks like that's where they let them sleep – kind of depot, I guess.'

Newman, ill-tempered, was watching the dogs scrabble round the lime-green container. 'We'll check it out. But my guess is they've changed their routine. Roe's death must have put the fear of God into them. They'll be finding a new route.'

189

Two PCs with bolt-cutters got to work on the tailgate restraints on the container. But Dryden knew what they'd find. An empty container full of filth. The one abandoned in the lay-by had been the worst, the sixteen illegal immigrants inside had not been let out for nearly four days. The toilet had started in one corner and then trickled across the whole floor. Sickness had, not surprisingly, been a problem. Food had consisted of cans of Coke and clingfilm-wrapped pasties from a Seven-11 at Felixstowe.

And then there was the dead dog. Curled around a spare tyre. The only fatality and the only occupant of the container with a real name.

The bolts sheared and the container door swung open to emit an overpowering wall of stench.

Pork, thought Dryden, the smell of cloying grease immediately unbearable. Dead pigs, about thirty of them, scattered the floor. The heat in the container drifted out. The meat was slow cooked, no crackling, but plenty of juices. A slick of animal fat began to trickle over the tailgate. Between the pigs were the telltale signs that people had shared their final journey – but had got off just in time. Ice-cream wrappers, some burger bar cartons and the usual shipment of human faeces.

'Unbelievable,' said Newman, spotting a heron on a rotting wooden post just off the beach. Then he checked the ever-present clipboard. 'Nark told us there were two.'

The next container along was lime green as well. It still had a cab attached. Same markings: ZKA-RAPIDE. The cab was blue, dusty, with a black oil-slick under one tyre, which Dryden noticed was slightly flat.

The same two PCs got to work on the tailgate. But this time Dryden didn't watch, his complacency already shattered by the casual slaughter of the dead pigs. One of Inspector

Newman's DCs had broken open the cab door, and he climbed up after him. On the first three jobs this had made the best copy, giving Dryden a chance to examine the detritus of the real villain – the driver who knew he had a human cargo. Maps, fags, sweets, and always the soiled copy of the *Sun*. He looked at the date: 10 June, seven days old. He sat on the wide driver's seat and picked through the evidence. Tape in the deck: Indian pop songs, glove compartment, packet of condoms (unopened), map of Birmingham, some black sticky binding tape, and an alarm clock.

He knew something was wrong when he looked in the wing mirror. Newman was smoking. He'd given up a year earlier after an autopsy on a down-and-out who died in a ditch of lung cancer, but he was gulping in the nicotine now. And the change in the atmosphere was tangible, the squad of cynical coppers tautly alert. The dogs went berserk as Dryden jumped down and ran to the back.

Pork, he thought. But this time it wasn't pigs; this time it was people. Three of them were crawling on the ground throwing up what little they had in their stomachs on to the sun-bleached tarmac, where it sizzled obscenely. Those in the van were alive, but another few hours in the heat of the afternoon sun would have done for them. All of them were black and soaked in sweat and urine. They blinked in the sun and cracked bent limbs. There was an almost complete lack of any human sound, except that of lungs sucking in air. The heat and smell formed an almost physical barrier. Gradually Newman's team helped them out, down from the tailgate, while Dryden took a walk up-wind, gulping in lungfuls of sea air.

When he got back there was only one person left in the back of the container. He knew immediately it was a corpse. The lower limbs were rigid and ugly, the torso's upper body slightly raised from the floor of the van on one side. One arm was flung behind the neck, which craned up for air, while the other stretched towards the place where light would have been. He didn't want to see the face but he did. Later, he couldn't describe it even to himself, but he knew what it wasn't: it wasn't 'Died Quietly in His Sleep'. It was Emmy Kabazo.

27

Did Jimmy Kabazo kill Johnnie Roe? It was a thought Dryden could not dislodge as he sat in the Capri, the doors open, and drank in the big sky over the sea like some visual antidote to the image of Emmy Kabazo's tortured body. They'd parked by the beach at Old Hunstanton so that Dryden could phone over the story – single paragraphs for the tabloids, but more substantial stories for the white broadsheets: *Guardian*, *Telegraph*, *Times* and *Independent*. He got the basics over to the BBC's *Look East* and made a note to bill them for the tip-off fee. The spate of work helped him deal with the helplessness he felt. Jimmy had to be a suspect. When Dryden had talked to him at the old airfield he claimed to be waiting for Emmy's arrival. But what if his son was long overdue? Had Jimmy tried to track him down through the Ritz? Had he tortured Johnnie to find out where his son had gone? Had Johnnie died not knowing how to give him the answer he needed, the answer which would have saved his life?

Dryden filled his lungs with ozone but failed to eradicate the lingering aroma of cooked pig. Humph, silent, looked out to sea. He liked the beach, principally because there was so much to look at before you needed to get out of the car. 'Gonna swim?' he said, scrambling in the glove compartment for a miniature bottle of gin. He'd bought a large bottle of tonic and a lemon at a roadside service station. He produced two plastic cups and sliced the lemon with a Swiss Army knife marginally smaller than a fork-lift truck.

'Sorry, no ice,' he said, trying pathetically to cheer Dryden up.

'What's Emmy short for?' asked Dryden.

Humph gave him the drink, and sipped his own. 'Emerson? Emmanuel?'

Dryden gulped the drink, failing to blot out the double image of Emmy's corpse and Johnnie Roe's skin grafts. Then he rooted in the Capri's boot for his swimming shorts and a towel. He wanted the North Sea to dilute whatever was left on his skin of the odour of rotting flesh. And worse, much worse. He walked off into the dunes to change, then ran towards the sea, a sprint which turned into a long-distance run. The water was a Mediterranean blue but the temperature of meltwater off a snow-covered roof. That was the problem with the Norfolk coast, the ice-cream vans were manned by Norwegians. Dryden's testicles jockeyed violently for re-entry to his body.

The shock helped. He managed to dislodge from memory the sight of that single, juvenile arm stretching up to the light. But the slick of putrid pork fat still lapped at the edge of consciousness. Thankfully the fizzing white spume of the waves gave off a cleansing rush of ozone.

He sat in the dunes and thought about being there with Laura four summers ago. They'd talked about the two cottages they'd seen, on Adventurer's Fen: Flightpath Cottages. Derelict and sodden with damp they would cost less to knock down than restore. It had been a discouraging day and Laura had seemed distant, preoccupied by some inner anxiety she seemed reluctant to share. The cottages weren't right, they'd agreed that. And there had been something mean and pinched about the man who'd shown them round. But they shared a view which redefined the concept of panoramic. The wide snaking river running north, the reed beds to the east and west, and the deep cut of the Thirty Foot Drain providing the final defence against the outside world. And Laura's reticence seemed coupled with another emotion, just below the surface, like the snaking green weed of the river. Excitement? Perhaps. Dryden sensed a coiled spring of elation somewhere within her, something brimming towards the surface but constantly hidden from him. He was growing impatient with their search and suspicious that Laura was avoiding the commitment the house, the home, would symbolize. She'd hugged her secret to herself, for that is what Dryden knew it to be that day, like a lonely child. It was a bad memory, but one of the last ones with any vividness before the crash in Harrimere Drain which had changed their lives for ever.

The memory didn't improve his mood. He felt depression sweeping over him like a cold front over a trawler at sea. He took evasive action, retrieving a white folded piece of paper sticking out of his trouser pocket. It was the printout from Laura's COMPASS machine that he had failed to read the night before. Now he laid it in the sand and put two pebbles at either end to hold it firm.

He saw the name but didn't recognize it, even though he felt his skin goosebump, despite the eighty-degree heat. Until now Laura's messages could have been simply the product of her unique view on the world. A view of hospital visitors whispering and discussing family secrets around the deathbed of Maggie Beck. But this? This was a warning.

WATCH WHITE

He knew that if he concentrated on something else the memory would come back. He watched a trawler running in on the gravy-brown tide, while on the beach a child stuck lollipop sticks into the tops of sandcastles.

Then he had it: Freeman White, Lyndon Koskinski's

fellow prisoner in Al Rasheid jail. Koskinski had said he was stationed at Mildenhall, undergoing medical treatment.

They were back at The Tower within an hour. Dryden sensed now that Laura had been at the centre of what had happened to Maggie Beck in the last days of her life. The life she had recorded on tape.

He climbed the stairs to Laura's room. The COMPASS machine was silent but a length of tickertape hung motionless in the room's fetid air. She was getting more expert at using the machine, Dryden could see that now. The gibberish was probably all involuntary movements. But when the message came it was separate and clear.

SHDUTUF F GKO GLDJUCN TAPESECORDER
FDHGFI FHGO SHSYGFKF DHDYWISJ SJSOSOJ

He felt the hair on his neck prickle. She was one letter out. He should have noticed before, the tape deck Estelle and Lyndon had left on the window ledge was gone.

The nurse on duty at the desk in the foyer seemed mildly affronted that Dryden could suggest one of the staff was a thief.

'I can't imagine anyone has taken it,' she said, a practised smile revealing sharp teeth.

'So where is it?'

'Perhaps Mrs Beck's family took it?'

'They said they left it, it's mine. But I'll double check,' said Dryden. 'In the meantime, perhaps you could ask around. If it turns up, no questions will be asked – OK? Otherwise, I guess it's the police.'

He showed his teeth back.

Then he told Humph to take him home. They drove in silence to Barham's Dock where *PK 129* lay motionless under a large moon.

'Drink?' asked Dryden, getting out, and not looking back.

He knew something was wrong before he reached the boat. It lay low in the water and he could see now that the bow was much lower than the stern. Some of the pots in which he grew herbs on the deck had spilled on to the bank.

He heard Humph behind him. 'Shit.'

About three foot of black, stinking river water lay inside the main cabin. A crude siphon pump had been set up to draw the river water up, over the bulwarks, and into the cabin well. He plucked one end of the pipe from the river and climbed aboard. He submerged the pipe in the water in the wheelhouse and then flipped one end of the pipe back overboard, reversing the flow and beginning the long task of draining the boat dry. Peeking through the forward portholes he saw debris floating: a picture of Laura's parents in Turin, some plastic plates, and a half-full bottle of malt whisky, bobbing cork up.

They edged on board, aware that *PK 129* had a dangerous list to port. Humph found the newspaper cutting – identical to the one left on the Capri's windscreen. It was pinned to the chart board in the galley. Pinned with a carving knife.

The childless house had mocked Maggie Beck from the first day: the day they'd driven through the military monotony of the Forestry Commission estates. The windows mocked her with their identical views of pine trees and sandy paths. And the ivory dress mocked her too, even now, from its crêpe-paper package above the wardrobe. She longed for the view across Black Bank Fen, wondering at the same time how she could miss, so much, something she had hated so much. The memory of an amphitheatre sky haunted her claustrophobic life. She longed for a horizon, a distant view of miniature people, a cloud casting a shadow half a county away.

She'd married Don two years ago. The best wedding picture was in the front room over the gas fire. He could have been her dad, she knew that's what everyone was saying behind their hands. Sometimes she wished he was. Then she could have shared the memory, the memory of the falling star that had taken Matty away.

Why had she married him? Children, security, kindness, decency. Four powerful reasons she knew now did not add up to love.

She went to the front room and touched Matty's picture: the one she'd taken when he was a week old. She loved this image, the one she saw every day, but she loved her secret more. So she ran, up the stairs, to the laundry room where the chest was. It was burnt too, like her cheek, and she ran her finger down the scar with an almost sensual caress. She lifted it open and slipped her hand down beside the old clothes until she found the waxed wallet that held the air-letters. They'd started to arrive last year on Lyndon's first birthday. She'd had to ask, by registered letter. She'd lost Matty, they knew that, she only asked to see how the boy she'd saved was growing. And he was growing. Her favourite showed *him naked, just two, standing in a lake with a smile like a searchlight and a plastic Captain Hook cutlass.*

She flipped it over but she knew the inscription, knew all the inscriptions: 'Tokebee, Michigan. Summer 78. Lyndon plays pirates.'

That's all she had until now: pictures of a memory. Until now. She checked her watch: 9.38.

Where was Don? He should be here, they'd agreed that, together. She ran to the nursery and checked the temperature: 74°F, just like the book had said. She rested her hand on the blanket in the cot and felt the familiar surge of grief, of loss, the almost overwhelming conviction that she could feel his body warmth even now, two years later.

She cried at the funeral. Cried openly for the little boy she didn't know, and secretly for the little boy she'd sent to live another life 5,000 miles away. Her lover's tears were real. They burst out of him like a spring and he'd knelt in the red dust and wept like a child who can find no logic in the world's cruelty. It was the only time she'd felt like touching him since the night she'd seen the pictures. The pictures of her. She could have reached out, told him even then, and ended those tears. But she kept her secret, and bathed instead in his grief.

The doorbell rang. She slipped on the stairs and clattered down into the hat stand. She fumbled with the latch and threw it open, knowing it was Don: two long rings and one short. It was his warning signal. To summon her from the depths of the old farmhouse. He was trying to smile, trying to hide what he felt: 'There's something wrong. The boy's gone, Maggie. The boy's gone. We have to talk to them again.'

She hated his farmer's face then, with the cheeks nipped red by the frost.

Wednesday, 18 June

28

Dawn: the sun broke on the eastern horizon and swung a searchlight beam over the landscape. From the observation platform on which Dryden stood he looked down on the canopy of trees which seemed to cover the earth. To the east a large freshwater lake broke the sea of feathered, sunlit green; motionless except for an excited flock of flamingoes, an impossibly pink blotch on the eggshell blue water. He was the only one in the tree hide forty feet above Wicken Fen. An elephant could have ambled out of the tall rushes and drunk at the water beneath him. Exotic bird calls cut the silence which had come over the waterscape with the start of the day. Dryden felt his spirit swell at the sheer scale of the landscape below him, and the skyscape above. In spring and autumn, when dawn was later, it was a sight which brought the crowds to see the feeding: but not today. He could see the reflective flash of binoculars from some of the other hides, but he was alone in his: a sentry against a purple sky.

The grain boat was in position. The warden sat, scanning the sky. Dryden listened. Nothing. They always managed to surprise him: either early and soundless, or late and clamouring. He heard weary footsteps climbing the wooden ladder. He didn't need to turn to know it was Andy 'Last Case' Newman, climbing reluctantly to their meeting, despite the promise of some on-duty birdwatching.

He got to the top and walked to the safety bar. 'There,' he said, pointing south. He was right. A tiny cloud, like a puff of smoke from a distant locomotive, was wheeling in towards the open water.

'I've got a paper to fill,' said Dryden. Wednesdays were tough on *The Crow*, with three inside news pages to fill in a circulation area as lively as Sleeping Beauty's castle.

Newman fixed his binoculars on the distant flock. 'I would have thought one emaciated corpse in a pillbox would do.'

'Old news,' said Dryden, manufacturing a yawn which turned into the real thing. He'd spent the night with Humph in the Capri and sleep had eluded him. He'd been up at dawn to check out the damage on *PK 129*. And he'd rung August and requested a background interview with Freeman White, Lyndon Koskinski's fellow prisoner in Al Rasheid. He yawned again, hearing the plastic pop of the jaw joint as his muscles stretched. 'How about confirming the ID?'

Newman dropped the glasses and gazed over the painted water. 'Can't do. But you know anyway, we both do. It's got to be Johnnie Roe – mobile tea-bar owner and general low-life.'

'Ex-wife?'

'She only reported him missing because the cheques stopped. Johnnie had a nice house, by the way – out at Nornea on the West Fen. Vermin and cat's pee – unusual combination, that.'

Dryden nodded. 'You were watching the Ritz. Why?'

'Like I said, the immigrants. We'd got most of the staging posts nailed between Felixstowe and the Midlands. A necklace, every thirty miles, like Little Chef. They picked up food, gave 'em air, and unloaded a handful for the local labour market. Then the rest went on. Or, in the case of the shipment we opened yesterday, got dumped.'

Shipment, thought Dryden, seeing the boy's twisted arms reaching for the air. 'Local labour market,' he said. 'You'd been into Wilkinson's. Only them?'

Newman nodded to say no. 'There were others. Same business. Itinerant labourers, high turnover. It's perfect for them. Some of them moved on, some didn't.'

The warden in the boat began to spread grain on the water. 'ID on the kid in the lorry?' Dryden tried to make the question sound as casual as possible.

Newman laughed. 'Nobody's talking. We haven't got names for the ones that survived yet. But we will. The passports are fake and once they realize they're heading back to the Channel ports, they'll talk.'

Dryden had promised Jimmy Kabazo he wouldn't go to the police. But that was before his son had turned up dead in the container on the coast. Dryden had always distrusted promises, and this one begged to be broken. He told Newman about his meeting with Kabazo at Wilkinson's, and again at the old airfield, and the snapshot he'd shown him of Emmy.

'It's the same kid?' asked Newman.

'Pretty sure,' said Dryden.

Newman made two mobile phone calls: one to the station at Ely to get out and interview Kabazo at Wilkinson's, the second to a scene of crime unit to re-examine the Nissen hut the people smugglers had used as a dormitory. He'd visited it himself after Dryden had told him it was being used, but now he had a child's death on his hands. Any forensic link between the hut and the HGV could be crucial in tracking down the people responsible for Emmy Kabazo's death.

Dryden let Newman watch the flamingoes in silence for a few minutes, but he figured he was now owed some information. 'The dirty pictures. Is it the same pillbox in which the pictures of Alice Sutton were taken. And if it is, where's her father?'

Newman sighed, tearing his eyes away from the pink

splodges of the birds. 'It's the same box. I can tell you that detectives from the East Midlands force will be re-interviewing our friend the pornstar stud tomorrow morning. He's already facing a holding charge relating to the possession of pornographic material. So far he's not talking. The fact that a corpse has been found on the film set may loosen his tongue – but I wouldn't bet on it.'

'Name yet for the stud?'

Newman slipped out a notebook from his windcheater. 'Selby. Peter. Aged twenty-six. No further charges as yet, although there are developments. I can't be more specific. You want the address?'

Dryden was forced to produce a notebook.

'Caddus Street, Rushden. Worked for a haulage company in the town: A. Ladd & Sons.'

Dryden produced a squiggle and snapped the notebook shut. Facts always made him nervous. 'Thanks. So you think what . . . ?'

Newman was listening, not to Dryden, but the rhythmic crack of the great wings and the plaintive cawing. The warden saw them too and stood in the grain boat to pebble the motionless water with more feed. They watched in silence as the cloud grew into a flock of forty swans. By the time they'd landed in a riot of flailing legs, feet, and wings, another flock had crept up behind them from the east, swinging suddenly overhead and obliterating the sun.

Dryden looked at Newman's face. Joy had rubbed twenty years off it. He looked like a kid in the front row at *The Jungle Book*. The detective produced a camera with a telephoto lens and Dryden heard the automatic shutter whir.

'What do you know?' said Newman at last.

'Well – I know Maggie Beck swapped the body of her own child for that of a US serviceman's in the 1976 air crash.'

'I can read the paper too,' said Newman.

'Should it be that easy?'

Newman shrugged: 'It's a thirty-year-old case. I need a statement off Koskinski for the record. We'll accept written affidavits from the grandparents. Then we can authorize the change of passports. There should be no problems. Just red tape. But he shouldn't travel until it's been completed.'

Dryden nodded, watching the water crease with an early morning breeze. 'And the pillbox killing? You found finger-prints at the scene,' said Dryden.

'Yup.' Newman slipped the binoculars into their case. The entire flock had landed now. A jostling snow-white field of raised wings and necks on a purple sea. He sighed. 'Beautiful,' he said, pausing briefly before adding: 'Bob Sutton. Don't tell his wife. In fact don't tell anyone until *The Crow* comes out on Friday. OK? '

It was Dryden's turn not to listen, he was thinking too fast. So Alice Sutton's father had gone looking for her and not come back. Now the body of Johnnie Roe had been found in the pillbox where the pornographic pictures had been taken. According to Alice, her father had been to the Ritz and was probably aware of Johnnie Roe's role in running a depot for the people smugglers.

'Jesus! Did Sutton kill Roe? If he did, he could run far enough we'd never find him.'

Newman shrugged. 'It's getting pretty crowded in this pillbox. Alice Sutton and the stud. Then Johnnie. Now Sutton looking for his daughter. If it had a turnstile they could have sold tickets.'

Newman pocketed the binoculars: 'When you write the Bob Sutton story I'd like you to add an appeal for infor-mation. There's no body yet – we can't presume he's dead. We can't presume he killed Roe. Anything anyone knows about him, and his recent movements. And that goes for Johnnie Roe too. He's been a loner for ten years. Doesn't mean his life was empty. Any information dealt with sympathetically – you know the form.'

A third flock of swans joined the mêlée around the grain boat.

'Two things,' said Dryden, following Newman down the vertical wooden ladder to the reed bed below. 'Someone's following me. Bloke on a motorbike. Red leathers, black bike. He attacked Humph's cab, vandalized it, left a copy of the story I wrote about Black Bank. Not very subtle, really.'

'Your mate all right?'

'He wasn't in the cab.'

'Bloody hell,' said Newman. 'I thought he was welded to the Capri – you know, like a luggage rack.'

Dryden ignored the insult. 'Anyway, he was back last night. The biker. He tried to scupper my boat at Barham's Dock. She'll take a week to pump out and everything inside is a write-off.'

They'd reached the cars parked at the National Trust centre. Humph was in the Capri and immersed in his tapes. Newman got in the Citroën and wound down the window. 'And you're telling me for why? You've reported it in the normal way?'

'Sure. Just insurance. A patrol car might make the occasional visit to Barham's Dock – it might help.'

Newman snorted.

'One other thing,' said Dryden. 'Someone stole a tape recorder from the room in which Maggie Beck died at The Tower, the room she shared with Laura. I've asked the staff, and it may turn up. If it doesn't turn up in the next twenty-four hours I'd appreciate a visit from a uniform. It might do the trick.'

'Anything else?'

Dryden's mobile rang, so he let Newman drive off. It was Gillies & Wright, solicitors. 'Mr Dryden? Just a courtesy call. The man who claimed to be Lyndon Koskinski's father – the name does not match that left by Maggie Beck, I'm afraid. The £5,000 has been withheld. And I've informed the police. Clearly it was an attempt at fraud – although he did seem to have known Mrs Beck when they were teenagers.'

'Thanks. I see.' Dryden felt a wave of disappointment that Maggie's last wishes had again been thwarted. 'By the way – can you tell me how Maggie's will dealt with Lyndon?'

'Yes. Yes I can – it's not usual, of course, but as you know Mrs Beck was very keen that all aspects of her estate should be above board and open to public scrutiny. And the will has now been read. The estate is left entirely to Mr Koskinski, as the eldest child. She stated quite clearly, however, that it was his duty to provide for his half-sister.'

Dryden rang off. He wondered how Estelle would take the news. She'd gone from only daughter and sole heiress to younger sister and dependant in a few days. Did she hate Black Bank so much she'd be happy to lose it?

29

The only things moving on the Tudor Hall Estate were the net curtains. The object of this twitching interest was obvious: Humph's cab was lowering the tone of the neighbourhood. The legoland houses brooded in their suburban desert trying to rise above the image of the rusted Capri. Inside the cab Dryden slumped in the passenger seat and let the tune from 'Little Boxes' play in his head. It helped block out the sound of a Greek street party on Humph's tape, for Nicos was celebrating and everyone in the village was invited. Even, apparently, Humph. Dryden hoped they'd ordered extra portions.

Dryden eyed the front door of No. 36, the home, according to the telephone book, of Robert L. Sutton, avenging father of Alice. A Barratt-style semi, it was adorned with fake carriage lamps and a couple of equally dubious Doric columns. Dryden tried to look like an insurance salesman as he rang the bell and stood smartly to attention. After fifteen seconds of that he peeked through the nets. Inside was a leather three-piece suite and a panoramic TV screen more than adequate for a short-sighted audience at a drive-in movie.

He tried to remember what Bob Sutton had looked like when he'd come into *The Crow*'s offices to report his daughter missing. Squat, muscle-bound, and industrial, the human cannonball. His house didn't suit him, but perhaps it had been chosen to suit someone else. Sure enough the someone else opened the door. It was 10.20 in the morning but she was dressed to kill: tall, dark and shaped like a model: and it wasn't a Hornby Dublo.

Elizabeth Jane Sutton put one high-heeled shoe ahead of the other and let her knees kiss in a classic photo-call pose.

'Sorry. Can I help?'

Her daughter Alice appeared behind her. She was a model too: a model teenager. She was wearing what Dryden guessed might pass for nightwear in teenage-daughter-land.

'Oh, God,' said Alice, recognizing Dryden from her visit to *The Crow*, and fled.

'It's Bob, isn't it?' said the mother. The make-up drooped and she looked her age instead of her daughter's.

'Philip Dryden. *The Crow*. There's no news,' he said, lying effortlessly. 'I'm sorry to disturb you but it might help to get some more publicity in the paper. Five minutes?' Dryden felt like a fraud. He had little choice but to claim ignorance about the fact that the police had found Bob Sutton's prints inside the pillbox. The police would be round that afternoon to break the news. Either way, events had taken a disturbing twist: the chances were that Sutton was either Johnnie's murderer, or another victim yet unfound. In the meantime Dryden needed an interview and a picture of the missing man. And, much more importantly now, he needed to know what had happened in that pillbox.

Thirty seconds later he was standing by the leather sofa. 'Nice,' he said, lying again, and sat down.

Mrs Sutton sat down herself and went out of her way not to offer Dryden a coffee.

'Bob's gone,' she said, and nervously played with an earring.

'I know. He came to see me at *The Crow* about the pictures, the pictures of Alice. But she came home, didn't she? What did your husband say?'

She looked away and lit a cigarette with an onyx lighter the size of a beach ball. 'He was gone. He hasn't seen Alice – I doubt he knew . . . knows . . . she's back. That's the bloody stupid . . .' She was either blinding herself with cigarette smoke or beginning to cry.

Dryden studied the seascape poster framed over the gas fire so that she could cry unobserved, never contemplating the possibility that she wanted an audience. 'I need to find him too,' he said, still looking away. 'Did he say what he was doing exactly, how he was going to find Alice?'

On the wall hung a picture of Bob Sutton in uniform. Dryden guessed it was the military police. It was a sunny picture, with the white light bleaching out the edges, and a colonial mansion in the background fringed with palms. He nodded at the frame. 'Overseas?'

She lit up. 'Yes. I was born in Hong Kong. Dad was Royal Engineers. Bob was MP. It was a glamorous life – then.'

'Could I borrow it? I'll get it back within twenty-four hours, I promise. If we run a story appealing for witnesses, it would help,' said Dryden.

She nodded and Dryden carefully took the picture down. There was a long silence in which he could hear the kitchen fridge humming.

She stood up and came over to take the seat next to him. 'You married?' she said.

'Yes. Five years. But there's been an accident – in a car. She's in a coma. She probably won't come out of it. Well, that's what they say.' He considered just how easy it was to tell strangers the truth.

They smiled at each other. 'He found something,' she said at last. 'One night. He went out and when he came back he was . . .'

'What?' said Dryden, beginning to like her.

'Excited. But he wouldn't talk about it. He never wanted to talk about what had happened to Alice. I was angry about that, still am. It wasn't up to him to put it right. It was up to both of us.' She stubbed out the cigarette and lit a fresh one with surprising grace.

'One of his so-called mates in the force sent him the pictures of Alice. Jesus!' she said, thumping the onyx football down on the table top where it left an ugly dent. 'He couldn't take that. He sat on that sofa and cried like a child. Clutching the pictures. As if it mattered. At least it showed she was alive. Sometimes I think he was more interested in proving she'd been made to do those things, than finding out if she was alive. That's a terrible thing to say, isn't it? I've never seen him cry before. I was frightened . . . frightened about what he'd do to make things right again.'

'Frightened he'd hurt someone?'

She nodded twice, taking two lungfuls of nicotine in and expelling the smoke in a fierce downdraft which almost reached the shag-pile carpet. 'I begged him to tell me what he'd found – not the pictures, what he'd found out there,' she said, nodding out through the fake mullioned windows towards the fen. 'He said he would, the next day . . .'

She took a magazine from the coffee table and put it on her lap. 'Blood,' she said, flicking the pages. 'There was blood – all over his handkerchief. I found it later – after he'd gone. He'd chucked it in the bin in the kitchen so I wouldn't see. Lots of blood, really. I checked his clothes, it was just the handkerchief.'

'So when was that? The first time he came home?'

'The police asked that,' she said, unblinking.

'And what was the answer?'

'Last Friday night. We were going out, that new Italian on Market Street. I'd dressed up.'

Dryden tried to imagine it.

'He dragged himself in at midnight. Sober. I could always tell – can always tell.' She looked out through the windows at the empty driveway.

'What did he say?'

'Said he was near. Close to finding her. Her,' she flicked her chin upwards. 'And all the time she was in some fucking bedsit in Camden Town.' She regretted swearing but felt better for it. 'Some fucking bedsit,' she said again, but louder, prompting a nervous movement from the top of the stairs.

'She's OK?' said Dryden.

'She can't remember. Not the pictures. So she ran away, and I don't blame her. What did anyone expect her to do – the police said she'd almost certainly been given that drug – the date-rape thing. She can't believe it's her in the pictures either.'

'And he went out again when?'

'Next night. The Saturday. He wasn't scared. I know when he's scared, it wasn't like he wasn't in control of whatever it was . . .'

'But he didn't come back . . .'

She lit a fresh cigarette with the onyx boulder. 'You could see his office . . . the police did,' she said, standing. It was the spare room next to Alice's. There was a PC, a card file box, and a telephone and fax. He clearly liked to bring his work home. Dryden flicked through the card file. Each one was for a separate job – the client's details poorly spelt out in childish capital letters.

'Bob Sutton Security,' she said, and at last began to cry. 'The job was the best he could get after the army. He didn't have much of an education – no certificates. Nothing. It's tough when you're his age.' Alice came in and wrapped her arms around her mother's neck.

'In the blue folder,' she said, leading Alice away.

And they were. The same stud. Different girls, but all in the pillbox. But they weren't pristine, like Alice's shots, they were dog-eared, they'd been through many grubby hands.

And police statements, photocopied transcripts of taped interviews. Dryden guessed Sutton's police contacts had come in useful again. He'd used his contacts in the lorry trade to pick up the trail of the people smugglers who'd traded in the pornography at the same time as illegal immigrants. He'd almost certainly identified the Ritz as a dropping-off point. Then he'd made contact with the police about the man they'd arrested in connection with the pictures of Alice – which in turn had led to other interviews, other raids. In the end he'd had enough information to act. He'd gone out and found something that Saturday night. Was it the pillbox? Had he confronted Johnnie Roe and got a confession? Or had he dragged Johnnie there himself? Whose blood had been on his handkerchief? According to his wife he'd then returned the next night – the Sunday. Did he return to kill Johnnie?

Dryden picked up the blue folder and chose a page at random.

DS John Tucker: I'd like you to describe the picture if you would, Mr Shah. It's one of those recovered from under your bed at the house in Tomkins St, Nuneaton, on the day of your arrest.

Panjit Shah: There's a girl, isn't there?

DS Tucker: Yes. There is, Mr Shah. What age would you say she was, Mr Shah? You have a sister I believe . . . aged 12. Would you say the girl in these pictures is older or younger than your sister, Mr Shah?'

Mr G. Evans (*suspect's solicitor*): Is this really necessary, detective sergeant? We can all see the pictures.

DS Tucker: It would be helpful to me, Mr Evans. I think your client wishes to be helpful, does he not? His passport is a forgery and he's no right being in the country. If he doesn't answer the questions he'll be back on a boat and retracing his journey . . . He understands that, does he?

Mr Shah: She is the same age, yes?

DS Tucker: Yes. She is – or thereabouts. Does the girl look happy, Mr Shah? Do you think so? Do you think she wanted to have sex with this man, Mr Shah? . . .

Dryden replaced the pictures in the folder with the statements and washed his hands before going downstairs. The two women were standing at the door, still locked in an embrace: 'You showed the police the documents?'

'Yes. Yes,' said Elizabeth Sutton. 'They took some. They seemed to be more worried about where Bob had got the stuff,' she laughed. 'Bob could teach them a thing or two.'

'When he went out the second time, Mrs Sutton, what did he take?'

She shrugged. 'Torch, I think. That's usually in the car but he changed the batteries. It's one of the torches they give the Red Caps, it's got a heavy rubber covering so it can double up as a blackjack . . . And his nookie kit.'

'What?'

Alice and her mother laughed. 'His nookie kit,' said Alice. 'He did a lot of private detective work – mainly husbands cheating on their wives. He had to spend a lot of time sitting in the car watching, with his cameras. So he had a nookie kit – chocolate bars, sandwiches, crisps, cake . . . a bit of a feast.'

Dryden was standing outside now in the sunshine. The temperature was rising. 'Anything to drink?'

'He always took a flask of tea. But that night he took water too. Which was odd – he doesn't even like it in his whisky. Two big bottles, Evian.'

30

Humph pointed the cab south across the Great West Fen. Dryden peered out through a windscreen made greasy with the bodies of eviscerated insects which had begun to multiply alarmingly in the continuing heat. The drought was frying the landscape now, anything left alive in the fields was sizzling on the dry, baked earth. At one crossroads an orderly line of OAPs stood dutifully waiting for the social services to take them off to the civic baths in Ely. The drought had resulted in mains supplies to several villages being cut off indefinitely.

'Great at queues,' said Dryden. 'Old people.'

Humph grunted. 'Why bother to wash?'

Why indeed? thought Dryden, lowering the window still further. The smell would have embarrassed a skunk.

A text message had been waiting on Dryden's mobile when he got back in the cab outside Bob Sutton's home. He'd rung Garry straight back. *The Crow*'s junior reporter had been monitoring emergency calls and had picked up a violent incident at the City Mortuary, outside Cambridge, where Emmy Kabazo's body was waiting for an official ID.

They pulled off the main road at a sign which said MORTUARY with brutal simplicity. The building itself was a long, brick two-storey block in 1930s fascist style. It could have been an abattoir, and in an odd way it was. Two ambulances stood silently at a 'goods in' entrance. The place reeked of blood, and violence, thought Dryden, like a bull ring.

Jimmy Kabazo was standing outside the plate-glass

entrance foyer with a crowbar in his hands. Even from fifty yards Dryden could see that sweat bathed his blue T-shirt. As Humph pulled the Capri up beside a police car Jimmy ran at the plate-glass doors of the main entrance and delivered a shattering blow with the iron bar. The reinforced glass splintered in a complex pattern, like expanding crystals.

Dryden got out of the cab, but carefully left the door open so that he could retreat. He understood Kabazo's rage. If he'd read the national newspapers or listened to the local radio he'd know about the body found in the van at the container park at the coast. He'd know it was the body of the only sixteen-year-old in the human consignment abandoned by the people smugglers. In other words, he knew, almost certainly, that it was his son.

Kabazo waited for him as Dryden walked the fifty yards between them. 'I'm sorry. I'm sure they'll let you see him . . .' said Dryden.

Tears bathed Jimmy's face. 'They said I had to wait – talk to the policeman.' The water was pouring out of Kabazo's eyes like a river over a weir. Dryden knew that anger and despair were a high-octane human emotional cocktail, so he kept a safe distance from the crowbar.

'I was there when they found him,' he said.

Kabazo dropped the crowbar, and in the silence they listened to it roll away. Dryden noticed that it left a thin trail of arterial-red blood in its wake.

'It is him?' said Kabazo.

'I think so,' said Dryden honestly. 'But you must see him. You will.'

Then they heard a car skid off the main road and head towards them across the tarmac. At the wheel was DS Peter Crabbe, Newman's sidekick, and pushy enough to be after his job once retirement had claimed a willing victim. Crabbe was insensitive, brusque, and lacked people skills to the same degree that deserts lack water.

Jimmy ignored him. 'You were there?'

Dryden nodded and held out his arms. 'We should talk. Inside?'

'I must see him,' said Jimmy simply, seeing DS Crabbe advancing, accompanied by the two PCs from the squad car. Some of the anger had washed out of him, and his shoulders sagged. Crabbe left the PCs to take Kabazo into custody and led the way towards the mortuary doors. He pushed a button to one side which opened up an intercom to the desk inside. 'OK. Open up now, please – the situation is under control. DS Peter Crabbe.' He held up his warrant card to the glass.

An orderly edged forward to read it before the doors slid electronically open, spilling shattered glass as they did so. One of the PCs from the squad car slipped handcuffs on Jimmy as they waited in the reception area. He didn't resist, his eyes set on the interior doors to the mortuary. One of the two medical orderlies behind the foyer counter held a bandage to his head, from which a thin trickle of blood had run down to his collar.

'I've radioed for medical,' said Crabbe, turning to Kabazo. 'While we're waiting, Mr Kabazo – I presume?'

Dryden nodded. 'Mr Kabazo wished to identify the body of his son,' he said.

Crabbe turned to him. 'Mr Kabazo. Are you responsible for this?' He gestured towards the orderly with the head wound.

'They wouldn't let me see him,' said Kabazo, his eyes still on the mortuary doors.

'We called at Wilkinson's, Mr Kabazo, to invite you to a formal identification. They said you were sick.'

Great stuff, thought Dryden. *His son is dead and you're lecturing him about taking a sickie.* But he said: 'Perhaps. While we are waiting, detective sergeant?'

Crabbe decided that he might as well press ahead with the ID while he had Kabazo in the building.

One of the mortuary assistants hit some security buttons on the desktop and the interior set of doors swished open. Beyond that Crabbe led them through two sets of industrial doors, the kind that have plastic sheeting attached to stop draughts. The floors were concrete and streaked with stains which turned Dryden's stomach. There was a smell in the air, a scent really, which Dryden could not identify. It was sweet, and medicinal, and it brought a lump to his throat. They stopped in front of a door marked: 'Autopsy Unit'. They were there too quickly. Dryden didn't know why he was there at all. Inside, the room was lit by sunshine from skylights, while metal boxes, like those in left luggage, were in serried ranks on either wall. A row of surgical tables stood in the centre. There was a body on one and the sunshine fell on the zip-up hospital-green bag in which it was wrapped.

A woman in a white body-suit appeared out of the blaze of light and stood by the table with her hand on the zip. Crabbe took Kabazo's arm, marched him forward to the table and nodded briskly, almost cheerfully, and the bag was unzipped to the chest of the child. Dryden had waited too long. He felt rather than heard the breath leaving Kabazo's body. He watched as Kabazo bent stiffly to kiss the child on the forehead. When he stood, Dryden noticed Emmy's face was splashed with tears, as if turned up to a summer shower. Kabazo sank to his knees by the table and they all stepped back, even Crabbe feeling it was time to release his custodial hold.

Dryden fled the room, and so he only heard the scream of despair. He waited outside in the car park in the long silence that followed, and thought about Johnnie Roe, staked out in the pillbox. What did his torturer want to know? Did Jimmy Kabazo track him down when his son failed to turn up with the people smugglers?

They put Kabazo in the back of the squad car and waited for Crabbe to appear. He came out clutching some paperwork and a plastic zip-up bag. Dryden guessed it was the boy's clothes and other belongings retrieved from the HGV container. He could see a green T-shirt and a pair of trainers and what looked like a notebook. Kabazo took it and as they drove him off he bowed his head and hugged it to his chest, as if it were the son he had lost.

31

The US air base at Mildenhall lay somewhere near the heart of the mystery of Black Bank. Humph edged the cab forward in the queue at the security gate, behind a Cadillac with two rear exhaust pipes like the entrance to the Channel Tunnel. The air-base wire ran into the distance like the edge of a giant chicken run. A Doomsday-grey B-52 was coming in to the main runway leaving a streak of lead half a mile wide hanging like a dirty washing line in a ceramic blue sky. His request for an interview with Captain Freeman White had got a prompt response from August Sondheim by text message: INTERVIEW NOON. Dryden wondered what was in it for August.

'No wisecracks,' said Dryden, as they edged towards the heavily armed military guards.

'Where are we?' said Humph, looking around him with indignation.

'It's not a hijack. You drove here. Where do you think we are? Vladivostok?'

In truth Dryden shared his disorientation. USAF Mildenhall was a world of its own. The Stars & Stripes hung from a flagpole with no enthusiasm. They could have been on the Great Plains. The sentry probably thought he was. He ambled up to Humph's cab dragging a size-10 arse behind him in combat fatigues. Then he made the mistake of tapping on Humph's window, a little military two-tap.

The cabbie wound it down. 'Wing Commander?' he said, beaming.

Dryden leant across with his wallet open to show a press pass. 'Excuse me. Major Sondheim is expecting us.'

The guard wore 100 per cent reflective dark sunglasses which meant Dryden could only guess how vacant his eyes actually were.

The barrier went up and the sentry barked. 'Follow the red lines, sir. To the red car park. Major Sondheim will meet you there, sir.'

Humph saluted as they sailed past at a stately twenty miles an hour.

The base was home to 7,500 people; a town crowded round a single runway long enough to take the big transatlantic planes. One and a half miles of reinforced concrete scattered with scurrying hedgehogs trying to avoid the ultimate roadkill. Dryden shifted in his seat, immediately aware that his claustrophobia had kicked in as they slipped inside the high-wire cordon of the base. Military hardware dotted the horizon, from the bristling communications masts to the rocking radar dishes which swept the sky for aircraft or, worse, incoming missiles. Some of the buildings were pre-war and smacked of the great days of aviation in the 1930s: the tailplanes of the latest modern aircraft sticking out of their open doors. A now-disused mast had once anchored giant airships over the Fens before they set out for the four corners of the Empire. The more modern buildings, mostly associated with the arrival of the US Air Force in the 1950s, were squat and ugly by comparison. They swept past one of the many on-base canteens which was built of blood-red brick and boasted a single, neon sign for McDonald's.

Since the terrorist attacks of September 11 security had been stepped up at all US bases abroad. Signposts and information boards had been taken down to confuse the enemy, and everybody else. A GI with a brutal crewcut stood

at a crossroads consulting a map. Traffic lights controlled
the runway crossing. A sentry waved them on, before changing his mind and waving them down to ask where they were
going.

'On-base communications unit,' said Dryden.

The GI looked bemused. He scanned the horizon as if
August's unit were hiding out there. Then the GI took
an executive decision: 'I'm lost, mister,' he said, genuinely
exasperated.

Dryden nodded happily. 'I'll ring Major Sondheim – he's
our contact.' But there was no need. August thumped his
hand on the roof and leant in on Humph's side.

'Hiya. Over there.' He pointed to a group of pre-war
hangars. Humph parked and began to inflate the in-flight
pillow he'd bought at Stansted Airport for just such
occasions.

August took Dryden by the arm and led him to a US
military Jeep. It was 11.45 and August was sober, but the
strain was showing. His diction was as sharp as the crease
on his trousers. In the back of the Jeep was one of his junior
PR staff, a woman in fatigues with a clipboard which Dryden
noted with approval held a piece of clean A4 paper with
nothing on it.

'Meet the enemy, Sergeant DeWitt,' said August. She
nodded into the rear-view mirror. Even in a partial reflection
Dryden could tell she was a woman of impressive credentials.
Her uniform tried but failed to encompass a heart-stopping
bust. August squirmed slightly in his seat in a way which
answered all the questions Dryden hadn't asked.

'Right,' said August, gunning the Jeep past two green lights
and crossing the runway to a group of post-war three-storey
dormitory buildings. Over them a water tower stood on stilts
like an alien invader from the *War of the Worlds*. Behind a wire

enclosure a bunch of GIs in blotched sweatshirts played a languid game of basketball.

They drove past a 'Shopette', a 24-hour laundromat, a K-Mart and a drive-in McDonald's.

'Makes ya proud,' said Dryden. August grinned but the woman in fatigues bristled. Through the distant perimeter wire Dryden could see the tall pines which marked Mons Wood and the edge of Black Bank Fen.

'We have a problem,' said August, pulling up outside one of the dormitory blocks. 'Lyndon Koskinski has gone AWOL.'

'I thought he was on leave.' Dryden got out and, deserting the air conditioning in the US-built Jeep, felt the heat from the tarmac slap him in the face. Now he knew why August had agreed to his interview request: he needed help.

'He was. But if you live on base you have to report; daily. If you leave base you have to sign out. He's done neither for more than a week. The police – civilian at Ely – want to talk to him about his mother's death. More precisely about his own – reported – death. Procedure, nothing suspicious, but they want him and I ain't got him. There is also the issue of his passport. Clearly, alterations need to be made. Red tape again, I'm afraid. He's fought for America – nobody is going to block an application for citizenship, but he needs to make it. His current passport is invalid. And a British one would take months to issue.'

'What would happen if he tried to leave the country?' asked Dryden.

August adjusted the forage cap held beneath his epaulette: 'Well, technically they'd have to refuse exit permission. But he might get through – we haven't put a stop on the passport number. But we'll have to if we can't talk to him soon.'

'Have you tried out at Black Bank?'

'Ms Beck? She says she hasn't seen him since her mother's funeral.'

'So you want me to interview the roommate. Run the story with an appeal for Lyndon to come forward and help the police clear up loose ends. Bit of a heart-sob piece. That it?'

August didn't answer, but led the way. The block smelt of carbolic and old trainers, an oddly reminiscent aroma which made Dryden uneasy. A pilot sat on the stairs, his head between his legs, breathing deeply. A pool of sweat was spreading on the concrete step. He didn't look up as they climbed to the top floor.

'Exercise,' said Dryden: 'Why do people do it?'

August stopped in front of one of the dried-blood-red dormitory doors marked:

R145
Major Lyndon Koskinski
Capt Freeman White
Base Fire Team

August knocked smartly like he owned the place. Lyndon's roommate was black, with grey curly hair and watery brown eyes. He was a big man, heavily built, with the manner of someone who finds it tiresome to carry around their own bones. Dryden and August sat on one bunk, White opposite. His bed was covered in several layers of newspaper in the middle of which was a jumble of oily machinery: cogs, cables and bolts. His fingers showed the grease where he'd been working.

And there was the wound. Lyndon Koskinski had said he'd been injured ejecting from their plane over Iraq. A welt about six inches long had healed on White's skull but could still be traced from his right cheekbone up into the hairline.

The right eye was cloudy and Dryden guessed from the way he held his head to one side that it was blind.

'Mechanic, eh?' asked Dryden.

'I ain't seen Lyndon for days,' he said, ignoring the question. His face was a smooth ebony black, polished like a banister, and impossible to date.

Dryden tried to recall the stature of the motorcyclist who had vandalized Humph's cab. The height was right. The shoulders maybe.

'We weren't that close, you know . . .' He spread two huge hands on his knees. 'Guy's got a life to lead, yeah? He wanted time. Space.'

August folded a knee flat over the other. 'But you were in Iraq together. You had to ditch. That's right, isn't it?'

White glanced up at a picture pinned above Lyndon's pillow. An F-111 on a hot white runway somewhere sandy where the tide never came in. He had a hi-tech flying helmet under his arm. White was next to him and they wore the expansive smiles people often affect just before they think they might get killed.

Dryden flipped open a notebook

'Yeah. Lyndon was the pilot that day – I was navigating. We bailed out, got separated . . .'

'How come?' said Dryden standing and looking at the snapshots pinned to a cork board.

'We parachuted down a few miles from each other. I got picked up right off by a field patrol. Republican Guard. I'd hit the canopy on the way out when we ejected. Made a mess of my head. I don't remember that much about it. They was happy guys though, you know? Jumpin'. Lyndon came down over the horizon. They sent a squad of the local militia after him – took 'em a week to find him. We both ended up in Al Rasheid. Some cell. It was grim, you can guess.'

'So you had that in common,' said August. 'Eight weeks together in that cell. That was a bond. You must feel close, no?'

'Sure,' said White, beginning to rearrange the cogs and bolts on the newspaper. 'Lyndon saved my life in there. Fed me, gave me his water, kept the wounds clean. I really don't remember a lot – but I'd be dead otherwise.' Dryden sensed he hadn't wanted to say this, but couldn't help himself.

'So you owe him your life. That's a big debt,' said Dryden, probing.

White ignored him again. 'Three months ago he was great, when we got back. He was going Stateside once he'd got his weight back. Then he went out to the farm – Black Bank. You know . . . ?' Dryden and August nodded.

'That seemed to go OK. He was kinda pleased. He loves his grandparents. That's dem.' He pointed at a colour snap of Lyndon on a beach. The grandparents stood stiffly on either side. She'd been beautiful once, he looked distinguished now, but nobody touched anybody else. 'Maggie was really pleased to see him. I went out too, a coupla times. I guess she wanted to get close.'

'He saw a lot of them?' asked Dryden, looking through the small barred window. A platoon of junior airmen were drilling while an orderly with a ladder was painting a white line down the side of a Nissen hut.

'Yeah. He stayed out there – they gave him a room. Food was good, that's what he wanted. It got him off the base. He looked great. Got a tan, this summer of yours is unreal.'

Dryden sat on the bunk beside him. 'It's a one-off. Even we don't believe it. So – then Maggie died.'

'Yeah. Then she died and, well, he kinda collapsed.' They left the silence for him to fill. 'He came back the next morning. Brought his stuff.'

'Stuff?' August leant back against the wall. Dryden appreci-
ated the classic interview technique. Relax when things get
interesting.

'Clothes. Books. Everything he'd taken. I asked him what
was up. He said Maggie had died, that everything was different. Then he shut up. Packed a kit-bag with his washing stuff
and fresh clothes and went. Didn't say goodbye, didn't say
anything.'

Dryden spoke from the window: 'Did he leave anything
valuable – anything that you knew was precious to him?'

White shook his head. Dryden was looking through the
window when he saw the box. He guessed it was made from
an exotic hardwood, almost ruby red, and constructed in a
carved fretwork like a confessional screen.

'That's nice,' said Dryden being careful not to touch it.
'Middle Eastern?'

'Yup. Aden, the souk – what a hole. Anyway, good for
presents, I guess.' White looked at his watch. 'I'm due on
duty, gentlemen. Flying a desk. Then physio.' Neither Dryden
nor August believed him, but they stood anyway.

Dryden thought, *There's always one more question.* 'And you've
not had contact with Lyndon at all – telephone, text, letter
. . . nothing?'

'Like I said. Nothin'. Nothin' for days.'

'Can I?' said August, pointing to the bathroom.

'Sure.' White made himself busy collecting some papers
while Dryden looked around. He waited until August pulled
the chain and then he stepped in close and picked up one of
the fly-wheel cogs on the bed.

'Motorcycle?' he asked.

White looked him in the eyes. 'Yup.'

'Thought so,' said Dryden, tossing the cog into White's
hands. 'Dangerous things. You should be careful.'

August appeared, so he grabbed White's hand. 'Thanks. You've been really helpful.'

Back in the Jeep August set out the ground rules. 'There's no hiding the fact Koskinski's gone AWOL, I know that. But he deserves some sympathy too. Two months in a cell can mess up anyone's head. Then he gets home and discovers he isn't who he thought he was. He gets a mother twenty-seven years after he was made an orphan.'

Dryden held his hands up. 'I hear you. No problem. I never planned to label him Most Wanted Man.'

'You can quote White, but no name, OK? Just a friend on base. Pilot – you can say that in *The Crow* this week. Yup?'

Dryden felt a line had been crossed. 'I can say what I bloody well like, when I like. But, as it happens, I won't name him, and yes, it will be in this week's paper. OK?'

'I owe you a drink,' said August, but really he owed it to himself, so they drove in silence to Mickey's Bar.

32

The primary school at Barrowby Drove was on the wrong side of the Sixteen Foot Drain. A graceless iron bridge crossed the snot-green water. The main building was a post-war prefab which appeared to be entirely constructed of asbestos sheeting. The heat outside was ninety degrees and rising; inside, under a corrugated iron roof, it must have been higher. As soon as Dryden went through the door the heat hit him, just before the smell did.

'Fen kids,' he said, trying to shut his nostrils by willpower. Humph was in the cab outside baking, but at least he was pot-roast; this was cabbage and socks.

Dryden was standing in an ante-room full of pegs marked with names. He'd gone to a similar school himself on Burnt Fen, fifteen kids from six families, and he'd smelt of cabbage too. There were about thirty names here, but very few surnames. Family inter-marriage wasn't a crime out here, it was a necessity.

Dryden peeked through a glass porthole into the single classroom. The classroom of the future, much trumpeted by the government, had missed the Fens by about eighty years. This could have been a Victorian snapshot: five rows of wooden single-unit desks with bench seats, a roll-round blackboard with triple dusters with retread felt, and a large map of the world. At least India had been removed from the Empire.

But the teacher looked thoroughly modern: Estelle Beck was at the front of the class perched precariously on the teacher's desk, her legs up in the lotus position. On the blackboard were some mathematical symbols Dryden didn't dwell on. Every head in the class was down, tiny fists holding pencils in cack-handed grips.

She didn't look much like a teacher and she certainly didn't look like a teacher who should be at Barrowby Drove. She was wearing sports gear and an array of pencils stuck out of her hair like punk spikes.

Dryden knocked and every head turned except hers. The silence dissolved in excited whispers as Estelle beckoned him inside. By the time he got to the front the class was in a state of nearly hysterical agitation.

'OK, OK,' said Estelle, holding up a hand for silence. 'Let's try and remember our manners. Remember what we've learned about how to behave with visitors. Jonathan . . . ?'

Jonathan stood. 'Welcome to Barrowby Drove School,' he said, turning scarlet.

She then introduced Dryden to the class. 'This is Mr Dryden,' said Estelle: 'He's a reporter with *The Crow*.'

Jaws dropped universally, indicating that visitors to Barrowby Drove School were rarely as exotic.

'OK – little ones around the art table please with crayons and paper. Middle group please read the next chapter of *Harry Potter and the Chamber of Secrets*. Jonathan is in charge.'

Estelle led the way out through another door into a small grassed playground which, looking south, was a stranger to shadows. The sun hammered down on a wrought-iron set of swings and a slide which were, as a consequence, radiating heat like boiler pipes.

'It's Lyndon,' said Dryden, looking north towards the only thing on the horizon – the giant grain silos at King's Lynn twenty miles to the north.

When he turned back he saw that the electric-green eyes

233

were extremely bright, almost preternaturally alive. Dryden could pick up most human emotions on his own antennae even if he was largely incapable of feeling his own. He was picking up an odd double transmission of anger and fear.

'My brother,' she said. 'What about him?'

'Well, officially he's AWOL from Mildenhall.'

'They seem pretty relaxed about it. Lyndon's under . . . pressure, he's confused, I think everyone understands that. I'm sure you do . . .'

On the Forty Foot a small motor launch swept past, a man at the tiller protected by a large sunhat.

'Have you any idea where he might be? Did he attend the reading of the will?'

She shook her head. 'No. He'd said from the start he wanted nothing. Which is a bit awkward as he got everything.'

'How do you feel about that?' said Dryden, cursing himself for a maladroit question.

'Mum knew I hated Black Bank. I hated it almost as much as she did. I think leaving it to Lyndon was a master-stroke. I feel free of it for the first time in my life. That answer your question?'

Dryden ignored the hostility. 'The last time you saw him, what was his mood?'

She looked out over the fen. 'He's very angry. He's certainly desperate. I worried about him when he was at Black Bank. Now he's gone, it's worse. I think he's gone away so he can't hurt anyone he likes. Loves.'

'Could he hurt himself?'

She shook the neat blonde bob and said: 'Maybe.' She forced herself to go on. 'I think so. Yes. Don't you? He's an American, he fought for his country, and now that's been taken away from him. And a life which I think he would have loved, here, was stolen long ago. He spent nearly thirty years thinking he'd lost his mother when he was two weeks old – then he discovers she's alive with almost her last breath. How much grief can one person take? What would you feel?'

Dryden felt the familiar panic sweep through him as he faced answering a question rather than posing one. 'I guess I'd want to know why she'd done it, why she gave me away.'

'Which is exactly what we don't know. She was unhappy at Black Bank, she hated her life in many ways. The tapes are very clear about that. About what my mother suffered . . .'

'You've listened to all of them?'

She answered immediately, as if under cross-examination in a courtroom. 'Yes. All those we found under the bed. Each one. From her earliest memories on Black Bank to her final illness . . .'

'Forgive me,' said Dryden, stepping closer. 'Are you sure? Did you get the sense that she'd completed the story? Does the last tape end abruptly, run out, what?'

She climbed effortlessly on to the playground see-saw and sat, perfectly balanced, at its fulcrum: 'It just runs out. You think there's more?'

'Possibly. The tape recorder's gone – you didn't take it?'

She shook her head, shading her eyes from the sun. 'No. I said, we left it for you.'

Dryden looked at the shadow condensed at his feet. 'And she gave no hint about her decision that night. Why she gave Matty away?'

'She said she had no choice,' said Estelle.

'Those are her words?'

'Yes. She said she had no choice and that she'd never regretted what she'd done, even though she grieved for her son for nearly thirty years.' She walked off to tap a barometer mounted on the schoolhouse wall next to a thermometer.

She had her back to him when she spoke: 'So who's looking for Lyndon?'

'The local police need to talk to him about Maggie's confession. At the very least his ID needs to be changed, records amended. I doubt it makes much difference to his nationality in reality, but it might. They've asked Mildenhall to help – they don't want to push it but they need to get Lyndon back before it becomes an issue, an incident.'

She turned with a smile on her face. 'If you find him first, Mr Dryden, tell him to speak to me. Will you take that message to him? Tell him to ring the mobile.' She touched her breast pocket to check the phone was still there.

Dryden walked back with her towards the classroom where a crescendo of babble indicated that Jonathan had lost control of his charges. 'One question. Did Lyndon take the Land Rover?'

'Yes, yes he did.'

Dryden spun on his heel, taking in the perfect circular horizon of the Black Fen. 'That's going to be difficult to hide. You can see for ever.'

She considered the view; a shimmering expanse of tumbling hot air. 'Sometimes the truth's a lot closer.'

33

Humph drove him to Barham's Dock as the sun fell. He left Humph rummaging in the drinks compartment and rang his landline answerphone: still no further word from Gillies & Wright. How could Maggie have miscalculated so badly? She'd been convinced Lyndon's father would come forward. If there was no further news soon Dryden needed a new lead on the story to run the appeal again – this time in *The Crow*.

He checked his watch: 8.45pm – time for night calls. Every evening he did the round of six: police headquarters at Cambridge, local cop shop at Ely, fire station at Cambridge, county ambulance control at Histon, the coastguard at Cromer, and the AA regional centre at Peterborough. Most nights it was six blanks, which was a good job as Dryden usually made the calls having taken a series of nightcaps with Humph.

Tonight it was miniature *crème de menthes*. Sickly green bottles of alcoholic medicine.

Dryden waited a full minute with the bottle vertically poised above his lips to allow the last of the green slurry to seep out. Then he hit the mobile. He knew something was wrong when he finally got through to the duty officer at the county police HQ.

'Yeah. We've got two units on the perimeter wire at Mildenhall. Request from the base commander. Fire. No other details at this time.'

'Shit,' said Dryden, cutting straight to fire HQ. Humph

carefully screwed the top back on to his second bottle and started the cab's engine.

'We've got three tenders on the airfield,' said the control room operator.

'From . . .' said Dryden, hoping his luck would hold.

'Mildenhall, Ely and Soham.'

The military at Mildenhall had three tenders of their own on the air base. If they'd called for assistance something had gone off with a big bang. He flicked through his contact book. He knew one of the Ely firemen whose wife was a nurse at The Tower. They'd met at a fund-raising barbecue four years earlier, the summer before Laura's accident. He'd been on the *News* then but could never let a social occasion pass without ruining it by asking someone for their mobile telephone number. He rang it now, it picked up, but all he could hear was garbled shouting and a mechanical roar like the sound of the sea, heard underwater.

'. . . here. Darren Peake here. Darren . . .'

'Hi. Hi. It's Philip. Philip Dryden from *The Crow*. Sorry. We met at one of the fund-raisers. Are you at the Mildenhall fire?'

Generally firemen were press-friendly. They liked seeing the pictures taken from the at-scene videos in the local paper and *The Crow* covered all their sports sponsorship events. During the firemen's strike Dryden had done a vox pop for the *Express* which had thrown up unexpectedly strong support for their claim.

'Yeah,' said Peake. 'It's a sight. Fire training facility has gone up, then a petrol tank. It's right by the wire on the south side – near the road to Beck Row, half a mile north of the junction with the main Ely road. I'm officer in charge at the scene for the civil – give us a wave. The yellow hat. Ciao.'

Dryden checked the back seat for *The Crow*'s office

cameras and a decent pair of binoculars. Humph already had the cab on the road going east, while overhead the sky was turning from blue to purple like a giant bruise as the sun set. They saw the single gout of fire ten miles short of the end of the main runway, a vertical eruption of fuel-blue flame closely followed by the crump of exploding metal.

The approach roads to the base were closed by military policemen with mobile road-blocks but Humph swung the Capri off down an unlit drove road around the perimeter wire. They big-dippered along the rock-hard farm track until they bounced out into a large field of unmown grass gone to seed. It was a camp site run by an enterprising local farmer exclusively for plane spotters. Their caravans and trailers stood well back from the twelve-foot security wire while in front of each stood a small fisherman's tent from which the spotters could train their telephoto lenses on the arrivals and departures at Mildenhall. It was, Dryden had often thought, the village of the sad.

The entire population of this dysfunctional holiday camp was up against the perimeter wire including half a dozen kids in stripy pyjamas.

The fire was 200 yards beyond the wire. An alcopop orange flame curled up in a single sickly cone of ear-splitting combustion. Dryden pressed his face against the diamond-webbed fence with all the rest. The guy next to him made Humph look like a bathing belle. He could only dream of pressing his face against the fence. On his huge chest a pair of binoculars rested unused, as he shielded his eyes by pulling down a cap peak slightly smaller than a garage door.

'Fucker,' he said, burping. A small boy at his knee, with suspicious quantities of puppy fat still adhering to his tiny limbs, looked up with adoring eyes. There was a lot to look up to.

'What happened?' said Dryden, hoping the guy wouldn't swing round and flatten him.

'The fire house went up.'

Dryden realized immediately that the big man didn't know he was not one of the brothers, one of that intimate band that knew the difference between an FK-109 and an FK-109XA, or even the secret society within that, which actually cared.

But being a reporter is all about owning up. 'Actually. I'm a reporter. Just driven out – what's a fire house?'

Dryden took an evasive step back as the big man swung round. He looked at Dryden as one would greet an alien life form, spitting effortlessly over Dryden's head and then cracking his knuckles. It sounded like he was dislocating the legs on a turkey.

'Fire house is where they practise fire fighting, OK? It's just a brick shell – but with concrete floors. Only difference is they have metal hatches over the windows, doors, chimney – all the outlets. That way they can control the fire. This one's got a fake fuselage attached, and a wing with an engine. They flood 'em with high-octane fuel and then – Bang!'

Dryden jumped. The big man liked that. So he did it again. 'Bang!'

They returned to the diamond mesh fence. 'So what went wrong?'

'Guess they didn't have this one under control.'

Dryden saw Darren Peake's yellow hat bobbing on the edge of the fire zone. He rang him on the mobile and waved, stupidly, from beyond the wire. Darren strolled over, removing the hat and the breathing gear, and Dryden took some pictures through the fence as he approached with the fire in the background.

'There's a body,' he said, sucking water from a bottle attached to his protective suit.

'In there?'

Darren nodded. 'Guy's a crisp. Not a lot left, even the teeth are carbonized.' Dryden felt a *crème de menthe* ease itself into his lower gut. 'How?'

He replaced the yellow hat. 'Between you and I? There was a practice scheduled for tomorrow morning; they usually let us know, just in case, so we can stand by. So everything would have been ready. There's a reservoir of aircraft fuel inside which was full. Looks like someone took their chance, dumped chummy and lit the fuel. Bingo – crispy bacon. There are ventilation grilles on all four outside walls which provide the fire with air – they were all open. Some sparks got out and lit the runway grass. That heated up the waste oil tank, which ignited.'

'Bang!' said the man-mountain, who had been listening intently.

They all looked back as a hissing sound overrode the screaming of the flames. Several jets of foam were being played on the flames which fluttered before dying in a cauldron of steam. The fire house was instantly buried under a snow drift.

'Send us some prints, eh? Show's over,' said Darren, walking off.

But it wasn't. The oil tank, capped with white foam, blew itself up. Darren, and everyone behind the wire, hit the grass, the big man going down with surprising grace. As cinders fell like black smoke Dryden left everyone else trying to pick him up.

He woke Humph up. 'There's a body in there. Human bacon. This place will be crawling with police when they get the call. Let's go.'

Humph, horrified, fired the Capri into life.

34

'I'd like you to come with me, OK?'

Humph studied the Capri's rear-view mirror.

'I've never asked before. I won't again. Once.'

'Last time,' said Humph, fingering the retied ends of his beloved fluffy dice.

'Jesus,' said Dryden. 'He slashed the seats. It wasn't Pearl Harbor. This is important. I need your help.'

Dryden got out of the car, slammed the door and took the steps two at a time into the reception area of the hospital. Humph followed carefully, picking his way up each individual step, and when he got to the top he surveyed the plush carpet-muffled interior of The Tower. 'Is there a lift?'

They rode up to the third floor in a silence punctuated by the bronchial whistles of Humph's pulmonary system coping with the shock of physical effort.

Humph had never actually seen Laura. His partnership with Dryden had begun in the desolate weeks after her accident when the reporter needed ferrying from the hospital to his mother's house on Burnt Fen. Wordless journeys of unshared grief which had somehow forged between them a bond of mutual alienation. Humph was dissolving in a toxic combination of anger and grief after his wife had walked out with the kids. Dryden was coming out of shock after the accident and wishing he wasn't. They were made for each other.

Humph felt guilty seeing the figure in the bed for the first time, as if he was peeping into a private nightmare. Dryden's rare excursions into memory had given an impression of his wife characterized by an exuberance of warmth: Latin temperament, Italian colouring, and ample curves. Humph had seen a picture reluctantly withdrawn from the zipped pocket of the wallet: a broad face blessed with perfect skin, brown eyes with a slight cast, and a jumble of auburn hair. The cabbie was not surprised to find the real Laura dramatically different. Her skin was ice-white and lifeless. The eyes open, brown, but blank; the arms laid straight at the sides, and the lips pale and parted by a centimetre. The teeth behind were perfect, linen white, and dry.

'She's beautiful,' said Humph, lying.

Dryden nodded, pleased at the lie, and oddly moved. 'Tear it off,' he said, pointing at the tickertape from the COMPASS machine.

'Why?' said Humph, tearing off the sheet and sitting down on two bedside chairs.

'Tell me what it says. It's beginning to freak me out. She told me to watch Freeman White. I'm pretty sure he's responsible for the threats, the attempt to sink my boat. How the hell does she know?'

Humph shrugged and studied the tape. There were a few lines of jumbled letters.

SGARTFN FH F F DGFDHFYRND LOPQJFCYOID SGSH SI I H SHSJOSD SDHFUTKG SHFDGFYTO GHLL

'Nothing,' said Humph.

'There's gotta be,' said Dryden, snatching the paper back.

There was a long silence in which Dryden tried to force meaning from the jumble of letters.

Then the tickertape machine bashed out a single letter: T.

They both jumped, Humph's return to earth producing a perceptible after-tremor.

The COMPASS machine ticked and printed a second letter: H. They jumped again and Humph began to edge back from the COMPASS machine. Dryden held his ground, holding the paper. 'Tell me, Laura,' he said, looking into her vacant brown eyes.

THE. Then she stopped. A minute passed in which they could hear a B-52 overhead droning in towards Mildenhall while the string of letters slowly lengthened.

THE WHISSLES

Dryden tore off the sheet and studied the letters again. 'Wait in the car,' he told Humph.

Dryden sat beside Laura's bed. 'I need help,' he said. 'Not this.'

He waited by the COMPASS machine for an hour in complete silence.

She knew the moment when she'd made the decision: the unilateral decision that she loved him. She'd always loved the idea of him, ever since she'd understood what America was. But that day at the track, she'd gone to get hot dogs and Cokes while he strolled round the cars before the first race. Running his fingers sensuously along the beaten metal, the way he'd run his fingers over her.

When she got back with the food the first race had begun. What she remembered was that he seemed to be the only thing that wasn't moving. The backdrop was chaotic. The stock cars raising dust even that early in the summer, the metal screeching as two clashed on a bend, then heaved over together as if in a brawl. The crowd, mostly US military from the air bases, had run to the rail to view the wreckage, to cheer the two drivers emerging from the dust.

And he'd just stood there, on the grass with his leg up on the running board of the Land Rover, flicking the Zippo. His self-contained stillness made her want to be near him always. It was the antidote to her own life, which had never seemed to have a centre, let alone one which would always hold. Even as she approached with the food and the drinks he didn't turn.

She touched his arm. 'Lyndon?' And that was when he knew he'd fallen in love with her, the point when he knew he wanted to come back to the world he'd lost in Al Rasheid. He'd been lonely ever since, avoiding strangers because they could ask questions, and friends because they couldn't, because they felt that saying nothing was the kindest cure for what he knew they must call many things – his illness, his injuries, his imprisonment, his lifelessness.

In truth he'd always been lonely. His lifelessness was older than his *imprisonment. His childhood had been oddly passionless, an orphan doted on, but never loved, not with the unconditional love of a parent. An orphan placated by money and education. A friendless boy who loved only an heroic image of his father, the Vietnam hero. A figure of intoxicating excitement always just beyond his reach. So he'd been lonely all his life: which is why he'd survived Al Rasheid.*

Estelle had ended that loneliness because their shared history made her unique. She'd known him all his life, but he was a stranger. Ever since he could remember they'd sent her presents from Texas, dolls when she was a child, then clothes, CDs, pictures of the desert, and the city where they lived: the pool, the Christmas tree, the people-carrier. And she'd sent pictures back, from the awkward Fen child in farm clothes clutching her American doll, to the blonde teenager with the all-American smile.

'Pretty kid,' said his grandfather, sourly. They'd resented the contact, his grandparents, he knew that now. He knew that it was Maggie who had kept them together, persisted, and used their guilt to keep the link alive.

And Estelle had envied him his family as well, with all the cruelty of a child. The lack of parents, the doting grandparents, the freedom. Her father had died when she was four, long before her memory had been born. And her mother had loved her as her second child, precisely that and nothing more. A great love, but always, she sensed, short of its absolute potential. Estelle knew that even before memory began.

And so they'd shared a childhood, an adolescence, despite the 5,000 miles that had always separated them. When he'd been stationed overseas he'd flown out via the Pacific – but they'd told Maggie he was posted in Iraq and that if he came back through the UK he'd visit. He'd dreaded the thought, the reality of the contact after all these years, but his grandparents had insisted it was only right. Only what Maggie deserved. She'd saved his life. But after Al Rasheid he couldn't face them, despite the calls from home telling him Maggie was ill.

But his depression had deepened, alone in his room at the base. He had to drive, drive anywhere without a map. Perhaps he knew it would happen. He'd seen the sign and felt the past pulling him towards the centre of his life: that moment when the plane had disintegrated in a fireball of burning aviation fuel. He'd never wanted to see it: the spot where his parents had died. But just after the sign came the stone, the memorial stone. He'd always carried the picture in his wallet. But now he got out and ran his fingers over the raised names on the stone, back and forth like a prayer said in Braille.

He'd left the car and walked to the house. There was no answer so he walked round to the yard. She had a towel out on the grass by the greenhouses. A bikini, in sky blue he remembered, contrasting with the corn-yellow hair. A CD player belting out country and western. She hadn't heard him so he stood and considered her, trying to recall what it was like to hold such a body. He couldn't remember the name of the last woman he'd made love to. It seemed like an episode from a book he'd read, on a forgotten train journey. Or even the last time he'd held anybody, or been held. In the cell, at Al Rasheid, he'd held Freeman, to hold someone, and to keep him alive. But now he wanted to hold this woman.

So he'd said hello. She'd jumped up and removed her sunglasses. And that was the start of it, and now there was an end to it.

Thursday, 19 June

35

'The pillbox,' said Dryden to himself, looking up at the shimmering bulk of the cathedral where a mirage already played above the lead roof. On Palace Green a gaggle of Japanese tourists had surrounded an ice cream van, but otherwise the town centre was deserted. The wet pools beneath the hanging baskets in the High Street had long since been burnt dry.

Dryden checked the court list again. He was first up on the rota for the magistrates: Peter Selby, of Caddus Street, Rushden. The stud from the pillbox porn show. Dryden zig-zagged through the streets from shade to shade until he reached the imposing façade of the courthouse. Inside, an assortment of Ely low-life shuffled about in ill-fitting suits, and they were the solicitors.

In the main courtroom the press bench was empty except for Alf Walker, a veteran wireman who had the county magistrate circuit stitched up, making a decent living filing anything juicy to the nationals. But he was no Rottweiler. He cut *The Crow* in for a nominal fee, which saved Henry Septimus Kew a fortune every year in staffing the court, while in return *The Crow* tipped him off if they heard something lively was on the court list.

Normally Dryden would have left this one to Alf, but he was beginning to take a strong personal interest in the pillbox on Black Bank Fen and everything that had happened there.

Alf was the opposite of the Fleet Street stereotype. Teetotal, with 180-wpm perfect Pitman shorthand, he dressed in country tweeds and sported a hat with a bird's feather sticking out of the band. His hobby was birdwatching and his notebook pages alternated between beautifully inscribed shorthand verbatim notes and mildly gifted line drawings of British birds. He was half-way through a fine kestrel when Dryden slumped on to the bench next to him.

At that moment the court clerk entered and promptly called the court to order with an 'All rise!' The magistrates trooped in.

'How's Andy?' Dryden whispered. Walker was a member of the same birdwatching society as Inspector Andy Newman. Dryden had noticed that he and Alf were occasionally blessed with the same inside information as a result.

'Chasing his arse. He's got two corpses and no idea. But I doubt he's losing any sleep over it.' Alf nodded at the dock: 'Hey up.'

There stood Peter Selby, the stud from Newman's pornographic snaps. Dryden reckoned he was six feet two, blond lifeless hair cut short and trendy with a French peak. He'd been given bail at his last appearance and was in a casual T-shirt which showed off the flawless muscles Alice Sutton had, at first, found so sexy. Even more so after she'd been slipped the date-rape drug in her drink.

But it was a face that was most forgettable. It was odd but true that a complete set of perfect features can make a face repellent: a hymn to symmetry without a trace of character. He looked like a computer-enhanced superhero; a somewhat pathetic one, given his inability to fly the confines of a chipboard dock in a small town magistrates court.

His lawyer stood, which was the first clue that Peter Selby had friends with wallets. This was no country circuit solicitor; the suit was navy blue, pinstripe, and cut to perfection. The legal bags were black leather and reeked of fees in excess of

£400 an hour. Behind him sat two juniors armed with papers, mobile phones, and bottles of Evian.

'I think we can assume Selby has wealthy friends,' said Alf.

The prosecuting solicitor stood slowly as two court ushers brought in four cardboard boxes and set them on the solicitor's bench.

For the first time Dryden noticed the group sitting behind the legal team. There were five men, four were black and smartly dressed, the fifth was white and but for the company he was keeping Dryden would have had him down as a member of the British National Party: a close-shaven head, military fatigues and an ugly botched attempt at a Union Jack tattoo on a bulging bicep.

'Sir,' said the solicitor, addressing the chairman of the bench. 'We are opposing the renewal of bail set on June the tenth at ten thousand pounds. We believe the accused may abscond.'

'What has changed since his last appearance?' The chairman of the magistrates was a local farmer Dryden had interviewed before when the drought had first struck. His face was ruddy, as if it had been recently slapped.

The court ushers opened the boxes and handed some of the contents to the court clerk, who passed them up to the magistrates. The skinhead leant forward to chat to the legals.

'These were found in a lock-up garage rented by the accused in Melton Mowbray, sir. There are nearly twelve thousand separate items.'

The chairman looked like he might want to see all of them.

'As you can see, sir, the scale of this operation is far wider than first thought. Large amounts of similar material, some involving girls clearly below the age of consent, have been found in containers at both Hull and Felixstowe. They had been prepared for export. Senior officers of the Cambridge-shire constabulary are investigating what they believe to be a two-way trade: people smuggled in and this, er, literature, smuggled out. Interpol is co-operating with the inquiry, as is the Serious Crime Squad. Police forces throughout the Midlands are now involved in the operation – Operation Pinion.'

The chairman of the bench nodded. 'I see. Mr Smith-fforbes?'

The expensive lawyer stood slowly, one hand clutching notes, the other resting with exaggerated ease on his hip. 'Sir. I am sure my client is as impressed as we all are by the scale of this operation, but I am afraid the Crown has put forward no facts to link the defendant to the mass production for export of this material. He is, if I may say so, a victim as much as these poor girls. It is his contention that he was unaware that his, er, activities were being photographed and he intends to establish his innocence of the charges in the Crown Court. He has agreed bail and he has volunteered to meet very strict bail requirements.'

The prosecuting solicitor stood. 'I think your worships will have noted that the defendant appears in many of the pictures I have shown the bench. Of the two thousand items recovered so far he appears in nearly six hundred. It is our belief he is a central figure in this illicit trade and we fear that those who have garnered considerable wealth from this traffic would find it convenient if he were to disappear. We believe they will see ten thousand pounds as a small price to pay.'

The skinhead said something to the legal team, who passed it on to Smith-fforbes. He stood smartly. 'If it is any help to the bench, sir, I can say that my client is willing to meet fresh bail conditions – including a considerably higher bail figure.'

The three magistrates conferred with the clerk. 'Very well,' said the chairman of the bench. 'We were minded to agree to remanding the defendant in custody, given the new evidence put before us today. However, am I right that the police do not think they will be able to move to a trial of this matter before Christmas?'

The prosecuting solicitor stood slowly, sensing the court was about to brush aside his request that Selby be held in custody. 'That's correct, sir. The enquiries are extremely complex . . . and several other arrests are imminent,' he added, casting a glance back over the court which was clearly designed to embrace the skinhead.

'I see. Well, we do not think the defendant can be rightly held for that length of time. We therefore grant bail at a figure of fifty thousand pounds. Mr Selby will report to his local police station twice daily during that period.'

Selby's advocate was on his feet again. 'Ah, if I may just comment, sir. My client is, of course, a long-distance lorry driver – that condition of the bail was waived at the last hearing to allow him to continue in gainful employment.'

The chairman looked unimpressed, and his cheeks flushed further. 'I know. But not this time. I'm afraid he will have to find other gainful employment.'

'Court rise,' said the clerk.

Outside, the WRVS ran a tea bar when the court was sitting. Dryden and Alf got their drinks and grabbed one of the wooden pews.

They watched as the four black men in suits from the back of the court got into two smart powder-blue Jags that pulled up at the courthouse steps. The skinhead sat back in one of them, studying documents while he used a mobile phone. The London legal team waited for taxis to take them back to the station.

'What do you reckon?' asked Dryden.

Alf shrugged. 'Well, it was about four grand's worth of lawyers. So I think we can rule out his Post Office savings, don't you? And it wasn't their only case of the day – they've earned their money twice.'

'Another case? I thought Selby was first up?'

Alf flicked back through his notebook. 'Nope. Remand. Jimmy Kabazo. Up on a GBH charge – cracked a mortuary attendant over the head with an iron bar. Our friends in suits argued that it was down to emotional distress. Police suggested they were also investigating the possibility that he was an illegal immigrant – but the bench kicked that out as they had no evidence to support it. Then they said – a bit belatedly if you ask me – he might be a suspect in that nasty killing out on the fens – the bloke in the pillbox.'

'Jesus – so they freed him?'

'Yup. Bit of a cock-up. Police solicitor looked a bit sick. Mind you, a bench in a small place like this gets very nervous when they've got a black in the dock. Don't want to put a foot wrong. Anyway, he was out – and into the waiting arms of that creepy skinhead and his mates. Bail of five thousand agreed by the advocate. Passport had been withdrawn already for examination.'

Alf grimaced as he finished the last of his tea. 'Put me right – this is actually dish-water, isn't it?'

'So he just walked off?' said Dryden, his patience draining away.

'Nope. There was a bit of a row outside the court. They tried to get him into one of the Jags to shut him up but he wasn't having it – you'd have thought he'd have at least said thanks for the five grand. He hung around the PC on duty for a bit and they got the hint – left him alone. Then he walked off – into town. If he's planning to give them the slip I don't rate his chances. He has to report at Ely twice a day – 9.ooam and 5.oopm. They'll pick him up later.'

Dryden walked back to *The Crow* wondering where Jimmy Kabazo would go and, more to the point, what he would do next. If the death of his son had been an accident someone had been reckless in dumping the van. If the van had been deliberately dumped then the driver had effectively left them all to die. Did Jimmy know the truth? And did he know who was responsible?

When he got back to the office there was twenty minutes to the deadline so he knocked out the remand on Selby. There'd been a fire at a school on the edge of town and Garry was attempting to write the story which would be that week's splash on the front page. His narrow forehead was furrowed while his fingers remained motionless, poised a few inches above the PC's keyboard. Dryden wandered over and looked at what he'd written. It was a hopeless scramble of facts and bad English lashed together with doubtful punctuation.

'Why don't you try this . . . ?' said Dryden. 'Police have launched a countywide hunt for child saboteurs after fire swept through a secondary school yesterday leaving a million-pound trail of damage.'

Garry nodded, tapping it out.

'Then mention the school's name in the second half of the story – that way readers don't turn off at the start if they don't come from Ely.'

Garry lit a cigarette, the panic which had made it imposs-ible for him to write coherently instantly replaced by mis-placed confidence. Dryden helped himself to some coffee and stood by the window looking down on Market Street. It was shadowless and shimmering mirages made the occasional late shopper appear to dance in the tumbling air. Dryden's thoughts were just as insubstantial but dominated by images of the bright scarlet blood dripping from the crowbar Jimmy Kabazo had wielded at the City Mortuary. Dryden feared that the next time Jimmy drew blood the victim wouldn't live to see the bandage. Paying Jimmy's bail must have been a real quandary for the smugglers. They needed him out of police custody to make sure he didn't talk. But once freed he would be out to avenge Emmy's death. Dryden guessed the number one target was the skinhead driver Jimmy had described at the airfield. He was undoubtedly the tattooed yob who had sat through the stud's appearance and was now lolling in the back of the Jag. The only real question was whether the skinhead would be Jimmy's first victim, or his last.

36

In Dryden's imagination a wounded Lancaster trailed black smoke behind a shattered tail, while Glenn Miller played on the Home Service. It was summer: summer 1940. The Battle of Britain. Overhead, fighter aircraft left a white cat's cradle hanging in the blue skies. But if Dryden had actually been there in that pivotal summer he would have been too scared to do what he was doing now, which was putting his feet up on the wooden verandah rail and listening in his head to Glenn's giddy dance numbers. Humph was in the parked cab about fifty yards away across the grassy overgrown runway. Dryden had an overwhelming urge to call him Ginger.

He'd been at Barham's Dock supervising the cleaning of the *PK 129* when he'd taken the call from August. A press conference had been set up to deal with enquiries over the fire-house fatality. 'Is it linked to Black Bank?' asked Dryden, knowing it must be.

'Who knows?' said August, and Dryden could tell he was sober. 'We may never even know who chummy was. Anyway – one o'clock at the new press centre at the old RAF huts.'

Dryden checked his watch: 12.50pm. USAF Mildenhall lay on the far side of the wire, laid out like a giant picnic blanket. He was sitting outside Hut B: Squadron A. The sign smacked of a simpler world, a world where you could spot a swastika at 3,000 feet and Dame Vera Lynn at 100 yards. The huts had been in use since the September 11 attacks on New York. Outside the perimeter wire, they offered a convenient place for community and press liaison without testing the security on the main gates. The hut next to Dryden had been used for base staff education on water conservation. A huge poster twenty yards long shouted 'Don't be a waterhog!'

Dryden felt the globes of sweat forming on his forehead and turned his eyelids up to receive the ritual shower of imaginary snow flakes. He thought about his floating home awash with river water and asked himself again the pressing question: Why did someone so desperately want him to stop writing about Maggie Beck? Was it Freeman White? And if it was, *why* was it Freeman White? Freeman and Lyndon were close, a relationship fused during their incarceration in Al Rasheid. Was Dryden a threat to Lyndon Koskinski? Or were the attacks on Humph's cab and *PK 129* somehow linked to the murder of Johnnie Roe, or even to the people smugglers?

His brain swam, unable to compute the interlocking facets of three stories which had become fixed in a baffling embrace. Was there any way forward? He sensed that if he could find the last tape that Maggie made before her death he could begin to unravel the truth. He would visit The Tower that night, and begin his own enquiries.

When he opened his eyes it was to see a crocodile of walkers making its way across the grass runway from Gate B. Her Majesty's Press had arrived en masse, and were being escorted by Sergeant DeWitt, August's statuesque assistant. The bedraggled group were hot, bad-tempered and in search of a decent story. Sergeant DeWitt promised cold drinks, a buffet lunch, and best of all – alcohol.

Inside, the old hut had been turned into a mini-conference centre. Plush seats with flip-down note tables were set in rows. A generous spread of sandwiches and nibbles had been laid on a new pine table down one side of the room. A dozen bottles of wine had been provided – although Dryden noted with suspicion the usual trick: they'd been opened and then re-corked, the contents thereby being unlikely to bear any relation to the labels. On the opposite side of the room an identical table had a series of six PCs linked up to the internet with the base website permanently online: USAF Mildenhall: The US Gateway to Europe.

August had invited Inspector Andy Newman along to take questions too. Technically the base was sovereign US soil while the 120-year lease ran its course. In practice a suspicious death on a US air base had attracted the interest of the Home Office in London and the US Embassy. Discreet calls had been made to secure the cooperation of the local constabulary in clearing up the crime as quickly as possible. Newman's first job was to settle nerves at HQ in Histon that the killing was not a terrorist act. Post-September 11 nerves amongst the top brass were still frayed.

Joey Forward, the local man for the *East Anglian Daily News*, played idly with his trouser zip as he considered his first question. 'So, this body that was burnt up – like a cinder the camera man said. Nasty business. Any ideas, sergeant?' He studied a briefing pack they'd all picked up on the way in.

'Major. Major August Sondheim. The murder victim . . .'

'Murder?' cut in Dryden. 'Why so sure?'

'All windows and doors on the fire house were locked from the outside. We don't know if the man died inside, or was dead before the fire was lit . . . we never will, I'm afraid. We'll be lucky to get an ID off the dental records. Not a piece of flesh left on him.'

Mike Yarr, the PA wireman, was working a piece of gristle out of his teeth, having hastily eaten a beef sandwich. He burped loudly without covering his mouth.

'Murder then,' he said, still working at his teeth. 'Any link with the Black Bank killing?'

August shrugged. 'Local CID investigating, gentlemen. Inspector Andy Newman will take your questions on that.'

There was a short but audible groan.

Newman stood and pinned a large Ordnance Survey map on the display board at the front of the conference room. Red circles marked the pillbox in Mons Wood and the fire house on the air base.

'For any strangers who may have wandered in, we are here,' said Newman, pointing to the old RAF huts marked outside the base's perimeter wire. 'Clearly, two such incidents within five miles of each other give us cause for concern, gentlemen. At the moment we will be operating two incident rooms and two enquiries – but I shall head both. I shall keep Major Sondheim's superiors briefed at all times. If there are links, I can assure you we will not miss them.'

'Timing on the ID?' said Dryden.

Newman consulted some notes. 'It has to be forty-eight hours. This is no ordinary medical examination. The inside of the fire house is essentially a crematorium. We are dealing with bones and ashes.'

'Any clues at the site?' said Forward.

August shot the cuffs on his uniform. 'All I can say is that there are no fingerprints on the metallic locks. The victim was male. Lot of bridgework on the teeth, which might help with the ID. Oh – and a metallic cylinder by the body could be the core of a heavy-duty torch.'

'Racial type?' asked Dryden.

'Indeterminate,' said August, who was beginning to lose a battle with a raging thirst. He fingered a bottle of Buxton water he'd brought into the briefing. Dryden might have been imagining it but the fluid inside seemed to leave a suspicious film on the inside of the bottle.

'Anyone missing on the base?' asked Forward, wandering

over to the food to add to a plate already resembling International Rescue's Tracey Island.

Good question, thought Dryden.

August didn't miss a beat. 'No member of the base complement is unaccounted for. Nor outside civilian staff.'

Lyndon Koskinski, of course, was neither: a nice distinction.

August ploughed on before anyone could delve deeper. 'As to timing. The last fire exercise was two weeks ago. The building was cleared then. So any time between then and now.'

Mike Yarr had been told by PA's news desk in London to get a terrorist line on the killings. That would ensure the copy was used nationwide. 'Clearly there are concerns about terrorist attacks, Major. Can you comment on that?' he asked.

August sighed. 'We are ever vigilant here at USAF . . .' As August began to run through a tedious prepared line on the terrorist threat Dryden stood, stacked a paper plate with individual miniature pork pies and sat before one of the PC screens. He'd pulled the cork on a bottle of red wine and poured himself a large glass. The PC was logged on to the USAF Mildenhall site. He scrolled on through the site to the official 'Welcome' from the President, short statements from the USAF and RAF commanders on the base, and fifteen pages of on-base sport which proved to be fifteen too many. Local baseball teams lined up for pictures. Endless league tables read like a roll-call of Middle America from the Big Rock Busters to the New Jersey Fliers. The social pages pointed up a production of *A Street Car Named Desire* at the base theatre, and *Die Hard 3* at the cinema. Ten Pin Bowling was now available twenty-four hours a day at the Lincoln Leisure Center.

And finally 'Noticeboard' – a message page dominated by vital events.

B Block Stateside congrats to Jaynette and Mike on the arrival of Mike Jnr. Go Fella!

· Friends of Michael J. Doherty, base medic 1975–2000 will want to know that he died peacefully in his sleep here at home in Salt Lake on June 5. A long illness bravely borne.

Then he saw it. He read it three times before shutting the PC down to think. Then he booted it back up and took a verbatim note.

This is a long shot but it's a message for the love birds. I was really privileged to be the witness – I guess it was the uniform that made you choose me. But look – the snapshots are great, especially the ones in the white Land Rover, and I thought that maybe one day you might want to share the memory after all. So just e-mail me and I'll send them online, if that's OK. The guy at the register office said I should do it this way coz you'd mentioned the base. So, no names! But e-mail me if you want to remember Cromer – I always will.

Dryden called up a fresh e-mail form and hit REPLY. The PC automatically reprinted the sender's e-mail address: jon.cummings@norfolkconstab_cromer.
He typed:

It was great to hear from you. We'd still like to keep our secret here but we'd love the pictures. Please send them to the e-mail below – it's a friend who's online and he's got a color printer. And thanks for being there!

Dryden added his own hotmail address and poured him-self another large glass of red wine.

He wondered how many white Land Rovers there were in the Fens and was appalled by the consequences if there was only one. He rejoined his colleagues and tried to smile at August's bad jokes. August was smiling too, but by then the Buxton water bottle was empty.

37

If he hadn't tried to track down Johnnie Roe's wife he'd have never known the dog track was there. This was Thursday night out, Fen-style. The stadium was a little cauldron of electric light in the wasteland beyond the Mildenhall wire. Darkness was beginning to fall, but even in broad daylight it would have taken you a week to find the Billy Row International Greyhound Stadium. Flags of every nation flew, rigid in an imaginary wind, supported by hidden aluminium frames. But every other one was a Stars & Stripes.

Dryden sat on the cab roof eating a beefburger. The Capri's windows were open in the heat and he heard the seven pips on the radio. She'd said 7.45 – after the first race on the card.

A couple of Fleet Street nationals were still interested in the bizarre pillbox killing – now they wanted family, friends, anything that could put a real life to a grisly death. He'd told Newman he wanted a telephone number to do some more background work on Roe's life. Newman had given him the ex-wife's full name and told him to find the number for himself. Luckily, she was in the book. A house on the outskirts of Newmarket, a council estate infamous for petty drugs offences. The call had been awkward but at least she'd agreed to meet. Her voice had been tough, disfigured by suspicion.

Already the punters were arriving. The Fens were a celebration of Americana, Mid-West variety. Stock-car racing was the most popular sport and large numbers of people had never seen the sea or the city, and were proud of it. Most of the cars rolling in for the dog racing were playing one or other of Dryden's two least favourite forms of music: country and western. Humph had his headphones on and was reading the book that went with his language tapes: *Greek Language and People*.

Then came the real Americans. The state plates, the blonde wives and the kids weighed down with enough dental work to embrace the Golden Gate Bridge.

Dryden sipped Coke and burped for fun. He liked Americans. He liked the brash good humour, the lack of two-faced English subtlety and the simple determination to have plenty of fun as loudly as possible. Dryden slid off the roof, down the windscreen and across the bonnet of the Capri to land lightly on the hot tarmac. It was a good trick, and one the crowd in his head always cheered.

By the turnstiles was The Greyhound 'Nite Spot'. Neon strip lighting picked out the shape of a racing dog. Class in spades, thought Dryden, as he ordered a pint of imported Bud at the bar and watched two US pilots playing pool on a table with a blue baize top. Two middle-aged guys at the bar played with their cigarette packs and vied, in a half-hearted way, for the attentions of the barmaid.

Dryden had another Bud and left at 7.29 precisely, but was still able to find an empty half-acre of terrace by the time the first race began. The bell rang. The dogs were paraded in their neat waistcoats. Handlers, in mock-lab coats, tried to look disinterested. The dogs were bundled into the starting gate with indecent haste, like murderers into the noose. The hare did a lap and Dryden laughed at its silly teetering progress, but as it lapped the starting gate the dogs exploded out of their traps. Their speed and beauty thrilled him, and they took the first bend in a tight hurtling pack of sporting colours. By the time they crossed the finishing line after three laps he was cheering with the rest. He didn't know which mutt had won, and he didn't care. The punters dropped their torn-up betting slips, a tiny snow shower of disappointment. The winners swaggered, but only as far as the bar.

She was beside him suddenly, with a tray of race cards and cigarettes. She was probably under fifty but she'd been given a double helping of wrinkles, and none of them were laughter lines. The hair was once blonde, but now it was grey and cut lifelessly short. She had the slight stoop of the habitual smoker and the nervous searching fingers of someone feeling for a filter-tip.

'Well?' she said, and sat down on the concrete terrace. She searched in her pockets for cigarettes, then stopped herself by clasping her hands in her lap.

'Sally Roe?' asked Dryden. She nodded, looking at her hands. 'You were married to Johnnie Roe?' he asked, trying to think fast and talk slowly at the same time.

'In 1978.'

'Thanks for agreeing to meet.'

'Not a lot of choice once you had the number.' She smiled in half-apology for the aggressive tone.

Dryden smiled back. 'The police said you were divorced. Years.'

She nodded, watching the dogs being led towards the starting booths again.

'Yeah. I got out in 'ninety-three.'

'Any reason?'

'Loads. Private now. Best forgotten. But one thing Johnnie never forgot was that kid. When he'd had too much that was what it all came down to. Every argument. Every fight. We never had children. So he grieved for Matt. It brought it all back – what you wrote in the paper.'

268

Dryden was thinking fast, but he'd just been lapped.

She turned to face him. 'Johnnie and Maggie were quite an item. We all thought they'd stick together, you know – not like the other teenage flings. He really wanted the kid – that's why he went back into the fire that night. That's how he got the burns – you should have seen his back.'

I have, thought Dryden. 'Johnnie Roe was the father of Maggie Beck's boy?' he said.

She nodded. 'Oh yeah. It made Johnnie what he was.'

'And what was that?' said Dryden, picturing the pillbox on Black Bank Fen.

Her resolution failed, she found the packet in her breast pocket and lit up in a single fluid movement. Then she took in the nicotine and waited that two or three seconds it takes before the effect floods the bloodstream.

'A bastard, really. But he could have been something else. If he'd come out of that fire with that kid his life would have been worth something. He said that. Drunk, I know, but he meant it. As it was, he amounted to nothing, so he didn't see the point in trying to be anything better. He said he was a zero. Mr Zero. Which was nice for me, of course, being Mrs Zero. But by the time I left him zero was an over-estimate.'

'But at the start?'

She laughed. The bell for the next race was rung and those of the crowd still interested moved down to the rail.

'The heat was bad then,' she said, and pressed her hand against her forehead. 'In 1976. I knew both of them. They broke up after the crash. I got the impression he'd offered to marry her. Anyway, the crash changed everything. We'd known each other before and we drifted back.' She watched the dogs being manhandled into the stalls. 'It was good at the beginning.'

The starting pistol cracked and a fresh set of dogs burst out of their traps. Dryden watched the dust the dogs kicked up drift across the floodlit sky.

She put her arms around her knees and drew them up. 'She must have hated him. To do that. Give his son away.'

'Any idea why?'

She looked at him then and he could see her eyes were in the past. A hot night more than a quarter of a century ago.

'No. Johnnie was local. Webbed feet, the lot. He was even glamorous – for the Fens. Blond. What passed for trendy. And nineteen, with a good job driving vans for the building company. That's glamorous round here.'

The race was finished and the dogs, suddenly robbed of the incentive of the speeding hare, milled about while their trainers tried to collar them.

'And the baby – Matty – was, what? Rebellion, passion, a mistake?'

She laughed again, this time for real, and Dryden glimpsed the fifteen-year-old in the mini-skirt.

'All three. Rebellion for her, passion for both of 'em. A mistake, too: what a start in life.'

'They were a couple, then. Everyone knew?'

'No way. Her just sixteen? They met on the QT. That's where Matty come from. She used to tell me, you know. Romance then, I guess. Moonlight meetings in the woods. They had a secret place. She wouldn't tell me where it was – that was their special secret. So they made Matty. She was proud of that, it wasn't a problem for her. She'd have brought him up on her own if she had to, but they wouldn't have it at Black Bank. Her father was a tough man. Fen farmer. She brought the bruises to school sometimes. He wanted her to bring the father home. Any father.'

'But Maggie didn't want him?'

270

'God knows why. There were worse; most of 'em were worse. He turned out bad, but it didn't have to be that way.'

There was a break in the racing. Kiosks were selling hot-dogs. Dryden bought two and they ate in silence. He tried to imagine the scene that night: the smoking ruin out of which Maggie had walked. 'So she saw her chance, and gave the boy away. And she never said why? Even to you?'

She stood, smoothing down the cheap blue uniform with the sprinting greyhound on the shoulder. 'She never visited him in hospital afterwards. She was out in a few days but Johnnie was in and out of hospital for weeks. Skin grafts, stuff like that. They didn't get it right first time, made a hell of a mess of his hands. She wouldn't go near him. So I visited him. I guess I knew what I was doing, but life isn't fair, is it? And if she didn't want him, why not? He was a charmer was Johnnie.

'Anyway, she married the following year. A Breckland farmer. At Black Bank she was lonely, haunted. So she found herself a husband and a new home. He was in his fifties . . . a bachelor, I think. Don? Yes, Don. They moved away and got a manager in at Black Bank. Bit of a surprise when she came back with the baby – Estelle, wasn't it? Don died young, so she sold up and returned home. I never understood why. I think she liked being haunted. Perhaps the ghosts were all she had.'

Dryden nodded. She stood, clipping on her sales tray with its race cards.

'But they weren't all ghosts. She knew Matty was still alive. Perhaps she thought he'd come back one day. Why do you think she gave him away?' asked Dryden, rising. It was the only question without an answer. 'Did you ever hate Johnnie?'

'Constantly, and with a passion at the end. The only

passion by then. But that was because of what he was. And he was what he was because of Matty.'

'He got into trouble – the police.'

She laughed. 'You could say that. After Maggie his life fell apart, really. I was there, and I think that helped, otherwise it would have been worse. But he was into anything that would make money fast – petty theft, porn, all sorts. He went inside a couple of times . . . but I was long gone by then, although I guess I got a cut – he never missed on the divorce payments. Odd sense of duty, he never showed it when we were married.'

Dryden scanned the crowd, looking at faces, looking for answers. 'Did anyone else live or work at Black Bank who might know why she gave Matty away?'

She lit up a fresh cigarette. 'Yeah. Early on. There was an aunt at Black Bank. The father's sister. Spinster – that's what we called them then. Constance. OK, really. In her forties then, I think. She'd be seventy-odd now. She came to help on the farm, in the house. But she was gone by the time the crash happened. I guess it didn't work out . . . she was a lot smarter than Maggie's parents. She didn't fit in. She left for a job – librarian? Possibly . . . I've got it in my mind she got married in the end and emigrated.'

'What was her new surname?'

She shrugged. 'Tompkins I think. Thompson? They had family in Canada, the north.' Dryden imagined the snow again, falling in ice cold flakes on to his upturned face.

'Canada?' he said, opening his eyes. She was ready to go, so he tried a last question. 'Did you ever see Maggie again?'

'Once. I was out in Ely, shopping. It must have been five years after the crash, more. She was with the daughter and I remember thinking how lucky she was. That kid was beautiful. Maggie wasn't ugly, you know, but she was a Fen farmer's daughter. Heavy bones, and the skin – potato white we used to call it at school. But the little girl was perfect, like kids can be. Cute, that olive skin, and the butter-yellow hair.

She stood. 'Kids are a blessing,' she said, and left.

38

The river slapped itself against the bank like a wet fish as the last of the pleasure cruisers swept past the quayside and turned into the marina. Customers on the verandah of the Cutter Inn sat happily, oblivious of the fact they were being eaten alive by Fen mosquitoes. It was the end of another long summer's day, and a hint of a mist was hauling itself out of the river.

Dryden left Humph parked up on the bank with his Greek language tape, six diet chicken and mayonnaise sandwiches, and a miniature bottle of Metaxa 3-star brandy. He got himself a pint of bitter in the pub and cradled a well-wrapped bottle of decent whisky under one arm. He needed more information about Johnnie Roe's secret life, and the Water Gypsies traded in best single malt.

Did Lyndon or Estelle know Johnnie was Maggie Beck's lover? Did they know that they'd met at the pillbox as lovers?

He set off south along the river bank past the ghostly white forms of the floating gin palaces which made up 80 per cent of the summer traffic on the main river. Each one was a hymn in fibreglass to the enduring bad taste of the English middle classes. Brass bristled at every vantage point while miniature ensigns and Union Jacks hung from useless masts.

Life, such as it was, within these floating suburban semis was oddly public. In one, a large middle-aged woman was lying on a bunk bed eating chocolates in her bra and knickers, presumably under the impression that while she could see passers-by on the towpath they couldn't see her. In the next a couple traded insults over a folding dinner table stacked high with a takeaway curry and a two-litre bottle of Chianti. In a third a large Dobermann pinscher scrabbled its paws along the porthole windows as Dryden hurried past with his pint.

Soon he left the up-market tastelessness of the summer tourist trade behind. The bright lights of the Cutter disappeared round a bend in the river and the moorings were taken up with narrow boats. Some were in darkness and even in the late evening of a long summer's day the accumulated damp of a dozen spendthrift winters was in the air. Most bore the scars of homemade patches and makeshift repairs. A few sported wind generators, and even cheap solar panels.

Dryden took a gulp from his pint, pausing by the *Solar Wind*, a narrow boat painted jet black but studded with hand-painted stars. The windows showed no light but from somewhere the distinct aroma of hash drifted with the mist off the river. Dryden treated himself to half a dozen lungfuls and pressed on. He found the *Middle Earth* at the end of the line. It had four rectangular windows at towpath level and light flooded out of all of them. This far out along the towpath passing walkers rarely strayed. There were no lights on shore and the reputation of the boat's crews guaranteed a certain exclusivity.

Dryden approached the first lighted window and watched without surprise a male bottom rising rhythmically, accompanied by faint whimpers of pleasure. Dryden expected similar scenes might be viewed in the other windows, but he checked each to make sure.

'Excellent,' he said, finishing the pint of beer. 'An orgy.'

He put a foot on the narrow boat's back landing stage and thumped hard on the roof of the *Middle Earth*, settling his now empty pint into one of the flower pots.

A motheaten man with no clothes and a wayward erection threw open the rear double doors.

'Nice out,' said Dryden, grinning.

'Dryden. What the fuck do you want?'

Dryden looked suitably affronted. He held up the bottle of malt whisky. 'I've got this for Etty – and a tenner for information received.'

Etty appeared, having recently extracted herself from under the pink bottom. Dryden felt a brief but intense surge of jealousy.

'Dryden. Welcome. Why the clothes?'

'Call me conventional. Can I . . . ?'

Garments were being hastily draped over various genitalia and all the blinds on the *Middle Earth* were belatedly drawn. Dryden counted five girls and three men and tried not to work out what had been going on. Someone produced glasses and he poured out the malt.

There was a satisfying fug in the closed compartment enhanced by the aroma of a recently devoured vegetable curry. Tin dishes with livid green stains obscured the map table. The light came from a single storm lamp with a gas wick. A calendar hanging by the sink listed organic recipes while on the draining-board a pile of freshly picked carrots waited to be washed. Dryden guessed these had been liberated from a nearby field.

Etty sniffed the tenner Dryden had given her and secreted it amongst the underclothes which surrounded her. 'I was actually looking for some more information,' said Dryden, sipping his own malt.

The bloke with the erection and one of the girls shuffled off towards the forward cabin, presumably to conclude unfinished business.

But Etty had sharpened up, overcoming the effects of whatever she'd been smoking. 'About . . .'

'Johnnie Roe. The people smugglers. They used to use the Ritz, but now that's closed down. And they had people living up at the old air base at Witchford. The police are on to that too. So – unless they've stopped the lorries, which I doubt, they must be operating out of somewhere else. Any idea where?'

'Why would we know . . . ?' It was Etty's partner. He was thin, with sandy hair, and a pointy beard like Catweazel. He began to roll a plump spliff. When he lit it he took about a centimetre off the beard, and there was a faint smell of old-fashioned barbers in the air.

Dryden ignored him and looked at Etty. 'There's some new pickers out for the harvest,' she said. 'They arrived the day before yesterday. My guess is their papers are phoney. They get dropped off by van for the night shifts. They don't know exactly where they're living and their English isn't great, but I heard them talking. There's a lot of languages, but English is the only one they share. They call it the silos – where they're sleeping. They're pretty unhappy with it as far as I can gather – no shops around, no nothing.'

'Silos?' said Dryden.

Etty finished her malt and licked her lips. 'A cluster of them. It has to be Sedge Fen. The old grain works.'

39

Laura's room was silent and flooded with light. The COMPASS machine trailed a six-foot tickertape. Dryden knew, sensing the incoherent patterns, but sat by the bed and studied the letters anyway. Half-way down, still lost in the random signals, he took Laura's hand, knowing it was for his own comfort rather than hers. When he reached the foot of the tickertape he kept his eyes down, folded the tickertape, and kissed her once.

The messages had stopped, he knew that now. He stood by the window in flat, cheerless heat and thought about what it meant for him if she had finally retreated, back into the coma which had engulfed her after the crash in Harrimere Drain. It meant that the nightmare was coming true. A lifetime spent at the foot of a hospital bed pretending to talk to a comatose figure which used to be his wife. A dialogue of self-deception he felt he could neither face nor abandon. As in all true nightmares, escape was beyond his control.

'If you're not there, why do I have to be?' he asked out loud.

He waited for an answer, feeling the anger lift his pulse rate. The silence in The Tower was complete, until he heard the caretaker in the corridor outside.

It was Ravel this time, *Bolero*.

'The whistler,' said Dryden, and kissed Laura's hand.

Out in the corridor he heard the sound of a pail of water being slopped on to a floor. Through a door he found his way on to a cast iron spiral stairway. When the door slammed behind him the light fled, leaving him blinded. Looking down through where he imagined the open metal rungs of the steps to be he sensed rather than saw the faint glow of distant, reflected light. Edging down he stumbled repeatedly on the narrow, triangular steps.

The light came from a series of four bulbs strung, like half-hearted illuminations, along fifty yards of cellar corridor. The pools of darkness between were deep and cool, the lights picking out a brutal black and white pattern of shadow along the bare brick walls. Under the far light the caretaker was working, expertly using his weight to push the mop forwards, backwards, and forwards again.

Dryden watched from the shadows. The caretaker was perhaps sixty, tall, but with a spine bent into a curve by years of labour. A minute passed and then a kettle's whistle blew. He straightened his back, took his mop and pail and disappeared through a doorway. The whistle died. Then the music began. Bruch, the violin concerto, swelled to fill the damp air.

Under cover of the London Symphony Orchestra Dryden walked to the door and looked in. It was a sitting room of sorts. A single table, single chair, and a single bed were the only furniture. A bookcase, made of planks on bricks, filled one wall. On the other narrow, vertical, wooden tape holders. There were hundreds, possibly thousands.

'Quite a collection,' said Dryden, in a pause in the Bruch.

The caretaker wheeled round, the tin cup he held shaking instantly. Dryden could only imagine what kind of life had produced a face like that. In the cellar's half light the deep lines were as sharp as knife wounds, the eyes hooded and cast down. Without looking at Dryden he walked to the tape recorder and hit the stop button, holding his finger on it for a few seconds before speaking. It was the recorder Dryden had bought Maggie. Its predecessor, a moulded 1970s version three times as big, stood beside it still.

The voice was a revelation, pitched high, clear and pleasantly musical. 'I'm sorry, I thought they'd left it behind. I . . .'

Dryden held up his hand. 'Keep it. It's not important. Was there a tape inside?'

The caretaker looked puzzled. 'A tape? Yes, yes . . . I'm sorry. I didn't think . . . Again. I'm sorry. So sorry.' He rummaged amongst the flotsam and jetsam of a kitchen drawer. He held up the tape, the fingers of his hand trembling clearly, and Dryden took it, turning it like a diamond in his hand.

Dryden left and as he climbed the stairs he heard the Bruch swell out again.

Outside, Inspector Newman had parked his Citroën next to Humph's cab. They were busy ignoring each other as Dryden appeared, flopping into the passenger seat beside the policeman. 'Anything new?'

The back seat of the car was nearly obscured by Newman's photographic equipment. He'd clearly been up to the coast in pursuit of the Siberian gull.

'If you count an ID on the body in the fire house at Mildenhall, yes,' he said. 'This is unofficial, OK?' Dryden nodded. 'Bob Sutton. Teeth gave it away – military work. We got the X-rays from Singapore. He was a Red Cap. Perfect match. Wife's upset.'

'Getaway. Some people, eh?'

Newman refused to take the bait. 'Which sort of cuts him out as number one suspect for torturing and killing Johnnie Roe.'

'Why does it rule him out? He had a great motive. His only daughter had been lured into that pillbox, raped, abused. She'd been drugged, and for all he knew at that time murdered as well. He must have thought Johnnie Roe knew where she was. Perhaps he was trying to get it out of him.'

'So who killed Sutton?'

'You tell me. But he's still my call on Roe's torturer,' said Dryden, watching Humph tear open a pre-wrapped sandwich.

'Great,' said Newman, viewing the cabbie with distaste. 'Two killers, not one.'

As he got out Dryden tried a last question: 'The bag in the pillbox. The picture, the food. It was Emmy Kabazo's?'

'Yup. Dad identified it for us during questioning before his release on bail. Doesn't put him in there though, does it? And it's Bob Sutton's prints on the knife, anyway. Work that one out.'

Jimmy Kabazo hugged himself and thought of Emmy, his son. He smelt his hair and the memory quickened his heartbeat. Then he lifted the rifle barrel to his lips and kissed the cool stock, leaving two lips of condensation on the dull yellow gunmetal. He watched the lips fade and then whispered 'Emmy' as he lowered his eye to meet the icy metal oval of the gunsight. The target crosshair swam slightly through a tear, and then cleared to reveal a crisp cross.

He swept the telescopic sight across the familiar contours of Sedge Fen. The main silos stood in an urban cluster rising out of the black peat flatlands. The Victorians had built them, and the New Elizabethans had let them rot. Each, empty now, was an open throat to the sky. The crows circled in the early morning heat, rising from their roosts inside.

At the foot of the silos clustered the little agricultural city which had been Sedge Fen. Storage sheds, machine shops, offices, canteens, a first-aid block and the charge hands' tied cottages. And at the edge of the complex, beneath an elevated and dilapidated conveyor belt, the loading bays where the produce had been dumped into the railway trucks for Ely Dock, and then London. Through the gunsight Jimmy watched a rat investigate some rotting grain sacks, its long tail stiff and silvery.

He shivered, not because the cool morning air was warming, but because he knew he would use the gun today. It would be Emmy's last revenge: the skinhead.

He'd botched his first revenge. Jimmy sobbed with the memory, the tears welling again. He thought of Emmy, and the body in the mortuary that was all that was left of Emmy, and the pain doubled him up. He clutched his arms around his chest and waited for the despair to subside.

He looked around him, but the room was comfortless. Red brick stripped of plaster, the concrete base where the diesel pump had stood, and the single window through which the sun poured on to the dusty floor. It had provided him with the perfect eyrie. A lonely water pumping station, long abandoned, far enough away to avoid their perfunctory patrols, but within range. Well within range.

He pressed his forehead against the floor and spoke into the dust. 'Cheated,' he said.

He'd waited that first time too. By the Ritz, in the Wilkinson's van, half a mile along the main road by an emergency telephone. He'd waited all night for Emmy with the bag, so that he'd have something to eat while they took him to the old airfield. Something for comfort. An excuse really, an excuse to see his son after nearly eighteen long months of lonely exile. And just after midnight a lorry had swung into the lay-by and the driver killed the lights. But Jimmy didn't move. He knew the warnings the smugglers had given. That the police would run a lorry too one day, to catch the middle-men. So he waited for the driver to unload, for Johnnie Roe to appear from the Ritz. But the minutes had slipped by and nobody had come. And so the lorry had powered out, the gears crashing angrily.

So Jimmy left the bag with the presents behind the Ritz, hanging from the door handle, and went to work. Smiling to work. The next evening the bag still hung there, like a head in a noose. So he switched to day shifts and watched each night from the van. He'd thought how much he loved his son, and how stupid he had been to entrust his life to the people smugglers. To the skinhead.

Two days gone. On the Friday night the square man full of muscles had parked up and examined everything like a policeman. He'd held open the top of the Tesco bag with a pen, using a miniature spotlight to look inside. With a bunch of keys he'd worked on the Ritz' locks until the back door had jumped open. Inside, he'd made the unit rock as he searched, the spotlight occasionally shooting out through the gap around the serving hatch. Outside, he'd found something on the ground. Jimmy sensed the excitement as the man squatted down on his haunches in the dust and then, straightened, had walked carefully eastwards towards the fen. Jimmy had feared for Emmy then. What did the man want? What had he found? And then the square man had returned to his car. Swiftly, as though a decision had been made. Not tonight, perhaps. But the next night he'd come again, and this time he'd brought a larger torch, and a rucksack, and he'd taken the bag, Emmy's bag, and walked off across Black Bank Fen.

So Jimmy followed, taking the car jack from the boot to keep his courage hot. Across Black Bank Fen, behind the square man with the Tesco bag that held his son's life. Across Black Bank Fen until they reached Mons Wood, and the pillbox in the moonlight.

Was Emmy inside? Jimmy waited as the square man went in and he listened, hoping with such a violent intensity to hear his son's voice that he conjured it up. He heard 'Papa'. He heard 'Help'; an hallucination more powerful than any sound he'd ever really heard. So he called out Emmy's name – but it was the square man who came out. And he had blood on his hands. He wouldn't have killed him if the muscled man hadn't been so strong. He hit him with the jack from the car, across the chest. But the fool ducked and took the blow across the forehead and just grunted, standing there, stupidly. Even in the moonlight Jimmy saw the shock in his eyes. So Jimmy hit him again and recognized the sound; the sticky soft crunch of the cranium folding into the brain. That's how his father had killed the cow a lifetime ago, a single blow, destroying the head and turning the eyes white.

So he left him in the grass and ran inside but Emmy wasn't there. Only the man from the Ritz. The man with the cigarette hair, strung out across the floor, reaching for the empty glass. Pathetically he thought Jimmy had come to save him. So he begged for the glass. Begged for the water. There was blood around the man's mouth which trickled as he spoke. Jimmy guessed the square man had hit him. A bruise, oddly green in the moonlight, was rising quickly over the man's cheek and eye, distorting his face.

The contents of the Tesco bag had been dumped on the straw floor. Jimmy looked down at them stupidly and the man from the Ritz saw his chance.

'I told him. I don't know – don't know whose they are. I missed the lorry. Tuesday. I missed it. Perhaps it was for them? I don't know.' Then his eyes turned again to the glass on the shelf and he almost whispered it this time. 'A drink?'

So Jimmy asked him where Emmy had gone. Where they'd all gone. What was the plan if the drop was missed? Was there a plan? But he wouldn't say, or he didn't know. And then when Jimmy didn't give him the water he made something up, babbling rubbish to win himself the water. Jimmy had felt anger then, and humiliation. He felt a fool, manipulated always by the white men who ran his life, the men who had lost his son. A simple bargain they had failed to keep. They'd taken the money and his son. The anger made him swoon.

So he left the glass on the ledge. And then he ran, hearing the man's screams diminish slowly, until he could only imagine them in the silence of the fields.

The humiliation came back now, fresh and powerful. He stood, and took up his post at the open window again, pulling the gunsight to his eye and training it on the loading bays. 'It's where he sleeps,' he said, out loud this time. The skinhead who had driven the lorry. The skinhead the black men paid to do the job. His hatred for the skinhead made him vomit, heaving up over his chin, but at least the taste of the bile stopped him shaking, so he put the crosshairs of the gunsight over the red door they always used, and waited, counting the seconds into minutes.

He thought of Emmy's body in the morgue, but this time there were no tears. He'd kissed him that one last time and although his skin had been cold, as the barrel on the gun was cold, he'd made him a promise as the lips touched his cheek. The skinhead. Then the red door opened and he led them out, the metal in his teeth catching the sun. A truck must be coming. The skinhead blinked in the sunlight and spread his arms wide in an embrace of life, while the others went to flag the truck *in off the drove road. Arms wide, his face to heaven; the skinhead grinned and rubbed his hands in his short, cropped hair. So Jimmy put the crosshairs on his neck, waited a second to make sure they were both still, pulled the trigger, and sent him to hell in a spurt of bright, arterial blood.*

Friday, 20 June

40

Dryden had considered playing Maggie's last tape on the Capri's deck. Did he have the right? Technically it was Maggie's testament, and it had been left for Estelle and Lyndon to hear. But he couldn't wait. He'd try Estelle at Black Bank first, then he'd play it. Still he had one other option to try to find his own answers to the mystery of Black Bank. What he needed was to talk to someone who had been there in 1976, but was prepared to tell the truth now about the Beck family, and its secrets.

Tracking Constance Tompkins down had been easy enough. Estelle was not answering calls at Black Bank and Johnnie Roe's ex-wife had offered him few details. But she must, he reasoned, be close by to have attended Maggie's funeral. He'd checked with a contact at County Hall and they'd traced her through the files on the county library service. She had emigrated, but she was back now, and drawing a pension. They were happy enough to give Dryden the address once he explained that Maggie Beck's children wanted to contact their great-aunt.

Which had led him here: Fenlandia. The wooden sign on the stone gate post said 'Rest Home', and Dryden felt a familiar surge of nausea at the euphemism. The house stood somewhere in a stand of pine trees at the end of a dreary, dead-end lane out of town. An unnecessary and undiplomatic sign added: DEAD SLOW in letters so large they were hard to read.

Dryden left Humph ordering a bottle of make-believe

retsina at Nicos's taverna and crunched his way up the gravel drive until the building came into view. He was surprised to find it was ultra-modern, boasted two satellite dishes and solar-powered roof panels. In a nod to the more traditional model it had a large conservatory along the building's front-age, overlooking lawns. Wisteria drooped from the eaves in a splash of washed-out purple and ivory.

'Wisteria,' said Dryden happily, thinking it was the perfect plant to reserve for old age.

A line of Lloydloom wicker chairs stood in firing-squad formation behind the smudge-free glass of the conservatory. All were empty except one. He'd rung ahead and the woman who had answered the phone said Mrs Constance Tompkins would love to see him. But she might not say much: 'Mrs Tompkins is with us sometimes, and sometimes not. She's happy either way.'

The rest of the residents were in a TV lounge at the rear. The heat was stifling, but try as he might Dryden could not detect the tell-tale odour of stale urine. Faintly disappointed not to have his prejudices confirmed he talked loudly to everyone he met on the assumption they were deaf. The woman who ran Fenlandia wore a dark suit and could have been a director of a City insurance company. She led Dryden to the conservatory at a military pace.

Mrs Tompkins was reading a novel with rapt concen-tration. The paperback cover was frayed and stained, a Pen-guin Classic from the sixties, lovingly re-read. She didn't look up when they arrived and, while she might have been deaf, Dryden suspected she was just ignoring him.

'I'll leave you alone for a few minutes,' said the proprietor, touching Mrs Tompkins on the arm. 'This is the man I mentioned, Connie. From the newspaper.'

She carried on reading pointedly until she finished a chapter. Then she folded the book and put her reading glasses away. She looked sprightlier than she had at Maggie's funeral, but Dryden guessed she must be seventy-five, perhaps more. She looked like Queen Mary, but in colour. If there was a family resemblance with Estelle he couldn't see it, except, perhaps, around the darting, playful eyes.

'Hello,' she said, and laughed. Dryden felt he'd made a misjudgement somewhere, sometime, about seventy-five-year-olds. 'You want to know about Maggie, don't you? I read the piece.' She pulled a copy of *The Crow* from the side of the cushions she sat on. 'It's got your name on it.'

Dryden sat down. Outside, the sunshine was burning the grass lawn quietly to stubble. The antimacassar on the seat oozed lavender water; he suddenly felt very tired. It took an effort of will to summon up the first question. 'Maggie died before she could tell Matty why she did what she did. I think she planned to tell him. She left some tapes – about her life. Estelle says she never explained, at the beginning at least, why she swapped the children. We know she wanted to give Matty a new life, but what was wrong with the one she could have given him herself? Matty should know – it's what Maggie would have wanted. Do you know, Mrs Tompkins?'

She'd been looking out at the pine trees until then, but now she turned, and smiled again.

'I'm letting go of the past now, Mr Dryden,' she said, leaning forward and tapping his knee with her book. 'It's very therapeutic.'

'But you went to the funeral . . .'

He had her then. He could tell she wasn't sure if he'd been there. 'Do you know? Why she did it?' he asked, and knew instantly that she did. There was pain in her face and he sensed she was tumbling back, towards a period of her life that Dryden guessed had been humiliating – the poor relative taken in out of charity, into an insidious order which put an unmarried woman at the bottom of a tiny social pyramid.

'Maggie was a sweet girl. I don't think Johnnie was all bad, either. Rudderless sort of man, lost, and angry about something. I knew they were seeing each other. He'd done some work on the farm as a picker. She'd been protected at Black Bank, perhaps over-protected. It was a very old-fashioned place, as I'm sure you can imagine. I found it so . . . stifling.'

Dryden watched Connie's bright eyes dancing over the lawn.

'I watched her several times that summer, she'd leave the house in the evening and set out across country. I don't think she thought I was a threat to her so she didn't seem to care that I knew. Assignations,' she added, hugging herself. 'Romantic, I thought then, so I said nothing.'

The pain showed again, even after nearly thirty years. 'She told no one about the baby until she had to. She was very brave about that. She told me first – I think she wanted advice about what to do and how to break it to my brother. She was very matter-of-fact about it, and I think then she believed Johnnie would be her husband. He was scared, of course, but I felt he wanted the child too.'

She let a silence begin to lengthen. A gong sounded discreetly from somewhere within Fenlandia.

'Morning coffee,' said Miss Tompkins, with relief. A woman in a white nurse's uniform brought a tray. Dryden noted the superior biscuits.

'You like it here?' he said, taking one.

'As Maurice Chevalier said in a different context, Mr Dryden, it's better than the alternative.'

'Must be expensive though?'

'Very. I married late and well. Ideal,' she smiled. She

slurped coffee and pressed on. 'Then something happened – to Maggie. She stopped seeing Johnnie.'

'This was when, exactly? Sorry – if you can remember.'

'Oh – I can remember all right. It was her birthday – Maggie's. It was 1976, she'd be sixteen then. February the tenth.'

She stopped then, lost again in the past. 'It was her birthday?' prompted Dryden.

'Yes. Yes. I'd been at Black Bank five years, five wasted years, five years of my life. I'm angry about that, even now. But Maggie had spent her whole life there. It was remarkable she was as normal as she was. I saw her grow up in those years, from a child to a mother in that time. Very little perturbed that child. She was innocent, I know, that's what my brother said when they found out she was pregnant, but innocence isn't stupidity. She was never that.'

'Her birthday?' prompted Dryden a second time.

'Yes. There'd been a party at home. A bit half-hearted, I'm afraid. The baby was a cloud over her parents. Maggie was an only child and I think they had high hopes for her. Suddenly those hopes seemed misplaced. Then Sally had called, that was her friend. She was quite different, very modern. She wore a low-cut blouse that could stop a plough team.'

Dryden thought of the disappointed woman he'd met at the dog stadium. They laughed and sipped their coffee in perfect synchronization.

'I think they'd gone dancing – the old Mecca in Broad Street. It's a bank now but it was pretty much the most exciting place on earth then. I got the impression they'd meet the boys there, as a rule. Anyway, I heard her come in. They'd given me a room in the attic at Black Bank. Servants' quarters, how appropriate!'

The old woman's eyes narrowed with malice. 'Maggie was up there too — a teenager's room next to the old retainer. Ha! That's the problem with my life, things have gone too fast.' She sipped the tea and looked beyond the sunlit garden.

'She came home?'

A nurse approached to remove the tray and touched Connie on the shoulder. 'Connie?' he asked.

She laughed again. 'I'm enjoying Mr Dryden's visit,' she said, clasping his hand.

Her smile vanished with the biscuits. 'Horrible man,' she said. 'Pinches the senile ones for fun.'

She looked into Dryden's eyes then, making her decision. 'I found the photos on the stairs. I got up to see if she was all right; I could always tell. The quick steps and then the sound of Maggie throwing herself on the bed. So I went out and the moon was pouring in through the skylight above the stairwell. And they were there, three of them.'

Dryden didn't help her then. Only she could finish Maggie's story.

'At first I thought they were all of Maggie. I was shocked, of course. But my life has been a lot less cloistered than people seem to think. They were naked, both of them, making love. Tangled up together. I could see it was Johnnie. But then I sat and looked at them when my hands had stopped shaking. And they weren't her at all, they were other girls.'

She tapped Dryden's knee firmly with her book. 'Then I picked up the one she'd torn up. I knew, of course . . . I was putting them together when she came back out. I knew it was her this time. Just like the others. Naked with Johnnie.'

'What did she say?' asked Dryden, the scene Connie had brought to life as vivid as a memory of his own.

'We never said anything. I just gave them to her and said

something reassuring and bland – something about fish in the sea, or experience, or such rot. She took them and went back to her room.'

'And Johnnie didn't come back after that?'

'Apparently. Not for some time, anyway. I left within a few weeks. I'd got a job – a library assistant in Peterborough. I was glad to go. They'd shown charity but never bothered to disguise it as anything else. I wrote to Maggie often. She wrote back. Guarded, of course, but she told me things, about the baby. About how Bill – my brother – wanted her to bring Johnnie to Black Bank, to give the baby a father. I think she was in despair, actually. I even thought she might take her life. I told Bill not to push. But he was quite rude, told me to leave family matters to the family. Very pointed.'

Dryden stood and dropped the blind on one of the windows so that a slatted shadow fell over them.

'What do you think the pictures meant?'

She pushed a call button on the wall beside her. 'Does it matter? Johnnie was always decked out with a camera. He was a pornographer – that's clear, I think. Perhaps he thought the pictures were funny. Perhaps he sold them to his friends. Perhaps he thought it didn't matter. But it did, Mr Dryden. And Maggie made him pay for it in the end by giving away the one thing he really wanted – a son. I don't think she could have faced life with Johnnie, so she gave Matty away and there was no need to marry any more. She'd give Matty a life away from Johnnie, and herself a life away from him. It was very neat, but she paid a terrible price, didn't she? And the worst thing, of course, is that the price went up as the years went on.'

The proprietor came up behind them.

'Goodbye, Mrs Tompkins,' said Dryden, rising. 'One last question. You didn't keep in touch with Maggie, or Estelle?'

'We move on, do we not? I told my husband about my life at Black Bank and he was horrified – he said it sounded Dickensian. He didn't want anything to do with them, and Maggie moved anyway – from Black Bank. A few Christmas cards . . . then it was easier to send nothing.'

'Lyndon needs to know why . . . Perhaps, could you?'

She took his hand for the last time. 'You tell stories for a living, Mr Dryden. Tell this one for me.'

Back in Humph's cab Dryden sat and tried not to think. He flipped down the vanity mirror and looked again at the picture he had downloaded to his PC that morning: a happy wedding-day shot, confetti on the groom's smart pilot's uniform, brother kissing sister. The visceral age-old revulsion swept over him again, and he tried to imagine what it felt like for them.

He found Maggie's last tape in the glove compartment. 'Black Bank,' he said, and hoped it was for the last time.

41

'Dry lightning,' said Dryden, as Humph's cab bumped through the gates to Black Bank Farm.

The bolt struck some trees at Mons Wood with a crack like an artillery shell, the light and sound in almost perfect harmony. The tallest pine torched itself, a crackling suicide of sudden purple flame. The sight of fire seemed, incredibly, to deepen the heat. The featureless horizon appeared to pulse, the hot air on the fen boiling over the shadowless fields.

Humph's Capri skidded to a halt in the red dust before the old farmhouse. Estelle was at the door, one hand clutched defensively to her throat. She looked a generation older, but nothing like her mother. Maggie's almost Victorian stoicism was beyond her reach. She looked very modern in the time-less surroundings of Black Bank. And very frightened.

Dryden produced the tape from his pocket and held it up like a trophy: 'I think we should listen to this. It's the last one. She said everything would be explained.'

'Everything is,' said Estelle, her voice crackling like the air. She turned on her heels and disappeared inside the cool blackness of the farmhouse. He found her in the kitchen, up on the wooden worktop with her legs folded beneath her. Beside her was a portable tape recorder.

'Your husband?' said Dryden, leaning against the white-washed wall.

She flinched at the word, then began to twist the draw-strings of her sweatshirt in a tight knot. 'I told him you'd find out. He had some crazy idea we could just live in the

States – Austin, perhaps. Say we were married in the UK. Keep the other secret. Pretend we didn't know about that.' Her hands shook as she lifted a can of Pepsi. 'But you can't keep a secret from yourself. And the passport was wrong. They'd have to change that. So we couldn't just go. Could we?'

Dryden sensed time opening up to let them talk. 'And the tapes . . . she did say why she gave Lyndon away?'

She nodded, not trusting herself to speak. Another lightning bolt struck the peatfields to the east and she jumped, every nerve alive to the fact that her world was being ripped apart: shredded by the lie Maggie had told twenty-seven years before.

'I know too,' said Dryden. 'Constance Tompkins just told me. I went to see her this morning.'

Estelle looked at him. 'We listened to the tapes after the funeral. Lyndon was there. Mum wasn't very explicit, I guess. But it's pretty clear. About Johnnie, Johnnie and the pictures . . . pictures of them, pictures of others. I think Mum was sick. Sick with anxiety. Sick that Lyndon – that Matty – would be abused – sucked into that life. How could she have married him? And in shock. She'd just seen her parents die, die horribly. And then she made that decision, almost instantly. I told Lyndon . . . he has to see it through the eyes of the girl, the girl Mum was.' Water welled freely out of her eyes and down her chin. 'She loved her baby,' she said, as if insisting on a great truth which had been disputed.

'But Lyndon doesn't believe that?'

'I think he feels it's not the reason he wanted. He wanted something else . . . I don't know what, Dryden. Just something that made it OK. This doesn't make it OK. I don't think anything could . . .'

'You knew who the father was, didn't you?'

She looked scared then. 'Mum never said. I think she wanted it forgotten. That's one of the reasons she went away. And Johnnie went away too for a bit. When he did come back he must've kept his distance. She never mentioned him. People forget, even in a place like this. But I knew. Kids, they talk. When we got back to Black Bank I was twelve. I went to the secondary school and I was famous – infamous. I came from the place where the plane had crashed. At the time, everyone knew Johnnie was the father. Why else would he have run into the flames? But you can imagine the scandal. So I found out pretty quickly. Sometimes, for a dare, we'd go to the Ritz and I'd buy a Coke. It was weird. He never knew I hated him.'

'Did Lyndon know?'

'Not before Mum died. But I told him that night – and it was on the tapes.' She bit her lip.

Dryden walked towards the tapedeck. 'Maggie said that the tapes would answer all the questions. We should give her that chance,' he said. He took the last cassette and slipped it into the recorder, and as he did so he felt some of the burden of his promise to Maggie lift. They listened to the silence together and Dryden wondered if it might be blank. Somewhere he could hear seagulls trailing a tractor. Then they heard Maggie's breath, laboured and intimate, unnaturally close. It filled the kitchen with a tangible sense of her, like an answerphone message played back for the first time.

Estelle watched the spools turn with appalled concentration. This was her mother's last testament, save for those few words on her deathbed; the two words nobody ever heard: 'The tapes'.

'Estelle?' The voice was an echo of the woman, speaking directly from what she knew would be her grave. It sounded extraordinarily strong and vital.

'My love,' said Maggie. 'I lied to you as well.'

Estelle covered her mouth and waited to see which way her life would turn.

'We promised each other we'd tell you. But then each year came and went and we wondered why. It made no difference to us. No difference . . . Every Christmas. Every birthday. All those chances missed . . .'

The breathing interrupted her, the failing heart bruising her ribs.

'Then Don died. Don died and it was all down to me. I just couldn't. He loved you too, Estelle, loved you more than anything – more than his life. He said that before he died – believe me – I haven't the breath to lie. He didn't count for anything without you. He told me that for you. His daughter . . .'

She took a breath and held it.

'But you weren't, love. Or mine. We tried to have a family, but it didn't happen. I think it was a punishment for me, although the doctors said it was Don. But it was my punishment for giving Matty away. For walking away from a child. And a punishment for both of us for wanting a son. Only a son.'

The tape clicked off, then almost immediately back on. 'The adoption service promised us a son. It was easier then, even with Don's age. But it went wrong, the family took the boy back at the last minute and it broke my heart, Estelle, broke my heart again. So we said we'd be happy to take the next child. We didn't mind then if it was a boy or a girl. We just wanted it . . . wanted you. And when Don brought you home I loved you from the minute I first saw you. I loved you like my own . . . more than my own.'

Estelle was frozen. 'Mum,' she said, and began to cry again. 'More than my own,' said Maggie again. 'A few people knew. But Connie had gone, and I didn't really have anyone I could tell at Black Bank. So we thought it was best left. School: it worried us. That you might be teased. So we brought you back to Black Bank as our child. You are our child, love.'

Out on the fen seagulls wheeled, calling, sensing the long drought was about to break. The laboured breathing on the tape returned and slowly tapered into sleep. Dryden switched it off.

'My God,' said Estelle, and Dryden knew instantly that she was thinking about Lyndon. About the consequences of another lie.

'Where is he?' said Dryden.

'My God,' she said again.

'Laura told me to watch out for Freeman White – Lyndon's roommate.'

Estelle just said 'Laura', and cried again. 'We didn't know she could hear us. I'm sorry. We just used to talk. About us. About what to do after Mum died. We didn't do it in front of Mum because she could hear us, even, sometimes, when she slept. We couldn't be sure. We wanted to surprise Mum – about us, when she was better. We still thought that then – that she would get better. And after she died we went back to pick up her things. Laura must have heard. We talked about what to do. We thought she was in a coma. I'm sorry.'

Dryden nodded so that she could go on: 'We asked Freeman to follow you. We were desperate. You were asking questions, so many questions. I couldn't refuse because you were right, it was what Mum wanted. She wanted it all out. And you came out to see us. We thought you were close to finding out about the marriage.'

'And the fire at the register office? White too?'

She looked him in the eyes, a silent affirmation. 'We

thought it would destroy the evidence. Give us some time to think. We told Freeman not to hurt you. Lyndon told him that. But Freeman owes him everything, his life, really, because of Al Rasheid. Lyndon kept him alive, gave him water, food. When the Americans got to Al Rasheid they were both nearly dead. Freeman knows that, the loyalty's fierce. So he agreed to help, when we told him we just needed to know if you'd got close. And if you had, we wanted to stop you. Warn you off.'

'Where's Lyndon?' asked Dryden.

'I have to tell him,' she said. 'Before . . .'

In the silence thunder rolled. 'Has he ever talked about suicide?'

She nodded. 'Sometimes, since Mum died. It got worse – when I wouldn't go back. Back to the States. He left, left here, the night before Mum's funeral.'

Dryden thought *Mum?* but asked: 'And you've no idea where he is?'

'He took the Land Rover and went. Said he'd find somewhere to think. Rent, I guess. He didn't have any friends outside the base. He just wanted to go somewhere that wasn't here, somewhere that wasn't the air force. He wanted space. He said he knew a place . . . out there.' She looked out over Black Bank Fen as another lightning bolt zig-zagged down into a stand of trees.

Dryden counted the seconds before the thunder struck, 1–2–3–4, and then the rumble which made his joints vibrate. She was still looking out. 'He said you'd told him of a place he could go.'

'Me?'

'To be on his own. That's what he said . . . a place you loved. Somewhere like Texas – somewhere he could be free.'

Dryden saw it then as he'd seen it last; the black peat of

Adventurer's Fen stretching out to the reed beds by the river.

'Does he have a mobile?' he said.

'Yes. But he never answers. Just listens to the messages.'

'Ring him. Ring him quickly. Tell him about the last tape. And tell him we're coming.'

The jailer cried, that last time, when Johnnie asked him what he'd done to deserve the torture of the pillbox.

'Just tell me,' said Johnnie, as though the answer marked the only difference between the real world and the hellish distortions of his hexagonal cell.

'I'm being punished. I know that. I'm going to die here. Tell me why.'

Lyndon took the decision then. He'd planned to stay silent, but the appeal was so direct, and he had such an overwhelming answer, he knelt before his victim and took his face in his hands.

'What do you see?' he said, feeling his nails puncture Johnnie's bristled flesh.

Johnnie felt his life hinged here: in an airless pillbox where he'd once made love to Maggie Beck. His jailer's voice, he noticed, was American. It surprised him, where the educated cadences did not.

'I can't see the glass,' he said. Lyndon's head obscured the diamond-like beauty of the water on the shelf.

Lyndon dug his thumbs into the sallow dehydrated flesh. 'What do you see?' he said again, knowing now he would have to give his father the answer. And he knew why he'd avoided speaking until now, for he felt an urge to be tender, to cradle the head of the man who had run into the flames of Black Bank to save his son.

He fought it back, and thought instead of his mother, tortured too by the knowledge that to save her son she must give his life away. 'Think of a mirror,' said Lyndon.

Johnnie tried to think. His mind screamed for water, for the glass beyond the jailer's eyes. His head swam and those eyes filled his world.

'My eyes?' he said, knowing instantly he was right, feeling his heart contract with dread.

'I'm your son,' said Lyndon, and let him, brutally, fall to the ground.

Johnnie fainted then, the thirst beginning to destroy his brain, as it had ravaged his flesh.

When he came to the pain had gone. His mind floated free, and he could consider what he knew with shocking clarity. 'You can't be,' he said, angry that the jailer should torment him further. 'Matty died. In the fire.'

'Maggie switched us. Me and the American kid. She did it to cheat you. Because of what you were.'

Lyndon stood and Johnnie noticed that his fingers shook violently and a nerve in his lean, tanned face was in spasm. 'You made her do it, and it's destroyed my life. Our lives.' He showed Johnnie the wedding ring on his finger, balled his fist, and hit him hard. The cartilage of Johnnie's nose collapsed, pushing up towards the brain, and the blood flowed out in gouts.

But this time Johnnie didn't pass out. He sat back on his haunches despite the cramp in his legs. 'What was I?' said Johnnie, trying hard to remember how he'd lost Maggie, how he'd lost the life he could have had.

'You took pictures. Making love to Maggie. Was it in here? Or did that come later?'

Johnnie remembered then, and felt ashamed that he had forgotten this crime, rather than all the others. 'Later,' he said, looking at the water in the glass as the thirst returned.

Lyndon hated him then, not because of what he'd done to Maggie, but because he couldn't know what he'd done to him. So he wrapped his bleeding hand in his T-shirt, took the glass, stood before his father, and drank it dry.

42

They drove towards Adventurer's Fen under a rotting sky. The drought was dying, overblown with heat, and ants had invaded the dashboard of the Capri, in anticipation of the final storm. The lightning-struck pine tree burned beside the road as they left Black Bank, the crackling static fire in counterpoint to the dull rolls of thunder. Dryden had the window down, and as they pulled past the memorial stone to the victims of the 1976 air crash, he felt a wind on his cheek. For the first time that summer it carried the taste of rain.

In the rear-view mirror Dryden watched Estelle. She'd left a message for Lyndon telling him about the last tape, about her adoption. 'We're OK. It's OK,' she'd said, but none of them, least of all her, believed it now. Her eyes told Dryden what she feared. That if they found Lyndon on Adventurer's Fen, they'd find him dead. That the real tragedy was that he'd risked so much for nothing. Had done so much which could not be undone.

Dryden's mobile rang, the signal splintered by the storm: 'Hi. Police have just issued a statement . . .' It was Garry. The signal broke, then made contact again. 'Newman is out there now.'

'Repeat that. Lost most of it,' said Dryden.

'They've found a body at Sedge Fen. At the old processing works under the silos. Gunshot to the head, apparently; high-calibre rifle. Guy at the station says they think it's linked to the people smuggling . . .'

'Arrests?'

'Kabazo. Your mate from the mortuary. Gave himself up at the scene. Sergeant said he was as happy as Larry. They found him standing over the corpse.'

'Get out there. Ring Mitch. He needs to get out anyway, the drought's breaking. These lightning strikes will start fires – some will spread. And there's a wind. These fields are like moondust – there's bound to be a blow or two as well. Tell him to get some shots at Sedge Fen and then cruise round. Got that?'

Garry was gone, lost in a hail of static.

They drove north on the old A10 past fields the colour of sackcloth. Before Southery they turned east beneath a sky beginning to boil with clouds. To the east, coming towards them on an angled path, Dryden spotted the first Fen Blow – a dust storm a mile high and rolling forward like a giant tumbleweed from an outsized Western. It rolled across the sun and a burnished gold shadow dashed across the landscape.

Humph suddenly slowed the Capri, swung it off the metalled road and hit the shingle of a drove road. A small copse of half-hearted pines was a sheaf of fire in the middle of Adventurer's Fen. The rest lay before them as it had always done in Dryden's dreams: 300 acres of blissful solitude and beauty. To the north and west the Little Ouse was its boundary, edged by fields of reed marsh. To the east lay the razor-sharp edge of Thetford Forest, the ancient border between the black peat of the fen and the sandy brecklands.

A single drove road ran down to the river past Flightpath Cottages. A hogweed grew from an upstairs bedroom window and both doors had crumpled in the damp of the last winter. Two 'For Sale' boards stood at crazy angles in the peat.

'I guessed wrong,' said Dryden, amazed that intuition had led him astray.

'There!' said Estelle, at the moment he saw it too. Leaning between Dryden and Humph she pointed down the drove road to the edge of the reed marsh. It was a new house, despite the old reclaimed bricks. It was roofed in slate and an old-style wooden verandah appeared to surround it at ground level. At the southeast corner a tower rose above the second floor, a tiny folly. A kitchen garden had gone to seed on the south side. A gate stood, but no fence. Dryden's heartbeat quickened, but he kept at bay the knowledge that it was with recognition.

Humph rattled down the rutted track to within a hundred yards of the house and then pulled up as the Capri's suspension groaned and cracked under the strain. The white Land Rover, until now hidden behind the house, had come into view.

'Tell him I love him,' said Estelle, terrified, Dryden guessed, at what she would find inside the house. 'Tell him it's OK.'

Dryden swung the door out and in the oppressive silence heard the rust scrape.

He leant back in through the open passenger window. 'I've got something to tell him. Something he still doesn't know,' she said. 'If he's alive, tell him that.'

Humph struggled out on the driver's side, sure testimony that he thought Dryden was about to do something stupid. Dryden nodded to the Capri. 'Stay with her.' Humph simply raised a finger and pointed east to where the forest edge had stood a minute earlier. Not now. The tumbling front of the dust storm rolled out from the trees towards them. Dryden felt his guts liquidize and in the panic of the moment he simply repeated himself. 'Stay with her.'

So Humph ducked back into the Capri and Dryden was

alone when the dust fell. At first it merely shimmered over his skin, accompanied by a slight fall in the light level. A hissing of minute particles of dry earth seemed to fill Adventurer's Fen. Then the light dipped again, the sun disappeared, and the wind began to drive the dust into his eyes, nose and ears. The house had disappeared but the path remained at his feet. Dryden staggered down it, away from where the car had been. He choked once, then stopped, doubled over, and filled his lungs with the air close to the ground. For a minute, less, he ran in a void of orange-brown dust. Then the façade of the house appeared, like cheap scenery, a one-dimensional grey, featureless outline. He threw himself against the door and tried the handle, knowing it was locked. He took another breath from below his knees but this time it too was clogged with dust. The muscles at the back of his knees fluttered with fear. He needed to find a door that opened. The windows, if they were all like the one beside the front door, were double-glazed and locked.

He sensed the lightning bolt before it struck and turned to see it plummet through the gloom, followed by the frenzied crackle of trees burning.

He began to skirt the house, cupping his hands at the first window to the right of the door to view a sitting room, furnished cheaply, with rugs on the polished floorboards, job-lot pictures and unmatched lightshades. There was no sign of life. 'Rented,' he said out loud, pressing his forehead against the window for coolness and sucking in air by pressing his lips to the glass. He left the kiss on the pane and moved on, past another locked door, and round the far corner. The wind here dropped and looking up he could see the weight of the dust storm tumbling over the pitch of the roof. He could smell the earth now, a stringent aroma of blood and rotted wood. The smell of the grave.

French windows extended the length of the verandah at the back of the house. Lyndon Koskinski sat inside, unmoving, on a cheap white sofa. In one hand he held a mobile phone, in the other his GI Zippo lighter. Both hands rested on his lap and his eyes appeared to be closed. The rest of the room was sparsely furnished. A three-shelf bookcase held some cheap volumes, a coffee table a single mug. To one side of the French windows a door stood open. Dryden slipped through and into the kitchen, and closed the door behind him. He gulped the relatively clean air but a layer of dust already covered the MFI fittings and the lino felt gritty under his feet. As soon as he closed the door the hissing stopped, the dust soundlessly pounding the double-glazed window.

The next door was glazed and opened easily into the room with the white sofa. Lyndon didn't turn his head but Dryden saw that a curtain of sweat gave his lean face an oddly reflective sheen. But his eyes were open now, although they were empty of light.

'Lyndon,' said Dryden, and nothing moved.

He took a step forward and caught the smell. He guessed it was petrol – but aircraft fuel was possible. The fumes were rising and billowing out from the sofa. Dryden could see now that it was soaked, the damp dark stain only lightening at the armrests and behind Lyndon's head. Dryden breathed in deeply and felt a wave of fume-induced nausea which almost knocked him down.

'Things have changed,' he said, trying to control his voice.

Lyndon blinked again, slowly like a lizard, but did not turn from the view from the window. 'I know. Estelle told me everything.' He held up the mobile and let it drop in his lap. An empty spirit bottle lay in the folds of the sofa.

'It changes things,' Dryden said again.

'For Johnnie Roe? He's still dead.' He laughed then, and made a frighteningly good job of it. 'The only thing that's changed is that he died for nothing.'

'And you killed him.' As Dryden said it he knew it must be true. The motives were compelling and multiple. Johnnie Roe was the father who had denied him a life, a mother, and finally a wife.

Lyndon smiled then, and Dryden knew the end was near. He fingered the Zippo lighter expertly at his chest. 'Yes. I suppose I did. I never planned to. At first I just wanted to hurt him. You know?' Dryden nodded stupidly. He didn't know. He didn't want to know.

'Hurt him bad. My life – everything, was down to him. Losing Mum was down to him. Al Rasheid was down to him. So I thought I'd recreate it for him. The prison. My cell. I enjoyed that.'

'What did you want?'

'At the beginning I wanted him to confess. We'd listened to the tapes. Maggie told us why she'd given me away. But I wanted to hear him say it. Tell me what he'd done to make her do it.'

'You used the knife,' said Dryden, recalling the intricately decorated Arab dagger.

Lyndon nodded, almost distracted by the memory. 'I got it in Aden – in the Souk, with Freeman.'

Dryden nodded. 'And the manacles? The chain you used?'

'Mine. The jailer at Al Rasheid gave me the key when the invasion of Baghdad began. They let all the prisoners free. He was scared, I guess. It was a final gesture. I walked out.'

'So did he confess?'

'No. But then, I think now, he didn't know his crime. Or hadn't guessed. I wanted him to know. I wanted to punish him for making Mum do it. Telling the lie that's done all this, brought us here. He was dying from the thirst. I could see that. So I watched.'

'Why don't you give me the lighter?' asked Dryden.

Lyndon smiled again. 'Then I just found that guy's body – his head stoved in. Sutton? I read it in the paper – the name. I cried . . . You know? I cried for that guy. I'd seen worse in the Gulf. But he looked kinda innocent. I guess he was.'

He heaved in a breath and choked on the monoxide. 'And then I thought he must have told someone he'd gone to the pillbox. He had a family, people who cared. They'd come looking. And someone had killed him. So someone else knew Johnnie was there. They'd find out what I'd done to him. How I dragged him there, through the dust, and chained him up.

'I had to get rid of Sutton's body.' He looked out at the drifting smoke and dust, untroubled by anything outside his own head.

Dryden tried to stem the fear that was constricting his throat. 'And Freeman White took care of that. He's on the fire crew at the base – it says it on his door. Your door.'

Lyndon tipped his head by way of assent. 'Then Johnnie died. That was the Sunday. I just found him. Taut, like that, and reaching out for the glass.'

'I presume we met at the pillbox,' said Dryden, fingering the blue-black eye.

'Another five minutes and I'd have had the body out . . . I was shocked, you know – shocked that he'd died so suddenly. I didn't expect that.'

Lyndon flipped open the top of the Zippo. Dryden tried to think. 'You can put it back together again. Your life. Lyndon's life. She's in the car.' Lyndon looked up then, but outside there was now only the drifting pall of the dust, darkening by the second. 'She's got something to tell you. She said there was more,' said Dryden.

Lyndon shrugged. 'Murder. In Texas they give you the chair,' he said, fingering his throat. 'Burn. That's what they say: Let 'em burn. Killed his own father. That's me.'

'But not here,' said Dryden.

'Civilized,' said Lyndon, sneering. 'But hey. They might deport me. US citizen . . . but then again. The final laugh on me. Well, well, he ain't a Yank after all. So he can rot in one of our jails. Ten years . . . fifteen? Maybe more.'

'She loves you. Estelle. That's why she's here. She doesn't need to be.'

He held the Zippo at arm's length and lit it once. In the gloomy penumbra of the dust storm it was a brilliant flame. 'She wouldn't come with me. She wouldn't just leave. I knew it was right. She didn't trust me. Didn't believe. She knows that. We'll always know that.'

He flicked the turning ignition wheel on the Zippo lighter and held it to his chest: a tender gesture of almost religious beauty. Like most moments which change people's lives it was enacted slowly, almost mundanely. He was, Dryden knew, dead already. A cold blue flame spread over Lyndon's sweatshirt for what seemed like a miniature eternity. Then the flame flapped like a wing and jumped silently to his arm, and the doused leather seat beside him. Lyndon raised a fluttering hand, despite himself, to ward off the heat. Then the blue flames engulfed him in what looked like a cool shroud. The colder orange flames slipped down to the bare floorboards where the petrol ran in a river towards the kitchen. A beaded curtain of heat rose, blocking the exit.

Then Lyndon began to scream. Even in the moment Dryden thought of Johnnie Roe, his vocal cords shredding in that long hot night.

But this cry was muted, contorted within the blue shroud of flame which was burning his skin. He turned his head rapidly from side to side as the heat bit in, wanting to end his life with the dignity of self-control. But the pain was too much, and the scream broke through the blue shroud and Dryden ran from it, ran anywhere, to escape the agony.

He closed the heavy wooden door behind him as the fire leapt across the room. He was in a corridor as familiar as a nightmare, at the end of which stood a front door like any other. He ran to it, his heart leaping, and turned the Yale lock to open but the door wouldn't move. There was a Chubb below it, locked fast, and no key. So he turned to face the fire which he could hear buffeting the door he had closed. It was an odd place, he thought, to die.

'Not here,' he said, without conviction, as he considered the smoke slithering under the door, and then the tongues of flame which began to curl under, like searching fingers.

Then the door imploded with a silent percussion which popped his ears. In slow motion the wood became kindling. Then a tumbling fireball swept towards him and as he turned his back on it he was yelling – Humph said that later – yelling for water. Then he yelled for anything that would stop the pain which was eating into his back. As he screamed he imagined the worst because he could not see: imagined the flame digging in to the bones of the spine, uncovering them by burning away the thin layers of flesh and muscle. Firing the bone like human pottery.

Which is when he thought of Laura. It was the coolness of her bed which called him. The lack of fire and warmth. The iciness which he desperately craved now. He wanted to be by her bedside for ever, forever cool, under the falling snowflakes which he could summon up when his eyes were closed. They could lie together in a drift, the antithesis of fire.

'Please, God, let her see me again,' he said, and gagging on the gases, he dropped to his knees.

It wasn't his own death that scared him. It was the idea that she'd think he'd left her again, left her like he had in Harrimere Drain, in the flooded car. There were many things he had said since the crash, but only one thing had he repeated each night at The Tower: 'I'll be back.'

'Please, God,' he said, silently this time. 'Let her see me again.'

When he opened his eyes he was an inch from the lock. It was the Chubb: gold, and oddly icy. He put his lips to it and the kiss was as cold as Laura's skin. So he pulled the chain at his neck and the key rose, and he put the key in the lock and even in the screaming chaos of the house in which he should have died he heard it effortlessly tumbling, the locksmith's wheels falling nicely into their allotted slots.

Then he thanked God, shouted his name, and pulling the door towards him, fell out, back into the world which wasn't on fire, his arms flailing in a fiery semaphore.

43

When he came to, Estelle was kneeling, holding him, with his back to the dust storm. Ahead the house still burned, a single column now of cherry-red flame fifty feet high. The pain along his spine was distant, but he knew that it was shock which had dulled it, and that it was blossoming slowly, but relentlessly. The dust storm blew, and somewhere in the hiss of the cloud in which they existed he could hear Humph, up close, on a mobile. 'Yup. Quickly. It's serious,' he said, and Dryden wondered how the cabbie had hurt himself. Dryden was unmoved by the fact that he was still alive. He glugged air, choked on the carbon monoxide, but glugged some more. Estelle's eyes were locked on the burning house, while she held her sweatshirt to her mouth to block the fumes.

Dryden's chest heaved. 'You knew,' he said. He took what air he could. 'Lyndon died thinking he'd killed Johnnie Roe. Thinking he died of thirst. But that's not right, is it?'

She didn't try to deny it. 'No.'

Dryden closed his eyes but could still see the brilliant outline of the house on his retinas. 'You'd been there – to the pillbox. At Maggie's funeral you said Johnnie had been tortured like Tantalus. It was too perfect a description. None of the reports had the details. But you knew . . .'

She watched the fire with the same intensity Lyndon had reserved for the Zippo lighter.

Humph's voice floated into their world. 'They're coming,' he said, and was gone.

She coughed back the fumes. 'He disappeared – after the night Mum died. He knew about Johnnie then, from the tapes. He came past a couple of times and we met at the hospital – to clear away her things. Freeman came too. But I knew Lyndon was struggling, struggling, with all of it. We had to talk. He just wanted to go back home – as if nothing had happened. It was crazy. He was crazy. It wasn't something you could just forget. Then I saw the lights one night – out at Mons Wood. And the Land Rover, in the trees.'

'You found Johnnie?'

'Yes. In Mum's pillbox, she'd talked about it on the tapes. Where she'd met Johnnie. And I knew then that Lyndon had taken him there. I'd thought of revenge too. But what could I do? Then, suddenly, he was there. And I had that power, of life and death, given to me without asking. So I went back the next night with some of the chemicals they use for the fields. Weedkiller. Dad . . . Don, Don always said they were lethal, and to keep them away from kids because they were tasteless. Like water. And colourless. We kept supplies locked up at Black Bank. I thought if Johnnie Roe was that desperate, he could drink that. So I filled the glass with the poison and I gave it to him.'

Dryden said nothing, trying not to see Johnnie's body twisted on the pillbox floor.

'He started screaming. Saying it burnt him inside. So I left.' She turned to Dryden and he sensed she'd taken a decision. She smiled. 'I don't regret it. I never have. I just wish I'd told Lyndon. Why didn't we talk? I wouldn't go back with him. We couldn't get past that. So we hid in silence and then he left.'

They watched the house burn. 'Now Lyndon's gone too,' said Dryden, shaking badly as the shock subsided. The pain was making it difficult for him to think: a pulsing electric pain, branching out from his spinal cord.

'I had something to tell him,' said Estelle, and she let her hands drop to her stomach, where they cradled the flesh. Dryden's head swam, but he knew she was rocking, rocking gently to the sound of the fire.

He knew then why Laura had told him there was another baby.

'A child,' he said, and she turned to him again.

'I wanted to tell him that I didn't go.'

'Go where?'

'The hospital. The last time we spoke we decided. I wouldn't go with him so he said that it would be best if the child wasn't born. I wanted to hurt him then, for being brutal. So I said OK. I said I would get rid of the child. He must have died thinking I had. That's terrible, isn't it? Terrible that he died not knowing there's still a baby.'

Humph appeared before them and the green tinge of sickness on his face told Dryden everything he didn't want to know. 'Your back,' he said. 'There's some burns. They'll be here soon, so sit.'

Dryden nodded and leant on Estelle. The dust storm had vanished as quickly as it had descended on Adventurer's Fen. In the silence the house crackled like kindling.

'Lyndon. How did he die?' she said, standing and taking a step towards the fire.

'The lighter. Petrol, I think. It was over very quickly.'

She twisted her head back in despair: 'Oh Jesus! We never escaped, did we? Any of us. From that fire. From this.'

And she started to walk towards the flames. Dryden stood, felt the fen sweep around him in a dizzy vision, and lunged after her. He clutched at Estelle's arm and then his knees buckled and he brought her down into the dust with him.

The front of the house was charcoal black, but where the door had been a sheet of ruby-red flame still burnt like a shimmering curtain of beads.

'The child can escape,' he said, and blacked out.

Postscript

As the ambulance took Dryden away from Adventurer's Fen the rain fell. Fizzing droplets turned to tiny clouds of gas over the burning forest and dripped from the open rafters of the house that Laura had built. The house she had built for them.

It hadn't just been her secret; she'd shared it with her parents. Six months before the accident at Harrimere Drain they'd come back from Italy, from retirement, on a visit. She wanted to take the money left to her in trust to build the house Dryden wanted, for the family they both wanted. She took them out to the spot and let them feel the thrill of the secret too. The secret she hugged to herself that last summer, even as she understood the shadow it cast over Dryden. But with her parents she agreed to keep the secret, at least for a few more weeks, until his birthday.

After Laura's accident her parents flew back to be at her side in The Tower, and after the weeks in which she might have died had passed, they asked Dryden what he wanted to do with the money in the trust fund. They'd agreed a plan on the flight: if he said he wanted the money they'd tell him about the house on Adventurer's Fen. If not, they'd rent it, bank the money as an investment, and keep the secret in the hope that when Laura came out of the coma she, and Dryden, could enjoy the surprise — at last. It was a sound investment, and a clever compromise. Dryden had told them to invest the money safely. He carried the key she'd given him, and they carried Laura's secret.

Which is why Dryden's key was made to fit a lock in a house which should have existed only in a dream.

Andy 'Last Case' Newman retired happily a month after the deaths on Adventurer's Fen. All three killings, of Bob Sutton, Johnnie Roe, and Winston the people smuggler, appeared on his file as solved. Lyndon Koskinski was Johnnie's presumed killer. Dryden and Estelle kept her secret to themselves. Newman was commended by the Chief Constable. He moved to the north Norfolk coast and shortly afterwards identified a new sub-species of Arctic Tern: Borealis Newmanii.

Estelle gave birth to a baby girl on Christmas Day at Black Bank Farm. She was christened Margaret at St Matthew's. Dryden was invited and they stood before Lyndon's grave in the churchyard afterwards. He'd been buried with Maggie and Don. Dryden, hospitalized after the burns he received at Adventurer's Fen, had only just escaped a wheelchair.

'*What will you tell her?' he'd asked.*

'*Everything,' said Estelle, hugging the baby.*

Lyndon's onetime grandparents in Austin had sent a wreath, which carried a small flag: a white star on a blue background with broad stripes of white and red – the flag of the Lone Star State. But there was no message. Privately, they approached the parish authorities responsible for St Matthew's and paid over an endowment of £500 for the upkeep of all the graves, in perpetuity.

Estelle asked Dryden to ring them. They'd taken the call, listened to a factual account of what had happened, and thanked him. He sensed few emotions, except bitterness and loss.

Jimmy Kabazo pleaded guilty to the murder – reduced to manslaughter – of Winston Edgeley (real name Wayne) on the direction of the judge at Cambridge Crown Court. A similar plea was entered and accepted for the killing of Bob Sutton. The judge, reported verbatim in the Daily Telegraph, *said the crimes were heinous, but the agonized mental state of the defendant was sufficient to warrant a plea in mitigation. Jimmy Kabazo didn't care. He was deported to Nigeria to serve his sentence: ten years, concurrent, on both charges. Dryden saw him briefly at Whitemoor Prison, north of Ely, three months after the trial, and on the eve of his deportation.*

'*How am I to tell her?' said Jimmy of his wife, the smile now gone* for ever. He saw her briefly at Poorloon Jail, Lagos, a week after his return on a scheduled flight handcuffed to immigration officers. The couple never met again. Their son Emmy was buried in the corporation cemetery at King's Lynn and the grave carries no marker.

Alice and Ellie Sutton buried Bob in the cemetery at Ely. The gravestone said: 'Gave his life for his daughter'. They emigrated to Hong Kong.

The memorial stone to the victims of the 1976 air crash still stands: the name of Lyndon Koskinski has been added, as Maggie requested.

Major August Sondheim was diagnosed with cirrhosis of the liver. He took sick leave and flew home to see his daughter. After three months in a Vermont nursing home with Sergeant Rachel DeWitt at his side his health improved and he took early retirement. He is still an alcoholic, but hasn't taken a drink since his disease was diagnosed. He will be a father again in six months' time.

Johnnie Roe's body was released for cremation after a formal inquest returned a verdict of murder. Sally Roe cried alone at home for what might have been. Peter Selby, eventually charged with aggravated rape and indecent assault, asked for eighty-three similar charges to be taken into account. He named five other defendants before his appearance at Peterborough Crown Court. All were found guilty on all charges. Selby got twelve years, the rest fourteen. He was murdered in prison with a Stanley knife, the killer unknown.

Captain Freeman White was released from police custody after being questioned about the death of Bob Sutton. Owing to insufficient evidence no charges were ever brought. He was discharged from the US Air Force two months later at Edwards Air Base, New Mexico. His record remains clean and distinguished by the award of a Purple Heart for valour in Iraq. He cashed in his military pension for a lump sum and bought a motorcycle repair business in Austin.

Humph spent the following Christmas in Thessalonika. He is now learning Walloon.

Dryden suffered third-degree burns to his upper back, left shoulder and left arm. Extensive skin grafts were needed. The operations were performed at The Tower. He took Maggie's bed to be near Laura, and told her the whole story. The COMPASS machine delivered no further messages.

When he was well enough to walk he stood at the foot of Laura's bed and told her what he was going to do. The insurance money had come through after the fire. He would rebuild Adventurer's Fen and rent it out again. It would be their home one day. One day soon. Then he went out and met a surveyor on the land.

While he was out the COMPASS machine chattered into life.

SAHDNF HGY DSPP DFHGI SIOOOOIFIWFOWEF ADG S S HJGUT I LOVE YOU FGFKJSHJAO AAJA

The Moon Tunnel

JIM KELLY

Now available in trade paperback
Michael Joseph £10.99

In the past. In a claustrophobic escape tunnel beneath a PoW camp in the Cambridgeshire Fens a man crawls desperately forwards. But ahead only death awaits him.

In the present. Journalist Philip Dryden is reporting on an archaeological dig at the old PoW camp when the body is uncovered. But there is something odd – death was from a gunshot to the head, and the position indicates the man was trying to ge *into* the camp not escape it.

Then a second – more recent – body is discovered . . .

Read on for a taster . . .

The man in the moon tunnel stops and listens to the night above, shivering despite the sweat which trickles into his ears, making them flutter like the beat of pigeons' wings. He stops crawling forward, bringing relief to the agony in his elbows and knees, and places his torch ahead, resting his forehead on his hands, shielding his face from the damp clay floor. The ring on his finger glitters by his eye and he thinks of her, feels her skin and traces, in his imagination, the S-curve of her waist and thigh. He holds the image like a talisman, pushing back the panic which makes him choke, feeling the mass of the suffocating earth above his head. His heartbeat fills the narrow space and he tries to conjure up the image of the sky above.

At that moment, as he lays paralyzed below, the shadow of the night cloud begins to drift across the harvest moon. Over the Fens life freezes as the shadow crosses the land, bringing darkness to the soaking fields and the silent river. Rats float with the sluggish stream on the Forty Foot; and pike in The Old West, moonbathing, slip to the safety of the banks. Eels, thrashing through the long grass to forage on the rotting carcass of a sheep, turn instantly to stone. Finally, the newly shrouded moon is gone, and the world below lies still and waiting.

He must go on, or die here. So he feels for the wooden panels in the tunnel side and counts on: 185, 186, 187. He focuses only on the numbers, blocking out the reality of what he is doing, of where he is, and what is above. The camp sleeps inside its flesh-tearing wire. A village of shadows, more substantial than the men themselves had ever been, diminished by their exile. The dreams of prisoners still pushing that night at the double-locked wooden shutters.

'Buried alive,' he thinks, and the fear makes him cry out despite himself.

He counts again, trying to ignore the panic which constricts his throat: 230, 231, 232, 233. He stops and curls his body so that he can play the torch light on the wood. There it is: emblazoned on the single pine board in faded stencil: *RED CROSS*.

He slips the jimmy from his belt and between the panel edges, easing the wood out from the earth behind. A neat chamber beyond, panelled, like a subterranean letterbox. Inside a tall waxed oilskin pouch. He grasps it, like a tomb robber, knowing his face will be ugly with the greed which had driven him there.

He lays the torch down again and taking his penknife cuts the twine so that the pouch falls open. The candlestick catches the light, the silver tarnished. Judging its worth he sets it aside. Only the rolled canvas remains, and so his anger mixes with disappointment: is this really all? He cuts a second thread and the picture unfolds: sepia clouds, a visionary shepherd looking up, and the half-obscured disc of the full moon, and lying on the picture the pearls, as white as teeth, making him smile.

'Beautiful?' asks a voice, but not his own.

He fumbles with the torch but is too slow to see his killer. The flash of gunshot lights the tunnel ahead like the arcing lightning that marks the passage of the night train. Deafened, he never hears the sound that kills him. But he feels the hand, clawing at his fingers and the ring, before the panels above his head, splintered by the percussion of the blast, begin to twist and the earth first trickles, then falls. And, as the weight of the clay crushes his ribs he hears a scream, and knows it isn't his.

The gunshot, heard above, breaks the spell. A cloud of lapwing rises, like smoke over the river and a starburst of light touches the upmost edge of the darkened moon, and time begins again for almost everyone.

I

Thursday, October 21st

Humphrey H. Holt's licensed minicab stood on Ely market square in the dense, damp heart of an early morning smog. 'Humph' cleaned a fresh circular porthole in the steamed-up windscreen and peered out: nothing, he could have been shrouded on an icefloe in an Antarctic mist. Shivering, he realized he could just see the outlines of the nearest buildings, the old Corn Exchange and the Cinema, and a single postbox like a hunched figure, just on the edge of sight. Beyond them the vast bulk of the cathedral loomed, but only in the memory. A duck stood on one leg on the glistening red bricks of the square, its head tucked under a damp wing, while a cat tiptoed by and was gone.

The first leaf of autumn fell from an invisible sycamore and settled on the windscreen of his beloved Ford Capri. The cabbie considered it morosely before swishing it aside with the wipers. The smog had enveloped the town for three days now, a suffocating blanket which left an acrid taste on the tongue and made Humph's small, baby-blue eyes water. He rubbed them, and thought about a nap, but decided the effort was too great this early in the day. Instead he turned up the cab's aged heating system, and gently wriggled his body until every one of his sixteen stones was comfortably arranged. He was not so much sitting in his cab as wedged into it.

He punched the 'on' button of the tape deck with a nimble, lean finger. The first instalment of his latest language course flooded the cab with sound: conversational Polish, for beginners. As he repeated Justina's greeting to the old village lamplighter he looked east himself, down Fore Hill, towards the Black Fen below. The mist buckled briefly, like a giant duvet being aired, and through the gap he glimpsed the blue smudged horizon as distant, and flat, as any on the great plains of Eastern Europe.

Philip Dryden, chief reporter on *The Crow*, slapped his hand on the cab roof, pulled open the passenger side door and crashed into the seat. At six- foot-three inches his angular frame had to be folded to fit into Humph's cab – the knees up, and the neck slightly bent. He wore a heavy black overcoat which was spangled with droplets of mist.

'Well that was highly entertaining,' he said, by way of greeting.

He tossed his notebook into the glove compartment, swapping it for one of the tiny miniature bottles of liquor Humph collected on his regular trips to Stansted Airport. Dryden snapped off the bottle top and took a swig of Talisker, single malt. Humph, sensing a sociable moment in their otherwise adversarial relationship, helped himself to a small *crème de menthe*.

Dryden closed his eyes and threw his head back. His face was early Norman, a medieval arrangement of sombre, geometric features which could have graced the back of any coin from the Conquest to Henry V: a straight brow, jutting cheekbones, and deep-set green eyes, while the black hair was thick and short. His age was thirty-something, and would be for a decade yet.

'I feel like I've been injected with concrete. I was so bored I nearly passed out,' said Dryden. 'Two people did.'

Humph laughed inaudibly, emitting a vaguely suspicious odour of cabbage and curry. Dryden lowered the window despite the damp, and took a second swig. One of the shops on the square had just reopened after a decade of stately dilapidation and now specialized in camping, climbing gear and outdoor pursuits. A mildly famous Alpine climber had been drafted in to cut the red tape. Dryden had been there to find a story.

'The Fens' own mountaineering supply shop. Brilliant. That's really going to bring 'em in.' said Dryden.

'It might take off,' said Humph, firing the aged Capri into life.

Dryden considered his friend. Humph might be at conversational level in eight obscure European languages but his conversational English was as underdeveloped as the East Anglian Mountain Rescue Service.

'That's quite a recommendation from the owner of the only two-door taxi cab in Ely. That's your unique selling point is it?' said Dryden, enjoying himself. 'You have a Hackney cab accessible to only half the population. And only half of those who can get in, can get out again.'

'It's good for tips,' said Humph, defensively.

'I bet it's good for bloody tips!' said Dryden, enjoying himself.

Humph allowed his rippling torso to settle slightly, indicating an end to the subject. He scratched his nails across the nylon chest of his Ipswich Town FC replica shirt and brought the cab to a sharp halt in a layby in the cathedral close. The mist, suddenly thickening, obscured a buttress of the cathedral down which the damp was running in rivers.

'Where next?' said Humph, by way of a challenge.

Dryden was in no hurry, and indeed had not been a hurry for several years. He turned to the cabbie: 'So. What did the doctor say?'

Humph's physical deterioration had been almost completely masked by the fact that he never got out of his cab.

But a recent bout of breathlessness had prompted a surgery visit that morning.

'Well?' Dryden foraged in his overcoat pocket, and discovering a slightly bruised sausage roll, began to munch it with the Talisker.

'He said I should lose three stone – quickly. He gave me a diet sheet. No chips.'

Dryden nodded: 'What you gonna do?'

Humph swung the cab out into the street: 'Get a second opinion. Where next?'

'Where next?' It was a good question, and one which would have haunted Dryden if he had allowed it to. Humph, a divorcee who pined for his daughters, was stalked by the same ghost. They shared an aimless life punctuated by the relief of regular movement. Today, tomorrow, for the rest of my life, thought Dryden: where next?

There was no copy in the shop opening. *The Crow's* deadline was just a few hours away. The mountaineer was strictly C-list celebrity status. Dryden couldn't remember what he'd said if he tried. He'd taken a shorthand note, but like all his shorthand notes, it was unreadable. In fact, come to think if it, he'd forgotten the bloke's name.

'Let's check the dig,' he said, running a hand back through the close-cropped black hair. The dig. Dryden had picked up a series of decent tales that summer from a team of archaeologists working in a field on the western edge of town. The onward march of the Barratt Homes generation threatened the site – indeed the whole western side of the town.

'The Invasion of the Little Boxes,' said Dryden, as they swept past the latest outcrop of executive homes, their carriage lamps dull orange in the gloom.

'You're an executive,' said Dryden, turning to Humph: 'An executive operator in the rapid transit sector.'

Humph burped. The Capri turned off the tarmac road onto a gravel drive and trundled forward, mist-wrapped pine trees just visible on either side. As they crawled forward Dryden felt they were leaving the world behind: the world of shop-openings, deadlines, and doctor's appointments. Ahead lay the past, buried for more than a thousand years in the sticky clay of the Isle of Ely, and around them the trees dripped rhythmically, like clocks.

The cab edged its way forward, lifting and separating the folds of smog like some ghostly snowplough, its lights dim replicas of the invisible sun. Dryden, his head back on the passenger seat rest, closed his eyes and thought about his new nightmare, which had woken him now each morning for a month. The one it had replaced was hardly a Freudian mystery. For the last five years his wife, Laura, had been in a coma following a car crash. They'd both been in the car, forced off a lonely Fen road at night time by a drunken driver. The car had plunged into Harrimere Drain, one of the placid pebble-black sheets of water which crisscrossed the marshlands. Dryden had been pulled clear by the drunk, unconscious, and came to outside the hospital, abandoned in a wheelchair. Laura had been left, trapped in a diminishing pocket of air in the total darkness of the submerged car. When they got her out she was in the coma, locked away from a world which had deserted her. Locked away from him.

The nightmare had been brutally graphic. A river of blood in black and white, with Laura floating by, her outstretched hand always, always, just beyond his stretching fingertips. And then it had changed, for the first time, a month ago. Childhood, summer, on the beach at Lowestoft. His parents, distant figures by the beach hut they always rented for the two weeks after the harvest. He had been five, perhaps six, and enticed away from his modest castles by the bigger children playing down by the waterline. They'd dug a pit, the base of which was black with shadow. Beside it, an identical one, and between them the tunnel. He'd watched, hypnotized, by the children crawling through. Then they caught his eye and he looked wildly for an adult nearby who might step in and save him. But his parents looked skywards in their deck chairs. So he'd gone down, feeling sick, egged on by the girls who said he shouldn't.

Even now in the overheated cab he could feel the damp sand around him, the distant sounds of the beach growing dimmer as he crawled forward to the smiling faces by the tunnel exit. Then came the crump of the failing sand above, the sudden weight on his back, and the sand in his mouth as he tried to scream.

He'd wake screaming, his rescue postponed, screaming with his mouth full of sand. Even now the sweat broke out, trickling down by his nose towards his dry lips. 'Claustrophobia,' he said, kicking out his heels in irritation at the cramped space of the Capri.

Out of the mist loomed a signpost with one sagging arm: 'California', the name of the farm which had once covered the site. The farmhouse and outbuildings had been demolished in the early years of the war, opening up the space for a PoW camp. The area was dry, and good for fruit trees, the clay preserving it from the damp black layers of the peat of the fen just beyond the site perimeter.

A year earlier, builders ripping up the old PoW huts and their concrete bases to make way for a housing development, had found a tiny amulet amongst the rubble. It was the figure of a charioteer, beautifully executed in a soft yellow gold. They'd tried to hush the find up, fearing it would wreck their timetable, but Dryden's halfhearted band of local contacts had, for once, come up trumps. Taking half a whisper and a series of 'no comments', Dryden had written a story in *The Crow* headlined 'Secret treasure unearthed at Ely dig', and the council had put a stop on building for six months, later extended to a year as more was uncovered: a gold pin and a silver pommel from a sword, amidst a tonne of broken Anglo-Saxon pottery.

Over a newsless summer Dryden had drummed up various experts to muse on the chances of finding a fabulous treasure in the clay of the Isle of Ely, perhaps to rival the famous Suffolk Viking burial site at Sutton Hoo. Dryden, who had an eye for detail even if the other one was largely focused on fiction, had supplied plenty of copy for Fleet Street. He'd stretched the truth but never consistently beyond breaking point. The nationals had finally moved on, leaving him with a watching brief, so he'd added a visit to the dig office to his necklace of weekly calls to places which just might give him a story in a town where a car backfiring could warrant a radio interview with the driver.

Humph's Capri clattered though the site gates towards the dig office – a Portakabin flanked by two blue portable loos, all of them pale outlines in the shifting white skeins of mist. A radio mast, rigged up to provide a broadband internet link for the office, disappeared into the cloud which crowded down on the site. An off-white agricultural marquee, like some wayward beached iceberg, covered an all-weather work area. Here pottery and other artefacts were cleaned and categorized by the diggers if bad weather had forced them off the site.

The cab's exhaust pipe hit a rut with a clang like a cow bell and Humph brought the Capri to a satisfying halt with a short skid. Dryden got out quickly, as he always did, in a vain attempt to disassociate himself from his mode of transport. The Capri was a rust bucket, sporting a Jolly Roger from the aerial and a giant Red Nose fixed to the radiator. It was like travelling with a circus.

Humph killed the engine and silence descended like a consignment of cotton wool. Clear of the town visibility in the smog was better, but still under fifty yards. The site was lit by four halogen floodlights at the corners, an echo of the original guard towers of the PoW camp. The lights were on in the gloom, but failed to penetrate with any force to ground level. The Portakabin was open, and inside a neon light shone down on a map table on which were some shards of pottery.

'Professor Valgimigli?' asked Dryden, in a loud voice damped down by the mist. Nothing. Luckily Dryden had a map of the site in his head: the archaeologists had dug two trenches which met like the cross hairs of a gunsight at the centre of the old PoW camp. The trenches avoided the concrete bases of the 24 original prisoners' huts – six of which lay within each quarter of the site. The Portakabin stood at the southern end of the main north – south trench. Dryden surveyed the ditch ahead, which seemed to be collecting and condensing the mist. He found the top of a short ladder, took three steps down, and jumped the rest, effortlessly pulverizing a shard of sixth-century pottery as he landed.

Light levels in the trench were very low, the mist denser, and he felt his flesh goose bump as he walked slowly forward straining to find a recognizable shape in the chaos of the shifting air. Disorientated by the lack of visual landmarks he tried to estimate visibility, but looking down realized he could barely see his feet. The acrid mist made the back of his throat ache, and he covered his mouth with his hand as he edged forward.

Ahead of him, funnelled along the trench, he could hear the susurration of the distant pine trees, and then something else: the brittle tap tap of a digger's trowel on clay and pebbles. He moved north and the sound grew suddenly clearer, preternaturally close, almost – it seemed – in his own head. He coughed self-consciously, and suddenly a figure in grey outline stood before him.

'Dryden. Welcome to the kingdom of the mist.' 'Professoro,' said Dryden, recognizing the voice of Azeglio Valgimigli, the academic leading the dig, an international collaboration between Cambridge, Lucca, Prague and Copenhagen. He was a deeply cultured man, a facet of character which bewitched Dryden, who was not. But there was something of the charlatan about him as well, something a little too mannered in the precise academic movements of the slim hands and the perfectly manicured fingers. Dryden imagined him working in a cool tiled museum expertly caring for the artefacts in glass-fronted exhibition cabinets, which like him, had been arranged for effect. He was lean, but slightly too short to carry off the half-moon professorial glasses, and the deep terracotta Tuscan tan. Dryden knew his age – 41 – thanks to a press release issused when the dig began. But the Italian looked older, the academic manners slightly archaic, the constant attempts at gravitas strained.

The clothes, although caked in dust, were the finest: moleskin trousers, a leather shirt and a faded silk bandana, the last an affectation which made Dryden wince. To combat the Fen mist he wore a thermal vest, but even this was a fashionable matt black.

Dryden, who made a point of making friends with people he didn't like, greeted him warmly with a handshake. 'What today?' he asked, peering into the hole Prof Valgimigli had dug in the trench face. 'Today Philip, we are what you say? Up page?' Dryden had given the archaeologist a brief drunken tutorial on the various gradations of newspaper story: from splash to filer, from page lead to down page. The

336

Italian had been enticed into the Fenman Bar opposite *The Crow*'s offices after the finding of the silver pommel – a conversation which had resulted in the headline 'Royal sword found at Ely dig.' Which was a shame, as it was almost certainly something else, but Valgimigli was unable to demand a correction due to the confusing effects of six pints of dark mild and a fervent desire for publicity of any kind. The story had, after all, got him a page lead in the *Daily Telegraph*, complete with a flattering picture.

'Up page' was encouraging, but Dryden didn't trust the academic's news judgement. 'Can I see?' Valgimigli crouched down on the damp clay and folded back a piece of tarpaulin. Against the dark green material the archaeologist had arranged what looked like six identical rusted carburettor rings.

'I found them by this.' Valgimigli picked up a curved shard of pottery decorated with blue smudges.

'Note the design,' said the professor. Dryden studied the pot. Heads perhaps? Pumpkins? Banjos? Was there anything duller than old pottery, he asked himself. Yes, old carburettor rings.

'It's a bull's head,' said Valgimigli and the smile that spread across his face was a living definition of the word smug. 'And these?' said Dryden, pointing at the rings. 'They don't look like much do they?' asked the archaeologist, not waiting for Dryden to confirm this judgement: 'They're rein rings.' 'Like for horses,' asked Dryden. 'Chariots,' said Valgimigli triumphantly.

'So?' Dryden had bright green eyes, like the worn glass you can pick up on a stony beach. When he knew he had a story, they caught the light. The archaeologist covered up the rings. Dryden whistled, knowing just how annoying it could be. 'Chariots. Like Bodekka. Charlton Heston.'

'If you like,' said Valgimigli, letting him build any story he wanted. 'I like,' thought Dryden, disliking him even more for underestimating him so much.

They looked up as a shadow fell across the trench. The crew had appeared, and stood in grey silhouette against the white sky, ghosts on parade. Dryden had got to know them over the months, Prof Valgimigli's 'muscle' – a team of six postgraduate students from Cambridge. The other senior archaeologists only made occasional visits to the site. Valgimigli ran the show, Lucca having provided the biggest single financial contribution to the costs.

There were five of them. 'Josh has found something, professor,' said a woman Dryden knew as Jayne. He noted with appreciation the curve of the hips and the tight jeans, fashionably bleached. Her voice lacked confidence and held an edge of anxiety: 'Something he shouldn't have.'

The crew stepped back into the mist, leaving Valgimigli and Dryden to continue north to the central crossroads where the two site trenches met. Here they turned east and continued for a further 25 yards. They reached a large hole dug in the north side of the trench. The diggers stood on the trench lip, while a large floodlight had been set up in the ditch floor aimed into the exposed cavity. Valgimigli stopped. 'Josh?'

'Here professor.' The voice was so close Dryden jumped, exhibiting the nerves which he generally hid so well. Josh backed out of the hole, dragging with him a set of trowels and a torch. Josh was tall, blond, and well-built, an ensemble undermined by heavy features and weak grey eyes. 'The light's bad, but have a look.' Dryden saw now that the hole was about 2ft 6 inches square, and the sides were roughly panelled in what looked like old pine slats.

Valgimigli emerged and handed the torch to Dryden without a word. Dryden, faced with an unknown fear, did what most children do – he ran towards it, thrusting his torso into the hole, and crawling forward three feet, bringing his trailing arm, which held the torch, around in front of his body.

His face was less than six inches from a skull. Its dull yellow surface caught the light like rancid butter. Only the top of the cranium was visible, with part of the brow exposed towards the ridges above the eye sockets. Around the head newly exposed earth trickled and shifted, a pebble dropping from the tunnel roof struck the exposed bone with a lifeless hollow tap.

Dryden drew back a foot and saw that the head was not the only bone unearthed. The fingers of the right hand were clear of the earth as well, giving the impression that the skeleton was emerging from its grave. A snail, its shell threatening to topple it forward, descended the cranium towards the unseen jaws.

Dryden backed out, feeling with relief the caress of the cool moist air. 'And that?' said the archaeologist, kneeling down and using a long metal pointer to gently tap the exposed bones of the finger. Something manmade caught the light, something folded into the exposed finger bones. Valgimigli stepped into the opening, and reaching forward lifted it gently out of the creeping earth. The rest of the digging crew had climbed down into the trench using a portable ladder and had laid a clear plastic artefact sheet on the trench floor. Valgimigli placed the object centrally with the kind of meticulous care reserved for a religious icon. It was a folded wax pouch, the kind smokers use for tobacco but much larger, A4 size. The archaeologist prised it open using one gloved hand and the metal probe.

A string of milk-white pearls spilled on to the plastic sheet. The clasp, in silver, untarnished. Valgimigli put his hand into the envelope and extracted a large candlestick, tarnished silver with an inlaid ebony collar, placing it beside the pearls.

'It's a tunnel,' said Josh, redundantly. He was standing against the opposite wall of the trench where a corresponding square of loose earth could be seen. 'We sliced through it. The digger smoothed the clay across the opening – it looks like it had already collapsed.'

'Killing our friend here,' said Valgimigli. 'The bones, Josh? What's your guess?' Josh, flattered by the question, thought for ten seconds: 'Fifty years?' Valgimigli nodded: 'Indeed. A man in a tunnel on the site of an old PoW camp,' he said: 'A mystery solved, Dryden?'

Dryden put a knee on the tunnel edge and pressed his body to the side, allowing the floodlight's white-blue beam to light the skeleton. The loose earth moved again, exposing the forehead and a shoulder blade, and a corroded ID disc hanging from the neck by what looked like a leather thong.

'Hardly,' he said, stepping back and taking the probe. 'I'd say that was a bullet hole,' he said, indicating a neat puncture in the cranium just below the brow. 'The ID disc will help of course. But there's still a mystery here . . .'

Dryden waited for someone else to spot it too. In Valgimigli's eyes he saw a flash of anger at being treated like a student. Dryden took the metal pointer: 'As I understand it the PoW camp huts are behind us over there . . .' A few of the students looked into the thick mist to the north.

He waited another few seconds, enjoying himself: 'And the perimeter wire would have been over there,' Dryden swung the pointer 180 degrees. 'So our prisoner of war was on a very unusual journey indeed: he was crawling in, not out.'

JIM KELLY

THE WATER CLOCK

In the bleak snowbound landscape of the Cambridgeshire Fens, a car is winched from a frozen river. Inside, locked in a block of ice, is a man's mutilated body. Later, high on Ely Cathedral, a second body is found, grotesquely riding a stone gargoyle. The decaying corpse has been there more than thirty years.

When forensic evidence links both victims to one awful event in 1966, local reporter Philip Dryden knows he's on to a great story. But as his investigations uncover some disturbing truths, they also point towards one terrifying foggy night in the Fens two years ago. A night that changed Dryden's life for ever ...

'An atmospheric, intriguing mystery with a tense denouement' Susanna Yager, *Sunday Telegraph*

'A sparkling star, newly risen in the crime fiction firmament' Colin Dexter

'Beautifully written ... The climax is chilling. Sometimes a book takes up residence inside my head and just won't leave. *The Water Clock* did just that' Val McDermid

SHORTLISTED FOR THE 2002 CWA JOHN CREASEY AWARD

JIM KELLY

THE MOON TUNNEL

In the past. A man crawls desperately through a claustrophobic escape tunnel beneath a POW camp in the Cambridgeshire Fens. Above, a shadow passes across the moon, while ahead only death awaits him.

In the present. Philip Dryden is reporting on an archaeological dig at the old POW camp when a body is uncovered. But there is something odd: the man appears to have been shot in the head, and the position indicates that he was trying to get *into* the camp, not escape it.

It's a puzzle which excites Dryden far more than the archaeologists or the police.

That is, until a second, more recent, body is discovered . . .

'The sense of place is terrific: the fens really brood. Dryden, the central character, is satisfyingly complicated . . . a good, atmospheric read' *Observer*